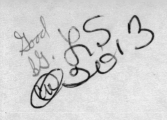

Surrender

"Get this straight," Ryan said. "The reason I'm marrying you is that you drive me crazy wanting you, and marriage seems the only way I'll have you." He leaned across the desk. "And believe me, my darling, I'll have you any time I want you, any place I want you. The sooner you understand that, the better off you'll be."

She slapped him.

Hard.

For an instant, he didn't move. Then he grabbed both her wrists and pulled her into his arms.

Erin was on fire. As much as she despised him at that moment, there was no way she could resist.

*$5
2013*

MIDNIGHT ROSE

PATRICIA HAGAN

HarperPaperbacks

A Division of HarperCollins Publishers

This is a work of fiction. The characters, incidents, and dialogues are products of the author's imagination and are not to be construed as real. Any resemblance to actual events or persons, living or dead, is entirely coincidental.

HarperPaperbacks   *A Division of* HarperCollins*Publishers*
10 East 53rd Street, New York, N.Y. 10022

Copyright © 1991 by Patricia Hagan
All rights reserved. No part of this book may be used or reproduced in any manner whatsoever without written permission of the publisher, except in the case of brief quotations embodied in critical articles and reviews. For information address HarperCollins*Publishers,*
10 East 53rd Street, New York, N.Y. 10022.

Cover illustration by Sanjulian

First printing: April 1991

Printed in the United States of America

HarperPaperbacks and colophon are trademarks of HarperCollins*Publishers*

10 9 8 7 6 5 4 3 2 1

AUTHOR'S NOTE

Although there are no recorded documents pinpointing the exact time when the Underground Railroad came to be officially recognized as an organization, desperate flights to freedom began long before it was known by that name. In 1741, the North Carolina colony passed an act providing for prosecution and fine on "any person harbouring a runaway." In 1786, George Washington wrote about fugitive slaves being aided in Philadelphia. And the first Fugitive Slave Law was passed by Congress in 1793.

By law, slaves were supposed to be kept illiterate, and most who could write were justifiably afraid to record their experiences. Many did, however, and it is from their diaries that underground activities could be studied.

The name "Free-Soil Party" had not yet been duly recorded in the time period for MIDNIGHT ROSE; however, it is correct to presume there had to be brave and courageous anti-slavery zealots working to bring fugitives to "free soil". Thus, I have taken the liberty of referring to these people as "Free Soilers".

Finally, I would like to thank the Philadelphia Maritime Museum for providing me with assistance in research, as well as the Information Centers at the Philadelphia and Richmond, Virginia libraries.

Patricia Hagan

Asheville, North Carolina
November 1990

CHAPTER

 1

Richmond, Virginia
Summer, 1819

Ryan Youngblood stirred, irritably protesting the sudden attack of daylight flooding into his room. Finally he raised his head, shook it to bring himself fully awake, then realized two things in shocking clarity. One was that he'd slept the day away, because that was late-afternoon sun washing over him; and two, a very naked woman was in bed with him.

It had been Ebner, his valet, who'd opened the drapes. He stood to one side apologizing, "Mastah, I didn't want to wake you up. I knowed you'd call me when you was up and wantin' somethin', but Mastah Roland, he's downstairs all in a dither and said I just had to get you up, 'cause you and him are supposed to go somewhere tonight."

Ryan groaned, sat up, ran his fingers through his hair in agitation. Keith Roland had been his closest friend as long as he could remember. Two years ago, Keith's wife and baby had died in childbirth, and he was understandably lonely, ready to get on with his life. Because he felt out of place and, didn't want to go alone, he'd asked Ryan to go with him to the annual Rose Ball, where debutantes were presented to Richmond society. So Ryan had reluctantly agreed, sardonically thinking how it was a waste of his time, because he surely didn't need to look for a wife. His mother, blast her, was taking care of that for him.

He waved Ebner away. "Tell him I'll be down shortly. Then come back up here and get my bath ready, lay my clothes out. I'll need some strong coffee and a shot of Scotch to get going."

"Yassuh." Ebner hurried to obey.

Ryan looked over at the naked woman sleeping so peacefully. Corrisa Buckner, her name was, and she was a cut above the others he'd caroused with in the year since he'd returned from France. He chuckled to think how his mother would doubtless have one of her attacks if she knew he'd dared bring a demimondaine into the house. But his mother was in Europe for the summer, thank God, along with Ermine Coley, his fiancée, he reflected bitterly, so he had a temporary respite from her nagging.

He gave Corrisa a sharp slap on her bare bottom, and she yelped, jolted from sleep. Then, dark hair tumbling across her face, she looked up at him and, smiling dreamily, began to wriggle seductively toward him. He quickly retreated from her beckoning arms. Reaching for his robe, he told her, "I forgot I had a previous engagement tonight. Ebner will see that you get back to town."

"Damn!" she cursed, disappointed for several reasons. Ryan Youngblood was not only a wonderful lover who satisfied her in a way she'd never dreamed possible, but she had also looked forward to a nice, cozy weekend at Jasmine Hill. It was considered one of the finest plantations and horse farms in all of Virginia, and he'd promised her they'd go riding, swim in a secluded pond, have a picnic. None of the other men in her life ever treated her so nicely. "Why can't I just stay here and wait for you?" she suggested, reaching to trail cajoling fingers down his back, loving the way his muscles rippled beneath her touch. "We can have a night as good as last night, and tomorrow you can keep your promise to take me riding."

Ryan shook his head. "You know I never promise a woman anything—except satisfaction." He winked.

"Oh, you do that, all right." She giggled, still disappointed but not about to get him to change his mind. In the short time she'd known him, Corrisa had realized Ryan Youngblood was different from other men, and he would never be manipulated by feminine guile. He seemed to be constantly on guard, cynical and suspicious.

She dressed hurriedly, lifted her lips for a parting kiss as Ebner appeared to receive Ryan's instructions for her departure by the rear entrance. He saw no need for Keith to know he'd had an overnight guest.

A parade of other household servants carrying buckets of heated water quickly filled the tub. He welcomed the bath almost as much as the Scotch-laced cup of coffee Ebner dutifully provided. Then he leaned back, allowed his mind to wander to the evening ahead, and tried not to dread it too much.

In the years before the war with Britain, when he'd been a student at West Point, he'd escaped his mother's annual nagging that he attend the damn thing. The few times he had yielded, the experience had been miserable.

Ebner moved to refill his cup with coffee, but he indicated straight Scotch instead, as he thought how he hated being so misanthropic where marriage, and women, were concerned but couldn't help it. Despite his parents' miserable relationship, he had been optimistic enough in his younger days to believe that with the right mate it didn't have to be like that. After all, he knew his mother for what she was—a conniving shrew who'd made his father's life miserable. It had probably been a relief for the poor soul when he dropped dead of a heart attack. That was the first year of the war, 1812, and Ryan came home long enough for the funeral and rushed back into combat as a panacea for his grief. Jasmine Hill was efficiently run by competent overseers in all areas, his father had seen to that. His mother could get along without him, and he sure as hell didn't want to be around her any more than necessary.

When the war ended, he'd been on a ship off the coast of England. He'd disembarked and journeyed on to France, in no hurry to return home. In Paris, he had met Simone, the femme fatale who would ultimately make a mockery of his belief in the possibility of a utopian marriage. She'd caught his eye in a cabaret on Place d'Anvers in lower Montmartre, where she sang lusty songs in a husky, mellow voice. He'd gone back again and again, and she began to single him out with hungry eyes. He sent her roses, asked that she meet him for dinner, and thus, the tumultuous romance had begun.

She'd told him she wasn't married, a lady disillusioned with love.

He vowed he'd make the painful past go away, replaced with a future laced only with rainbows.

In turn, she took him to her bed and carried him to heights of passion he'd only imagined in pubescent dreams. She was wanton and wild and held him a willing captive of love. He had showered her with expensive jewelry and gifts, and when he was totally and undeniably under her spell, he had asked her to marry him, return with him to America where she'd be treated as a queen at Jasmine Hill, her empire to rule.

Ryan was too ecstatic over her acceptance to wonder about her sudden eagerness. All along, she'd danced him about like a puppet on a string, making him crazy with worry that she was only trifling with him. But, she lovingly confided, she'd harbored the same fears as to his intentions, and now that they knew they truly loved each other, she couldn't wait to get married. However, she was reluctant to remind him, she was but a poor bistro singer and couldn't afford fancy clothes, couldn't bear the thought of traveling to America as his wife, to meet his family and friends unless she was stylishly dressed. Ryan had waved away her protests and gave her unlimited access to his bank account, which he had sufficiently established with money from his trust fund. After all, he pointed out, what was his would soon be hers.

God, what a fool he'd been!

The day the bank notified him his account was overdrawn, he had immediately confronted Simone, only to have her burst into tears and confess she'd used the money to buy her freedom from her *husband*. Every instinct told him she was lying, but his overwhelming love made him turn a deaf ear to the warning voices within. He wanted so desperately to believe her when she said she hadn't told him she was married, for fear of losing him. Her husband, she said, was in prison, had sworn if she tried to divorce him, he'd find a way to escape and kill her with his bare hands.

In desperation, when she realized how much she did love him, she had dared to beg her husband for her freedom, despite his violent threat. The husband had finally named a price, and that was where the money had gone.

Yes, Ryan stupidly recalled with chagrin, he had believed her and continued to believe her when she said the paperwork was being held up. She had assured him it was just a matter of time till she was free to marry him and set sail for their new life together in America. It was only when he'd lost patience and threatened to go to the French government to demand expediency that she agreed to set a date.

He had booked their passage, made ready to leave. She was to meet him at the pier, one hour before sailing. He waited, growing more anxious by the moment. Just as the anchor was being hauled up by the crew, and he was about to rush down the loading plank and go ashore in search of her, the messenger had come.

The messenger had been sent, he said, to inform Ryan that Simone would not be going with him, for she and her husband had reconciled their differences. She had been granted connubial visitation privileges by the prison authorities.

Ryan had gone crazy then, and by the time onlookers were able to pull him away, he'd beaten the messenger into admitting he was actually Simone's nephew, that she was, in fact, married to the owner of the bistro where she sang, and this wasn't the first time the couple had swindled an amorous and unsuspecting fool.

The terrified nephew had actually jumped overboard and swum ashore in his desperate haste to get away. Ryan then spent the entire voyage in a drunken stupor.

Finally, he was able to realize that the sting didn't come from learning it had all been a devious plan to get his money. Oh, no, he could live with that. What needled and tormented was the undeniable reality that he'd loved her and firmly believed she returned that love. How could he have been so naive? But then, on the other hand, how could she have been so goddamn convincing? He could take solace only in the affirmation that never again would he be so stupid. Not that he intended to avoid women. Far from it. Simone had taught him well, and he'd left Paris a far better lover. He had every intention of partaking the joys of the flesh, but that's all he'd ever want from a woman. He would make sure they didn't feel used, would promise only that they were properly pleasured.

By the time he got home, he had locked himself in a shell and turned a deaf ear to his mother's fury over his staying away so long, nearly two years. He needed to settle down and take the reins of Jasmine Hill, she said, needed to take a wife and start having sons to carry on the Youngblood name, for he was the last in the line. He paid no attention, went about his business of drinking and gambling and keeping company with ladies of the night. Then, when he'd been back about six months, she bluntly told him she'd found the perfect wife for him—Ermine Coley. The daughter of one of Richmond's most prominent attorneys, she could trace her ancestors all the way back to the Mayflower and even beyond, with distant claim to royal blood.

Ryan acknowledged that Ermine was pretty, petite, with long blond hair that fell in natural ringlets and eyes the color of cornflowers. Quickly, however, he discovered she was also a spoiled brat, given to ugly tantrums when she didn't get her way.

She also reminded him of his mother.

But so what, he asked himself. She would make a regal hostess for Jasmine Hill, and they would, no doubt, produce fine heirs to carry on the family name. He'd tolerate her long enough to impregnate her, then have a mistress to give him the warmth and affection he knew he'd never receive from his wife.

Ebner held out a towel for him as he stepped out of the tub. Perhaps, he mused, drying off and glancing at the ivory tailcoat and matching trousers laid out on the bed, he ought to start looking for a suitable mistress right away, before his mother and Ermine returned. The wedding was set for Christmas, and it'd be nice to know he had a passionate, willing woman waiting for him while he endured a superficial honeymoon. He also knew it wasn't going to be easy to find the kind of woman he wanted, because he required more than just a voluptuous body and a tigress in bed. She had to be intelligent, as well, someone with whom he could enjoy something besides sex.

Keith was waiting in the parlor, enjoying a brandy. He leapt to his feet as Ryan walked in. "I really appreciate this. Frankly, I got worried when Ebner told me you'd been in bed all day and thought maybe you wouldn't feel up to going."

"I don't," Ryan was quick to confirm, eagerly taking the glass of brandy he was offered. "I just hope you can actually find a suitable wife among those silly, giggling debutantes."

"Sometimes a man gets lucky. I met Lareina at the Rose Ball, remember?"

Ryan was politely contrite. "Of course, I do, and she was one of the few treasures to be found. Believe me, I'm hoping you'll be lucky twice."

"Well, again, I appreciate your going to give me moral support. Granted, I could start searching for a wife without going to a presentation ball, but the fact is, I'm kind of looking forward to it just because it's the first time I've done anything social since Lareina died."

"Life goes on, Keith," Ryan said dryly, meaning the words for himself, as well.

In an attempt to lighten the mood, Keith pointed out, "Well, you can just relax and enjoy yourself, drink champagne and feel sorry for the rest of us nervous blokes. You've found *your* bride."

"My mother found her. I wasn't looking."

Keith nodded, wondered again what it was that had happened in France to make Ryan change so. Once, he'd been cheerful, outgoing, but now he seemed bitter, almost cynical. "Well, Ermine might not be your choice, but what difference does it make? You've never been satisfied with one woman, anyway. You'll have your mistresses. The one I caught a glimpse of being spirited away in your carriage was quite a charmer, from what I could see," he said with a grin. "But you'd better learn to be more discreet. You can't be bringing them home with you, you know."

"That was a special occasion—not a special woman." He downed the rest of his brandy, then, attempting to be genial, said, "If you don't stop wasting time worrying about my love life, you're going to miss out on pursuing your own. Shall we go?"

Keith nodded vigorously, again expressing gratitude for Ryan's company. "It's just a shame for you to have to waste your time. Maybe they should have presentation balls for potential mistresses."

Ryan pretended to take him seriously. "Hey, that's not a bad idea. Do you think we could arrange one?"

They looked at each other and burst into laughter, then headed for Keith's waiting carriage.

Erin sat patiently as Letty styled her hair. Noting Letty's pensive expression in the mirror, she once more wondered what had happened to change her so. They had played together as children, till Erin's stepfather happened to notice and said it wasn't proper for her, a white child, to play with Negroes. But the two had still managed to find time to enjoy each other, giggling and sharing secrets. Then Erin had gone to Atlanta, and when she had returned nearly five years later, nothing was the same. Letty was like a stranger, quiet, withdrawn. It was as though they had never shared all those wonderful times together.

Attempting to ease the tension, Erin complimented her. "Mother was right. You really do have a knack for doing hair, Letty. It looks nice." Wanting to remind her of their past friendship, she continued with a soft laugh, "Now who would've thought back when we were playing such rough and rowdy games you'd grow up to have such a genteel talent?"

Letty's round, anxious eyes met hers in the huge oval mirror above the dressing table. She didn't want to think about the past. "You've got to be the most gorgeous lady at that ball. That's your mama's orders."

Erin made a face. "As if I care. I don't even want to go."

"You shouldn't talk like that," Letty dared to say. "Your mama got the finest dressmaker in all of Richmond to make that gorgeous gown especially for you. Why, those are real black pearls sewn into the netting, and no telling what that cost. I've never seen a dress so fine, and none of the other house workers has either. Everybody's eyes are gonna pop out when you walk in."

"Oh, I'm sure of that," Erin said bitterly. "But not over my dress. They'll be staring out of shock that I dared go where I wasn't invited. This whole thing is ridiculous, and if I had anywhere to run to, I would."

"That's just no way for you to feel, Miss Erin. You might meet your husband tonight, and—"

"Don't call me *Miss* Erin!" she cried, unable to keep still any longer and implored, "Oh, Letty, what is wrong with you? You're not the same. We've known each other almost all our lives, but since I've come home, you're different. And you know you don't have to be formal with me."

"Folks change," Letty murmured, trying to concentrate on what she was doing, despite the way her hands were starting to shake. She wished Erin had stayed in Atlanta but didn't dare say so. Instead, she pointed out, "Besides, if the mastah hears me call you anything but Miss Erin, he'll have me whipped."

"Not with me around, he won't! And I'd better not hear of any whippings going on, anyway. Dear God, I hate slavery. It's wrong, and—"

"And nothing for you to concern yourself with, my dear." Arlene Tremayne breezed into the dressing alcove.

Slender, not as tall as her daughter, she was stunning in a gown of champagne silk. Letty was just interlacing the delicate white and smoked pearl band among the tight ringlets at her crown. "Magnificent! Absolutely magnificent!" she praised as she set down the bowl she was carrying. "You're a jewel, Letty. You have such a talent. I don't know how we'd manage without you, but you can run along now. I'll finish adjusting this. Erin and I need some time for a mother-daughter chat, you know." She dismissed the woman with a patronizing smile.

Letty nodded and quickly backed out, obediently bowing and curtsying as Master Zachary required all his slaves to do.

The moment they were alone, Arlene sternly admonished, "You should never say such things in front of the servants. What if your stepfather heard you?" She shuddered, envisioning his reaction. "Ladies of good breeding never discuss such things anyway, to anyone. Remember that."

"You don't like slavery any more than I do," Erin tartly reminded her. "You won't even refer to them as slaves. Like now, you said servants. Slavery is just as detestable to you as it is to me, but you won't dare admit it."

Uneasily, Arlene countered, "Well, some things you have to accept whether you like them or not. Now here—" She abruptly changed the subject, gesturing to the bowl she'd brought. "This is fresh. I made it this afternoon."

Erin knew what it was. For as long as she could remember, her mother had insisted she scrub her skin vigorously with a solution concocted of lemon juice, unripe grapes, parsley, and horseradish water. For nice skin, she said, smooth and soft.

Arlene continued, "When you've finished, I'll help you with your gown. It *is* lovely, isn't it?" She turned to look beyond the alcove to where the shaded rose gown was spread across her canopied bed. "Now what did we decide to do about your corset? Madame Cherise says most women aren't wearing them anymore, but I feel naked without mine. I forgot to ask her what you should wear, and—"

"Mother, don't worry about it," Erin interrupted, then rushed to beg desperately once more, "Can't we just forget this madness? I wasn't invited to the ball, and we both know why. Zachary has never been accepted by the social elite of Richmond, and neither have we. It doesn't matter how much money he's got. Everyone knows how he got it—by cheating and swindling people."

"Erin, no!" Arlene said, quickly sinking into a nearby chair, because her trembling legs would no longer support her. She drew closer, leaned to whisper, even though they were alone in the alcove. "You musn't talk like that. Ever. He might hear you, and it wouldn't do. He'd be so hurt to hear you say such things. I know he's not a perfect man, far from it, but he is my husband, and he's your stepfather, and you should try to get along with him, show some respect."

Erin's heart went out to her, but still she couldn't hold back her loathing. "I can't stand him. I wish I could have stayed in Atlanta, because I can't hide the way I feel about him, and I'm sorry, for your sake."

Arlene's lower lip trembled as she fought to hold back the tears. In only a little while, both she and Erin were expected by Zachary in his study to have a glass of sherry before they left for the ball. He wasn't going, thank goodness, said he had to go away for a few days on business but had expressed a desire to see them in their new finery. She didn't want him to think she'd been crying.

Reaching to give Erin a gentle shake, she tremulously begged, "I want you to try and get along with him, please, for me. It was time for you to come home, because this is your home, and it's also time for you to take a husband, get married. You couldn't go on living with your father's sister forever, and I didn't want you to meet someone and marry and settle down there, so far away.

She paused on a melancholy sigh. "I never understood why you were so hysterical to leave here, anyway. I knew you and Zachary just couldn't seem to get along, but I never dreamed it was so bad you'd want to go away."

Erin wasn't about to tell her just how bad it had been, knew it would crush her to learn what that fiend had tried to do to her when she was twelve years old. Instead, she pointed out, "I can't stand the way he treats the servants, and he's always ranting and raving about something." She shook her head in dismay, wished things were different, but knew they never would be.

Arlene ignored that. "You have to remember, if it hadn't been for Zachary asking me to marry him right after your father died, we'd be as poor as your Aunt Sarah and her family. No man from a wealthy and prominent family would have ever courted me, because I didn't come from a similar background."

Erin gave an unladylike snort. "So you married a man of disrepute, because he had money."

"Erin, please. . . ." Arlene choked back a sob, the tears she was fighting beginning to sting her eyes. "I had no choice. I had you to think about, and I didn't want you to grow up in a life of poverty like I did. I was pretty then, too, and that's why Zachary wanted me, and I held out for marriage, and now look what I have. . . ." She waved her arms in a gesture to the opulent surroundings. "He isn't all bad, Erin," she rushed on. "He just gets mean when he's drinking."

"Which seems to be all the time."

Arlene ignored that painful reality and continued her

plea. "All I'm asking is that you try to get along with him. Maybe tonight we'll find someone suitable for you, so you can hurry and get married and move out of the house.

"But I don't want just anybody for you. And tonight you'll be exposed to the cream of Virginia's most eligible bachelors. I want you to stop worrying that we weren't invited. We'll just behave as though we were, because we should have been, and no one will say anything, because no one will dare make a scene. Now then . . ." She got to her feet and forced a smile she didn't truly feel. "After you've had your bath, Letty will help you with your gown, and then I'll meet you in the parlor."

Alone in the alcove, Erin looked at her reflection and wasn't surprised to see the resentment and rebellion mirrored there. She didn't want to be put on display like a slave at auction and had no intention of marrying only for monetary and social reasons. She'd gone to school in Atlanta and studied hard; she considered herself to have above average intelligence for a woman. Accordingly, she dared hope there might be more for her in life than being subservient to a man she didn't love, giving birth to a baby every year, and filling her boring hours with tatting and sewing. Why couldn't she find a job and support herself? Surely, there was something she could do. Why did she have to adhere to unwritten laws that said she had to have a husband to take care of her, as if she were some kind of dependent simpleton? She wasn't worried about finding one if she wanted one; she was not at all conceited about her looks. And men seemed to find her height of nearly five feet nine an interesting contrast to dainty, fluffy girls of diminutive size. Well, she might have to go to the ball, but she'd do absolutely nothing to entice or encourage any man.

With that firm resolution, Erin had her bath, finishing, as always, by vigorously scrubbing with the strange solution. Letty helped her into the gown, marveling at her tiny waist, envying once more her generous bosom.

"You don't need no stays, and you don't need them new type corsets with the cup-shaped bust sections, either. I'd say you've got a figure any woman would die for, and a body any man would kill for," she added with a rare devilish grin.

It was like the old Letty, Erin thought, relieved things were starting to seem a bit more normal between them.

She turned in front of the mirror. The bodice of the dress was crusted with tiny, precious pearls in white and smoke shades. From the narrow waist, the cascade of shaded colors began, from palest pink to deepest rose, with an overlay of pearl-studded chiffon. The sleeves were pouffed, also interspersed with precious nacres.

For any other occasion, Erin knew she'd be thrilled over such elegance. The concept behind the Rose Ball, however, she found degrading to women. "You know something, Letty?" she couldn't resist proclaiming. "In a way, the only difference between tonight's ball and a slave auction is hypocrisy."

At that, Letty scurried from the room, not about to indulge in such a delicate topic of conversation.

When Erin entered the parlor, her mother cried, "Dear God in heaven, child, you're beautiful!" Quickly she set aside her sherry and crossed the room to embrace her gently and exclaim with shining eyes, "I'm so very proud to be your mother."

Zachary Tremayne felt anything but fatherly as his eyes drank in the stirring sight of his stepdaughter. He didn't dare stand, lest the desire she'd so instantly evoked be obvious in his tight trousers. He raised one hand, still holding his drink, in a toast. "To the most gorgeous enchantress Virginia has ever seen," he said.

Erin murmured an obligatory acknowledgment but

didn't look his way. She could actually feel the heat of his stare from across the room and wondered why her mother didn't sense it. Yet Erin knew it was a blessing she didn't. The man was evil, a reprobate, and she couldn't stand even to be in the same room with him.

"I think we'd better leave now," she said, declining the drink that Roscoe, the butler, offered.

In a thick, husky voice, Zachary protested, "You've got time for a sherry. After all, you're supposed to be fashionably late, make a grand entrance." He didn't want her to leave, wanted to drink in the sight of her as long as possible.

Erin bit back a sharp retort. She didn't want to make any kind of entrance. She intended just to drift in quietly, then find a place to hide till it was all over. Let her mother do the mingling. But, for the moment, she wanted to escape Zachary's company. With a stubborn lift of her chin, she turned toward the door. "I don't want to be late. I'll wait in the carriage."

She hurried out, and Arlene fearfully turned to Zachary and apologized. "I'm sorry. I know you wanted this little family gathering for us. I'm afraid I don't know what's wrong with her these days."

"Your sister-in-law spoiled her, that's what's wrong with her. She needs to taste the lash, learn her place, just like the slaves." He tossed down his drink angrily.

Arlene whispered, "I'm sorry, Zachary. I'll talk to her and make her see she's hurt your feelings." Quickly, she ran from the room to follow after Erin, lest he lose his temper and forbid them to go.

CHAPTER

 2

$\mathbf{T}$*HEIR CARRIAGE PROCEEDED SLOWLY ALONG* the curving driveway, which was crowded with fine saddle horses and other conveyances. It was not yet dark but already lightning bugs performed their glowing dance of twilight beneath the canopy of spreading oaks. The velvet green lawn of Pine Tops plantation was a rainbow of pastel-gowned debutantes. Their glittering jewels vied to outshine the eager eyes of potential beaus.

The mansion was huge and impressive. Wide marble steps led up to the terrace, which swept the front and sides. White columns stretched to the overhanging roof, which shaded both porch and second-floor balcony.

Erin tensed as the carriage pulled up in front of the steps. She could see the receiving line waiting at the top: Tyler Manning and his wife, Opal. Opal was this year's chairwoman, the reason for the ball being held at Pine Tops. No doubt that was Carolyn, their daughter, standing beside them in a flounced white gown. Erin, who hadn't seen her in years, wondered if she was still haughty and conceited. Fearfully, she asked, "Surely we aren't going in the front entrance."

"Well, of course, we are." Arlene's laugh was forced, because she was every bit as dubious and nervous as Erin but determined not to show it. "What did you think? That we'd sneak in the back way?"

Erin was mortified. "But they'll know we weren't invited, and they might not let us in. I thought we'd just sort of drift in and out, not stay long . . . and, oh!" She pounded her knees with her fists. "I was a fool to let you talk me into this."

Arlene crisply reminded her, "You had no choice. And you're overreacting, anyway. It's not as if I don't know the Mannings, as well as almost everybody else that will be here, for that matter. Zachary might be a heathen and never darken the door of a church, but *I* try to live a Christian life, and I've met these people either through church or charity work. I consider them my friends, even if I'm not on the invitation list for their parties. Now just relax and be yourself. Act as though you have every right to be here, and no one will say a word."

"This is the most ridiculous thing I've ever heard of!"

"It's the only way to introduce you to Richmond society, Erin. We have to let everyone know that you've reached a marriageable age, and the only way to do that is for you to dazzle them here, tonight." She flashed a spirited smile. "So now, my beautiful daughter, go forth and dazzle!"

It was only with great effort that Erin forced her reluctant legs to carry her up the stairs. Before she was halfway in her ascent, she could see the expressions on the faces of the hosts. First, confusion and bewilderment, then, astonishment, and, finally, resentment and controlled anger.

Reaching the receiving line, she couldn't bring herself to utter a word, but Arlene was the epitome of charm and composure. "Tyler. Opal. Carolyn," she cooed, grasping their hands in turn. "How wonderful to see all of you again. Erin was so thrilled she arrived from Atlanta in time for your little soiree." She abruptly whirled away, calling out to someone she knew from church, not about to linger before their contemptuous glare.

Erin was slower, hesitated a fraction of a second too long, and was thus vulnerable to Carolyn Manning's loud whisper. "You weren't invited, and you know it! You're no debutante," she added with a sneer, turning away as she felt the warning jab of her mother's elbow in her side.

Erin was well aware of the young men turning to stare appreciatively as she followed her mother inside the grandiose house. She ignored them and turned her attention to the lavish decor. There seemed to be an overabundance of everything—furniture, sculptures, paintings, crystal, gilt—as though the Mannings were desperate to display their wealth.

All around, the ladies were conspicuously gowned and bejeweled, striving, it seemed, to flaunt every precious gem in their collections.

They accepted champagne from a white-gloved servant who looked hot and uncomfortable in a red velvet coat and black velvet trousers.

Arlene led the way to the ballroom, with its waved parquet floor and mirrored walls reflecting myriads of flickering tallow candles that other servants were just beginning to light.

A string ensemble was playing in one corner, and along one wall were banquet tables filled with sumptuous foods. Beyond the French doors opening onto the rear terrace, the huge fountain had been transformed to offer a steady stream of bubbling champagne which flowed over the strawberries lining the bowl. Already, young girls with hopeful suitors hovering were giggling, becoming tipsy.

"Isn't it like something from a fairy tale?" Arlene breathed in awe. "I've never been to a party so lavish."

Erin felt a wave of pity, as well as guilt, over having protested attending. The sad truth was that her mother had probably never been to a ball, or even a tea party, in her entire life. Oh, there'd been attempts to be accepted, always ending in heartache. She could remember the occasion of her tenth birthday, when her mother had planned a gala event, even engaged a traveling circus to perform on the lawn. Couriers were sent to hand deliver invitations to every prominent family within a thirty-mile radius that had children in the household. But nobody came. So, for her mother's sake, she made up her mind, then and there, to endure the evening and to pretend, at least, to have a good time, as long as she didn't have to indulge in flirtatious contrivances, as she noted the other girls were doing.

Arlene was delighted as Erin easily became the center of attention. The unmarried men flocked about her, begging for introductions, the opportunity to bring her more champagne, asking for dances later on. She truly was a beauty.

Despite herself, Erin was starting to enjoy the ball. Thrilled by the contagious gaiety of her would-be swains, she couldn't help but be dazzled by so much attention and beguiled by the romantic and lovely music, the wondrous ambience. Her emotions were displayed in her shining eyes and radiant smile.

Erin wasn't aware of the tall, broad-shouldered man who stood watching her from the shadows of the side terrace.

Ryan had sought escape, tired of coquettish girls who disregarded the fact he was engaged to one of their friends as they clamored for attention. Keith, he was relieved to note, had apparently fallen in love on sight. He and the young lady of his choice seemed to have paired off for the evening. So Ryan had fled to the deserted terrace, willing his boredom to hurry and end, but suddenly found himself fascinated by the tall, tawny beauty that seemed to have mesmerized every male in attendance. He couldn't figure out who she was, couldn't remember ever having seen her at any social gathering. But having been away so long, he'd lost touch. He'd even had difficulty in some instances recalling the names of neighbors he hadn't seen in a while, but, regardless, he knew there was no way he would have ever forgotten one so lovely.

There was also, he noticed, something startlingly different about her. He could tell by the sparkle in her eyes and the way she laughed so easily that she was enjoying herself. Yet, the undercurrent of tension and desperation present in the other debutantes, as they sought to bewitch the beaux of their choice, was missing. It was as though she had not a care in the world.

As Ryan continued to observe the raven-haired lovely, Keith appeared at his side. He'd been searching for Ryan, wanting to extol the qualities and charm he'd discovered in Miss Mary Susan Hightower. But Ryan seemed preoccupied. Keith followed his gaze, a frown creasing his forehead as he discovered the reason. He'd overheard Mary Susan and Carolyn Manning whispering furiously about the brazen appearance of Erin Sterling and her mother. With an exaggerated sigh, he airily declared, "Well, I guess I was wrong in thinking there's no such thing as a ball for potential mistresses. Seems Erin Sterling is turning this into one."

Ryan looked at him then and sharply asked, "What do you mean? Who is she, anyway?"

"Zachary Tremayne's stepdaughter. That says it all, doesn't it? She's no debutante. She wasn't even invited. She and her mother just barged in, hoping, no doubt, to find her a husband. But they're wasting their time. The only thing the men are thinking about is a quick tumble in a hayloft. They know they'd be disinherited if they dared court such trash. Like I said, she's turning this into a ball for those looking for a mistress, because that's all she's good for. Granted, she's beautiful, and I wouldn't mind—"

"Trash?" Ryan echoed curiously, cutting him off. "Why on earth would anyone think of her as trash? What's she done?"

"Why . . . nothing that I know of." Keith shrugged, unnerved by his question, then recovered to snap, "Come now, Ryan, you know what an unscrupulous bastard Tremayne is. America banned slave trading from Africa and the West Indies over ten years ago, but he's still into it, and everybody knows it. They say he makes regular runs into the Carolinas to buy slaves illegally smuggled in, then sells them to plantation owners farther south. He's making a fortune.

"I've got nothing against owning slaves," he airily continued. "Goodness knows, I've got my share, but I also got them honestly."

Ryan couldn't resist a wry grin. "Maybe you're angry because you paid more for them on the block than if you'd bought them privately from Tremayne."

Keith stiffened with indignity. "That's not so."

Returning his gaze to Erin, Ryan probed, "Do you know her personally?"

He shook his head. "I used to see her in church with her mother, but that was a long time ago. I think she went away somewhere. One thing is for sure, she's made a lot of people angry tonight, and you can believe those drooling young men are going to catch hell from their parents for wasting time fawning over her instead of doing what they came here to do—look over this season's crop of debutantes."

"Well, from what I've seen, she's not only gorgeous. She has the ability to make them enjoy themselves.

There's none of the stuffy demureness and artificial charm the others ooze with. I'd say she seems to be the most appealing woman here."

"But class is what it's all about, my friend, and you'd be wise to keep your observations at a distance. Victoria Youngblood would sooner invite that strumpet you had in your bed last night to tea, than walk on the same side of the street with a member of Tremayne's family. Now I think I'd better get back to Mary Susan. The dancing is starting."

He went back inside, but Ryan stayed where he was, even more fascinated than before. If Erin Sterling had, indeed, dared to show up without being invited, then there had to be a good reason. And, since she also had to be aware of the low esteem with which her family was regarded, then she'd realize not one of the eligible bachelors attending would seriously consider courting her.

What, then, was her motivation?

Could it be that she was, actually, searching for a wealthy paramour in the only way she knew how?

He intended to find out.

With a faint smile teasing the corners of his lips, he remembered he just happened to be seeking to fill such a position himself.

A persistent young man named Carl Whitfield was standing next to Erin as the dance music began. Before she could protest, he exuberantly grabbed her arm and pulled her toward the center of the ballroom floor, where men and women were lining up in two opposing lines to do the fast paced reel. She hadn't planned to participate but found herself caught up in the excitement, started clapping in time to the music, having a wonderful time— till a waspish voice said, "You've got your nerve! Barging into my home uninvited and then throwing yourself like a hussy at all my male guests!"

Erin whipped about to see it was Carolyn Manning who had spoken, her face flushed with rage. Several of the girls behind her were also glaring furiously.

Just then, the caller began singing out instructions, and the lines began to move.

Erin couldn't join them, because all at once she knew she had to escape, for never in her whole life had she felt so resented or out of place.

No one paid any attention as she slipped away, moved to the side, melding with the crowd of onlookers. Carl would soon discover he didn't have a partner, but she couldn't be concerned about that.

Glancing quickly about, she was disappointed not to spot her mother. If she had, she'd have begged to leave then and there. Knowing she had to try and compose herself, she darted through the doors and out to the terrace, where there was no longer a gathering around the champagne fountain. She took a glass from a table, held it beneath the delicious sparkling spray, then gulped it down. She was shaking all over, but not from embarrassment. The reality was that her temper was rapidly reaching the boiling point, because who the hell did they think they were, anyway?

Personally, she didn't give a damn to be invited, but her mother certainly deserved the courtesy. There wasn't a more charitable or kinder person in all of Richmond. Arlene Tremayne was always doing something nice for someone, yet, these snobs had the nerve to exclude her from their intimate circle, merely because she happened to be married to a rogue.

Erin filled her glass again, scowling through the open doors at the merrymakers. Then, unable to bear watching any longer, she left the terrace and walked out into the formal gardens. She was assailed by the intoxicating fragrance of roses and took a deep breath to drink in the sweetness. Beyond the terraced steps was a winding path. She had no idea where it went, didn't care, for what she sought was a momentary respite in order to calm down and be able to go back inside.

She paused to take a single red rose, her favorite over the yellow, pink, and white blossoms that were everywhere. Pressing it to her lips, she was about to move deeper into the perfumed night, when she was startled at the sound of footsteps. Whirling about, she realized a man was approaching, slowly, deliberately, almost as though he were stalking her.

"I beg your pardon," she said curtly, "but are you following me?"

"No," Ryan glibly lied in response, then challenged, "Do you think you're the only one who has a right to escape the boredom?"

She didn't miss the humor in his voice, took a few steps to see him in the light filtering down from the terrace lanterns. He was tall, broad-shouldered, and, she noted, powerfully built. He had a nice face, not handsome, but ruggedly appealing. His hair was the color of sand, thick, only slightly wavy where it brushed the collar of his well-fitting coat. She found herself drawn to his eyes, a shade of indigo blue; she also liked the warmth she perceived. He was almost caressing her with his gaze. He smiled down at her, and she actually felt her cheeks grow warm. What was wrong with her? Men never affected her that way. But then, some tiny little warning bell rang inside, and suddenly she knew this wasn't just any man. For one thing, he was much older than any of the hopeful bachelors inside, probably near thirty. But it wasn't merely his age that made him different. There was an air about him, she noted at once, of strength, confidence, yet, she was sure she sensed tenderness, as well. Politely, she held out her hand. "I don't believe we've met. I'm Erin Sterling."

He caressed her fingertips and said, "Yes, I know." Then added with candor, "You're the daring young lady who came without being invited but wound up being the proverbial belle of the ball. I admire your temerity, but if you don't mind my asking, why did you do it?"

She withdrew her hand. Stiffly, because she really didn't feel it was any of his business, she explained, "Because my mother wanted me to come. She seems to think I'll find a husband here. It doesn't matter to her that I'm not looking for one." Then, matching his audacity, she informed him, "You haven't told me who you are, and I might ask why you're out here, instead of inside with the other wife hunters."

He saw the twinkle in her lovely brandy-colored eyes, took note of the undercurrent of contempt in her voice as he thought how she was even more beautiful up close. Her skin was like rich cream laced with coffee, soft and begging to be caressed. There was a voluptuousness about her, as though her body reached out, begging to be touched. He was shocked to realize he was actually fighting the impulse to take her in his arms then and there, to kiss her full, sensual lips. He gave himself a mental shake and drew in a deep breath before responding, "The name is Youngblood. Ryan Youngblood. I came here at the request of a friend who's a widower, making his own debut to let everyone know he's out of mourning. As for why I'm out here instead of in there, I don't happen to be a wife hunter, as you call it."

"Then where is your wife?"

"I don't have one." He didn't feel the need to add that was only a temporary situation.

Erin had at once connected the Youngblood name as being associated with one of the most prosperous horse breeders in the state. But she'd never heard of him, specifically. "So?" She cocked her head to one side and couldn't resist goading, "Why are you wasting your chance to find one? I don't remember seeing you even mingling about."

"Haven't seen anyone I wanted to mingle with . . . till now," he lazily grinned.

She felt a delicious rush, quelled it with feigned indignity. "I'm afraid you'd be wasting your time. Not only am I not looking for a husband, I happen to find this whole ritual degrading."

He raised an eyebrow. If she were opposed to the concept of the ball, wasn't there in keeping with it, then it was strange she'd subject herself to certain scorn and ridicule merely at her mother's insistence. He'd observed the brief scene with Carolyn Manning, figured when she took off like she did that Carolyn hadn't exactly been saying she hoped she was having a good time. So maybe Erin Sterling did have an ulterior motive, and perhaps her mother was a part of it. There was no harm in finding out, and it might turn out to be a spicy diversion to an otherwise boring summer. "Well," he said finally, "now that we understand each other, why don't we both enjoy the evening—together?" He held out his arm to her. "Would you care to dance?"

Yes, she realized with pounding heart, she would, very much, but was compelled to remind him with a mirthless chuckle, "They're doing the reel, Mr. Youngblood, and I'm not exactly welcome in the ladies' line. Next, they'll probably break into a four-couple quadrille. They won't want me there, either. So, if you want to enjoy yourself, I suggest you join them and leave me to my roses."

He burst into delighted laughter. She was so wonderfully different from the other women he knew, without guile and with a good sense of humor. He liked that. He liked her. It was going to be fun learning just what her game was, and with a sudden, unmistakable stirring in his loins, he couldn't help thinking how she might just be the woman he was looking for, the mistress who'd make his life with Ermine bearable.

"I think I've got the solution to that," he told her mysteriously, "that is, if you dare . . . and if you don't mind raising a few more eyebrows."

Erin was still so bitter over the way she and her mother had been treated that she was willing to take his dare. She also had to admit she found him intriguing, interesting, exciting—as well as attractive. She took his arm, acknowledging she wouldn't mind raising a few more eyebrows at all.

He led the way back into the ballroom. The reel had just ended, and everyone was standing about, waiting for another to begin. Excusing himself to Erin, Ryan made his way to where the musicians were resting. When he returned, he explained, "I was in Paris not long ago, and I learned a new dance, which is quite different from anything this country has seen. It's called the valse. It's done in couples, facing each other, embracing . . . like this." He positioned her left hand on his waist, her right arm raised outwards, palm pressed against his. Then, as the music began, a sweeping, light, melody, his other arm embraced her, and he whispered, "Just follow me, in a kind of sidestep, forward, side, and back, as though we're stepping off a box. Keep in time to the music, relax, and let me lead you. It's simple." He gave a smile of encouragement.

Once more she was warmed by his caressing eyes, oblivious to the startled gasps echoing throughout the ballroom as they began to dance. He swept her so easily into the steps, and they moved like skaters on ice, smoothly, gently, and all the while their gazes locked, held.

Erin wondered if the excited tremors within were mirrored on her face for everyone to see. Her cheeks felt so warm, flushed, and she became mesmerized by the tender moment. It was as though she were drowning in his embrace, and she closed her eyes and let the magic take her away, to a world where the music of violins enticed butterflies to dance on the nightwind, and amidst the splendor, there was the fragrance of roses forever. . . .

Arlene's eyes narrowed thoughtfully as she watched her daughter dancing so scandalously with the handsome and very wealthy Ryan Youngblood. It was obvious to her he was quite smitten. Yet, she'd heard his mother had arranged his engagement to Ermine Coley, so she was puzzled as to why he was even in attendance. Well, she wasn't going to be concerned about that, because the truth was she couldn't ask for a better husband for Erin. True, Ryan had the reputation of being something of a rogue where the ladies were concerned, and there was speculation as to why he'd stayed away in France so long after the war, instead of coming home. Some said he didn't get along with his mother, and she could certainly understand that. Everyone knew Victoria Youngblood was haughty, arrogant, and extremely difficult to get along with. Pity Erin such a mother-in-law, but that was a small price to pay for marrying into such wealth. Her future would certainly be secured for all time.

Opal Manning was also watching, but not in the same light as Arlene. She was getting angrier by the minute and whispered to her husband, "It's disgusting! Licentious. Why the nerve of them! Pairing off like that, touching so intimately. It's unheard of."

Tyler Manning was trying very hard to keep from smiling, because he thought Erin Sterling was a rare and treasured beauty, and he envied any man who could hold her in his arms and dance with her in such a manner. Making his voice firm, he informed his wife, "Actually, it's the new dance of Europe, I've heard. I don't see anything licentious about it."

"Well, I do," she said between gritted teeth, "and if you don't march yourself over to those musicians this very instant and demand they play another reel, I'll do it myself."

He knew she would, so, with a reluctant sigh, Tyler knew there was nothing to do but oblige her.

Ryan saw their host heading for the musicians, knew the golden moment was about to come to an end, and that once it did, their intimate encounter was over for the evening. He held her tighter, and her eyes widened in surprise at his boldness. "I'm about to have to bid you good night," he whispered, the play of a smile on his lips, "but if you feel what I'm feeling, Erin Sterling, we'll be dancing together in our hearts, till the next time we meet."

He released her at the same instant the music came to an abrupt halt. With a bow from the waist, he kissed her fingertips, then led her to the edge of the floor and took his leave.

Erin stared after him and realized, with a thrilling rush, that she would, indeed, like to see him again.

In fact, she would like that very much.

CHAPTER

 3

E*RIN HAD NO INTENTION OF TELLING HER* mother how Carolyn Manning had behaved. She was sure her mother had borne her own share of hurtful snubs and didn't want to add to them. However, as soon as they were in the carriage and on their way home, it was obvious their less than cordial welcome was the last thing on her mother's mind.

"I want to hear everything," Arlene urged excitedly. "Ryan Youngblood comes from a very fine family. He'd be perfect for you. Handsome, too! And I hear he's quite the charmer with the ladies."

Nonchalant, for she wasn't about to let on just how impressed she really was, Erin said, "He's nice. But there's really nothing else to tell. We just had a dance, that's all."

"That's all?" Arlene echoed dramatically, rolling her eyes. "Everyone was shocked over that intimate dance you were doing, just the two of you. But tell me, did he ask if he could call on you?"

Erin shook her head.

"Then what were you talking about while you were dancing? He was saying something to you just before Tyler Manning made the musicians change to a reel, wasn't he? He seemed quite taken with you, too. I recognized that look," she added with a nostalgic smile. "It's the same way your father used to look at me. So surely he said something about seeing you again."

Erin wasn't about to get her mother's hopes up by confiding what Ryan had said in parting, because if he did, indeed, have a reputation for being a charmer with the ladies, then he was probably just trifling with her anyway. "Sorry to disappoint you, Mother"—she reached to pat her hand in comfort—"but we just made polite conversation."

Arlene shook her head, nonplussed. She considered herself gifted at judging people's reactions, and she would've sworn that Ryan Youngblood had been awed by Erin and would, indeed, come calling. In fact, he was her best hope that the entire evening hadn't been for naught. The other young men were, no doubt, still tied to their mothers' apron strings, would court the young lady their family chose and approved. Ryan, she'd heard, was something of a maverick, a rebel, and if he took a fancy to Erin, his betrothal to Ermine Coley would be forgotten as quickly as last Sunday's sermon, especially since it wasn't his idea in the first place. Ermine just didn't seem to be the kind of girl who would normally catch his eye. Oh, she was pretty, but so were birthday cakes, and once past the frosting, nobody cared about the cake beneath. Erin, on the other hand, was not only extremely beautiful, she was also intelligent, witty, fun-loving, and full of life. A man as worldly and sophisticated as Ryan would surely appreciate those attributes in a woman.

So, all things considered, it was hard for Arlene to believe they'd heard the last of Mr. Youngblood. The more she thought about it, the more convinced she was that he'd be the perfect husband for Erin. She needed a man who could cope with her indomitable spirit.

"Don't worry." She smiled more to herself than to

Erin. "I've got an idea he'll be calling soon. Would that please you, dear?"

"I suppose." Erin shrugged and turned to gaze thoughtfully out the window as the carriage moved through the balmy night. "It was all a mistake, you know, our coming here. Nothing has changed. We're still social outcasts, and I'd be better off going back to Atlanta and trying to find work, instead of staying around here, looking like I'm desperate for a husband, afraid I'll wind up a spinster. And frankly, I don't care if I do. Anything is better than marrying somebody I don't love."

Arlene stared at her daughter's profile in the glow of the side lamp and sadly thought how she could empathize so well with her feelings. Marriage to Jacob Sterling had been so very happy. Each day was a joy to live, and the nights in his arms had been heaven. She'd loved him above and beyond everything in this world. She couldn't remember a single argument or cross word between them. Not only were they lovers and parents and helpmates and everything else that went with a good marriage—they were also best friends. When he'd died so suddenly, thrown violently from a horse spooked by a snake, she'd been devastated; she'd lived in a stupor for weeks. The only thing that had kept her from joining him in death had been Erin. For her sake, Arlene had struggled from the brink of insanity, knowing Jacob would have wanted her to dedicate herself to the child borne of their deep and abiding love. Then, when Zachary had proposed, she'd been well aware she could never love him as she had Jacob, but vowed to try to be a good wife to him. But how could she have known what he was really like? How could she have been aware, beforehand, that in exchange for future security she had actually signed away her soul to the devil himself?

Oh, yes, Arlene nodded to herself as she continued to

stare solemnly at the daughter she adored, how well she could understand her child's resolve to avoid a loveless marriage. But Ryan Youngblood was a man of class and good breeding. Surely, he'd never physically abuse or mistreat his wife. Zachary, on the other hand, might be rich, but he was selfish, mean, lacked scruples and honor, and life with him had been hell. She had, so far, managed to suffer in silence, not wanting Erin to know just how awful things were. Better, she felt, to lie with simpering remarks about how Zachary wasn't as bad as he seemed.

Erin, Arlene was well aware, could be quite stubborn. Getting her married as soon as possible was a formidable task. But it had to be done. Thinking once more of Dr. Bowman's grim diagnosis, she was raked with panic and desperation. He could do nothing, he said, for the illness that plagued her. Consumption, he called it, warning the coughing spells would become spasms, as the blood spitting worsened. He had no idea how long she might live, but assured her she would get weaker and weaker.

Arlene was not afraid to die, but she did want to have the peace of knowing Erin would be looked after when she was gone. Never could she trust Zachary to do so; she didn't intend even to let him know how sick she was.

Erin turned to look at her mother, curious as to why she'd become so quiet. Seeing her worried expression, she felt the need to offer, "Mother, it'll be okay. Someday the right man for me will happen along. We don't have to humiliate ourselves this way, and I don't want to, ever again. But I appreciate your efforts. I really do. This dress, everything. The evening wasn't entirely wasted."

Arlene smiled to herself as she murmured, "No, dear, it wasn't wasted at all." She then leaned back against the smooth leather seat and closed her eyes in complacency. Erin didn't know it yet, but she had found the right man.

Midmorning, the next day, Erin was still sleeping, because she'd lain awake for hours reliving the delicious moments in Ryan Youngblood's arms. She couldn't stop thinking about how he'd caressed her with his eyes, the feeling that at any moment he was going to kiss her, wondered what she'd have done if he had. In Atlanta there had been a few boys who'd called on her, but she never got interested in any of them, and the kisses they'd stolen on the wisteria-draped porch had been awkward, clumsy.

Somehow, she knew it would be different with Ryan. He was, she felt sure, quite experienced in such things.

Still, despite the sweet reverie, Erin was realistic, telling herself she'd never see him again. At least the memories were wonderful, even if they were all she'd ever have, she acknowledged as she drifted off to sleep.

Letty, forgetting her mother's stern warning that she'd best forget the closeness she and Erin had once shared, was beside herself to hear Erin's version of the ball. Miz Arlene had said not to wake her for church, that she was probably tired from all the excitement, but Letty wanted to find out just what kind of excitement she was talking about.

Quietly letting herself into Erin's room, Letty crossed to the bed and gently shook her awake to ask, "What was it like? Did you meet somebody real nice?" She crawled onto the bed to sit cross-legged, elbows propped on her knees, as she'd done so many times when they were children.

Erin stretched and yawned, smiling as it all came rushing back. She confided everything, as Letty listened with wide eyes, finally exclaiming, "I've seen Mastah Youngblood before, when we was—"

"*Were,*" Erin was quick to correct. "You haven't forgotten everything I tried to teach you about talking proper, have you?" she chided gently.

Letty rushed on, not wanting to be reminded of something else she could get in trouble for if it were known Erin had been teaching her to read, write, and talk as white folks did. "When we *were* takin' cotton into town one day, I saw him standing on the side of the street, and I noticed him, 'cause he was so fine lookin', and I asked Momma who that was, and she said that was Mastah Youngblood of Jasmine Hill, where they breed fine horses and have one of the biggest and nicest plantations in all of Virginia.

"But she also said," she went on to confide, "that he never beat his slaves, and when his daddy was alive he didn't, either. She said what a blessing it would be, if we ever got sold to somebody like Mastah Youngblood. Is he goin' to come courtin' you?" Letty asked hopefully. "Just think, if you marry him, you can talk him into buyin' me and Mama, and we could all be together."

Erin laughed, but not in ridicule. "Well, that's a wonderful idea, but not likely to come true. I don't think Victoria Youngblood, from what I've heard about her, would ever approve of her son courting Zachary Tremayne's stepdaughter."

Letty hooted at that. "He danced with you, didn't he? And he didn't care who saw! Why, as pretty as you is—" she saw Erin's dark frown and corrected herself, *"are,* he won't care what his momma says. You wait and see. He'll be knockin' on the door."

Erin lay back against the pillows in contemplation of that possibility, then admitted, "I'm not sure I'm ready for that, Letty. With any man."

"Ready for what?"

"Romance. Love. Kissing. Touching." She folded her arms behind her head, staring up at the blue lace canopy above. "Frankly, it scares me to think about it."

"But why? It's nothin' to be afraid of."

Erin lowered her gaze then, to stare at Letty and wonder once more if she should tell her about that awful night, then decided it best to keep it locked inside. As long as she didn't put it into words, it seemed more like a nightmare than reality. Forcing a smile she didn't feel, she said, "Enough about me. Do you realize since I've been home we haven't had one serious conversation about you and what's happened to you these past five years?"

Letty couldn't help snickering at such a ludicrous question, couldn't hold back the cynical retort, "What could change in five years for a slave? Oh, I don't have to work in the fields, anymore, and that's nice. Lord knows, I hate pickin' cotton, draggin' those big sacks behind me, while the stickers keep my hands raw and bleedin', and the sun beats down to fry my skin. Now I get to work in the kitchen out back, or here in the big house, 'cause Mastah Zachary says I'm breedin' age, so it's time for me to do some lighter work, leave the fields to the younguns and the bucks, and the older ones. Hmph!" She gave a bitter snort, then leaned to whisper, instinctively fearful, even though they were alone. "I ain't breedin' with just anybody, no matter what the mastah says. The truth is, I love somebody, Erin, and he loves me, and that's who I want to breed with, have a baby by, and marry!"

Erin was delighted, sat up once more to hug her knees against her chest and cry, "You see? Something has happened in your life since I've been away, and you've got to tell me all about it. Who is this wonderful young man that has fireflies dancing in your eyes?"

Looking absolutely blissful, Letty told her about Ben, one of the grooms at the stable, how they'd fallen in love during the past year. Then the happiness left her face and voice all at once, as she angrily told how they weren't allowed to marry. "Mastah Zachary says he don't want none of his slaves gettin' married, 'cause he wants to choose who we breed by, and he also says it just causes more trouble when he separates a husband and wife by sellin' one of 'em."

Erin was struck with fury and sympathy at the same time. "That's wrong. It's also sinful, and—"

Letty interrupted, anxious to finish venting her rage. "That's not all the evil that goes on around here. It's got worse while you were gone. He's awful, Erin. Just awful. He even beat my momma, and you know how good she is, how she minds and never gives nobody no trouble. But one night, the mastah, he came home drunk, and he got mad 'cause she didn't have his supper waitin', and she tried to tell him it was way past suppertime, nearly midnight, and Miz Arlene, she said he won't comin' in, and to put all the food away, but he'd dragged her out of the bed, anyway, but he was so crazy drunk he wouldn't listen, and he threw her down in the floor of our cabin and beat her with his belt then and there. If he hadn't been so reelin' drunk, hardly able to stand up, he'd have hurt her real bad, but he didn't have the strength, thank Jesus."

Erin sucked in her breath, felt the cold shiver in her spine as she tightly asked, "Does my mother know all this?"

Letty hesitated, not wanting to say more but knew she'd said too much as it was. "Yassum," she regretfully answered, falling back into the slurring speech of the colored and forgetting everything Erin had taught her about carefully pronouncing all the syllables in a word. "She knows. But she ain't gonna say nothin', cause she's prob'ly scared of him, too."

Erin clenched her fists, suddenly rigid with fury. She knew if she ever saw Zachary strike her mother, she'd want to kill him. Once upon a time, she'd been ready to, anyway, but pushed back that horrid memory as she focused on the present misery.

Maybe she was being foolish and unrealistic to think she could actually meet a man with whom she could fall in love and live happily ever after, like in fairy tales. Her only real chance at happiness might be in getting married as soon as possible, escaping this awful place, and taking everyone she cared about with her, and that included convincing her mother to go, too. And just maybe that somebody was Ryan Youngblood.

Finally she said to Letty, who sat watching her in apprehensive silence, "I suppose I'd better keep my fingers crossed that Mr. Youngblood was impressed, that he'll want to court me. It may be the only way out for all of us. God forgive me"— she was suddenly swept with emotion—"but I hate Zachary Tremayne!"

Letty could actually feel her wrath and shuddered at the intensity. She was not, however, going to join her in asking forgiveness for harboring hatred. No, sir! Instead, she was going to pray real hard for God to make it all work out, that Master Youngblood would ask Erin to marry him, and then they would all be delivered from the evil.

But most of all, Letty hoped to spare her from ever knowing just how evil things really were!

"I definitely think she's the right one." Keith tossed down the rest of his whiskey and held out his glass to Ebner for refill.

Ryan was only half listening. For the past hour, they'd been sitting in the study, while Keith droned on and on about the attributes of Mary Susan Hightower. In the span of only one evening, Keith had decided he was going to marry her and wanted Ryan to share his enthusiasm. Ryan was trying to be polite, but the fact was, he couldn't care less. He was too lost in thought over his own find at last night's ball—Miss Erin Sterling.

The image of her lovely face kept appearing before

him—limpid eyes framed by lashes that seemed to have been dusted with silver and gold, the ebony sheen of her hair and the way he'd lustily envisioned it fanned out on a pillow. He thought, too, of her luscious body, the way she'd moved as he watched from the terrace. Tall, she'd have long, curvaceous legs, and he wanted to see them, feel them, run his fingertips up and down and caress that creamy skin, move all the way up between her thighs to touch her in that magic place, making her moan and writhe as she begged him to take her.

Ryan not only enjoyed making love to women, he liked making it good for them, too. Watching their enraptured faces as he took them to climax, knowing he'd succeeded in giving them total ecstasy, served to make his own that much better. Never had a woman left his bed without being satisfied—and if she had, she was a damn good actress.

He looked forward to giving Erin Sterling pleasure. In fact, he was anticipating many good times with her, once she was established as his mistress. He'd be discreet, of course, but he'd make sure she was lavishly provided for. A small house in Richmond, perhaps, so the times he couldn't be with her due to his family or his business, she could find entertainment dining out, going to the theater, with escorts he'd provide, of course. He would see to it she lacked for nothing, that she had the most exquisite clothes, jewelry, any luxury she desired. He'd arrange servants, too, as many as she wanted.

Templing his fingers, Ryan looked through them, framing the lush, rolling pastures outside the window, thought how unfortunate it was he couldn't share his own treasures with her. She struck him as the type who'd enjoy horseback riding, farm and plantation life. A shame it would be to tuck her away in the confines of the city, in order to render her available whenever he wanted or needed her, but that's the way it was, the way it had to be. He'd try to take her with him when he traveled as often as it could be arranged, because after talking with her only briefly, he could tell she'd make a good companion.

Companion.

He smiled to himself.

Mistress.

Erin was the perfect choice.

Just as Ermine was the right pick for a wife, he supposed resignedly. She was good blood. They'd produce fine children. He knew nothing about Erin's background. In fact, the only thing he did know about her was that she set him on fire, and he had to have her, damn it.

"You aren't listening to a word I've said!"

Keith's sharp, indignant cry brought him out of his reverie, and he glanced at him, shook his head, and admitted, "I'm sorry. What did you say?"

"I was asking," Keith said, "whether you thought Christmas would be too soon for me to marry Mary Susan, because I thought it'd be nice if we made it a double wedding with you and Ermine."

"That sounds fine," he said, though he didn't know what he really thought, because he just wasn't concerned with Keith and his problems. What he wanted to concentrate on was how to approach Erin. Hell, as eager as her mother was to find her a husband, he couldn't just go charging over there and knock on the door as if he were commencing to court her officially. There had to be another way, a way to get the message across to Erin, who certainly had left the impression she was interested in anything but matrimony. That left only the position of mistress. She was smart. She'd catch on quickly—if he could just get to her.

Keith, watching him with narrowed, suspicious eyes,

finally accused, "You're thinking about Erin Sterling, aren't you?" Without giving him a chance to confirm or deny, he continued, "Now's as good a time as any for me to tell you I think you should know people are talking. In church this morning, I overheard several of the women talking about that dance you were doing last night, though the criticism was more with whom you were doing it with."

Regarding him cooly, Ryan said, "She happens to be gorgeous, Keith, in case you were blind to everyone but Mary Susan. And she certainly can't help who her stepfather is. Tell me, what do you know about her? I mean, where did her mother come from? What's her family background?"

"Oh, I don't know," Keith replied with an absent wave. He wanted to talk about Mary Susan, not some brazen female who'd dare go where she wasn't invited. "Not from around here. South Carolina, I think I heard someone say a long time ago."

"Well, I've never heard much about Zachary Tremayne, but you seem to know a lot, from what you were saying last night, implying he's into illegal slave trading."

"You've been away. He only got involved after America made it illegal, like I told you. Up till then he was just a rich plantation owner with no class or background and was just ignored. Still is. The same for his wife. Arlene, her name is. A very sweet woman. I know her from church, and when Lareina died, she was very kind, came to visit and brought me food, long after everyone else had gone back to their own affairs and were no longer concerned with my grief. But none of that matters when it comes to being accepted socially, Ryan. You know that. So, get Erin off your mind. She's pretty, but she's not our kind."

"Depends on what I've got in mind for her."

"And that would be?" Keith raised an eyebrow.

"As you said yourself," Ryan gave a lazy grin, "maybe they should have presentation balls for potential mistresses . . . and maybe we actually went to one last night."

Keith joined him with a smirk of his own. "I'm beginning to understand."

"Good. So tell me. Does Erin go anywhere that I might be able to run into her so it looks like a chance meeting?" He related his fears of calling formally, lest her mother jump to conclusions.

Keith obliged by telling him he'd seen Erin riding by the mill stream that fed into the James River at the southeast corner of the Tremayne plantation. "Before Tremayne won that adjoining tract in a poker game, which, I heard, he cheated to win, Pete Dabnem owned it, had a gristhouse there for grinding corn. Tremayne shut it down, ran everybody off, posted signs. I used to like to fish there, but he's such a maniac, I was afraid he'd shoot me if I kept going, so I moved up farther, but I can still see his place as I'm coming or going across the ridge. Twice, I've seen Erin headed there on horseback."

"Late in the day?"

"Around four o'clock."

Ryan nodded to himself. Now he knew how he would make first contact.

CHAPTER

 4

AFTER SEVERAL DAYS OF DRIZZLING RAIN AND overcast skies, Arlene relished the afternoon of sunshine and cool breezes. She could breathe better in fresh air, didn't cough as much, so she stayed outdoors as often as weather permitted.

Concentrating on her tatting, as she sat on the front porch, she hummed to herself, rocking gently to and fro. Maybe with the nice weather, she mused, Ryan Youngblood would come calling. If not, then maybe she'd have to be so bold as to send Roscoe to Jasmine Hill with a written invitation to tea. When she'd mentioned that possibility to Erin at breakfast only that morning, she'd been surprised that she hadn't protested, actually appeared to approve the idea, though she hadn't come right out and said so. The fact was, she seemed to have mellowed a bit since the ball, didn't seem quite so defiant, though she did appear to be deep in thought about something. But, when asked if there was anything she'd like to talk about, she'd said not. Arlene had noticed, however, that she and Letty seemed to have picked up where they left off in their friendship. She'd seen Letty slipping up the back stairs after dark, despite Zachary's decree that no servants, except Roscoe, were allowed indoors at night. He didn't trust them, he said, and Arlene didn't blame him. They all hated him, would probably love to stick a knife in his throat as he slept. She didn't blame *them,* either. Not that she was prone to violence or condoned it. She just candidly acknowledged they hated him, had good reason to. But it worried her about Letty and Erin getting chummy again. Zachary had made it very clear he didn't approve, and she feared he'd take drastic steps if he found out.

Rosa came out on the porch with a glass of cool lemonade topped with a sprig of fresh mint. Arlene felt a special bond with Rosa, who also happened to be Letty's mother. In fact, it was at her urging Zachary had bought the two at a slave auction in Wilmington. They hadn't been married but a few days and were heading for Richmond and her new home. Passing through the coastal North Carolina town, Zachary had heard there was a big auction going on, because a slave ship had just arrived from Africa. He'd told her it was a good opportunity for her to pick out some household help of her own liking.

She hadn't wanted to go, hated the idea of bidding on people, buying them as if they were no more than cattle, but dared not say so, any more than she'd expound on her hatred for slavery in general. But he'd insisted, and then when she'd seen Rosa standing there on the block, her heart had melted. The auctioneer, callous bastard that he was, had stripped her naked, made her turn around in front of the hundreds of spectators, most of them men. "A good breeder!" he'd bellowed matter-of-factly, pointing at her wide hips and large breasts with the crop of his whip. "Already got a pickaninny, too." He pointed to Letty, who was still a baby, clinging to her mother's legs in terror as she stared out at the sea of impassive faces. She had no way of knowing what was happening to her. The auctioneer had then barked, "She's bound to be a strong one. It ain't too often pickaninnies survive the voyage."

Something had struck Arlene right in her heart as she'd witnessed the pathetic scene. Perhaps it was the fact that she had a baby daughter, too, or maybe her reaction was provoked by her own close-locked secret. She knew only that she wanted to spare that wretched woman and her pitiful child any more humiliation. Clutching Zachary's arm, she'd whispered, "Please. Buy them."

He didn't hesitate. "Yeah, I guess I could use a good breeder." Then he made a bid so high everyone else backed off. When they left Wilmington, Rosa and her baby rode on top of the carriage, crowded in among the luggage and trunks. No amount of begging from Arlene could move Zachary to allow them to ride inside, out of the broiling hot sun.

Rosa had gone on to have three healthy sons whom Zachary had sold, and it was only due to Arlene's constant, desperate pleas that he'd not done the same with Letty. She intended to remind Erin about that, as a warning that he might now sell Letty if he found out the two were renewing their intimacy.

Rosa had begun to water the potted ferns that lined the porch. They both looked up curiously as they heard the sound of a rider coming up the road. Shading her eyes with one hand, Rosa speculated, "That looks like Mastah Zachary. If it is, he sho is comin' in fast."

Arlene saw it was, indeed, her husband, and tensed instinctively. She'd thought he'd be back the night before, and when he hadn't returned, knew he'd probably stayed over in town to get liquored up. She had no idea where he went on his business trips, as he called them. Actually, she didn't want to know, fearing he was up to no good. All she knew was that whatever he was doing, it made him a lot of money. Now, however, she'd have to cope with him either being sick from drinking all night, or, worse, he'd still be drunk. Getting to her feet slowly, she walked to the edge of the porch in fearful anticipation of what she'd have to deal with.

Rosa had started to go back inside, then hung back out of curiosity, sensing something was wrong.

Zachary reined in his horse so hard, the animal reared up in panic before landing on all fours to stomp about in agitation as he quickly dismounted. He threw the reins at Ben, who'd rushed from the stable at the sound of his galloping approach. Arlene saw at once he was not only drunk, he was livid with rage.

"You!" He pointed at Rosa, who had frozen where she stood. "Get inside. You know I can't stand you eavesdroppin'."

She rushed to obey, daring only to throw a sympathetic glance at her mistress.

Arlene was also frightened but mustered the bravado to meet his fiery glare. He was tall, heavy-set, with a big barrel chest. Heavily bearded, he had the eyes of a snake, and she wondered how she could ever have found him even remotely attractive. But that had been years ago, when heavy drinking hadn't caused broken veins all over his nose, and just plain meanness hadn't made him appear uglier than he actually was.

He didn't like the arrogant way she was looking at him and gave her a rough shove that sent her stumbling backward into the rocker. The jolt set off a coughing spell, and as she covered her mouth with shaking hands, he bellowed, "Don't start that goddamn barkin' of yours. You know it drives me crazy."

She tried to control herself, choked out the burning question, "What on earth is wrong with you? Dear God, you're like a madman."

"You're damn right!" He squatted before her, looked

up into her reddening face as she wheezed, tried to catch her breath. "I just came from Sully's Tavern in town, and I heard how the whole county is laughin' at you and Erin for showin' up at the Rose Ball without bein' invited. I should've known somethin' was funny when you said you were, after all the years when you weren't.

"Have you lost your goddamn mind, woman?" He raved on. "You think you can bull your way in and find a husband for Erin amongst them snotty, holier-than-thou, pompous asses?"

She drew in her breath slowly, trying to calm herself as she framed her answer carefully. "I knew it was just an oversight, a mistake, and we were really supposed to be on the invitation list, and—"

"Goddamn it, woman, that's a lie, and you know it!" He struck at the air with his fist. "You've never been invited to a ball or a social in this county, and you never will be. Folks look down their noses at me, 'cause I work for a livin'. I didn't come from a rich family to hand down wealth to me like those lazy, uppity sons of bitches. I had to work for everything I got. Folks can't stand knowin' that, and that's why I'm shunned and always will be, and the sooner you and that high-minded daughter of yours realize that, the better off you'll be.

"Furthermore," he went on, nostrils flaring, cords standing out in his neck, "they were also talkin' about what a spectacle Erin made of herself doin' some kind of lewd dance with that rake, Ryan Youngblood. And you let her do it, so that makes you guilty as she is!"

"Guilty of what?" Arlene was slowly getting to her feet once more, ire rising despite her fear of him, intensified in that moment by the way he reeked with the odor of whiskey.

Zachary also straightened, clenching his fists at his sides.

"I can't see that Erin has done anything wrong," she said. "And Ryan Youngblood is certainly no rake. He comes from a good family, but that's not the point. Erin can't help it if we're socially ostracized because of you. And you're wrong in your reasoning," she dared point out. "Folks don't look down on you because you had to work for what you've got. They shun you because of the way you behave, getting drunk and rowdy and always in a scrap. And they don't like the way you treat our servants. You try to hide it, but you're brutal and word gets out and—"

He gave her another rough shove that sat her back down, towered over her, and shook his fist in her face as he growled, "You shut up! You don't know what you're talkin' about, and you oughta know after all these years, I don't take sass off nobody, 'specially what I own, and I own you just like I own them slaves. And that's what they are—slaves! And it's nobody's business how I treat 'em.

"And I'll tell you something else," he went on raggedly, hoarsely. "Don't you ever throw off at me that it's my fault you ain't accepted, 'cause if folks around here knew the truth about what you are, they wouldn't even let you sit with 'em in church! You'd be up in the balcony with the rest of the darkies!"

Arlene gasped, stricken, instinctively glancing about for fear someone could hear him, relieved no one was about. "That's got nothing to do with it," she whispered, aghast that he had flung that in her face—again. Oh, there'd been times in the past when he had, but only when he was rip-roaring drunk and mean and not caring how bad he hurt her.

"Just remember your place, woman!" His upper lip turned back in a scornful snarl. "And don't you let me hear of you ever pullin' such a stunt again. Now I'm tellin' you to get that girl of yours down off her high horse before I do it for you! I'll see to it she gets a husband without makin' this family look like a fool!"

Arlene knew he couldn't stand for her to cry but had no more control. Covering her face with her hands, she bowed her head and wept. Enraged, he wrapped his fingers in her hair, yanked her head back, forcing her to look up at him as he continued his tirade. "You've made my life hell all these years, you know that? You connived to get me to marry you, put a spell on me, made me so goddamn crazy wantin' you I was willin' to marry you even after what you told me, but I ain't under that spell no more. And if you don't straighten up, learn your place, and do somethin' about that snotty daughter of yours, I'll do the same thing to you I do with slaves I get tired of fuckin' around with. You understand me? Now get out of here. I can't stand your sniveling!"

She fled quickly into the house to her sewing room, locking the door behind her before collapsing to the floor to give way to the flood of tears. Dear God, she asked herself for the thousandth time, why had she told him in a weak moment, all those years ago, that she had Negro blood, that her maternal grandmother had been a Negro? He had never suspected because she passed for white, with help from the skin-bleaching potion her mother had taught her to make, the same potion she insisted Erin use, so there'd never be a hint she was a mulatto. But back then she'd foolishly felt the need to be completely honest with Zachary, as she'd been with her beloved Jacob, who'd loved her so much he wouldn't have cared if she'd been green! Naively, she had believed Zachary when he professed to love her, thinking they would have a good marriage, also. So she had told him the secret, and he'd said it didn't matter. It was only later, when the fires of his loins had cooled, that she painfully realized just how terribly much it did matter.

There were times, when he was drunk, when she felt he truly hated her. He accused her of enticing him, holding out for marriage, making him so crazy wanting her he'd given in. He would beat her then, forcing her to perform the most depraved acts he could think of to humiliate her. Afterward, when he was sober, he would cry and apologize, beg her forgiveness, and swear he loved her. But that was years ago. Now he had no more remorse, no matter how brutal he became.

Too late, Arlene had realized her mistake. Devoting herself to Erin, determined she should not suffer, she resolved to protect her at all costs, even if it meant being totally subservient to Zachary. He knew that gave him the upper hand, that she would tolerate any abuse he handed out. When she lost the baby she was carrying, he said he was glad, because he didn't want to have a baby by a mulatto. What he didn't know, what she'd never tell, was that she'd subjected herself to an abortion by a Negro midwife Rosa knew about, who was also adept at ridding slave girls of unwanted babies conceived by their masters.

So life had gone on, becoming more and more miserable with each passing year. Arlene lived in fear that Zachary would one day, in a drunken rage, reveal all to Erin. He'd sworn never to do that, but she no longer trusted him to keep his word about anything. And she never intended for Erin to know the truth, lest she repeat the mistake and confide the secret to the man she married . . . and subsequently live to regret it.

Arlene knew the only reason Zachary didn't tell Erin was that he enjoyed holding the threat over her head more. Once, she'd asked him why he didn't divorce her, since he obviously didn't love her, but in fact loathed and despised her. In response, he had sneered, then taunted,

"Because I own you, Arlene, just like the rest of the darkies on this place, and I'll keep you as long as it pleases me to do so. When it doesn't, I'll sell you, just like I sell them. Remember that, and don't give me any trouble!"

She wasn't really worried. After all, no one else suspected there was a drop of anything but Caucasian blood flowing in her veins. So, through the years, she had learned her place, and when he wasn't drinking, he just ignored her.

When Erin had begged, almost hysterically, to go to Atlanta to live with her aunt, Arlene had given in reluctantly. Filling her lonely hours with charity and church work had been rewarding, and she'd made many friends, even though she accepted the painful reality that friendship could go only so far, due to community disregard for her husband.

And now she was running out of time. She was dying, and soon all the misery would end, but please, God, she prayed, huddled there on the floor, let me live long enough to see my daughter taken care of, so she won't suffer as I've had to suffer all these years.

A sudden knock on the door brought her scrambling to her feet. Dabbing furiously at her eyes with the back of her hands, she anxiously called out, "Yes, who is it?"

"Me," Erin responded. "I wanted to let you know I'm going riding."

Arlene made her voice light, "Oh, go ahead, dear, have a good time. Forgive me for not letting you in, but I'm in the middle of something."

Erin, bemused by the locked door, lingered only an instant, for she was anxious to be on her way. Horseback riding was one of her few pleasures since coming back, especially since it took her away from the house—and Zachary.

Ben had her favorite horse bridled and waiting outside

the stable. She suppressed a knowing smile over the secret that he and Letty were lovers. He tried not to appear shocked, as always, over the way she wore riding breeches, like a man, instead of a skirt, and rode bareback.

The day was hot, sun beating down on the fields of cotton and corn from a sky so deeply blue it appeared to touch the distant horizon in a solid mass. She set out on her favorite trail, which took her beyond the fields to the banks of the meandering stream that eventually fed into the James River. Her favorite spot was the site of the old mill. Zachary had closed it down some years ago, but the water was shallow there in one spot, if anyone wanted to ford to the other side. Beside the waterwheel and the tiny stone mill house, there was a delightful pool for bathing on a terribly hot day. A graceful weeping willow tree stood sentry atop the grassy, sloping bank.

Erin didn't feel like wading or bathing. She was in a somber mood, reflecting on how so many things had changed while she was away. It was as though an invisible pall had descended, oppressive and evil. Despite all Letty had dared to tell her, she'd already noticed how the other servants seemed subdued, moving about to do their chores with head down, shoulders stooped, spirit broken. Even her mother had no real zest for living anymore, though she tried to put up a front. Erin noticed the shadow of misery in her eyes, the desolation and despair mirrored there when she thought no one was looking.

Dismounting, she looped her horse's reins around a bush, then began to wander absently along the bank to the juncture at the river. Staring at the flowing current with envy, she thought how at least the river knew where it was going. She had no idea what the future held for her.

She was relieved that Zachary had more or less ignored her since she'd returned from Atlanta. Maybe his specialty was molesting children, she thought with a violent shudder of contempt and bitterness.

Never would she forget the terror and revulsion of that night when he'd sneaked into her room to crawl into her bed as she slept. She'd awakened in terror to feel his fingers probing between her legs, and when she'd tried to scream, he'd grabbed her around her throat and choked her till she started to lose consciousness, all the while being blasted by his whiskey breath as he whispered he'd kill her if she didn't stop struggling, or dared to ever tell a soul. She'd had to lie there, fearing for her life, as he touched her, squeezed her, rubbed his ugly, swollen thing between her thighs till he'd made a lot of grunting noises. Afterwards, she'd felt nasty, defiled.

She hadn't dared tell anyone, not even Letty, who sensed something was wrong. The next night, and all the nights after till she convinced her mother to let her go stay with her aunt, she had pushed furniture in front of the door, then hidden under the bed till morning.

Now that she was back, Erin no longer dragged furniture in front of the door, but she locked it, and she kept a kitchen knife hidden beneath her mattress. If he dared return to her bed, she was prepared to defend herself, to the death if need be.

Suddenly she was wrenched from the loathsome memories by the sound of a snapping twig in the woods just behind her.

A roll of panic assaulted at the thought that Zachary might have seen her ride out alone and followed her. She'd noticed his horse being rubbed down by another groom at the stable, so she knew he was back from wherever he'd gone. He might have taken another horse, planning to attack her far from the house, where no one would hear her screams. But by God, he'd have a fight on his hands!

Glancing around quickly, she spied a large stone and grabbed it for a weapon.

Then she felt a wave of sweet relief as the rider came out of the woods, and she saw it wasn't Zachary—it was Ryan Youngblood, and he was riding a magnificent white stallion.

Looking at the rock she was holding, he realized he'd startled her and apologized, "I'm sorry. I didn't know anyone was about." Glibly, he lied, "I was just out riding and must have wandered onto your place without realizing it." Actually, he'd been there every day, even in the rain, waiting for her. He'd about given up hope, figuring Keith had been mistaken, seen someone else out riding along the stream.

Bemused, she told him, "It's all right. You just took me by surprise." She noted he was wearing a white shirt, open to his waist, and her gaze helplessly moved from the thick mat of dark blond hairs on his broad chest, downward to rock-hard thighs in form-fitting trousers. He exuded strength, and, yes, there was something almost feral about the way he was looking at her with those smoldering blue eyes, making her tremble, not with fright, but a kind of delicious anticipation.

"Well, it was fate." He dismounted and slowly approached her. He was toying with the reins, wrapping them absently about his fingers as he drank in the sight of her. "I must say you've been on my mind almost constantly since the other night, and. . . ." With a teasing smile, he huskily reminded her, "As I said, I've been dancing with you in my heart ever since."

Erin was warmed by his words but maintained her cool demeanor. "Well, we certainly gave people something to talk about."

"You like to shock people, don't you?" He surprised her by bluntly asking.

"I don't know that I'd go so far as to say that," she replied with equal candor, "but I pride myself on having a mind of my own."

"We're a lot alike. I sensed that right away. Maybe that's why I'm so taken by you—your spirit, plus other attributes. . . ." His gaze raked over her appreciatively before he continued. "This is a nice spot. Do you always come here?"

"Always," she admitted, her voice even despite the tremors within. "It's private, till today."

He walked past her, as though looking for something, then pointed to the bank. "Lots of horses. Wagon wheels. Somebody comes around," he noted curiously.

" 'Coon hunters, probably," she speculated, noticing the tracks. "They must come at night. I've never seen anyone during the day."

He was quietly thoughtful for a moment, then told her how once, as a boy, he and a friend had built a raft and passed this very place as they ran away from home, heading downriver. "We intended to go all the way to Norfolk, where we hoped to stowaway on a ship and sail to England."

"How far did you get?" she asked, amused at such antics.

He laughed. "My father was waiting for us at Cooley's Bridge, about a mile on downriver, waiting with his belt, I might add." He rubbed his backside for emphasis. "I walked for the next two weeks, couldn't even sit on a horse. It was a long time before I thought about sailing to Europe again, believe me."

"But you eventually made it, or you wouldn't have learned the valse or did you make that up to tease me?"

"Why would I do a thing like that?" He frowned at such absurdity. "Of course I learned it over there. You caught on very quickly, by the way. We'll have to try it again, sometime. I enjoy shocking people, too," he teased.

She saw the mischievous gleam in his eye, sensed he had a rebellious streak, and she liked that—a lot. "I envy you," she said then, "being a man and able to travel to faraway places, do anything you want to do. I'd love to be so free."

"You should be able to afford to go anywhere you want to. I hear your stepfather is quite well off."

"I don't want to spend his money," she said quickly, sharply, then hastened to explain, "My mother wouldn't hear of me traveling alone. That's what I mean about envying you. Men can do anything they want to."

"Well, maybe one day you'll marry a man who likes to travel as much as you do."

She laughed, a soft, wistful sound. "If I wait till then, I'll be too old to travel."

"A beautiful young woman like you? Come now, Erin. I imagine you've got your pick of beaux."

"If that were true," she challenged with a sudden lift of her chin, "why would my mother have insisted I show up at the ball without an invitation? If men were flocking to my doorstep, it wouldn't have been necessary for me to humiliate myself, would it?"

"I only meant—"

"You were only being polite," she corrected sharply, "because I'm sure you know all about my stepfather, how my mother and I aren't received by Richmond society due to his less than favorable reputation."

"I guess I have," he admitted quietly, "and I think it's unfair."

Erin couldn't resist pointing out, "I don't recall my mother ever being invited to call at *your* home, Mr. Youngblood."

He stiffened, momentarily unnerved by her candor, then recovered to admit, "Frankly, I didn't know you or your mother existed till the night of the ball. I'd heard of your stepfather. Few people haven't, but where have you been?"

"Atlanta," she said with a shrug. "Living with my aunt. Otherwise, my mother would probably have been dragging me around trying to find a suitable husband for me long before now."

His lips were twitching, amused by her self-deprecating humor. "I think you're being too hard on yourself, Erin. I can't imagine any man letting animosity for your stepfather stand in the way of pursuing a lovely woman like you. I know I wouldn't—if I happened to be looking for a wife."

Erin was quick to inform him, "Well, I appreciate your concern, but I don't happen to think marriage is all life holds for a woman, whether she's pretty or not. I like to think there are options."

"Such as?" He raised an eyebrow, delighted at her spunk.

"I'm not sure, but there has to be something." Then, wanting to turn the conversation from herself, said, "I'd like to hear about France, Paris, tell me what it's really like."

Ryan was only too happy to oblige, for, despite the memories that were unpleasant, he had been entranced by the country and its people. He told her about Paris in October, when the days grew shorter. Dusk fell by four o'clock, and how cozy it was to have the *valet de chambre* light the logs in the fireplace, and sit there having tea in the cheerful glow while watching the violet twilight creep over the city.

He told her about the magic of Versailles in autumn when gold and russet leaves drift among the allées. He painted for her with words, a tapestry of beauty to be found in the chateaux of the Loire, the parterres of brilliant chrysanthemums in Chenonceaux, and the splendor of the Tuilleries gardens after a sculpturing snow. And he made her thirst as he described the taste of wine with roasted pheasant or partridge in Burgundy.

Absently, as he talked so spiritedly and she listened, enchanted, they had walked along the soft, grassy banks, finally resting beneath the whispering fronds of the weeping willow. It was only when fireflies began to dance in the gathering shadows that they realized the afternoon had passed.

Erin scrambled to her feet, brushing bits of grass from her skirt. "I have to get back. It's suppertime, and my mother will be worried, because I'm always home before now."

She started to turn away, but suddenly Ryan yielded to the longing that had been building all afternoon. Almost roughly he caught her about her waist and spun her about. Momentarily surprised, she had only to look into his smoldering eyes to know what was about to happen. As his lips began to descend to hers, she began to tremble, first in fear, then anticipation, as she yielded with a sigh.

As his mouth covered hers, Ryan could feel her quivering response. Shyly, slowly, her fingers lifted to his shoulders, and then she was clutching, clinging, her body unconsciously arching against his. She was swept away from reality by a dizzy ecstasy never before experienced. Time seemed frozen as he held her captive in his embrace.

Ryan felt himself being wrenched apart, ignited with desire fiercely above and beyond anything he'd ever known before. He was on fire with want and need, an almost frantic wave sweeping him from head to toe as he pressed her yet closer to him, knowing she could feel his hardness.

Erin was too naive to know what to do. She wanted to cry and laugh all at once in the sheer wonder of it all.

She was helpless, befuddled, could only continue to cling to him and savor the sweetness for as long as it lasted.

He raised his lips to whisper hoarsely, "God, you're driving me mad," then assaulted again, his tongue tracing a hot line between her lips, urging, coaxing them to part. But when she felt his tongue, at last, plunge inside her mouth, at the exact instant he reached to cup her breasts and gently squeeze, Erin found herself suddenly caught in the whirling maelstrom of a nightmare returning. Gone was the joy, the sweetness, and in its place was a terrified child, writhing in protest and terror as her stepfather tried to hold her still, hands clawing at her beneath her nightgown.

"No! Don't!" She screamed, tearing herself from him. "No . . ." She stumbled away from him, swiping at her mouth with the back of her hand, but was instantly horrified at what she'd done. The hurt in his puzzled, bewildered gaze was unbearable, and she could only stammer, "I—I'm sorry. It—it was happening so fast." Dear God, she couldn't tell him that he'd unknowingly conjured terrifying memories.

He stared at her in frowning disbelief. It was difficult to comprehend that one so sensuous and enticing could be so easily unnerved. Surely, she'd known what she was doing. He'd felt her pressing herself against him almost eagerly. Was she playing some kind of game, making him crazy with wanting her? She seemed far too sophisticated for such capricious nonsense, especially when she'd impressed him with intelligent questions, her own knowledge of worldly affairs. Seldom did he encounter such intellectually captivating company in a female, particularly in one so beautiful. Seeing the undeniable panic in her lovely brandy-colored eyes, he supposed an apology was in order and murmured he didn't mean to offend her.

She untied her horse and swung up into the saddle to

look at him beseechingly. "There's nothing to apologize for. It was my fault. I shouldn't . . ." Her voice trailed, and wildly, silently, she asked herself what it was she shouldn't have done, because everything she did, she'd wanted to do, right up to the time he'd touched her breasts and slipped his tongue in her mouth, bringing back all the ugliness.

She reined the horse around and dug her heels into his flanks to set him at full gallop. She could think of nothing else to do for the embarrassing moment except to escape it.

"Tomorrow," he yelled firmly after her. "I'll be waiting for you."

She was too filled with self-loathing to look back, or respond, yet felt the familiar thrilling rush.

She'd be there.

Oh, yes, she had to be there, for there was no denying that Ryan Youngblood had touched her heart, and she had to find out where all of this was going to lead, where she truly wanted it to lead.

CHAPTER

 5

L*ETTY LISTENED, ENTRANCED, AS ERIN TOLD HER*
about the chance meeting with Ryan. Then, when she got
to the part about him kissing her, how she'd reacted,
Letty was astonished and cried, "But why? Why did you
do that? You've been kissed by boys before, haven't you?"

"Ryan is no boy, Letty. He's a man, and it was different.
He obviously knew what he was doing. I didn't."

Letty's brows drew together as she thought about the
situation. "Maybe," she said slowly, evenly, "it's best you
don't act like you know what you're doing."

"What do you mean by that? I feel like a fool."

"You don't know Sudie, do you?" Letty didn't wait for
a response but rushed on. "You probably wouldn't. She's
in the fields all the time. Anyway, Mastah Zachary bought
her last year. She comes from someplace down in North
Carolina, and she was sold off by the family that owned
her, 'cause her mistress had to go away, and they didn't
need her no more. And you know why her mistress had
to go away?" Her eyes grew wide.

Erin shook her head. It all sounded terribly mysterious,
and she wondered what it all had to do with her own dilemma.

Letty proceeded to oblige with the information that,

according to Sudie, her mistress, Miss Coralee, was being courted by a young gentleman, and the family was already making plans for a big wedding. When he suddenly didn't come around anymore, gossip began to circulate that he'd got what he wanted from her and no longer had a reason to marry her. "Her daddy went crazy, from what Sudie said, half beat Miss Coralee to death, sayin' she shoulda known a man ain't gonna buy the cow if he gets the milk for free, and no decent man would marry her after everybody knew that. So he sent her away, to live with some kin in another state, where nobody would know what she done, and she'd have a chance to find her a husband."

Erin sighed and reached for another oatmeal cookie. She and Letty were piled into her bed. It was nearly midnight, and they'd sneaked some things out of the kitchen and up to her room for a late-night snack. "Why are you telling me all this?" she asked. "What does it have to do with me acting like a ninny when Ryan Youngblood kissed me?"

Letty also grabbed a cookie, stuffed it in her mouth, then talked around it. "Don't you see? If he can't get free milk, he's gonna buy the cow!"

Erin looked at her in the candle's glow. She looked so ridiculous, trying to be serious, while her mouth was full of oatmeal cookie. Then, thinking of being compared to a milk cow, Erin started to giggle. Letty joined in, and soon they were swept with gales of laughter.

When, at last, they calmed down, Letty grew serious and said that she didn't know anything about the courting ways of white folks, but it seemed to her that if Miss Coralee had lost her beau by giving him something he wasn't supposed to have until after they were properly married, that Erin would be wise to remember that and not make the same mistake with Mr. Youngblood. "So," she said with proud finality, "I think you're smart to look dumb, so he won't think you ever did give away any free milk. In fact"—she leaned closer to advise conspiratorially—"I think you oughta make him want that milk real bad!"

"Letty, you're terrible!" Erin laughed self-consciously. "What you're suggesting I do is to lead him on, make him want me something fierce, and then tell him he can't have me unless he marries me."

With a shrug, Letty asked, "What's wrong with that? That's the way it's supposed to be, ain't it? When are you gonna see him again?"

"Tomorrow. He said he'd be there tomorrow waiting for me."

"Just remember what I told you, and the next thing you know"—she waved her arms triumphantly—"you'll be Mrs. Ryan Youngblood, and your momma and me and my momma and Ben will all be livin' at Jasmine Hill!"

Erin looked at her thoughtfully and dared to wonder whether she might be right. If he did propose, and they did get married, so many lives would be made happy by their union, and wasn't that what really counted? Yet, she knew there was one obstacle—her fear and revulsion of any man touching her. She'd have to try very, very hard, because she had a feeling he would easily lose patience if she rebuked him every time he tried to kiss her.

He'd wind up not wanting the milk or the cow!

Zachary made his way slowly up the back stairway. This part of the house was used only by the servants and then only during the day, but he hesitated between steps anyway, to listen for any sound. The master quarters were situated all the way at the other end of the second floor. Erin's room, however, was right at the top of the steps. Very convenient. Just as he'd planned it to be when he had Arlene give her that room when she returned from Atlanta. And since he'd been waiting for this moment for five years, he figured he could be patient a little longer, take it slow and easy. He licked his dry lips in hungry anticipation. Lordy, she was worth the wait, because she'd really ripened into a lush and lovely piece of woman flesh. And he figured by now she was old enough to see how it was to her advantage to be nice to him. There'd be no more resistance, much less furniture shoved against the door once he made it clear he'd give her anything she wanted.

He was approaching the top. Just a turn to the right, and then five more steps, and he'd be directly outside her door. If she had locked it or tried to block him, he'd brought tools to take the door off at the hinges. Arlene wouldn't hear. She slept soundly, thanks to that cough medicine the doctor gave her for that infernal wheezing of hers. It was probably put on to get sympathy, anyway, he figured.

He stopped just as he was about to round the corner, because he could hear the familiar sound, muffled, like when she'd stuff a handkerchief in her mouth to try and stifle the rasping that got on his nerves. It was Arlene, right outside Erin's door!

Cautiously, he peered around the corner, and, in the shadowed darkness, could just make her out. It was then that he heard the laughing and giggling coming from Erin's room, and furiously realized Letty was inside with Erin. It was all he could do to keep from charging up there to kick the door down and drag both of them out and give them a harsh whipping. Yet, he fought for control to realize Arlene would wonder why he'd been creeping up the back stairs in the middle of the night.

He began to retreat, as quietly and stealthily as he'd advanced.

By the time he'd gone around and made his way up the main stairway, Arlene was on her way back to her room.

He heard her coming down the hall, waited to take his final step up as she got right on him. She gave a soft cry, choked on a sudden gasp, and began to cough. He caught her by her elbow. She was wearing a woolen robe and slippers. He could feel her trembling as he silently guided her back to her room.

Once inside, he pushed her roughly down on her bed, and, as she stared up at him in the lantern's glow, her eyes bulged with both fear and the effort to hold back the rasping pressure in her terrified lungs. "She was in there, wasn't she? Letty."

Arlene would not respond; she shook her head slowly.

"Yeah, she was there all right, and now I know what I gotta do." He turned to go.

Arlene found her voice, dared to plead tremulously, "Don't go down there, Zachary. Please. Not when you're so upset."

He turned to face her, gave a short, brittle laugh. "Oh, I'm not going to interrupt them right now. Let 'em have their fun . . . for the last goddamn time," he added with a snarl. He continued on his way, closing the door soundly behind him.

Arlene stared after him only momentarily before reaching for the bottle of green hoarhound juice on the bedside table and taking a big gulp. Sometimes it helped soothe the coughing, and she leaned her head back against the pillows to take short, shallow breaths as the doctor had instructed.

Panic was a lump in her throat, even after the attack had subsided, because she knew what Zachary had meant when he said it was Erin and Letty's last time together.

Nothing would stop him from selling Letty now.

Her teeth ground together so tight her jaws ached, and she shivered with the force of her determination.

It might be too late for Letty, but by God, nothing

would stand in the way of ensuring Erin's future by arranging her marriage to Ryan Youngblood.

With a chill of foreboding, Arlene knew it had to be soon. She was running out of time.

He was sitting beneath the weeping willow tree, absently chewing a blade of grass, as he gazed toward the honeyed water. Erin watched him from the bank just above, struck once more by his stark good looks. He was wearing a pale blue shirt of muslin, and she feasted on his wide, masculine shoulders, the corded muscles of his arms, tanned to a golden bronze. Worn denim trousers molded tightly to rock-hard thighs. Sunlight filtering down through the gently swaying fronds dusted his hair with gold.

She could not deny being drawn to him. But while she had sensed warmth and tenderness, she also felt an undercurrent that he should not be pushed too far, not taken lightly. She had no intention of doing either, and, taking a deep breath and gathering all her courage, she urged her horse forward.

He heard her approach and quickly got up to meet her. Lifting her down from the saddle, he continued to clasp her waist with firm hands. Mouth curving in a teasing smile, he said, "It's nice to know you decided I wasn't such a monster, after all."

Unable to quell a sudden stab of uneasiness, she moved from his embrace, feeling her face grow warm.

She was wearing a pale green riding habit. With gloved hands, she reached to remove the matching bonnet, and her hair tumbled freely about her shoulders. "I never thought you were a monster." She finally trusted her voice to speak and turned to him once more. "I just felt things were moving too fast. We hardly know each other."

He cocked his head to one side, amused by her reserved

demeanor. "Some things don't move fast enough, my dear." Then, before she could dissent, he pointed to the basket she hadn't noticed. "I thought a glass of wine might be nice. Some fruit." He took out a linen cloth, unfolded it to spread in the shade.

They sat down, and, to make conversation, he complimented her fine chestnut quarter horse. She asked him about his own, a Morgan, and he proceeded to tell her a bit about the ones raised at Jasmine Hill. She was fascinated and began asking questions, which he eagerly answered.

As they talked and sipped the wine, Erin began to feel mellow, relaxed. She made a pillow of the bonnet she thought silly anyway, and stretched out beneath the swaying willow branches, enjoying the afternoon. Ryan lay on his side next to her, making sure to keep her glass filled.

They talked of any and everything, laughing together, just enjoying each other, losing all track of time. Eventually, Erin prompted him to talk about his travels once more, and he said his next trip would be to New Orleans in the fall. "There's a big horse show and auction. I've been wanting to breed Arabians. They're magnificent horses, so I thought I'd look for breeding stock at the show."

"New Orleans," she said in wonder. "I've always wanted to go there."

"Then come with me."

"Oh, I can't do that, and you know it."

"But would you like to?"

She was puzzled as to why he was pursuing something that was impossible. "It's ridiculous to even talk about."

Ryan bit back a smile as he poured more wine in her glass. "If you'd like to go, it can be arranged."

"We'll see." She laughed softly, sure he was teasing.

He reached to brush back a lock of hair that had fallen

onto her face, struck once more by her natural beauty. He moved closer. "Erin, I've learned that in this world you have to make the good times yourself. You can't sit back and wait for life to just hand them to you. If you really want to go with me, we'll work it out, because I sure as hell would like to have you along."

She knew he was about to kiss her and wanted him to, while at the same time becoming frightened all over again. "It's—it's getting late," she said nervously. "I really have to be going."

Almost roughly, he jerked her into his arms, and she gave a little gasp of surprise. He rolled over on his back, pulling her on top of him. He could feel her startled resistance melting as his mouth claimed hers in a smoldering kiss. Slowly, his hands began to move down her back, molding about her incredibly tiny waist before trailing downward to cup her firm, rounded buttocks. He wanted to touch her all over, kiss her all over, yet knew he had to move slowly. Despite her attempt at sophistication, he knew her for what she was—a naive girl trying to be a woman in the only way she knew how. He also found her innocence refreshing. It was nice to have a challenge for a change. Yet, there was no denying he was nearly crazy with wanting her.

Erin was swept with overwhelming desire and struggled against rising terror at the same time. Commanding herself to relax, she tentatively parted her lips, allowing his tongue to meld against her own, then delighted at the sweetness. He had begun to run his hands up and down her body in exploration once more, and she was tingling, shivering at his touch.

He maneuvered to the side, and she felt as if she were being consumed, devoured, by his ravishing hunger. She could feel the swelling of his desire, and with primal instinct, her body arched against his. Then, as though shocked by awareness of how easily they fit together, she stiffened and began to pull away. He wouldn't let her go, but held her with one hand, while the other quickly began to shove her skirt up about her shapely thighs.

As his fingers began to move upwards, Erin tore her mouth from his and gasped, "No, don't, you musn't . . ." She grabbed at his hand, slipped, clutched at his wrist instead, attempting to stop his assault, but he continued to search for, and find, that nuclei of sensation that rendered her helpless to the sweet hot needles of ecstasy that fired up into her belly. He caressed and squeezed, and she felt herself going limp in his arms, whimpering softly, deep in her throat. Maneuvering with his knee, he spread her legs, then reached up inside her to feel the moisture of her own rampant passion.

He wanted her as he'd never wanted another. Yet, even in the sweet anguish of maddening hunger, he knew once would never be enough. Not with Erin. She was the personification of everything he'd dreamed of in a woman but never found. As he held her, stroked her, reveling in her shudders of pleasure beneath his touch, he knew he had to have her at his beck and call. She was all he needed to make his life complete, the perfect mistress.

Despite the liquid fire coursing through her veins, Erin knew she had to turn back before it was too late. He was confident of her surrender, and she mustered every ounce of strength and determination to take him by surprise and tear from his grasp.

Quickly, she scrambled to her feet as he stared up at her in anguished disbelief.

"I can't!" She shook her head wildly as she backed away from him, raven hair whipping about her face. How could she explain what she was feeling? To hell with what Letty said about making him want her so desperately he'd marry her despite everything. She didn't want to cajole or bewitch any man. If it were meant for them to fall in love, so be it, but she'd not be a party to deception. "I'm sorry, Ryan, but I can't. Not like this."

He stared after her as she headed to where she'd left her horse. Damn it, he fumed, he'd never forced himself on any woman and never would, but he hadn't been turned down by one, either, especially when things had reached the point they had only seconds ago. He leapt up to follow her, grabbed her, and spun her about. "If you say you don't want me, Erin, you're lying. To me. To yourself. Why are you torturing both of us this way?"

How could she explain her anguished shame? She'd actually set out to seduce him, to make him want her so badly he'd stop at nothing to have her. But the reality was, she didn't want it that way. She knew no matter what her motive, she'd never be able to live with herself if she cajoled him into marriage. "I'm sorry," she repeated, closing her eyes because she couldn't stand the way he was looking at her with such blazing contempt. "I didn't mean it to be this way."

"What did you mean?" He gave her a violent shake that sent her head bobbing to and fro. "What's this all about? Why did you even meet me here?"

Her own ire started to rise. Her eyes flashed open and she fired back, "Why did you ask me? Was this all you wanted? To take your pleasure on the ground like a—a rutting animal?" she stammered indignantly.

Despite the wrenching pain in his gut from being set on fire and then left to smolder, he thought how lovely her eyes when angry, like brandy laced with raging splashes of claret. Recovering some of his wit, he gave a taunting smile and told her, "Well, frankly, I prefer to make love in a real bed, my dear, but that's kind of difficult to arrange under the circumstances. I can't take you to my house, not when you're still living at home under your mother and your stepfather's protection. A man can get killed for that sort of indiscretion, you know, and the same holds true if I take you to a hotel. So until we knew for sure this was what we both wanted and dared to go on and make arrangements to get you set up, what in hell did you propose we do?"

Erin's eyes had grown wider with each word he spoke, and, at last, she was able to demand past her constricting throat, "What are you talking about? What kind of arrangements? Set me up to do what?"

He couldn't believe what he was hearing. "Erin, you know damn well what I'm talking about. I want you to be my mistress."

"Your—your mistress?" she echoed, aghast, then shook her head furiously, wildly, and exploded, "You bastard! You think that's why I came here? Because I want to be your—your paid whore?" Tears stung her eyes, and she bit down on her lip hard enough to taste blood, fighting to hold them back. She'd be damned if she'd let him know just how deeply she was wounded by his callous reasoning. Mustering as much dignity as possible under the circumstances, she rushed on, "I thought we enjoyed each other's company. I liked you. I wanted to get to know you better. Maybe I even dared to think that somewhere down the road our feelings might grow and you'd court me. I was wrong. I was a fool."

He could only watch, stunned by her outburst, as she mounted her horse, then, reining about, she fired her parting shot. "I think, Mr. Youngblood, it would be best if we just forgot we ever met. And I'll thank you to stay off this property in the future."

Ryan stared after her as she urged the horse into a full gallop, disappearing around a bend in the road in a cloud of dust.

Never had he felt such frustration.

What the hell did she want from him? Surely, she didn't expect him to pursue her with the idea of matrimony—did she? Or was she actually attempting to make him so crazy with wanting her that he'd do just that?

He picked up the empty wine bottle and sent it sailing through the air to land with a loud splash in the middle of the stream.

Never again.

Never again would he allow himself to become so bewitched by a woman that he'd lose all control. Yet he knew he had to have Erin Sterling, and by God, he'd find a way to do so.

He returned to where he'd left his horse, rode away so deep in thought he didn't notice the Negro boy and the white woman watching from the wagon at the edge of the woods.

Arlene Tremayne withdrew the handkerchief she'd been pressing tightly against her lips for long moments to stifle the sepulchral cough. Despite her misery, she managed a wan smile.

She motioned to Ben to start the horses for home.

She'd seen everything she needed to see.

Now she could begin to make her wish come true—if God would spare her a little bit longer.

CHAPTER

 6

"**H**E KNOWS LETTY HAS BEEN SNEAKING UP TO your room," Arlene bluntly informed Erin, not looking up from her tatting. They were in the sewing room, and she'd seen Zachary ride out earlier and knew they could talk without him eavesdroping, as he was prone to do.

Defiantly, Erin replied, "So what? I invited her, Mother. Letty is my friend. There's nothing wrong with her coming to my room and talking."

"You know it's forbidden."

Erin had been standing at the window, gazing out at the rolling green lawn, dotted with leafy pecan and magnolia trees. Billowy clouds in a turquoise sky provided a canopy for the perfect afternoon. She wanted to go riding, but where? She'd have to find a different trail, because she wouldn't be at all surprised to find Ryan waiting for her at the millstream, despite her explosion yesterday. She sensed he was the kind of man who was used to getting what he wanted, and after a sleepless night of tossing and turning, she had to admit she was afraid—not of him, but herself, because when he held her, kissed her, it was all she could do to resist, and—

"Erin, are you listening to me?" Arlene asked sharply. Torn from her agitated thoughts, Erin looked at her mother and shrugged. "What do you want me to say? Letty is my friend, and I don't think it's right that Zachary objects, just because she's colored."

"It's not only that. She's a servant, dear, and she has to remember her place, just as you should remember yours." Arlene hated having to talk that way, because she certainly didn't feel that way, but for Erin's sake, and also for Letty's, she had to try and make her understand the social impropriety of their relationship.

Stubbornly, Erin persisted, "I still don't see anything wrong with it."

"Zachary does, and I hate to tell you this, but I think he's determined to put a stop to it, which means he'll sell Letty."

"No!" Erin cried in horror as she hurried to kneel before her mother. "You can't let him do that! Not Letty!"

"There's nothing I can do to stop him." She laid aside her tatting to reach and cup Erin's face with loving hands. "But if you'll promise me it won't happen again, that you'll forget about being friends with her, regard her as a servant and nothing more, then I'll do my best to persuade him to give you one more chance to obey his wishes."

Erin clasped her mother's hands, pressed them against her lips, then stood and moved to the window once more as she thought about the futility of it all. If Ryan's interest had gone beyond his lust, and he had eventually proposed, a lot of problems could have been solved. Now, sadly, that hope was dashed. So what did the future hold? Everything suddenly seemed bleak, dismal.

Arlene was watching her intently. When she'd overheard her telling Letty of her planned rendezvous with Ryan Youngblood, she'd had Ben take her to spy on them in hopes of confirming they were falling in love. Instead, though she couldn't hear what they were saying, she knew she had witnessed an argument of some sort. Erin had left in a huff, and Ryan appeared vexed. But Arlene wasn't giving up. Oh, no, she had the ammunition she needed to induce him to propose to Erin, and that's exactly what she intended to do—after she attempted to save Letty from the auction block. Gingerly, she prompted, "If you don't promise, then Letty is as good as gone."

But Erin wasn't listening, instead she was set on venting long-held resentments. She'd hated slavery from the time she'd been old enough to understand what it meant. "It's not fair. It's not right. Oh, why couldn't Virginia have been a free state?" She threw up her hands in agitation. "All the debate in Congress over trying to balance free states with slave states isn't going to solve anything. It's still cruel to hold people in bondage. And if Virginia hadn't been admitted to the union as a slave state, this nightmare wouldn't be happening."

"Erin, you aren't being realistic. I don't like it any more than you do, but the divide on the slavery issue is only becoming wider. Industry in the North is growing," Arlene said, "while the South just becomes more and more dependent on agriculture for survival. The use of slave labor is the basis of that survival, cruel though it may be. That's the way it is, the way it always will be, and poor Negroes like Letty are slaves, and all we can do is try to make their lives a little bit easier every chance we get."

"My father didn't own slaves. You told me that."

A dreamy smile touched Arlene's lips to think of the man she had loved with all her heart. Marriage to Jacob Sterling had been the only true happiness she'd ever known. "No, he sure didn't, but you have to remember he wasn't a farmer, he was a fisherman. I told you how we lived in a shanty by the ocean near Charleston. We didn't have much, except each other, and then you, but that was enough for us."

"You told me once he didn't believe in slavery."

"That's true. If he'd owned a hundred acres of cotton, I think he'd have let it rot in the fields if he couldn't afford to pay pickers. He would never have used slaves."

"And Zachary?" she prompted. "Did you know he had slaves when you married him?"

A shadow crossed her face as she bit back the response that there was actually a lot she hadn't known about Zachary Tremayne back then. "He told me he had a large plantation, and I suppose that implied as much, but I didn't want to believe anything in those days except that I loved him, and he loved me, and that you and I were going to escape poverty to live in luxury in Virginia. Your father hadn't been dead very long, remember, and I was having a terrible time eking out a living at the waterfront. I cut bait, scrubbed floors, begged for handouts when there was no money at all. Then Zachary came along one day and decided he wanted me, then and there.

"It was only later," she went on dismally, "that I found out things weren't going to be as wonderful as I'd dared to hope, but then there's never anything certain in life."

Erin bit down on her lip thoughtfully. At the time, she knew her mother had truly been desperate—a starving, penniless widow with a baby depending on her for survival. She could easily understand how her mother had allowed herself to be swept off her feet by a wealthy man. Still, she was compelled to find out. "What if he hadn't proposed? What if, instead, he'd asked you to just be his mistress?"

"His mistress?" Arlene echoed, eyebrows rising. "Why would he want me for his mistress if he didn't have a wife?"

Carefully, with a flippant shrug as though she weren't really serious, Erin said, "Well, you said you were begging, scrubbing floors. That's not exactly the kind of background a rich man looks for in a wife, is it? So, if he felt you weren't good enough, but still found you beautiful, desirable, wanted you just for his mistress, what would you have said?"

Suddenly, Arlene was struck by what she suspected might be Erin's motivation in asking such a question. Could it possibly have something to do with the scene she'd witnessed yesterday? She'd got there late, yet saw them lying on the ground embracing, kissing, just before Erin appeared to become upset, angry. Embarrassed Ben should see her daughter in such a situation, she'd made him turn his head and look the other way.

"Well, what would you have done?" Erin persisted when her mother didn't respond, just sat there looking at her, her mind a million miles away.

Taking a deep breath, letting it out slowly as she carefully framed her answer, Arlene finally pronounced, "I can't say, because it didn't happen. I suppose, however, I'd have held out for the respectability and security of marriage, even though it would've been a tempting offer due to my situation. I would've thought how once I relegated myself to being his mistress, I'd have been at his mercy. He could've kicked me out any time he chose, and then what would I have done? As I said, it hasn't all been apple pie and peaches as his wife, but at least I had some security."

Erin nodded, for that was her way of thinking also.

Arlene knew then her suspicion was correct. Ryan had asked Erin to meet him at the stream, instead of properly calling, because breaking his engagement to Ermine Coley was the farthest thing from his mind. He wanted a mistress, and when he'd let that fact be known, Erin had balked. Good for her, Arlene thought with pride, washed with relief to have figured out this new development. Now she had another weapon to help her achieve her ultimate goal.

Wanting to end the conversation so she could move on with her plan, Arlene suggested, "Why don't you run along, take your afternoon ride? Zachary will be back later this evening, and I'll talk to him then, see if I can persuade him to change his mind."

Erin couldn't hold back any longer and cried, "He beats his slaves, you know!"

Arlene winced. "I know, but there's nothing I can do. Nothing you can do." With a sigh, she suggested, "Maybe Letty would be better off if she were sold to another family. Maybe her life would be a bit easier."

"But what about Rosa? She doesn't know what happened to her sons, as it is. If Letty is taken away, too, it'll finish breaking her heart. No." She shook her head firmly, adamantly. "That can't happen. I won't let it happen. You tell Zachary I've sworn to you the friendship has ended. I'll have nothing more to do with Letty except as a—a slave," she spat the word contemptuously.

"I'm sorry it has to be this way. I can't even guarantee that my telling him will make him change his mind."

"How did he find out she was slipping into my room, anyway? What was he doing prowling around the house in the middle of the night?" Oh, how she ached to come right out and tell her mother what a true fiend he really was.

Arlene felt a wave of guilt. If she hadn't been prowling around herself, eavesdroping to try and hear what Erin was telling Letty about Ryan Youngblood, Zachary probably wouldn't have found out. She could only say, "It's his house. He has a right to do anything he wants to in it."

Erin gritted her teeth. Her mother didn't know just how far he thought that right extended. She knew what he was up to. No doubt, he'd been lurking outside her door, gathering nerve to attack. He'd heard Letty's voice, knew she wasn't alone, and now he wanted to get rid of

Letty so he wouldn't have to worry about her next time. Well, by God, she fumed, if he did sell Letty, and he did find a way into her room, he'd live to regret it—if he lived at all! She wasn't hiding that knife under her mattress just to threaten. She'd use it if it came to that. "You have my word," she said finally. "Do what you can."

Erin left, shoulders slumped, deep in thought over what to do if Zachary did, indeed, put her beloved friend on the auction block. What could she do?

If only, she reflected sadly, Ryan had wanted to marry her, everything would have worked out. She'd found him handsome, appealing, warm, and sensitive—enjoyable company. Drawn to him, she knew he would've been so easy to love, and she'd have found a way, somehow, to make him love her.

Now, she could only feel loathing, due to his insult and humiliation.

And never would she forgive, nor forget.

Ryan sat in his favorite leather chair, feet propped on the table before him. He chewed an unlit cheroot absently as he stared into the clean-swept fireplace. A half-empty bottle of whiskey at his elbow, he'd lost track of time. What difference did it make, anyway, he moodily reflected, how long he retreated to his study? Jasmine Hill was still efficiently run by competent overseers. There wasn't anything for him to do, except ride into Richmond for another wild, passionate night with Corrisa, or any one of a dozen other eager doxies. But he didn't want them. What he did want, he contemplated with narrowed eyes, was Erin Sterling.

She was beautiful. Gold-dusted eyelashes brushing gently against peach-colored cheeks, her lovely ebony hair falling softly about her face. Her breasts, firm, pointing. Her incredibly long and curvaceous legs. Perfect, rounded buttocks that ached to be caressed. Erin was the finest woman he had ever seen, the lushest, most appealing body he had ever held in his arms. Feeling a tightening in his loins, he knew he wanted her more than he'd ever wanted a woman in his life. He wanted to enter her and stay there until everything in him was drained into her. He wanted her beside him through the night, every night. He wanted to kiss those pouting lips into submission, make her want him every bit as damn much as he wanted her.

He reached for the bottle, took a swig. Several drinks ago he'd stopped bothering with a glass. Now, as the afternoon sun began to move toward early evening, shadows were creeping about the room. He didn't care, didn't give a damn for anything right then except trying to figure out what kind of game Erin was playing. She knew, damn it, she didn't stand a snowball's chance in hell of ever marrying into wealth or prominence. Her mother knew that, too, or else she'd never have been so desperate as to push her way into the Rose Ball. But it hadn't worked, and now what else was there for her? As he saw it, she had two options: marry anybody that would have her, which meant the lower class, or live a life of luxury as someone's mistress.

She knew that, so why had she reacted with such surprise and indignity when he'd made his offer? She sure as hell had given the impression she knew what he was after by the innuendoes she'd made. And there was no mistaking her response when he'd kissed her. It was all puzzling, and he wished he could get her off his mind but couldn't. All he could do was sit there and drink and be miserable, and the truth was, he was mad because he hadn't gone ahead and taken her then and there. It wouldn't have been rape. He knew how to make women beg for it, but he'd never done so when they weren't willing in the first place. And Erin had made it quite clear she wasn't.

He wondered if he dared ride over there, walk right up to her front door, demand to see her, and then come right out and ask her why she had led him on. But the truth was, he didn't dare. It would be misconstrued as calling on her, and her mother would jump to conclusions, and it could turn into a bigger mess than it already was. The best thing to do was forget all about those limpid brandy-colored eyes and that luscious body. Just get up, take a bath, get dressed, and ride into town and find Corrisa. At least she was eager and willing, knew what he liked. He had nearly two months free before his mother and Ermine returned from Europe, so maybe he'd just move Corrisa into the house. The servants wouldn't dare gossip about it. Jasmine Hill was composed of nearly a thousand acres, so it wasn't likely anyone would even know she was about. Most importantly, he knew he had to get his mind on something else. He'd probably wind up making Corrisa his mistress, anyway—a possibility that didn't particularly excite him.

He reached for the bottle again and took a long swallow. He was just sober enough to realize he didn't have any business riding into Richmond alone. He'd either fall off his horse or make easy prey for any outlaws that might be about. He'd go in the carriage, get Ebner to take the reins.

With a yawn, he got up, stretched, and was about to ring for Ebner to have his bath drawn, when he heard a hesitant knock on the door. "Mastah," Ebner called softly, "I'm sorry to bother you, but you got company."

Ryan shook his head, which felt a bit cobwebby. He wasn't expecting anyone, and people knew better than to call without being invited. "Who the hell is it?" he barked, tone a bit slurred from drink. "Get rid of them and get my bath ready."

"She says her name is Mrs. Tremayne."

He quickly went to open the door, sure he'd heard wrong. "Erin's mother? Are you sure about that?"

"Yes, he's quite sure," Arlene stated crisply, as she breezed by Ebner and on into the room. She wasn't about to be put off, and when he'd instructed her to wait in the front parlor, she had stubbornly followed after him.

Ebner nervously began to explain how he'd asked her to wait, but Ryan waved him away. "Just get me some strong coffee. Tea for the lady." Closing the door, he wished he hadn't drunk the afternoon away so he could think, speak, clearly. "Mrs. Tremayne," he greeted thickly. He held out his hand, slightly swaying. "An unexpected pleasure—"

"Unexpected?" She raised an eyebrow. She was carefully removing her gloves, one finger at a time. Her gaze flicked over him critically. He was disheveled, wearing wrinkled trousers, a shirt with the tail hanging out. No shoes. His hair hadn't been combed, and he hadn't shaved. With an intimidating air, she said, "I would say so. I'd hate to think this is the way you normally receive guests."

He didn't like the way she was looking at him and instinctively began to stuff his shirt into his trousers and to glance about for his shoes. "Forgive me for saying so," he couldn't resist, "but you seem to make a habit of appearing unexpectedly, Mrs. Tremayne. Had you been an invited guest, you'd have certainly found me appropriately dressed. Sit, please." He gestured to the leather sofa. "And tell me why I'm honored with this visit."

"Honor?" Again she responded with sarcasm. "An interesting choice of words, Mr. Youngblood, since I'm here to discuss that very matter concerning my daughter."

She sat down primly on the edge of the sofa, keeping her back rigid, stiff, striving to appear imperious.

For an instant, Ryan could only stare at her, bewildered, trying to figure out amidst the damn buzzing in his head what the hell she was talking about. He lowered himself into his chair before tersely responding, "I think you'd better explain that remark."

"Certainly. You see, Mr. Youngblood, the matter of honor is what brings me here. You've sullied my daughter's by attempting to seduce her."

"Seduce?" He half rose out of his chair, eyes widening.

She regarded him cooly, motioned for him to sit back down, waited for him to do so before continuing, "I'm a witness to that shocking scene yesterday, when you met my daughter down near the gristhouse. I saw you try to get her intoxicated. I saw you trying to force yourself on her. And I saw her fight you off and run away."

Arlene paused, wanting to give him time to absorb everything she'd just said, before concluding, "I'm sure we can resolve this amiably, with a minimum of embarrassment to both families."

Again, Ryan gave his head a vicious shake, wondered what the hell was going on. "Now wait a minute," he said. "If you were there, then you should know I wasn't forcing Erin to do anything. I have no idea why she got upset all of a sudden, because she was sure acting like she enjoyed every minute of what I was doing to her."

Arlene hoped her grimace convincingly conveyed her embarrassment over such a delicate subject. "Surely, Mr. Youngblood, you will agree that it was very improper of you to invite my daughter to meet you there in the first place. When a man is interested in a young woman, he calls at her home."

"*If* he's interested in formally courting her," he pointed out sharply, leaning forward to grip the arms of the chair,

knuckles turning white with the pressure. "I'm not interested in courting Erin, Mrs. Tremayne. In case you aren't
aware, I already have a fiancée."

"I know," she said, unmoved, then added challeng-
ingly, "So why were you at the Rose Ball?"

"A friend asked me to go with him. Look here!" He
bolted from his chair to tower over her, eyes narrowed
in anger. "I didn't try to force your daughter to do anything. Now get to the point, Mrs. Tremayne," he said,
muscles twitching in his jaw. "Why are you here? Did Erin
say I tried to force myself on her, because if she did, she's
lying, and I'm afraid I'll have to call her a liar to her face,
if she persists."

It was only with great effort that Arlene was able to
keep from withering before him. Lord, he was angry, but
she told herself he'd get over it. Erin would make him a
much better wife than would Ermine Coley, and in time
he'd come to realize that fact himself. Meanwhile she
would just have to help things along. "To repeat myself,
I'm sure we can resolve all of this with a minimum of embarrassment to both families."

He laughed, incredulous. "Just what is that supposed
to mean?"

"That my husband will be very upset if I have to tell
him all this, how you tried to seduce Erin, even asked her
to be your mistress."

"Mistress!" he roared, then silently cursed. So, Erin was
going to use that to try and force him to marry her. Damn
the vixen to hell!

"And," Arlene smoothly went on, "we don't want the
scandal of a duel, for heaven's sake! After all, I shouldn't
have to remind that your family honor is also at stake in
this unfortunate situation. Now, if we can just quietly arrange the wedding, my daughter's virtue and reputation
will be assured, and your mother, along with your friends,

will think you met my daughter and it was love at first sight. Those things do happen. There will be no need for anyone to ever know you tried to seduce a young girl."

He threw up his hands in absolute frustration, then slammed them down to whirl about, even more agitated, at the sound of the door opening quietly.

Ebner entered the room, carefully balancing a silver tray with teapot, cream, a bowl of sugar lumps, a cup of steaming coffee, and a plate of lemon cookies. With a wary look at his master, he set the tray down on the table in front of the lady, then stood back as she obliged herself by pouring her own tea. "Anything else, suh?" he asked worriedly, sure something was wrong, because he'd heard much of his master's shouting.

"Yes." Ryan all but snarled. "Get my bath ready, and get the carriage ready. We're going into town. I have an appointment with a lady friend." He turned to glare at Arlene for emphasis.

While she waited for his servant to leave, she creamed her tea, dropped in two lumps of sugar, then stirred with a tiny silver spoon. Finally, she looked up at him to offer her most demure smile and sweetly say, "Since you seem to be busy this evening, Mr. Youngblood, we'll expect you to call tomorrow to discuss the wedding arrangements. Shall we say—tea at four?"

CHAPTER

 7

R*YAN HAD NOT GONE INTO RICHMOND. AFTER* getting absolutely nowhere with Mrs. Tremayne, who'd made it very clear when she finally left that if he didn't show up the following afternoon by four, her husband would be banging on his door by five, he was in no mood for either revelry or sex.

He'd consumed two pots of strong black coffee to clear his head fully, as he spent the next few hours railing at himself for being in such disreputable shape when she'd confronted him. Unshaved, unkept, just a few drinks short of being totally drunk and incoherent, he hadn't been in a condition even to attempt to defend himself.

It wasn't like him to drink himself into a stupor, anyway. Sure he imbibed now and then but could count on one hand the number of times he'd crossed the line to utter intoxication. The first had been the year he turned twelve. One of his friends found a jar of home brew, and they had hidden in a hayloft to guzzle it down and wound up being sick for two days afterward. The next binge was the night his father died. And, again, when he'd learned the truth about that bitch, Simone.

Now, misery over the beauteous Erin Sterling had provoked a bender, and as he sobered, he realized things were even worse than he'd first imagined.

It was all a scheme. He knew that beyond a doubt. Erin had planned to make him so crazy with wanting her, he'd ask her to marry him. She hadn't counted on his offer, instead, to be his mistress. So, she and her mother came up with the contrivance about his attempted seduction and subsequent dishonor to her virtue.

The more he thought about it, the madder he got. Who the hell did they think they were dealing with, anyway? Did they actually think he'd be intimidated by an unprincipled scoundrel like Zachary Tremayne? If the fool challenged him to a duel, he'd blow him away in the blink of an eye. And he sure as hell didn't care about embarrassment to either himself or his family. His mother had nagged him for years about his disregard for social mores and wouldn't be at all surprised to learn he'd had another dalliance. Neither would Ermine, who probably suspected he had other women and would continue to do so after they were married and wouldn't give a damn as long as he was reasonably discreet about it.

Why, then, he asked himself over and over as the miserable night passed, was he even upset about Mrs. Tremayne's imperious and ridiculous demand? Yet, when anger and indignity finally began to cool, he was washed with the reality that the idea of marriage to Erin was not totally repugnant. She was, he acknowledged, everything any man could desire in a woman—certainly all he had ever dreamed of possessing. Had she come from the right kind of family, made a proper debut, nothing would have stopped him from pursuing her with matrimony in mind from the instant he laid eyes on her.

It was not, he rationalized, altogether her beauty that triggered such emotions. Neither was it her sensual aura that made him want to take her in his arms and carry her

off to the nearest bed. Oh, no, there was much more—
like her wit and sense of humor and her spirit and zest
for living. No question but that she was keenly intelligent,
an interesting conversationalist.

With a wry grin, he was forced to realize how much
more he'd have to share with Erin than with the cotton-
headed fluff chosen by his mother. Something told him
that he wouldn't need, or want, another woman with Erin
in his bed every night. Taking her with him on his travels
would be a pleasure. And maybe, he dared envision, if
they both tried, his jaded opinion of a possible utopian
marriage would crystallize into reality.

Yet, despite the positive waves, he was still infuriated
by all the conniving. Erin, like her mother, was obviously
the sort who'd stop at nothing to get what she wanted,
and he'd be damned if he'd put up with their blackmail.

By sunrise, Ryan had made up his mind to settle the
matter as soon as possible. He'd be damned if he was
going to stew about it all day. He saddled his horse himself, because the grooms were all still asleep, and headed
for the Tremayne plantation. The air was sweet and cool,
and gentle mist was rising from the dew-kissed meadows.
A doe and her fawn curiously watched him galloping
along from where they drank at a stream. Ryan, in his determination, was oblivious to everything around him.

The ride took nearly twenty minutes at a moderate gait,
but he slowed as the house came into view. It wasn't so
grand, he thought, certainly nowhere near the opulence
of Jasmine Hill, but then it was highly unlikely Zachary
Tremayne's wealth could compete with the Youngblood
fortune.

He found himself wondering if Erin were aware of her
stepfather's real source of income. It damn sure wasn't
from cotton. Ryan had made some discreet inquiries after
the ball, wanting to learn exactly what kind of background

she came from. He had learned that Keith was quite correct in the gossip about Tremayne being suspected of illegal slave trading. Tremayne had frequently been seen in the company of Nate Donovan, one of the most brutal slave handlers and traders in the South.

Since the law had passed prohibiting the importation of Africans for slaves, a vast black market had emerged. Virginia was up in arms over the situation, and its dynasty in the White House had sent several messages to Congress calling for more effective legislation against it. Evidence had been mounting for some time that outlaws, some of them organized into bands of pirates, were operating in the Gulf of Mexico and pouring slaves through southern borders into the union. The British naval blockade during the War of 1812 had stopped much of it, but it was still estimated that in the past five years, over ten thousand Negroes had been smuggled in. Those who owned rich spreads, like himself, Ryan reflected, were opposed to the African slave trade, but for rather narrow reasons. They preferred to breed and trade their own, selling at auction to farmers with smaller operations. The danger came from those who bought illegally more slaves than they needed. Parvenus, like Tremayne, drove the price beyond the reach of most men. That hurt the smaller farmers, who still needed slave labor to survive with the demand for cotton increasing. Vigilante groups were constantly searching for the bands of traders smuggling slaves in from forbidden cargo ships, but it wasn't an easy discovery to make. Many a body had been found in a swamp or coastal area where traders who didn't like being spied on came ashore.

Tremayne, it was said, did his dirty dealing in another state. It was rumored he'd get the illegal slaves somewhere along the Virginia coast, then quickly transport them down into the Carolinas for auction. By moving out of the area fast, there was little chance he'd get caught. No doubt, he was a slick operator.

It was still quite early, and Ryan was sure no one was up and about inside the house. He circled to the rear, to a detached building that served as the kitchen. It was a precaution against rapid spreading should there be a fire.

Slaves eyed him curiously. They stood in line, tin plates in hand, as they awaited their breakfast of hominy grits and lard biscuits.

Other plantation owners gave their slaves Sundays off, but not Tremayne. His Negroes were obviously overworked. Ryan could see that in their weary faces, the way they shuffled doggedly along with shoulders stooped, as though every movement was an effort, even so early in the day.

The smell of fresh boiled coffee was in the air, and suddenly he wanted another cup desperately. What he had to say to Mrs. Tremayne wasn't going to take long, but he had been awake all night, and he wasn't feeling very alert at the moment.

A slave, obviously a stable worker, hesitantly approached, unsure as to what he was supposed to do with such an early morning guest. Ryan waved him away, tied his horse to a nearby post himself, then headed toward the kitchen as the others moved aside for him.

He was almost to the door when he heard it—the sound of broken sobbing coming from inside. Entering the small brick structure, he saw the woman sitting on a stool in a far corner, crying pitifully. A few other women hovered about her, but at the sight of a stranger in their midst, they began to disperse. The woman, however, was far too broken up to be aware of anything around her.

One of the others dutifully asked, "Suh, you need somethin' here?"

"Coffee," he replied, and she got him a cup at once.

He took a sip, still watching the hysterically sobbing woman. He couldn't keep from asking, "What's wrong with her?"

"Well, suh," she began hesitantly, then fell silent as there was a commotion outside. Everyone seemed to be talking at once, and above it all, he could hear a woman shouting to let her through.

Ryan blinked at the sight of Erin charging into the kitchen, but she didn't see him standing to one side; she was oblivious to everyone and everything about her, even the fact she was wearing only a thin, and very revealing, nightgown.

He drew in his breath sharply. God, she was exquisite. Silhouetted against the light streaming in from the door behind her, he could see the sculpture of her full, rounded breasts, her shapely thighs, and the shadowed treasure between. He'd envisioned how she'd look naked, and with a sudden wrench in his loins knew his fantasies were reality. And, for the moment, he forgot why he was even there.

He was, however, abruptly yanked back to the present as Erin ran to the woman, dropped to her knees, grabbed her hands in hers and fiercely demanded, "When did you find out, Rosa? How long has the bastard been gone with her?"

Rosa choked on a fresh sob, and Erin patted her back to calm her.

"Jus' befo' I sent 'em to fetch you. I got up this morning, and she won't in her bed, so I thought she was with Ben, and when I went to his shack to tell her she better get up and get busy, that's when I saw what they'd done to him." She looked at Erin in horror, shook her head as though still unwilling to accept it was so. "They musta hit him while he was asleep, bashed his face all in, and then took her. There was blood all over the floor, so I know she put up a fight." Covering her face with her hands, she began to wail as her body rocked to and fro in quaking misery, "They took my baby girl. Jus' like they took my boys. And I ain't never gonna see her again."

At that, Erin protested, "No, Rosa! I won't let them get away with it. I'm going to ride after them. There has to be a trail. I'll track them down and get her back, I promise, and—"

"You'll do nothing of the kind! You aren't going anywhere!"

Erin was jolted by her mother's unexpected entrance.

Unlike her daughter, Arlene had taken time to put on her robe. Walking across the room, she seemed in complete control as she continued. "What's done is done. You'd never be able to find them. Now Rosa—" she started also to kneel but began to cough, and had to back away as a spasm took over. Turning, she saw Ryan and gasped, coughing even harder in her sudden shock.

Erin followed her gaze and exploded at once, "What are you doing here? How long have you been standing there eavesdroping on things that don't concern you?"

She started to advance, but Arlene threw out a feeble hand in protest. It wouldn't do, she knew, for there to be a scene, here, now, in front of the servants. "Erin. Go make yourself decent!" To no one in particular, she desperately begged, "Water, quickly, please."

In horror, Erin glanced down to realize how she might as well have been naked, standing there in the sheer gown. Further enraged to know Ryan was staring at her, she lashed out at him as she hurried out. "I warn you. You'd better not be here when I get back."

With Erin out, and after a sip of water from the glass she'd quickly been handed, Arlene gathered her composure. "Yes, I think that would be a good idea." She glanced about, spotted Roscoe anxiously watching from a side window, and called, "Take Mr. Youngblood to my sewing room. Get him coffee or whatever he wants. Put his horse away."

Turning back to Ryan, she advised she'd meet with him after she was dressed. Then, with a sweeping gaze, she gave the orders. "Miss Erin is not to be told that Mr. Youngblood is still on the premises. Is that clear?"

Assuming it was, Arlene gave her attention to Rosa.

Ryan hung back only for a moment. All he could gather was that Zachary Tremayne had spirited away the heart-broken woman's daughter to sell her. A sad situation, but not out of the ordinary. Erin, however, had been strangely upset by it all.

He didn't have to wait long, hadn't even finished his coffee when Mrs. Tremayne came in, very calm and collected. Her hair was no longer streaming down her back but braided about her head. She was wearing a simple cotton dress of pale yellow that did nothing to compliment her sallow complexion. He hadn't noticed the previous evening just how unhealthy she looked, but then he'd been drinking—and also got mad pretty damn quickly after her arrival.

She didn't offer her hand, which was just as well, because he probably wouldn't have taken it.

She crossed to the cabinet where Roscoe had left the silver service and poured the coffee he'd left for her. After a quick sip in an attempt to quell her nervousness, she said, "You were invited for afternoon tea, Mr. Youngblood, not morning coffee."

He was equally curt. "Well, I knew if we didn't get this settled, everything in-between would sour my stomach."

"Which means you're ready to set a wedding date?" She walked over to the divan, head held high and knees shaking violently, praying he wouldn't notice.

Ryan actually started to tell her she was crazy, to recite

everything he'd planned, how there was no way he'd be cajoled, coaxed, coerced, blackmailed, whatever it might be called, into marrying Erin. Yet, as his lips parted to vehemently inform her of his feelings, the vision of Erin in that damn nightgown danced before his eyes. Her body was sculptured to perfection—breasts like honeydew melons with nipples as succulent and sweet as wild mountain berries. And the thought of those long, graceful legs wrapped around his back made his heart slam right into his chest.

He had never been a man given to impulse or irrational behavior, but with the familiar flames of desire starting to rage, he knew, beyond all doubt, he had to have her. To hell with his mother and her determination that he breed with aristocracy. Breed! The word rolled around in his brain amidst waves of contempt. That was what his horses did, for God's sake. And cows and hogs and other animals. He didn't want to breed!

He just wanted to be inside Erin, feel her velvet warmth wrapped around him.

He was also jarred to realize how the thought of being saddled with Ermine for the rest of his life had become unbearable in the wake of his passion for Erin.

Finally, in a voice he hardly recognized as his own, he surprised even himself by declaring, "Yeah, I guess so."

Arlene's hand flew to her throat, as she swayed ever so slightly in astonishment. When he'd appeared unexpectedly, she figured on an ugly scene of refusal. She hadn't had time, in the wake of the terrible situation concerning Letty, to plan her next course of action. Now, for him to yield so easily, she could only stare at him in wonder.

He saw that she'd been caught off-guard and couldn't resent goading, "Well, it seems you've amazed even yourself, Mrs. Tremayne, that you were able to actually pull it off."

"Pull it off?" she echoed, slowly regaining her composure to pretend innocence. "I'm sure I don't know what you mean."

"Of course, you do." She was good. Damn good, he mused, and if Erin inherited her talent for acting, heaven help him if he wasn't forever on his toes. "Come now, Mrs. Tremayne, do you take me for a fool?"

"Are you denying you asked my daughter to meet you with the intention of seducing her, intending to ultimately take her for your mistress?" She stared at him, mustering an indignant expression.

"I'm not denying anything. That's what I'm trying to tell you. I don't have to, because I'm not guilty of anything. You, on the other hand—" he sat down beside her, eyes twinkling—"have only one thing on your mind, and that's getting your daughter suitably married. And you're willing to do anything to accomplish that, even if it means blackmailing me."

"Call it what you will," Arlene snapped, not liking his arrogance. "I'm merely a mother protecting her daughter's good name. What chance do you think she'd have to marry a decent man after it was known you've been trifling with her?"

He raised an eyebrow, couldn't hold back a soft chuckle as he countered to challenge, "What chance does she have of marrying a decent man when her stepfather is an unscrupulous rogue?"

Arlene gasped, not at the effrontery but at his audacity in speaking the truth. "I resent that, sir."

He went on as though she hadn't spoken. "The fact of the matter is, I am willing to marry your daughter, Mrs. Tremayne, but not because I'm intimidated by your ridiculous threats. The fact is, Erin happens to be the most beautiful and exciting woman I've ever met. Had I met her sooner, under, shall we say, normal circumstances, I would have wanted to court her without any prompting by you, or anyone else.

"I want her," he concluded. "It's that simple."

Arlene fought the impulse to clap her hands together and scream with joy. Instead, she gave a satisfied nod and calmly said, "Justify if you will, Mr. Youngblood. I'm interested only in my daughter's good name and continued respect in this community."

"Oh, of course." He bit back a laugh. "And now that you've got what you wanted, how about telling me what's going on around here so early in the morning?"

She bit her lip, looked toward the window, and fought the impulse to cry. "My husband sold a servant Erin was quite fond of. Too fond, I'm afraid. He objected to their friendship. I was also fond of Letty. I tried to get him to change his mind, but—" she caught herself and fell silent, embarrassed to have drifted into family matters. "We have other things to discuss." She suddenly felt driven to settle everything, get him out of there, so she could start thinking about how she was going to break all of this to Erin. It would be even more difficult on top of Letty's disappearance. "I think the marriage should take place immediately."

So fast, so simple, Ryan grimly reflected. He wanted a mistress, and he was getting a wife, and all hell was going to bust loose when his mother and his fiancée returned from Europe, but he'd worry about that later.

A part of him said he should be fighting all this, while another was silently, warmly, telling him it was the way it was supposed to be. Still, he knew he'd always remember Erin's treachery and forever be on his guard. "All right, but I'll have to get back with you on the arrangements."

"Good." Arlene rose, signaling the conversation had ended. She was anxious to see about Ben and try once more to comfort Rosa. It was going to be a busy day, and she wasn't feeling at all well. What she wanted to do was go back to bed and rest her weakened body.

She rang for Roscoe and told him to have Mr. Young-blood's horse brought to the front door, then walked with him to the foyer. They stood there a moment in awkward silence, neither knowing quite what to say. Finally Ryan felt the need to compliment her. "You're an incredible woman, Mrs. Tremayne. Not many women could've achieved what you set out to do."

"It depends," she retorted, "on how driven a person is, Mr. Youngblood."

"Perhaps. I suppose I've just never encountered a woman so desperate to get her daughter married." Bitterness rang in his voice. No matter how damn much he wanted Erin, the harsh reality was that her mother thought she'd forced him into it, and he didn't like feeling his pride had been trampled to bits.

"Erin will make you a good wife. Just see that you don't hold your resentment for me against her."

"I won't mistreat her, Mrs. Tremayne, but bear in mind I certainly don't love her."

"Of course you don't. All I expect from you is to treat her well. And remember—" she couldn't resist adding with a triumphant smile, "I can be a formidable foe."

He chose to end the verbal warfare and hurried on out.

Arlene took a deep breath, which provoked a little cough, then leaned back against the door frame to watch him go. She felt a warm, happy glow spread from head to toe.

It was done!

For whatever time she had left on this earth, she could bask in the joy of knowing Erin would be taken care of after she was gone. Ryan was a handsome man, and they would, no doubt, have beautiful children. Maybe the gods would smile on them, and they'd even eventually fall in love.

Smiling to herself with the assurance that when her time came, she could draw her dying breath in peace, Arlene turned, then gasped in sudden, shocked, awareness.

Erin was standing midway down the stairs, and she knew, at once, by the stricken look on her daughter's face, that she had heard everything.

CHAPTER

 8

"How could you?" Erin raged. "How could you do such a thing? Humiliate me this way?"

Arlene reclined against the pillows as she sipped the green hoarhound juice to stave off a coughing spasm. She'd learned that being upset sometimes brought on the attacks, and it was only with great effort that she controlled herself now. Erin had followed her to her room and was raving like a maniac. It didn't help that she was already upset over Letty.

"I wish you hadn't been standing there listening. I wanted to tell you in my own way. When you calm down and think about it rationally, you'll realize it's all for the best. He comes from a fine family. He'll be good to you, and you'll never want for anything the rest of your life. I couldn't be more pleased."

Erin who had been pacing wildly around, finally sat down on the edge of the bed. "Tell me everything. I've got to know how you ever got him to agree to this madness."

Arlene shrugged, as though it were all quite simple. "It's a matter of honor. He tried to seduce you—"

"How do you know that?"

"It doesn't matter how I know. The point is, he added

insult to injury by asking you to be his mistress. The only way he can redeem himself, save your good name, is to marry you."

"He probably hates me, because he thinks I was in on your little scheme. Don't you see? I can't marry him now. I don't even want to.

"I'll admit"—she got up, began to walk around once more—"that I *was* attracted to him in the beginning, but that was before I realized he was only interested in making me his mistress and wanted a little sample of what he'd be getting. The nerve!" She fumed.

"You see? That's exactly what I mean. He's insulted you, and now he owes it to you to marry you and restore your dignity."

"I still have my dignity, Mother. He didn't get what he was after. He doesn't owe me anything, and all I want is never to see him again."

"Be realistic, dear. You have no other options. You have to take a husband. I won't always be here to look after you, and—"

"I can take care of myself. I'm not like you. I'd never be desperate for a husband, like you were when you married Zachary."

Arlene winced, and Erin was immediately contrite. "I'm sorry, I shouldn't have said that." She took a seat next to the bed and wearily shook her head. "I don't mean to hurt you. It just seems like the whole world is crashing down around me. First, Letty is dragged off to be sold, God knows where and to whom, and then I find out you're arranging for me to get married . . . to a man I happen to loathe."

Arlene hurried to explain. "I tried to save Letty. I told Zachary you'd promised to end the friendship, and I begged him to give you another chance. I dared to think maybe he would, but I see now his mind was already made up.

She rushed on, "But please, give up the idea of looking for her. It's dangerous, and it's a waste of time. He takes all his slaves he wants to get rid of all the way down into the Carolinas, to make sure they won't be anywhere around here. If you keep the others stirred up with hopes of going after her, he's just going to have them beaten when he gets back to settle them down. The thing for you to do now is convince Ben to just keep his mouth shut. It's over. I'll do what I can to comfort Rosa."

Erin said nothing, not about to admit she had no intentions of considering the matter closed.

"And please," Arlene went on, "reconsider your feelings about Ryan. He'll make you a good husband."

Erin saw the desperation mirrored in her mother's eyes, the way she fought to hold back her tears, but she remained staunch in her avowal. "No. I won't marry him. I know how much it means to you, but I'm sorry. I just can't. Not after finding out he never thought I was good enough to be his wife," she added bitterly.

Erin spent the remainder of the morning helping tend to Ben's injuries. His nose was terribly swollen, probably broken. He had a nasty gash on the side of his face, and Tulwah, the old root doctor the slaves depended on to care for them when they were sick or hurt, came to stitch him up expertly with a needle and fine strands of horse hair.

Ben sorrowfully said he couldn't remember anything. He had awakened only when Rosa started screaming, he explained, and that was when he realized he'd been injured. He figured they had knocked him out so he couldn't make a fuss when they took Letty. "I'd have fought tooth and nail," he fiercely assured. "They'd probably have had to kill me."

"He knew we'd all have tried to stop him," Erin was quick to point out. "That's why he did it in the middle of the night. With others, he just marches them off in broad daylight, but Letty was special, and he knew it."

"Ain't there nothin' we can do?"

"We'll have to wait till Zachary comes back, and then I'll try and find out where he took her. Till then, just don't make any trouble, Ben. Take it easy and let your wounds heal."

She left him to see about Rosa. Tulwah had already given her one of his potions. She had stopped crying and lay in a drug-induced stupor, pitifully calling out, not only for Letty but her long, lost sons, as well. Erin couldn't do anything except sit beside her for a while, holding her hand to let her know she was there if needed.

Time passed miserably, as Erin worried over Letty's fate. She blamed herself for what had happened, for underestimating just how cruel Zachary could be. She longed to be able to tell her mother everything, how he'd tried to force himself on her those years ago, and her fear that he would try again. If only they could leave, go somewhere else to live, make a new life. He was getting meaner. There was no telling what he'd do next. But she was afraid telling her mother would have a calamitous effect. Not only would it crush her, but more and more lately, Erin was becoming concerned about her mother's declining health, which she was obviously trying to conceal. Perhaps, Erin thought, that was her mother's real motivation in trying to persuade her to marry Ryan Youngblood. Well, too bad. Erin resolved there had to be another solution to their sad situation.

Anxiously, she waited for Zachary to return. There were always papers signed, exchanged, between buyer and seller, when a slave transaction was made. No doubt, he would have a record for his files. All owners kept a registration list of their slaves, to prove ownership, and she knew where Zachary kept his. As a child, she had been playing in his study one day, behind his sofa. He had come in with one of his overseers and didn't know she was there. The men had shared a few drinks as they discussed the slaves bought that day. Erin had peeked out to watch Zachary write in a ledger book, then saw him place it, along with several papers, in a wooden box. He had put the box in the bottom drawer of his desk. So, when he returned from selling Letty, all she had to do was find the papers, and she would know where she had been taken and who had bought her.

Arlene continued to beg Erin to change her mind about marrying Ryan. "He said he was going to make arrangements for the wedding. He thinks he's going to marry you."

"It's not my problem. I never agreed to anything, and I wasn't the one who talked him into it."

Arlene refused to give up but knew she couldn't go on letting him think everything was settled. Toward the end of the week, she decided to pay him a visit and explain Erin's reluctance. By no means, she would emphasize, was he to think the marriage would not eventually take place. Erin was willful and stubborn, she'd point out, and her feelings had been hurt by his insulting behavior. Eventually, she'd get over it.

She made it a point to tell Erin exactly what she planned to say. "I'm still hoping you'll come to your senses."

They were having lunch. The day was hot and sweltering, and Erin had no appetite. She toyed with a bowl of sliced peaches and sipped at mint tea. Irritably, she said, "I told you, Mother. I'm not going to be a part of your scheme."

Arlene sighed and shook her head. "You're making a mistake, and I'm praying you realize that before it's too late. I don't think I have to point out no other young man has come to call on you."

"Neither did Ryan Youngblood, Mother. He asked me to meet him elsewhere, remember?"

As Rosa came in with dessert neither of them wanted, Arlene wearily said, "Have Roscoe bring my carriage around. Tell him to bring a water jug, because we'll be gone till evening. I'm going to the quilting circle at the church, and then we'll be visiting at Jasmine Hill."

Erin wondered, as always, why her mother helped out with making blankets for the poor with the ladies at the church. They only tolerated her because she made generous donations now and then; they didn't really want her there. She'd be much better off helping out in other ways, without subjecting herself to their condescending attitude.

Erin was in her room reading when Rosa came running in, wild-eyed and frantic. "He's back, Missy. Mastah Zachary just came into the house. I rushed up the back steps to tell you."

Erin tensed, then sat up. "Where is he?"

"He went in his study with Mastah Frank."

Frank was one of his favorite overseers, and Erin figured they were having a drink, something Zachary always treated his men to when they returned after a trip. He would, no doubt, also file away his papers on Letty's sale.

Anger was a knot in her throat as she struggled to remain composed for Rosa's sake. "Now listen to me," she quickly advised. "I want you to go to your cabin and stay there. You're too upset to be working in the house, and you're liable to make him mad. If you see Ben, tell him to be calm, that I'm going to try and find out where they took Letty, and I'll let him know later if I succeed."

"Oh, child, do you think you can?"

She got up to give her a comforting hug. "I hope so. I'll try my best. Now go, please."

Erin waited for what seemed like forever, keeping a vigil at the window for Frank to leave the house. Zachary usually passed out from his drinking, and hopefully would make it to his room first. If, instead, he lay down on the sofa in his study, as he sometimes did, she'd have to wait till later to search his desk.

At last she spotted the two of them, crossing the side yard and heading for the path that led to the distant cabins that housed the overseers. She saw Zachary was staggering a bit, which meant he was well into his cups.

Curious, she watched as Zachary sent one of the slaves to ring the iron bell in signal for the overseers to gather. Something was going on, but she didn't take time to wonder about that, wanting to take advantage of having him out of the house to look for the papers.

She hurried down the back stairs. The first floor of the house was composed of four large rooms, divided by the entrance foyer and the main stairs. To the left of the foyer was the parlor, adjoining the dining room. On the other side was Zachary's study, with her mother's sewing room behind that. The back hall ran the length of the house, with a few small rooms beyond for storage and a preparation room for food brought from the kitchen.

Erin went directly to the study, hurried to the desk, and pulled open the bottom drawer. Taking out the wooden box with trembling fingers, she lifted the lid. The ledger was not there, only a sheaf of papers, but none with Letty's name on them. Frantic, she turned the box over to dump the contents and began to look through once more. It didn't matter if Zachary knew she'd been through his things; she would worry about that later.

Lost in her desperate search, she was unaware that Zachary had come into the room. Only when she heard the ominous sound of the door closing, did she look up to see him. Fright struck but an instant, for rage overrode trepidation. "Where did you take her?" she demanded.

At first, he was angered to find her snooping in his desk, but then threw his head back to laugh at such outrageous audacity. "You'll never find her, you little idiot."

"How could you do it?" She exploded. "Wasn't it enough you sold off her brothers? Letty was all Rosa had left!"

"Rosa is a slave, and slaves don't have nothin'," he said with a sneer. "And it's none of your business what I do. Now get out of here, before I teach you a lesson you won't forget."

"I hate you," she said coldly, standing her ground. "I hate you for selling Letty. I hate you for what you did to me that night. I hate you for the evil bastard you are. And I wish you were dead!"

He ignored her tirade. Eyes gleaming with lust, he began to walk slowly toward her as he taunted, "Well, now, how cozy this is. Your momma's gone to truckle up to them holier-'n-thou church ladies, and I saw how you sent Rosa high-tailin' it out of the house. So now, we're all alone . . . just like that night."

She began to retreat as he started to stalk her around the desk. Between clenched teeth, she ground out the warning, "Don't you dare touch me, Zachary!" Glancing about wildly, she looked for anything to be used as a weapon. "This time, I will tell my mother, and—"

He sensed what she was thinking, cleared the desk with one sweep of his arm. "And what the hell can she do? Nothing. Not a goddamn thing. I own her, like I own you, and everything and everybody on this place, and I do what I want to, and the sooner you learn that, the better off you'll be.

"All these years," he drawled, reeling slightly from all the liquor he'd guzzled, "I fed you, clothed you, gave you the life of a princess, and you can't even stand to be in the same room with me, you snotty little bitch. It's time you showed some gratitude. Now get over here and give your daddy a kiss."

"You go to hell!" She forced the words past the constricting terror in her throat, as he moved like a predatory animal.

"You know, sweet baby," he continued, "maybe we should go together and tell her about us, how I've had a yen for you all these years, and now that she's so sickly with that infernal coughin' of hers, you're gonna be nice and give me what she don't want to. Now you come here, damn you"—his voice rose shrilly—"'cause I been waitin' long enough to taste your little honey pot."

He lunged. She didn't move fast enough, and he grabbed her and threw her to the floor. She fought wildly, but he was big, strong, drunk, and determined. He grabbed at her dress, tore the front, and her breasts tumbled forth. He clutched, squeezed, oblivious in his lust to the frenzied raking of her nails clawing at his face.

"Look at 'em," he said hungrily. "Like melons, all ripe and firm for the takin'." He burrowed his face in her heaving flesh, at the same time reaching to grope below. He rolled from side to side on top of her, shoving up her skirt, rendering her vulnerable to the attack of his probing fingers.

"Gonna have it," he cried, his whiskeyed breath blasting her. He moved to cover her face with wet, eager kisses as he fought to spread her wildly thrashing legs. "Gonna have that honey pot any time I want, and you'll love it, beg for it, and maybe I'll even marry you when your momma dies."

Erin was terrified, helpless beneath him. He was lying

to one side, pressed against her thigh, as he forced her legs apart with his knee. Grabbing her wrists with one hand, he pinned her down, assaulting her with his other. She rocked back and forth, horrified, knowing any second he'd have his way with her.

His body was pressing down her other leg, and when he maneuvered to unfasten his pants and release himself, she felt the momentary laxity in his hold. Gathering all her strength, she jerked one arm free and sent her fist slamming into that giant, throbbing thing that was about to invade her. With a scream of pain, he tore away from her, doubling over in agony.

Erin was on her feet at once. Chest heaving, rage and terror melding together like hot, molten lava through her veins, she towered over him to gasp, "If you ever touch me again, so help me, God, I'll kill you!"

He managed to get to his knees, and fire was in his eyes as he glowered up at her. "Just who the hell do you think you are?" He was nearly choking on his fury. "You dare threaten me? I'll tell you something, you little strumpet . . ."

She began to back up toward the door, then snatched up a vase in case he tried to attack again.

Slowly, he struggled to his feet; then, leaning against the desk, he made his way around to the chair. "Next time, I'll be sober, and we're gonna talk about this, 'cause it's time you learned which side your bread's buttered on. You're gonna find out just how mean I can be. And re-member somethin' else, if you ain't good to me, I'll see your momma suffers for it, too." He fumbled in a drawer, took out a flask. Unscrewing the top, he tilted it up to his lips and drank greedily, watching her all the while.

She shuddered with contempt, and, yes, fear. In that frozen moment, Erin knew there was but one way out of the hell on earth her life had become, for both her and her mother.

She had to marry Ryan Youngblood.

Albeit a deceitful arrangement, Ryan deserved it, she rationalized, in a way. Like her mother claimed, there was a matter of honor involved. He had insulted her by presuming she wasn't good enough to be his wife, fit only to be a kept woman, a prostitute by any other name. Instead, he would have to marry her, according all the rights and privileges of a wife. She would enjoy a life of luxury and wealth, bearing, in turn, his children, perhaps a son and heir. Meanwhile, he could take some other woman for his mistress to endure society's censure.

She would make her position clear from the beginning, and how she also intended to persuade her mother to move in with them to escape Zachary's mistreatment.

"Don't worry," Zachary snickered between gulps of the whiskey, "we'll keep this from your momma as long as you keep me happy. The way she is lately, I don't imagine we're gonna have to bother with her much longer, anyway.

"If you play your cards right," he continued, "I might marry you, like I said. Now get out of here." He stopped sneering to command, "And send somebody in here to clean up this mess."

Erin quickened her steps, and as she reached the door, turned the knob, he yelled, "By the way, there's no need for you to snoop around in here. You won't find out where she went."

She turned to stare at him, wondering what fiendish torment he'd throw at her next.

With a deep scowl, he told her, "The damn wench got away."

Erin couldn't hold back a scream of joy, "Thank God!"

"We'll get her, though," he was quick to say. "Me and

my men are goin' right back to the North Carolina line where she got away, and we're goin' to fan out in all directions and hire vigilantes and slave hunters, whatever it takes to find her.

"She got away." He paused to snicker. "Next time, you won't."

CHAPTER

 9

AFTER THE UGLY ENCOUNTER WITH ZACHARY, Erin had taken time to change clothes, hiding the torn dress in the bottom of her armoire. Later, she'd make sure it was thrown out, for it was beyond repair, and she didn't want her mother to see it and ask how it happened. Then, she'd gone in search of Rosa, to tell her what she'd just learned.

As she left by the back door and hurried across the yard toward the outbuildings, she could see Zachary over at the barn. Evidently, the reason he'd gone back to the house, after she dared think it safe to go in his study, had been to take weapons from the gun cabinet there. She could see him handing over several to Frank and the other white men gathered. No doubt, he was sending out a search party, all the way to the vicinity of where Letty had managed to escape.

Beyond the outbuildings—the kitchen, blacksmith, weavers, brickmakers, and several storage facilities—a path began to wind down toward the creek. She made her way past the nicer overseers section—log cabins in a neat row along cleared, smooth banks sloping to the creek. Farther along, the area became almost swampy, with fallen trees and dense undergrowth to the sides of the path. Zachary didn't allow any clearing, wanting the denseness for a divider between slaves and white workers.

She walked the trail for nearly a half mile, ever on the lookout for snakes. In the summer months, it wasn't unusual to find a copperhead water moccasin curled up beneath a pokeberry bush. Several slaves had been bitten in the past, and one, a small child, had died from the venomous bite.

Finally, she reached the slave compound, where three dozen or more tiny wooden shacks circled a clearing. The dilapidated porches were clustered with curiously staring children—pickaninnies, Zachary derisively referred to them. She knew most of them had to be less than five years old. Zachary sent children older than that into the fields to do whatever work their strength allowed.

She knew which shack was Rosa's. She had been there so many times in younger years to play with Letty. Back then, she hadn't paid any attention to the pitiful way the slaves lived. Now it leapt out at her like a cat after a field mouse, to painfully grab all her senses. She saw the shabbiness—rough-hewn log shacks, the roofs speckled with bits of trash and rags that had been stuffed into holes to try and keep out the rain. Doors hung open to give as much air as possible in the sweltering heat, because there were few windows—Zachary's only offering for insulation against winter chill. As she approached Rosa's cabin, it was impossible to tell where outside ended and inside began, for the floor was just dirt, a coarse, yellow, sandy kind of soil.

As she walked in, she was blasted by the heat of the open hearth. Rosa, trying to focus on something besides her troubles, was busy checking a stewing opossum. The heavy air was pungent with the smell of smoke and melting animal fat.

Hearing her come in, Rosa swung around to cry, "Did

you find out where he took her, where he sold my baby girl?"

"No, I didn't," she responded quickly, wanting to just get it over with, "because it looks like Letty escaped."

At that, Rosa fell to her knees and began to offer up a prayer of thanksgiving. A few women who had gathered outside when they saw Erin come in to the compound heard and quickly rushed in to join the frenzy.

Erin stared in wonder, unable to figure out what they were so happy about. Didn't they realize the perils Letty now faced as a runaway slave? Not only was Zachary organizing a hunt, there were also ruthless vigilantes about, who made a living tracking down the fugitives, using trained dogs to flush them out of hiding. Letty wouldn't know who to trust, because informers were generously rewarded by enraged slave owners. She had no money, no friends, only the clothes on her back, and she was out there somewhere in the wilderness, between Virginia and North Carolina, scared, hungry, and lost.

To be captured, Erin had heard, was even worse. Some runaways were punished by having a portion of one foot brutally hacked off with an ax, and, at the very least, were mercilessly whipped. Yet, despite all the grimness, the women were rejoicing.

In the middle of it all, Ben came running in to pull Rosa to her feet and give her a big bear hug in shared jubilation. He was barefooted and shirtless, his baggy, ragged pants tied about his narrow waist with a piece of rope. Unlike other plantation owners who made an effort to keep their slaves in adequate clothes and shoes, Zachary didn't care. The women wore clothes made from burlap feed bags, and many of the children just ran around naked in the summer months, like the ones now gathered in the doorway, curious as to why all the grownups were shouting and crying.

Ben's face, still pitifully swollen, spread into a relieved grin as he called to Erin, "It's God's blessin', Miz Erin. Oh, thank Jesus, she was able to get away."

Before she could ask why on earth they were all celebrating, Tulwah appeared, as he had a habit of doing at odd times and places. He was a free Negro, much to the dismay of people like Zachary, and had the papers to prove it. Despite the heat, he was attired in his usual purple-and-red woven robe. His feet were bare, but he wore gold rings around his toes. A leather thong around his neck held tiny bags of foul-smelling herbs and weird-shaped charms. Erin thought she saw a dried chicken foot among them and shuddered.

He looked about suspiciously, and when he saw Erin, he frowned. Ben was quick to assure him, "It's all right, Tulwah. Miz Erin won't say nothin'. She's the one what brought us the news about Letty."

Tulwah remained skeptical, crossed the tiny cabin to put an arm about Rosa and whisper something in her ear. She nodded, looked pleased over whatever he'd said. Then, with another wary look at Erin, he left as quietly and quickly as he came.

Exasperated, she asked of no one in particular, "Will somebody please tell me what's happening here? Why are you all so excited? Don't you realize what Letty has done? She's now a fugitive, the same as an outlaw, and they can shoot her if they want to, and—"

"They always could, Miz Erin," Ben interrupted. "Don't you know that nobody cares if a slave gets killed? But what you got to understand now is that Letty has a chance to be free. Once she gets in touch with the Free-Soil workers, and. . . ." His voice trailed off at the admonishing gasps exploding all around him in the tiny one-room shack.

"Ben, you say too much!" one woman cried.

Rosa was quick to defend, "No, it's all right. Miz Erin can be trusted. She's our friend. I speak for her."

There were some disgruntled mumblings, and Ben waved everyone out. When the three of them were alone, he exchanged an affirming nod with Rosa, took a deep breath, and proceeded to tell Erin why they were all so relieved. "I guess it's all right for me to tell you, 'cause you've sure let us know you ain't like them other white folks, the ones what don't think of us no better than a hound dog."

"Go on," she urged, anxious to learn finally what was going on.

"There's a secret group callin' themselves 'Free Soilers,' that's helpin' runaways. It's made up of free blacks and runaways, and they're in every community along the way North. Letty will be fine, once she makes her way to one of them, and she's better off than most runaways, 'cause thanks to you, she's smarter. You broke the rules and taught her to read and write.

"I'm gonna tell you somethin' else, too," he went on. "Me and Letty had been talkin' about runnin' away, 'cause things here are gettin' so bad—" he paused to flash an accusing look at Rosa, "but she couldn't talk her mammy into goin' with us and wouldn't leave without her."

"I'm too old to run," Rosa said brokenly, wearily.

He ignored her to continue, "So you see, Letty is on her way now, and she'll find a way to get word to me where she is, soon as she can."

Erin was fascinated, dared to feel hope that maybe there was justification to rejoice. But she wanted to know more about this new group that she was glad to hear existed. "Where do you think she went? Where does this . . . this underground trail take the runaways?"

"The free state of—" he hesitated, not sure how to pronounce it, "Penn . . . suhl . . . vainyuh. A place called . . ."

He shook his head. He heard only smatterings of what went on up North, and if the words and names and places were unfamiliar, they slipped right over his head.

"Philadelphia?" she guessed. He nodded. Remembering her geography, she went on to point out, "Pennsylvania would be a likely state. It's the only one immediately north of the Mason-Dixon line that has an international port—Philadelphia. It would be a natural meeting place for boats traveling north from Virginia, Maryland, and Delaware."

Ben wanted to know what the Mason-Dixon line was, and Erin explained that between 1763 and 1767, two Englishmen, Charles Mason and Jeremiah Dixon, surveyed the two hundred thirty-three-mile line to define the long-disputed boundaries of the overlapping land grants of the Penns, proprietors of Pennsylvania, and the Baltimores, proprietors of Maryland. "Actually, it's considered the dividing line between slave and free-soil states. That's obviously where the group helping runaways got their name—the Free-Soilers."

When he seemed to understand, she prodded, "Do you know what happens to the fugitives once they get there?"

"Well, I've heard there's a bunch of folks up there called Quakers, and they're helpin' set up places where they can live. Like colonies, I heard somebody say."

"The Quakers," she clarified, "are a Christian group, and their church is also known as Friends. I'm not at all surprised to hear they'd oppose slavery. Pennsylvania would also be a perfect state for sanctuary for runaways, because once they cross the rough terrain of the mountains in the south central part, the same mountains will prove to be a natural fortress to protect them from slave-catchers.

"I'm glad you told me all this, Ben," she said, satisfied. "Now maybe I can help, too."

He and Rosa looked at each other, not understanding. Rosa asked what she was talking about.

Bluntly she declared, "I've always been against slavery, and if there's an organization to help runaways, then I want to be a part of it. I wish you'd told me all this sooner."

Ben spoke up to warn, "If Mastah Zachary was to even hear you talkin' like this, he'd likely drag you through them swamps to that whippin' post and have old Frank beat you bloody with that rawhide whip just like he beats us. You is a fine woman, Miz Erin, and me and all my people love you, but you just can't get messed up in this. It's too dangerous."

She dismissed his fears with an airy wave of her hand. "He's not going to find out. Now, I've got something to share with you two." She proceeded to confide her plans to marry Ryan Youngblood, sharing her motivation, and her ultimate goal for her mother to be able to leave Zachary. "Once I'm established as mistress of Jasmine Hill," she predicted, "I'll have access to Youngblood money. I can help the cause in many ways, and I think I'm smart enough to do it without getting caught."

Ben was quick to agree, "You're smart, all right, Miz Erin. If anybody can do it, you can. We just don't want you gettin' in no trouble."

Turning to Rosa, she assured, "I'm going to help you get out of here as soon as possible."

"Letty won't never be happy till she's got you with her, Rosa," Ben chimed in.

"I can't leave Miz Arlene," Rosa announced, casting her eyes downward, rubbed at them with the back of her hand as fresh tears stung. "I just can't leave her."

Erin quickly reminded her, "But I told you, I'm going to persuade her to move with me to Jasmine Hill. I'm sure the only reason she's put up with Zachary's meanness all these years, anyway, is that she hasn't had anywhere else to go, and she was also determined to make sure I'd never want for anything. It's all come together for me these past weeks, don't you see? She's wanted to get me married off, so she wouldn't have to tolerate his abuse. Maybe all along she was hoping she could go with me, and—"

"That ain't the only reason, Miz Erin."

Erin felt the cold fingers of apprehension twist about her spine. Perhaps, in the back of her own mind, she'd known all along something else was being kept from her. "Tell me."

"Your momma ain't well. It's nothin' I know for certain, now, so don't you go gettin' upset and thinkin' she told me somethin' she wouldn't tell you. It ain't like that, at all. It's just that I've known her so long, you see. Mastah Zachary, he bought me right after they got married, remember? While you and her was on the way here for the first time. I've known her and loved her, all these years, and I've seen lately how she's fadin' away, gettin' weak from that awful coughin'. Why, I tol' Tulwah just the other day about how bad it was gettin', and he's got some special syrup brewin' in his shack down in the swamp right now, just for her.

"She just ain't well, Miz Erin," Rosa repeated as she looked at her with worry etched in her dark face, "and I can't leave her right now, but you got to, 'cause she tol' me how powerful bad she wants you to marry Mastah Youngblood. Then you can talk her into goin' with you, but till then, I can't leave her, 'cause with you gone, she wouldn't have nobody."

Erin hugged her with gratitude and smiled through her own tears. "Thanks for sharing all this, Rosa, because I've been afraid something was wrong, and now that I know for sure, I'm all the more determined to get her moved in safely with me.

"Then you can be on your way to Letty," she added with a confident smile. "As for you, Ben—" she turned to him once more. "When do you think you'll hear something from her?"

"You didn't know about Micah. He run away from here just befo' Christmas, and it wasn't till two weeks ago we finally heard he's doin' fine and livin' in a colony called Meadville, up in Penn . . . suhl . . . vainyuh." He struggled once more to pronounce the word before he continued. "So we might not hear no news of her for a while. The man who told us about Micah is a secret Free Soiler. He pretends to be a peddler. Sells things like rheumatiz 'lixer from the back of his wagon. Letty will know to get a message to him when she can, 'cause she knows he comes through these parts often."

"But if you go ahead and run away, could you find your way to her?"

He gave a helpless shrug. "Don't know. I'd find the first free-soiler agent, and he'd send me to the next stop. I'd have no way of knowin' where I was goin'. There ain't nothin' regular about none of it, we hear. They change the way all the time, sayin' there's less chance of bein' followed after if they don't stick to the same route. But that don't matter. I'm gonna go as soon as I can, but there's no tellin' when that might be. When a slave runs away, the mastah, he keeps an awful close watch for awhile."

"I wasn't aware there were any slaves running away from here," she admitted.

Rosa was quick to inform her solemnly, "Miz Erin, all over the South, overseers are blowin' their horns every mornin', to rouse the slaves, and every time, they're findin' out the number reportin' to the fields is dwindlin'. They're runnin', Miz Erin," she said in a voice etched with bitterness and pain, " 'runnin' from bein' beaten and bein' thought of lower than the dogs trained to hunt 'em. It's gonna get worse, too, 'cause my people are gettin' tired of it. They'd rather go to their maker than be slaves."

Erin, overwhelmed by everything she'd just learned, began to experience an emotional and spiritual kinship with the wretched souls of all slaves everywhere. "I'm going to do everything I can to help," she vowed, there in the oppressive heat of the shabby slave cabin. "I promise."

"Then you might as well know somethin' else." Rosa looked to Ben for his consent that she tell all. He nodded, and choking on a sob, she hoarsely whispered, "Mastah Zachary, he been takin' his pleasure with Letty. That's why she was wantin' to run away so bad."

Erin became dizzy with flashing rage. It was all she could do to keep from marching straight back to the house and trying to strangle the devil with her bare hands. Instead, she told herself to be calm, that there was much more to be accomplished in secret. "I'm sorry," she whispered, barely able to speak beyond her fury. "You can tell your people that from this day forward, they can count on me to help them any way I can."

For now, she told herself fiercely, as she left them, it's time for me to make some wedding plans.

CHAPTER

 10

R*YAN WAS AT ONE OF THE STABLES, ASSISTING* with a difficult foaling. When one of the hands came rushing in to inform him a female rider was coming up the road, he frowned at the interruption. "Whoever it is, tell them I can't see them right now. Damn! When will people learn they aren't welcome here unless they're invited?" He returned to the task at hand, dismissing the potential intruder.

A few moments later, Erin walked into the stable. She surveyed the dramatic scene—Ryan with his sleeves rolled up, hands and arms smeared with blood, as he worked feverishly with what appeared to be a very anguished mare. The thought of just backing out didn't occur to her. Instead, she watched in awe as he ultimately succeeded in delivering a shaky-legged colt into the world.

"This one is going to be a fine stallion," Ryan announced proudly to the Negroes hanging on the railings about the stall. "It was well worth the effort to save him."

He stood and began to wipe his hands on a towel someone had handed over. It was only then that he noticed how the onlookers were staring beyond him, to the open stall gate. As he turned to see what held their interest, he was immediately jolted by a flash of anger.

Erin Sterling.

The bitterness came rushing back over the conniving way she'd set out to trap him into marriage from the very beginning. Yet, as he continued merely to glare at her in icy silence, rankled by her presence, there was no denying she was truly a splendid sight to behold.

She was wearing a pristine dress of pink cotton lace. Her long, thick, glossy hair was blue-black, like a moonless sky at midnight. Her skin, so soft, still reminded him of rich cream laced with warm coffee. He'd always thought her eyebrows so extraordinary, arched like raven's wings, above thick-lashed eyes of that strange color, cognac, with flame stars at their centers, like the fiery topaz jewel they simulated.

Late this humid July afternoon, Erin wore her hair upswept, tied with a pink bow. Her dress fit tight across her bosom, emphasizing full, round breasts and tiny waist. Gracefully, her skirt draped to offer a glimpse of slender, shapely ankles.

Disconcerted by her unexpected appearance, and also exhausted by having been at his task since before dawn, Ryan could only stand there and drink in the sight of her.

Finally, with a saucy smile, she tilted her head back to tease, "Goodness, Mr. Youngblood, is this any way to receive a lady who's come to accept your proposal of marriage?"

He tossed the towel aside, stepped over the exhausted mare and walked out of the straw-littered stall. He suppressed his amusement as he fired back, "That would be the last reason I'd guess you were here, after your mother's visit of a few days ago."

She fell in step beside him as they left the stable. With a shrug of nonchalance, as though it were mere whimsy, Erin reminded him, "Well, as you know, I was insulted, justifiably so, I might add, by your previous offer—"

"I never made any offer," he corrected. "I only admitted to intent."

"Whatever," she airily dismissed. "I thought it over and decided perhaps it was to my advantage to accept. After all, servants talk and word gets out, and I can't have my name sullied. So, I finally gave in to my mother's insistence that you owed it to me, after your disreputable behavior, to marry me and protect my virtuous reputation."

It was all he could to keep from bursting out laughing. She was quite the little schemer and played the role of indignant damsel to the hilt.

They walked along in silence for a few moments, and, as they approached the rear of the house, he realized she had slowed. He looked at her to see how her eyes had grown wide at the sight of the massive structure, how she just stood there, gazing in awe.

"I didn't know it was so . . . so impressive," she finally murmured. "How many rooms are there?"

"I haven't thought about it lately. Last time I counted, there were about twenty."

"My God!" She shook her head. "Unbelievable. What do you use them all for?"

"First floor has a ballroom. Two dining rooms, one large for formal dinners, the other is small, for regular family meals. There are two parlors, again, one large for company, and the other one small, intimate. My mother uses it to receive her friends for tea, or whatever. Then there's a library. A sewing room. Sun porch. A couple of rooms for serving food brought in from the outside kitchen. Upstairs there's a wing on each end, two bedrooms adjoined by a sitting room, and three bedrooms each side, hall down the middle."

He motioned for her to precede him up the back steps. "Would you like a grand tour?"

So far, she'd been able to hide her nervousness. Being

near him ignited memories of the way he had held her, kissed her. She didn't want to chance being alone with him in one of those twenty rooms. "I don't think so," she said finally. "There'll be time for that later."

Ryan was tired. He was also annoyed with her acting as if she was doing him a favor by her presence. "Is that the only reason you came?" he snapped. "To tell me you changed your mind? I figured you would, and you could have just written a note, or sent your mother. Now, if you'll excuse me, I've got other things to do." He took a step up.

"No," she cried, not liking his attitude. "I wanted to let you know that two weeks from Sunday will be fine. I'm afraid Mother was a bit anxious, but she agrees with me there's no real rush. Now, I'll talk to Parson Knight and make the arrangements for a simple service in his parsonage. You can send for my trunks the day before, and . . ." Her voice trailed off as she saw the astonished way he was looking at her, as though he were about to explode in anger. "Is something wrong?" she asked.

"I think," he said tightly, grasping her elbow firmly and abruptly steering her up the steps toward the back porch, "you do need to come inside, Miss Sterling, because I think it's time we got a few more things settled besides the wedding date."

"But—"

"This way!" He thundered, giving her a gentle shove into the house.

She saw they were in a small room, with cabinets on the wall filled with dishes of all sizes and quality. There were counter tops below, a large table in the middle. It was, no doubt, the room where food was brought for serving.

He guided her from there down a narrow, dark hallway, and she became angrier by the moment at the way he was acting. Opening a door at the end, she was greeted with late afternoon sun streaming in through floor-to-ceiling windows. There was a huge stone fireplace at one end, the walls covered in mounted heads of deer, bear, wild hogs, and other creatures of the wild. The air smelled of tobacco and leather. He pointed to a sofa. "Sit." Moving to a mahogany cabinet, he brusquely asked, "What would you like? Wine? A brandy? I can have Ebner bring tea, if you prefer."

"Wine," she told him, then rushed to protest, "I don't know why you're behaving like this, but I can't see that we've anything else to discuss for the moment, and—"

"No, we aren't going to discuss anything," he said, pouring her wine. He handed her the glass, then declared icily, "I am going to talk, and you are going to listen."

"I don't understand."

"You will."

He sat down behind his desk, leaned back, and propped his boots on the edge. He allowed his gaze to rake her once more, as though committing her beauty to memory while he concentrated on the task at hand, which was informing her of her future place in his life. He took a long swallow of whiskey, then began. "First of all, two weeks from Sunday is fine, but the wedding will take place here, at Jasmine Hill, in the formal gardens. My mother is still in Europe, but I've other relatives—uncles, aunts, and cousins—I'll want to invite. Then there are neighbors, friends. I don't want anyone thinking this marriage is anything I'm ashamed of, which is what it would look like if we just went to the parson and said our vows. I do not want any hint that I was, shall we say, coerced into this marriage? The story will be that we met at the Rose Ball and fell madly, hopelessly, in love on sight. We refused to let anything stand in the way of our getting married as quickly as possible."

"But—" she tried to protest, but he shook his head and held up a hand for silence.

"Never interrupt me when I'm speaking, Erin. You need to learn that I demand respect in this house, from all my servants, and—"

"Now you wait a damn minute!" At that, Erin leapt to her feet, slinging the glass to the floor, neither noticing nor caring that wine splashed across the delicate pink skirt to stain. She was across the room in a flash, slamming her hands down on his desk, as she cried, "I am not going to be one of your servants, Ryan Youngblood. I am going to be your wife, which means *I* also demand respect. Furthermore, I don't appreciate your sitting there like some kind of . . . of potentate, telling me you've made all the decisions about the wedding, who is to be invited, and the lies you plan to tell."

His eyes narrowed as he waited for her to finish her diatribe, then he continued calmly as though she hadn't spoken at all. "You will be accorded the rights and privileges of my wife by my servants, but you will serve me as they do. You'll give me pleasure, and you'll bear my children."

"Oh, I'll have your children," she was quick to assure him, "because I want them, too, but as for your 'pleasure,' I suggest you find yourself the mistress you were looking for when you found out I wasn't available!"

"A mistress?" He raised an eyebrow mockingly. "My dear, I don't think you understand at all what I'm saying. I won't need a mistress. I'll have you. You'll just be serving a dual purpose, however, when you bear my children."

Erin exploded, "You are mad!"

"No," he corrected with a gloating smile, "I'm afraid you're the one who's crazy, Erin, if you thought for one minute you were going to move into this house and make any demands. Get this straight—" He stood and leaned across the desk, only inches from her face. "Do you really think the only reason I agreed to marry you is because of your mother's threat to scream to the entire state of Virginia that I tried to seduce her virginal daughter? Are you that naive? The fact of the matter is, I don't give a damn what she says, and when you come to know me better, you'll find out I don't give a damn what anybody says.

"The reason I am marrying you," he rushed on, nostrils flaring, enraged eyes locked with hers, "is because you drive me crazy wanting you, and marriage seems to be the only way I'll have you, and believe me, my darling, I'll have you any time I want you, any where, any place! And the sooner you understand that, and accept it, the better off you'll be."

She slapped him.

Hard.

The sound of flesh striking flesh resounded in the silent wake of his harsh avowal.

For an instant, he merely maintained his position, not flinching or moving. Then, with a quick movement, he grabbed both her wrists and pulled her roughly across the desk. Papers, pens, books, everything went scattering to the floor as he dragged her, kicking and flailing, into his arms.

"Bastard!" She screamed, kicking her legs wildly as he held her wrists tightly with one hand behind her back.

Abruptly, he rolled her over, to imprison her viselike with one arm, as his hand moved quickly between her thighs. He began to massage, lightly at first, in a circular motion. Feeling her legs become limber as delicious ecstasy began to needle, hearing the pleasured moan she could not hold back, he began to press harder with his fingertips, moving up and down.

Erin was on fire. As much as she despised him at that moment, there was no way she could resist, or fight, the betrayal of her body as it yielded to arousal. Her head lay back upon the desk, and faintly she was thankful he still held her one arm, lest she experience the further humiliation of wrapping her own about his neck and clinging to him. Closing her eyes, her breath was hot and ragged, bosom heaving with the thunderous pounding of her heart.

Ryan saw the way her nipples hardened, visibly straining against the thin fabric of her bodice. She wore no stays, no corset, unnecessary for a body so perfectly sculptured. He licked his lips in hungry anticipation.

The exquisite torture he was inflicting upon her was almost more than he could bear. God, how he wanted her. It was only with the greatest of self-control that he was able to resist the temptation to heave her up onto the desk and take her then and there. Instead, he methodically continued the savage, heated torment, wanting her to learn, once and for all, that he was, truly, her master, and she, no more than a love slave.

She began to undulate her hips in complete surrender, all the while cursing and hating herself for being so weak.

Again, mustering every shred of self-control he possessed, Ryan sucked in a ragged breath and abruptly set her on her feet. He gave her bottom a pat and declared with mock seriousness, "Hey, for a second there, I almost forgot we've got to preserve your precious virtue, Miss Sterling.

"But don't worry," he goaded further, "I've got a good memory, in case you don't. Should you be so unwise as to forget your place and lose that temper of yours again, I'll remember what it takes to calm you down."

She whirled away, embarrassed, humiliated, hating him and wanting him all in one breath, one heartbeat. She smoothed her skirt, at the same time attempting to soothe her dignity by remaining silent. God, there was so much she wanted to vent at that moment—call him ugly names, make vile accusations, utter threats of violence. Yet, she resisted as she managed to hold her head up and walk swiftly, silently toward the door.

"Yes, I think it's best you do take your leave now," he called after her, amused at the way she was obviously struggling to keep from exploding all over again. "So, I'll send Ebner to get your trunks, two weeks from Saturday, and I'll write your mother a note as to what time I'll set the wedding. I'll see you then, Erin, . . . my dear."

She made her way out of the house, ignoring the opulent furnishings, the wide-eyed stares of several of the downstairs servants, and the butler, who discreetly glanced away as she passed.

Outside, in the golden haze of sunset against the shadowed trees to the west, Erin broke into a run across the velvet green lawn. Reaching her horse, she waved away the obliging groom who had hurried to help her mount. She'd ridden bareback, as usual, and hurled herself up angrily on the horse's back.

Digging in her heels, she set the horse into a full gallop. Down the entrance road she charged, hair coming undone to whip wildly about her feverish face. Ahead, she saw the gate, a slave moving to open it to set her free to the curving road that would eventually take her from Jasmine Hill boundaries. Instead, feeling driven to escape Youngblood soil without delay, she took a shortcut, reining her horse to cross the wide span of lawn. Without hesitation, she urged him to jump the split-rail fence.

Erin was so mad she gritted her teeth till her jaw ached. Damn him, she wished she could forget the whole thing but knew that wasn't possible. She had to go through with it for her mother's sake, as well as her new devotion to the Free Soilers. Those considerations were tantamount.

Finally slowing the horse to a comfortable canter, she

was struck by the realization that she hadn't felt terror this time when Ryan touched her. Only anger. And, yes, pleasure, she had to admit. The memories of Zachary's abuse had not returned to haunt her. As she thought about it, it became easy to understand how Ryan had only been salvaging his pride. What a blow it must have been to a man so strong-willed to be forced into a marriage he didn't want. She also admitted to being partially responsible, even though her mother had done the actual "persuading." After all, she and Letty had talked about how she should make him so crazy wanting her, he'd propose. Wasn't that her motivation for meeting him when he'd asked her to?

Yes, she acknowledged there were many things to be taken into consideration. She would marry him, of course, but he also had a few things to learn.

And one day, she vowed, Ryan Youngblood would learn she, too, could inflict sensual torture and humiliation. For if he thought he would ever succeed in relegating her to the lowly position of his love slave, as he'd taunted, he would realize he was sadly mistaken.

That day of retribution, she assured herself, would not be long in coming.

Ryan stood at the window and watched her go. He saw the way she expertly jumped her horse over the fence. She was a good rider. He was going to enjoy sharing his own love for horses with her in the future.

He saw her slow down and figured she was cooling off, getting over her anger. He had to admit he felt a little bad about what he'd done. But not much. After all, Erin was a schemer. He wanted her to know he was the master; he would never again be taken in by her guile.

He turned from the window with a wry smile. Sure, he'd shown her he was in control.

And all he had to do to maintain that control was to keep her from realizing he just might be falling in love with her.

CHAPTER
 11

T HE DAY AFTER ERIN'S VISIT TO RYAN, HE HAD
delivered to her several large bouquets of blood red roses
from his mother's gardens. With the fragrant blossoms
came a note inviting her and her mother to a formal party
he was hosting at Jasmine Hill the following weekend to
celebrate their betrothal.

Arlene was beside herself. "Erin, you've made me so
happy," she exulted over and over. "It's the beginning of
a wonderful new life for you. I just know it!"

Erin wished she could tell her then and there the reality
of what she was saying, how it was going to be a new life
for her, as well, but knew it was best to wait till things
settled down after the wedding. At least Zachary was
away, searching for Letty. Hopefully, he wouldn't return
till after she'd moved out of the house.

Arlene desperately wanted new clothes for Erin—for
the engagement party and, of course, the wedding. Zachary, however, had made sure she could no longer get
her hands on any of his money. It was his way of punish-
ing her for lying about being invited to the Rose Ball and
spending so much on that. Not to be outdone, Arlene
had Roscoe take her into Richmond, where she went to
a jeweler and sold the emerald necklace Zachary had given

her as a wedding present. Actually, it had been his only gift through the years. There had not been many occasions to wear it, and, actually, it had become a symbol over the years of broken dreams. It meant no more to her than he did, and she had no qualms over parting with it.

Erin obliged by being fitted for her new clothes, pretending that she had complacently accepted her fate. Actually, she was more concerned with her burning commitment to help the Negroes.

She was excited when Rosa arranged a meeting with a slave from another plantation who was the only person in Virginia, it was whispered, who had any connection at all with the Free Soilers. She was the one the slaves went to for directions after they escaped.

Her name was Mahalia, and, unknown to her present owner, she could read and write. He thought he'd bought just another illiterate slave at auction. Actually, she'd been planted there by the Free-Soilers to get her entrenched in Richmond as a secret contact.

Rosa and Erin slipped out one night to meet her a few miles away on the banks of the James River. At first Mahalia was wary, then warmed to Rosa's hearty endorsement that Erin could be trusted. She welcomed her into the group, emphasizing that her coming marriage to a wealthy man would put her in a position to be of great help. Funds were sorely needed to feed and clothe the runaways and aid them in getting established in one of the colonies. They were also desperate now and then for bribe money, to pay certain heads to turn as fugitives made their way north.

Erin assured her that she'd do everything in her power to help.

There had been no word of Letty, and Mahalia could not give them any hope there ever would be. Regretfully, she reminded them how she wouldn't have known who to contact in the area where she escaped, and unless she stumbled across someone willing to help, to point her in the right direction, she'd never stand a chance of making it across the Mason-Dixon line. Rosa cried at hearing that, fearing her daughter was gone forever, just like her sons.

Erin told Mahalia it was her ultimate goal to help as many runaways as possible but emphasized, "I will have to be very careful. No one can know that I am the benefactress. My identity must remain a secret among us, as well as your contact in the Free-Soilers. Runaways will seek your guidance, as they do now, and as soon as I can, I'll start getting money to you."

Mahalia swore she'd never tell, and Rosa likewise promised, speaking also for Ben and Tulwah, who were very much involved.

That taken care of, Erin turned her attention back to her impending marriage. She hadn't forgotten the humiliating scene in Ryan's study but had to admit thoughts of their first, pleasant encounters were overriding the latest bitter memory. Thinking about her wedding night inspired a warm glow, and she wickedly looked forward to learning ways to entice him, bewitch him, turn things around and make him a love slave. If she had to submit to his lust, she intended to make him suffer, too.

The gown her mother had made for the Saturday party was exquisite. No matter that the couturiere had haughtily pointed out that the Empire style was becoming passé in Europe. Arlene had crisply reminded this was not Europe, and she'd have the dress she wanted.

Low-cut, high-waisted, plain in front and gathered into folds behind, Erin's statuesque figure was perfect for the style. The material was shimmering satin the color of champagne. She wore her hair swept up high, caught with a garnet-encrusted band, tiny curls cascading to wisp about her slender neck. Her only jewelry was a pair of ear-bobs. Sunborn ruby.

When their carriage turned in to the main road leading to Ryan's mansion, Arlene gasped out loud. "Oh, dear Lord, look at all the horses and wagons in front of us. I thought this was to be an intimate party for his family, not a grand ball."

Erin was likewise impressed, but not happily so. The way the marriage had been arranged was still embarrassing to her, and she'd have preferred as little fuss as possible.

The drive was lined with stakes holding candles, and the lawn and gardens surrounding the house were also aglow. Guests mingled about on the porch that swept the front of the house, and she could even see them on the second-floor balcony, as well. There were urns filled with red roses lining the steps upward, and Erin felt a warm stirring to know Ryan had added that special touch just for her.

Ben pulled to a stop, and a uniformed groom waited to help them alight. Word quickly spread that the bride-to-be had arrived, and everyone on the porches began to move to the railings to look on. Arlene got out first, and Erin glanced about nervously, recognizing some of the same condemning faces she'd encountered at the Rose Ball. Oh, why had Ryan insisted on all of this? Was it his way of humiliating her further? Or did he actually believe that once she became Mrs. Ryan Youngblood, she'd be accepted by these snobbish people?

When she stepped out of the carriage, it was not the servant's hand that reached for hers but Ryan's, and Erin suddenly found herself looking up into his ruggedly handsome face. "My darling," he greeted loudly enough for those closest to hear, "you're prettier each time I see you. I don't know if I can stand it every morning of my life." He bowed to kiss her hand and, as he straightened, whispered for her ears only, "But it's the nights I'm looking forward to."

She did not stiffen or react with demure embarrassment the way he doubtless expected. Giving him a dazzling smile, she boldly fired back, "I, too, my darling, for the rest of my life."

It was as though she hadn't spoken at all, for Ryan was far too sophisticated to indicate any loss of composure. He was well aware everyone was watching. Still, on the inside, he was bemused by her change of attitude, and a warning bell sounded to remind him just what a great little actress she was. She loathed him, was marrying him strictly for monetary reasons, and was, no doubt, playing a new little game.

He was, she silently acknowledged, absolutely splendid in a simple blue frock coat, cut away in front, tails descending behind. His white shirt was adorned with a madras cravat, and his well-fitting trousers a shade lighter than his coat. No matter her personal opinion, there was no denying Ryan Youngblood was a fine specimen of a man.

She kept a smile pasted on her lips as he proceeded to take her inside and introduce her around. Arlene was likewise escorted, but there was nothing artificial about her happiness over the occasion. She was glowing with enthusiasm.

The names breezed by Erin, but not the way so many looked at her with cold scrutiny. A few attempted to conceal their disapproval, while she could actually feel the contempt of others.

Ryan didn't seem to notice as he offered vague justification for the sudden announcement to wed. "Isn't she as lovely as I told you she was?" he said over and over, or, now and then, "I knew I had to hurry up and convince her to marry me before somebody else spirited her away."

As he moved about, Erin's hand daintily tucked about his arm, she couldn't help marveling at the lavishness of the mansion. On her previous visit, she'd been too upset to notice just how magnificent the decor was. There were leaded and stained-glass windows that offered pastel hues from the fading light beyond. Elaborately carved oak doors with bronze fixtures stood open to reveal the interiors of the massive rooms with ornate friezes, frescoes, and fine wood paneling. There were elegant pieces of furniture, obviously valuable paintings, ivory and jade and marble sculptures.

Through open French doors that led to a marble terrace, Erin could see the inspiring view of the carefully manicured gardens sloping down to the riverbank. There were masses of brilliant flowers—zinnias, sweetpeas, and daisies, reflecting pools, fountains, even a statuary. Servants in neat white pants and shirts were scurrying about setting up linen-covered tables. It was far too warm for so many to dine inside, so a picnic would be served outdoors.

Ryan saw her fascination and walked her outside for a better panorama. English boxwoods, sheared into perfect geometrical designs, offered a maze daring to be explored. All about mimosas and magnolias were in bloom, and the air was intoxicating with the sweet fragrance of the white jasmine blossoms that seemed to be everywhere.

"It was my grandfather who built this place," Ryan told her, sensing her awe at the grandeur. He pointed to a smaller, intimate garden, farther down the lawn toward the river. "My grandmother's favorite flower was jasmine, and she had them planted everywhere, and that's how the place got its name. If she'd ever had a daughter, she was going to name her Jasmine, but, unfortunately, she only had one child, a son—my father—and she died having him. My grandfather adored her, never had any interest in taking another wife. He had her buried there, in that solitary little garden you see. The whole place is overgrown with jasmine, just the way he wanted it. While I like the scent, I have to admit it's a bit overwhelming at times."

She could see, amidst the greenery and blossoms, what looked like a white marble statue of an angel but nothing else that resembled another tombstone. "Is your grandfather buried there, too?"

"Oh, no. He couldn't stand the smell of jasmine. Said it made him sick. So he's buried in another place he had built for a family cemetery. Same as my father. I'll show it to you another day."

They turned to go back inside, just as one of the house servants came to advise the food was being brought out of the kitchens.

Erin saw her mother talking to someone she knew from church, oblivious to the fact the woman was looking at her with veiled disdain. Erin motioned to Arlene to come over.

Her mother's face glowed as she whispered, "Oh, it's wonderful. All of it. Just wonderful. To think you're going to be mistress of Jasmine Hill, live here, raise your children here." Ryan had stepped away for a moment to give instructions to the servant, and Arlene hurried to confide, "He's so handsome. As wicked as it is for me to say so, you should be looking forward to your wedding night."

She giggled, and Erin realized she was well in her cups from many glasses of champagne. Seeing that, she dared to ask, "Do you think I'd ever be able to convince you to come and live with us, Mother? To help me raise all those children you think I'm going to have?"

Arlene swayed, every so slightly, rolled her eyes and giggled again. "You never know. I just might." Then, spotting someone else from her tatting circle, hurried away.

Fatted calves and pigs were roasting on hand-turned skewers over pits of smoldering hickory chips. The delicious aroma of barbecued beef and pork filled the air. Fish and chicken were frying in the outdoor kitchens, as servants rushed around with crocks of coleslaw and potato salad, large tureens of creamed and buttered vegetables, plates of crisp dill pickles, chutney, and relish. There were large tables offering only desserts—cakes, fruit pies, berry cobblers, and creamy puddings. Little Negro girls stood with long-handled palmetto fans to shoo away flies and insects.

When they had their plates filled, Ryan directed Erin to a table he'd ordered set up away from the other guests. She noted workmen had been digging up the ground nearby, and before she could ask the reason, he proudly told her, "I'm having a rose bed planted. Red roses. Beneath the window of the master suite. Just for you."

She couldn't resist laughing. "Oh, give me a chance, Ryan. Who knows? We might actually be able to stand each other after all. Don't plan my grave yet, please."

"Hmmm." He pretended to muse, sitting down opposite. "I hadn't thought about it, but that is an idea."

Suddenly, amidst the light banter, Erin couldn't resist asking, "Why are you doing all this?"

"What do you mean?"

"You're being . . . civil, and after our argument the other day—"

"Oh, that!" He cut her off. "That was no argument, my dear. That was just my way of letting you know who's in charge around here."

She bit back an angry response. He'd find out soon enough she'd never bend to his iron will.

Erin was grateful that her mother came to join them just then.

Arlene was gushing over everything, and as Erin watched and listened to her pleasant conversation with Ryan, she found it hard to believe the two had ever been anything but close friends.

After supper, they all gathered in the huge ballroom. An ensemble was about to begin playing, but first Ryan led Erin to the center of the floor and and asked for everyone's attention. Then, with great flourish, he made his official announcement of their engagement. He invited everyone present to return for the wedding in the gardens the next Sunday afternoon. Finally, he took a ring from his coat pocket and slipped it on Erin's finger amidst gasps from the onlookers.

She held up her hand, reeling at the sight of the huge diamond sparkling in the lights of the glittering chandelier above. It was pear-shaped, set with tiny rubies, and was, without a doubt, the most impressive ring she'd ever seen on any woman's finger.

He signaled to the musicians to begin playing, and Erin was only dimly aware it was a valse. She was baffled not only by his generosity but also by the extent to which he was going to impress. The ring must have cost a fortune.

He held out his arms to her, and she was locked into his gaze. They began to move rhythmically to the lilting strains of the violins, and all eyes were upon them as they swung gently about the floor.

Despite everything, all her doubts and fears, Erin could not help but be fascinated by this handsome, enigmatic man, who would soon become her husband.

"So you have the beginning of what you want out of this marriage, my dear," he told her gently as they continued to glide fluidly around the dance floor.

Despite the sarcastic innuendo, she graciously responded, "Thank you. It's beautiful."

"Next Sunday night"—his appreciative gaze went to her bosom, so lusciously emphasized by the Empire style—"I'll have the beginning of what I want."

"Oh, really? You seem to forget that what you wanted was to have me for your mistress, not your wife."

"You don't intend to let me forget, do you?"

"I have to admit it stings to know you wouldn't be marrying me if you could've had me on your terms."

"Well, we'll never know, will we? But as I said, next Sunday night is only the beginning."

She blinked as though baffled, smiling with enjoyment at the sensual banter. "And what about the ending?"

"There won't be one, Erin. I could never get enough of a woman like you. Remember that, and never be so foolish as to refuse me. You're going to belong to me—for always."

CHAPTER

 12

*A*RLENE'S HAPPINESS OVER THE COMING WEDDING was dimmed only by concern for Letty. Her heart also went out to Rosa, who was more than just the household slave Zachary had bought for her as a wedding gift so long ago. Through the years, Rosa had become a dear and cherished friend—as much as decorum allowed. Unlike Erin, Arlene had never dared go against Zachary's decree that there was to be no fraternization with his slaves.

"I wish I could say, or do, something to make you feel better," Arlene offered one morning as Rosa brought in the usual breakfast tray of tea and toast. She was sitting at her desk, going over her list once more, to make sure everyone she knew from church had received a personally handwritten invitation to the wedding that Sunday. Gesturing to a nearby chair, she urged, "Stay awhile and let's talk. Mr. Tremayne is still away, so that means they haven't found her."

"And they aren't goin' to, either." Rosa flashed a confident smile as she took the offered seat. "I got a feelin' that she ain't nowhere near where they's lookin'. She's long gone from there by now."

Arlene glanced up sharply, surprised by the lilt in her voice. She was even more baffled by her expression—eyes shining, lips curved in a smile that was sanguine. "You . . . you sound almost happy, Rosa," she said hesitantly. "Is there something I don't know?"

A shadow passed, as Rosa checked herself. She realized she was arousing suspicion by letting her pleasure show. She trusted her mistress. Lordy, yes. But there was no way she was going to let her know about the Free Soilers, or let her become involved in any of it, not with her poor health. "No ma'm," she responded, lowering her head as she began to clasp and twist her hands, as though nervous, worried. "There's nothin'. I just leave it all to the Lord, put it in His hands, and I know He's got to be lookin' out for my little girl. After all, it was His will she was able to escape."

Arlene bit down on her lip thoughtfully. There was just something about the way Rosa was acting that made her feel she was hiding something. "Have you heard from her, Rosa?" she asked softly. "Has she got a message to you, telling you where she is?" She reached to cover her folded hands in assurance. "You know you can trust me. If there's anything I can do to help—"

"No ma'am," Rosa repeated, raising her head to look her straight in the eye and say, "I ain't heard from her, and it's not likely I'm goin' to, and there's nothin' you can do. And if I never hear from her again, I'll still have a feelin' in my heart that she's better off wherever she is, than if the mastah had sold her on the block."

Arlene turned to pour herself a cup of tea. "It's not right, Rosa. Any of it. And you know you've got my sympathy. I've tried through the years to make things easier for you and the others, but I'm afraid I haven't been very successful. Mr. Tremayne is a stubborn, willful man. I was never able to persuade him to my way of thinking, though Lord knows, I tried."

"I know that, and so do all the others. We all love you,

Miz Arlene, and we think you're a fine, Christian woman. We know the way the mastah treats us ain't none of your fault."

"If I had my way, Rosa, every one of you would be set free."

"We know that, too, and forgive me if it hurts you for me to say so"—she dared to add—"but there ain't a one of us what don't pray every night of our lives that the mastah will die befo' mornin', so you'd set us free by sunset."

Arlene closed her eyes, drew in her breath, and let it out slowly, washed with guilt over the inability to voice loyalty to her husband. All she could do was remain silent, lest her own loathing be revealed. Finally, she looked at Rosa and said, "Maybe it's best we don't talk about this, anymore."

Stiffly, Rosa nodded but ventured to ask, "Aren't you glad the mastah ain't here right now? Aren't you hopin' he don't come back before the weddin' is over?"

"Oh, yes. As selfish as it might sound, Letty escaping when she did made things a lot easier for me right now. All I want is to get Erin safely married and out of the house before he comes back."

"I hope . . ." Rosa began, then hesitated, but finally decided to come right out and say it, "I hope you move off with her, Miz Arlene."

Arlene had been tipsy on champagne when Erin had mentioned the same thing at the engagement party, but she had not forgotten and dared to hope such a possibility might become reality . . . if she lived long enough. Ryan Youngblood was a fine man, she believed, as well as strong and powerful and rich. Although he didn't realize it, yet, he was going to fall desperately in love with Erin and become absolutely devoted to her. And if she wanted her mother to move in and live with them, he not only wouldn't protest, he would also, Arlene felt sure, stand up to Zachary should he try to prevent it. "We'll just have to wait and see," she told Rosa. "We'll just have to take one day at a time.

"But," she hastened to add, "if that happens, you're going with me. I'd never leave you here. Remember that."

"He wouldn't let me go, but don't worry, I wouldn't stay after you was gone, Miz Arlene. I'd run away and try to find my girl."

Arlene gave her a probing look as she lightly accused, "I think you'd know where to look, too, Rosa. I think you know more than you're telling me, and—" She was struck by a coughing spell.

Rosa leapt to pat her on the back, try to get her to sip some tea. Arlene gestured wildly, desperately, to the bottle of green horehound syrup on the bedside table.

Even after she took a deep swallow, it was a few moments before the coughing subsided. As she gasped, trying to fill her lungs with air once more, there was a shrill, wheezing sound. Rosa watched her with wide, frightened yes, saw the blood on the linen handkerchief she'd used to cover her mouth during the spasm. It was getting worse, Rosa realized sadly. Gently, she related that Tulway had told her only the day before that the potion he was brewing was almost ready.

"He's been coming almost regularly since Mr. Tremayne has been away," Arlene warily pointed out, still struggling to get her breath. "You need to warn him that Mr. Tremayne could come back anytime, and if he catches him here, there's no telling what he might do."

"Tulwah ain't afraid." Rosa lifted her chin in a sudden flash of defiance. "If it won't fo' him, none of us would have no doctorin'. The mastah won't never let no doctor come for a sick slave. And he ought to be grateful, 'cause Tulwah has sho' kept some of his slaves from dyin'."

"Another plantation owner might care if their slaves die," Arlene said, more to herself than to Rosa. "Other men value their slaves and consider it a loss of property when one of them dies, but he doesn't care. He just goes out and gets another one."

"I think he's scared of Tulwah."

"I don't know about that, but he does feel Tulwah is a bad influence, that he teaches witchcraft and voodoo. The last time he caught him around the compound, he was in a rage for days, and I overheard him tell one of the overseers to shoot him if he came back."

Rosa shivered with instinctive fright. "I'll tell him to be careful. I knows where he lives, and I'll slip down there and get the potion, myself, soon as it's ready."

Wearily, weakly, Arlene shook her head. Rosa was the only person in whom she dared confide. "It won't help any more than this juice the doctor gave me. The attacks are coming closer together, lasting longer, and it takes more juice to ease them. I have good days and bad days, but the bad days seem to be getting closer together. All I pray for is to have the strength to get me through this wedding, and then I think I can curl up and die happy." She smiled wanly.

"Mastah Youngblood, he's takin' care of everything?"

"That's what he said. And I'm grateful, to be sure. I couldn't chance having anything here. What if Mr. Tremayne walked in right in the middle of the reception?" She shuddered at the thought. "Believe me, Rosa, I am very grateful Mr. Youngblood took charge."

"Were you surprised he didn't want to have it at the church? I thought most white folks got married in the church."

Arlene had to laugh at that notion where Ryan Youngblood was concerned. She might not be a member of the elite inner circle of Richmond society, but she prided herself in keeping up with what went on. It was said that Ryan Youngblood was a nonconformist, a rebel. So like Erin, she mused with private delight. And Arlene was not at all surprised he did not want to have a church wedding. "It's to be in the formal gardens at Jasmine Hill, quite lovely this time of year.

"You'll see it all," she went on brightly to assure. "I want you to go with us, so you can help Erin with her dress, and her hair."

That made Rosa remember, "There were two wagons here, first thing this morning, to deliver lots of packages."

"Two?" Arlene's brows shot up in bewilderment. "That's strange. I was only expecting a delivery from Madame Cherise's shop. Not only is she the best couturiere in the state, but she also happens to have Erin's measurements from her fitting for the Rose Ball. Erin isn't exactly cooperating in all of this, you know."

Rosa nodded in agreement. She had overheard Miss Erin say she saw no need in spending a lot of money on fancy clothes before the wedding. She'd just let Master Youngblood pay for them, afterward. Rosa also knew Miss Erin's reasoning was, no doubt, to get her hands on shopping money and then slip part of it out to Mahalia, but she wasn't about to say so.

Rosa described the boxes that had arrived, spelling out the few letters she knew that were marked on each. Arlene stared at her incredulously and asked, "Are you sure? It sounds like you're spelling out Fine Things, and I'd never shop there. It's run by Madam Estelle, and it's not just a boutique for intimate apparel, it's . . ." Her voice trailed off. She wasn't sure whether she wanted to speak to Rosa of such things.

Just then, however, Erin walked into the bedroom to finish the sentence angrily for her. "It's a whorehouse!"

Arlene and Rosa both whipped their heads about to

stare at her; her face was livid with rage. She was carrying several pink boxes, all trailing lavender-colored tissue and red satin ribbons. She crossed the room to dump all on the bed as though it were garbage. Turning to Rosa, she went on to explain, "Fine Things is a shop where very revealing lingerie is sold. Things like this." She reached among the boxes to pluck out a red lace gown with holes for nipples to protrude. Flinging it down in disgust, she extracted other items with equal exclamations of disrelish, then curtly said, "Madam Estelle runs a house of prostitution on the second floor."

Arlene's hand went to her throat, aghast that such garments had inadvertently been sent to her home and was also surprised Erin knew so much about the place.

Erin guessed what she was thinking and snapped, "Don't look at me like that, Mother. I do hear gossip, you know, and I don't think there's a girl over the age of ten in all of Richmond who doesn't know what goes on upstairs over Estelle's boutique. They eavesdrop on grownups every chance they get, just like I did, because they're curious, and that's how they find out."

"Well, I wonder why they made a mistake and sent those things here," Arlene said.

"It was no mistake."

Arlene blinked, confused. "It wasn't?"

"No! Don't you see? Those things were sent by that— that reprobate"—she sputtered indignantly—"that you insist I marry, and, oh!" She whirled around, threw up her arms, and began to pace furiously about the room. "I just can't believe he had the nerve to do such a thing."

Arlene and Rosa glanced at each other nervously. Finally, Arlene endeavored to change the subject. "Well, did you see your wedding gown, dear? I liked it when Madame Cherise showed it to me in her shop, and she

said she could alter it to fit you. There wasn't time to de-
sign one, and—"

"It's fine." Erin ground out the words icily. She
couldn't care less what she got married in, could hardly
think straight, anyway, past the blinding rage over Ryan
being so audacious as to pick out lingerie and have it sent
to her, as if she were some kind of whore herself! Damn
him, she inwardly cursed.

Arlene pressed on to divert her anger. "Rosa said there
were two boxes from Cherise. What was in the other one,
dear?"

"Don't tell me he ordered that, too!" She stopped pacing to stare at her mother. "It's a dove silk suit. Quite
lovely. Quite tasteful. Modest. Not like anything he
would choose. Now that, I would say, is accurate to call
a mistake. I'll check on that, too." She started gathering
up the boxes.

Rosa did not know what was going on but quickly
moved to help her repack the lingerie in the boxes and
retie them with the satin ribbons.

Arlene watched, bemused, for a moment, then cautiously asked, "What are you doing, dear?"

"I'm taking everything back."

"To Ryan? He had it delivered, and—"

"Oh, I'm returning it to the store. I want him to feel
like a fool when Madam Estelle has to tell him that his
fiancée was insulted that he'd pick out such naughty
things." She held out a black lace gown and laughed, but
inside, she had to admit she felt a warm tremor to think
of wearing it for him. Still, she had to put him in his place.
After all, selecting and sending such personal things was
not something a man did for his fiancée. That was something he did for his mistress, and—!

She froze, washed with fresh rage, for suddenly it
dawned on her exactly what his motive had been.

This was his way of reminding her she was no more to him than what he'd intended when he set out to pursue her in the first place.

Well, by God, she would show him.

"Tell Ben to saddle my horse," she snapped to Rosa as she hurried out of the room to change into riding clothes.

Arlene, stunned, called, "But why aren't you taking one of the carriages? If you ride into town with all those boxes strapped on the back of a horse, people will see, and they'll know where they came from, and they'll wonder what's going on."

"Fine!" Erin was quick to shout over her shoulder as she went down the hall toward her room. "I hope they follow me like they did Lady Godiva, and if Ryan Young-blood is watching, I hope he's struck blind or dead like the ones that dared look at her!"

Arlene shook her head and told Rosa, "Heaven help us when those two get together!"

Many heads did turn as Erin rode straight through the heart of Richmond. She had purposely turned the pink boxes so that the name Fine Things, emblazoned in red, shown brightly for all to see. They were also staring at her, for few women were ever seen riding astraddle a horse and wearing men's riding breeches.

Madam Estelle's place had been constructed in a space that had once been a very wide alley between two build-ings. Cozy and intimate, it was set back from a busy street, the short way paved in cobblestones. A red-and-pink-striped canopy sheltered the steps leading up to a porch hidden behind a thick cascade of lilacs and honeysuckle vines. There were several small tables with chairs and a few empty wine bottles, which evidenced waiting clientele from the evening before.

There was no hint that it was a house of prostitution,

or even a shop for ladies lingerie. Such unmentionables were certainly not advertised, so there was only a small pink-and-white plaque beside the door that simply stated, Fine Things.

There were two windows on each side of the curtained door, but the pink velvet drapes were closed, and Erin could not see inside. Not about just to walk right in, she lifted the brass knocker and let it drop loudly.

Almost at once the door opened, and a woman with bright red hair peered out at her. She had orange splotches of rouge on her cheeks, and her eyelids were dusted with a gaudy shade of purple. Her lips were painted blood red, and she was wearing a yellow satin robe with some kind of fluffy feathers all around the collar that made Erin want to sneeze.

The woman looked Erin up and down curiously, noticed she was carrying several of her pink boxes, and said, "Yeah? What do you want?" She did not recognize Erin as anyone who had ever shopped there, and Estelle prided herself in knowing, and catering to, every rich man's mistress in Richmond.

Erin gave her an equally thorough once over. Actually, she was dying to peek inside. She had no idea what such a place would look like and curiosity burned. She gave herself a mental shake. There was no time for wondering. She wanted to get her business over with as quickly as possible. Crisply, she said, "I believe Mr. Ryan Youngblood did some shopping with you recently."

Estelle continued to stare blankly, even though it suddenly dawned on her who this woman was.

Erin was growing impatient. People passing by on the main street, just a short distance away, could glance in and see her standing there on the porch, and she didn't want that. "Well?" She drew a ragged breath, struggling to hold all the boxes in her arms. "You do know Mr. Youngblood, don't you? And these things did come from your shop, didn't they?"

Estelle was also losing patience. "Look, I don't know what your problem is, girlie, and I don't have time to stand here and—"

"Neither do I!" Erin released her hold, let the boxes fall to the porch. With a wave of dismissal, she stepped back to declare icily, "Just tell Mr. Youngblood that his fiancée is very indignant that he would send her such insulting and degrading garments, and that your delivery person undoubtedly made a mistake in not taking them to his mistress."

With that, she turned and walked down the steps as fast as her shaking legs would carry her.

Estelle opened the door all the way and furiously began to pick up the parcels. Behind her, Corrisa Buckner, dressed to go out, watched. She had been on her way down the stairs but paused to witness the scene, curious when she had heard Ryan's name mentioned.

"Arrogant little chit!" Estelle fumed as she began to gather the filmy lingerie that had spilled out of the boxes. "Ryan must have rocks in his head to get himself involved with a cold fish like her. He sure ain't gonna find no warmth in her bed. I'll be damned if I'm going to be the one to tell him that, either. He's going to be madder than drawin' from a deck with five aces when he finds out what she's done. I'll just stack these things in the back room, and the next time he comes in, he can do whatever he wants to with 'em."

Corrisa couldn't help laughing as she stooped to help her. "He's going to be mad, all right."

"Maybe you'll wind up with 'em," Estelle offered, then couldn't resist adding tartly, "I haven't seen him around here lately. Maybe you need something new to entice him."

At that, Corrisa bristled. She was not at all happy over the way Ryan had stopped coming around. Straightening, she continued on her way and snapped, "Pick it up yourself."

She saw that Erin was heading across the street in the direction of Madame Cherise's shop.

So that was Ryan's future wife, she mused, the woman everyone was talking about as they tried to figure out just how she had managed to make him forget all about his betrothal to Ermine Coley. It was said she was quite beautiful, though Corrisa had not had a good look. She could see she had long, sable-black hair that fell silkily all the way to her incredibly tiny waist. And she was tall, with a well-rounded bottom that was presently swishing furiously from side to side in the tight men's breeches she was wearing.

Corrisa smiled to herself. Obviously, Erin Sterling had a lot of spunk, just the kind of woman Ryan needed for a wife. And, even though Corrisa had no illusions about who or what she was, and made it a rule not to get personally involved with any of her customers, she had to admit secretly she was quite fond of Ryan.

Deciding she wanted to see his future bride up close, she started to follow her.

She was about to step out of the cobblestone alley and cross the street, when she slowed at the sound of female voices—haughty, angry voices—and they were obviously talking about Erin.

"Look at her," one of them said waspishly. "Dressed in men's clothes. And she's supposed to be so devastatingly gorgeous?"

They moved onto the boardwalk directly in front of Corrisa, still watching Erin. Quickly, she stepped to the side, in the shadows, so as not to be seen. She recognized one of the two girls as the daughter of Tyrone Manning.

He was one of her regular customers, and Carolyn had been pointed out to her by Estelle when they were out shopping one day. She did not know the other girl, but since she seemed to match Carolyn in mannerisms and comments, decided she was equally snobbish.

"Did you know," Carolyn remarked snidely, "that my Carl had the nerve to say he didn't blame Ryan for being mesmerized by that little schemer, because he agreed with all the other menfolk who think she's absolutely ravishing?"

Her companion cried, "Why, that's ridiculous. Keith said the same thing, when I told him how all the decent folk of Richmond are appalled that Ryan could even think of marrying Zachary Tremayne's stepdaughter. Why, poor Victoria is going to have a fit when she gets home and finds out what her son has done.

"And I agree with you," she added with a sniff of disdain. "She's not so pretty. Why, she's tall and positively gangly looking. There's nothing feminine about her. Certainly not like dear, sweet Ermine, who looks like a dainty porcelain doll."

Corrisa pressed her fingertips against her lips to smother a giggle. She might not know who Carolyn Manning's friend was but sure knew the man she spoke of—Keith. He came at least three times a week to frolic with Josephine, one of Estelle's younger girls. And, she thought with wicked delight, she knew Carolyn's beau, as well. Carl Whitfield was also one of her regular customers.

Suddenly, Carolyn turned around but did not see Corrisa as she looked toward Estelle's place and cried excitedly, "That's where she came from! Why, I'll bet she was in there buying her . . . unmentionables." She gave a soft gasp, then laughed shrilly, "Oh, Mary Susan, now we know how she mesmerized poor Ryan. She's using the wiles of a whore!"

Mary Susan Hightower was quick to agree, her eyes narrowing with contempt. "Of course. She's driving him crazy and holding out for marriage. How shameful!"

Carolyn offered, "She knows that's the only way she'll ever get a *decent* man. Ryan is too noble to take a woman out of wedlock."

Now Corrisa was having a terrible time holding back her giggles. She clamped her teeth together till her jaws ached. The thought of Ryan being so noble as to keep a woman virtuous was hysterical.

Turning once more to stare after Erin, Carolyn cried, "She's headed for Madame Cherise's shop. Let's follow her and see what she's buying there."

"Yes, let's do." Mary Susan cried, lifting her skirts to step out into the street and hurry along beside her. "That should be very interesting, since Cherise sells decent things."

Corrisa followed close behind, not about to miss anything.

Madame Cherise glanced up at the tinkling sound of the bell above the door. "Ahh, Mademoiselle Sterling." She smiled in pleased recognition, then saw the box Erin was carrying. Frowning, she asked, "Is something wrong? Did the wedding gown not fit? I had your measurements, and—"

"No. I suppose the gown fits fine. To tell the truth, I haven't even tried it on." She laid the box on the counter, untied the string, and lifted the lid to reveal the dove silk suit beneath the layers of tissue. "I'm here about this. There's been a mistake. My mother said she didn't order it, so I wanted to return it."

Cherise was quick to say, "But mademoiselle. There is no mistake. Monsieur Youngblood, he came in and ordered this suit for you, to be delivered with your wedding gown. I worked day and night to have it ready," she added, almost defensively.

Erin pointed to the outfit, expression incredulous. "He ordered this?" She shook her head, bewildered. "But . . . why?"

"He said you would need it for your nuptial journey." She hesitated as she realized Erin was truly baffled. "Did he not tell you of his travel plans?"

Erin shook her head slowly, her gaze transfixed to the suit. Another surprise. And this one was lovely.

The bell after the door jingled again, but Erin was too deep in thought to be aware of anything going on around her.

Cherise recognized Carolyn and Mary Susan, gave a nod to let them know she would be with them soon. "So," she prodded Erin impatiently, "since there is no mistake, I can repack the suit for you to take with you, or perhaps you'd like to step in the back and try it on while you're here, to make sure it fits." She motioned to the curtain that concealed the dressing area.

Erin came out of her reverie and picked up the box. "No. I'm sure it's fine." She turned to go and bumped right into Carolyn Manning, automatically apologized, and brushed on by.

With a lift of her chin, Carolyn launched her verbal attack. "This must be a terribly busy time for you, Erin. You seem to have so many different places to shop—suits from here, lingerie from Fine Things."

Cherise gasped to hear such a thing and did not notice the bell ringing once more as Corrisa stepped inside the shop.

Erin stiffened at Carolyn's remark but maintained her composure, commanding herself not to be goaded into an unpleasant scene. She continued on her way.

"I'm not surprised, though, are you, Mary Susan?" Carolyn asked her companion in a shrill, nervous voice. She was eager to hurt Erin Sterling, because she was still mad over the way Carl had panted after her at the Rose Ball. She rushed on. "After all, when you aren't received by Virginia's prominent families, I suppose you have to rely on any means available to try and get a decent husband, even if it means buying whore's lingerie."

Cherise glowered with disapproval as Carolyn and Mary Susan began to giggle almost hysterically, covering their faces with their hands.

Erin opened the door but could not resist a taunt of her own. "Have you looked at your underwear lately, Carolyn? Maybe you should. I don't see a ring on your finger." She walked out, chin up in defiance. They could think whatever they wished. She just didn't give a damn.

Carolyn stared after her, eyes ablaze. "How—how dare she say such a thing?" She sputtered indignantly. "The nerve. . . ."

Mary Susan looked on but remained silent, not sure whether she wanted to endorse her friend's behavior any longer, due to the way Madame Cherise was glaring at her, along with the other woman who'd come in that she didn't know.

Enraged, Carolyn cried, "Let's go. I don't want to shop where she does." She bolted toward the door, then saw Corrisa staring at her so obviously with contempt and lashed out, "Well, what are you looking at? I know who you are. You're one of Estelle's girls. I've seen you lounging around on the steps, trying to entice men off the street. Get out of my way."

She jerked open the door and rushed out, but Corrisa was suddenly livid with rage. Damn the snotty little bitch, she fumed, following after her. If there was one thing she never did, it was stand outside and lure men off the street, and she wasn't going to let Carolyn Manning get away with accusing her of doing so. "You listen to me, you arrogant little twit," she cried, not caring who overheard. "Who the hell do you think you are accusing me of being a—a street whore? You don't know what you're talking about."

Mary Susan, mortified at the scene, dashed away in the opposite direction, not about to be involved.

Madame Cherise, totally disgusted, closed the door after them in curt dismissal.

Erin, across the street and about to mount her waiting horse, paused to listen as the two women squared off. All around, others were gathering to watch.

Carolyn was oblivious to everything, would later be horrified at her own behavior, but for the moment was too angry to care. "I know what you are," She screamed at Corrisa. "And I'll bet you helped her pick out her filthy fine things. Your kind knows what men like, don't you?"

At that, Corrisa threw her head back and laughed raucously. She could not resist taunting, "Well, I know what Carl likes, for sure."

A roar went up from the men standing around, as the women exchanged shocked murmurs.

Corrisa knew when word spread and Carl heard, she would lose a customer, but so what? It was worth it to see the look on that hateful girl's face as she turned and ran away.

Heading back to Estelle's, Corrisa glanced up to see that Erin was watching her from her horse. She also saw the way she was smiling with gratitude, as well as the wink of approval. She smiled back, thinking how Erin was every bit as lovely as she'd heard. Ryan had made a good choice, she decided, continuing on her way, and Erin was a lucky young woman.

Erin stared after her thoughtfully. So, she was one of

the women, the prostitutes, who worked at Estelle's establishment.

And Carolyn had said her kind knew what men liked.

She had not forgotten her vow for revenge after Ryan had humiliated her that day in his study. She found herself suddenly wishing she had the nerve to go after that woman and ask her for a few tips on how to torment him, as he had tormented her.

But she did not dare.

CHAPTER

 13

As THEIR CARRIAGE TURNED FROM THE MAIN road into the tree-lined driveway, Arlene felt a bit light-headed. The day before, Rosa had gone to Tulwah's shack, deep in the swamp, and brought back the potion he had concocted for her. It smelled terrible and looked worse, thick and dark, with all kinds of ominous things swirled in its depths. But when she had tried it, the result was nothing short of a miracle. Gone was the dry, papery feeling in her throat. And if she began to cough, one sip would take away the hacking. To make sure she would not have a spell during the wedding, she had taken several strong doses before leaving and felt tipsier than she had after the champagne at the engagement party.

Erin noted the glassy look in her mother's eyes and worriedly asked, "Are you all right? You look . . . strange."

"I feel strange," she confirmed with a dreamy smile. Not about to admit the true reason, she equivocated, "Why shouldn't I? It's not every day a mother sees her daughter get married, especially to a man like Ryan Youngblood, and, oh . . . . . look!" she cried, pointing out the carriage window as they rounded a curve in the drive.

Roses.

Everywhere, it seemed, there were blood-red roses—pots set under every tree on the lawn, urns filled with the fragrant blossoms on either end of every step going up to the porch, where baskets lined the edges. Even rose petals were strewn on the walkways, across the lawn.

Arlene breathed a sigh and wondered aloud, "I can't imagine why Ryan would have so many roses. After all, this is Jasmine Hill, known for that particular flower."

Erin felt smug. He knew red roses were her favorite, and, no doubt, this was his peace offering for having offended with the distasteful lingerie. Maybe one day she would tell him it was not the lingerie that had offended, but the intent. Frankly, she would have liked to wear it for him, but that time would come. First, he had to learn she was not going to be subservient.

Arlene felt compelled to say, "I know this wasn't the way you would've liked things to be, Erin. I know you wanted to fall in love first and have everything all nice and romantic. But it's for the best. You'll see. Look around you." She gestured to the opulent surroundings as the carriage rolled to a stop. "You're going to have a wonderful life. And I'm impressed, and appreciative, over the way Ryan has tried to make this a memorable day for you both."

Erin made no comment. All she wanted was to get it over with so she could get on with her plans for the future. Once Rosa confided in her, some of the other slaves had also opened up, eager to inform her of the atrocities they endured. It was with deep fervor that she now felt driven to help them in their cause. So many would not flee and seek freedom, for they were either too frightened or could not bear to leave their families and loved ones. But those who did have the spark to run away and make a better life, these Erin was firmly committed to help in any way possible.

Arlene sensed her tension and mistook it for the moment at hand. "You're beautiful, darling," she said, her voice a bit slurred from Tulwah's potion. "I'm so proud of you."

Erin gave her a grateful, loving smile. And when she stepped out of the carriage, she knew her mother was not just being kind with her compliments. An impressed ripple went through the crowd gathered in anticipation of her arrival, and she heard whispered exclamations—"So pretty!" "Oh, isn't she lovely?" "Beautiful, just beautiful!"

Her gown was silver satin, the bodice plain, the neckline high and delicately edged in lace. The sleeves were pouffed from shoulder to elbow, then tapered to her fingertips. The waistline was smooth and tight above the first, thick bouffant folds of satin that layered almost to the floor. Her black hair, as shiny as a crow's wing in the midafternoon sun, was first pulled up and held by a cluster of net intertwined with tiny satin bows, then trailed in ringlets down her back.

Arlene was dressed in a simple gown of shimmering blue satin, overlaid with cream-colored lace. As she stepped from the carriage to receive the hand of the uniformed groomsmen, the crowd likewise acknowledged her beauty.

Rosa had been sitting opposite them in silence, awed by everything she had seen on the near-hour-long ride. She got out on the other side of the carriage. She knew she was supposed to go to the rear of the enormous house to wait till she was called to assist, if needed, but hesitated to watch everyone's reaction over seeing Miss Erin. The gown was lovely, Rosa had to admit, but it was silver, and wasn't that the same as gray? She shook her head, remembering the saying her mamaw had recited about the colors a bride should and shouldn't wear. That had been a long time ago, when she was a little girl growing up on a big plantation outside Charleston, South Carolina, and her mamaw was loaned out to other families to make wedding dresses for their daughters. Rosa struggled to remember the lines—"Married in white, you have chosen all right. Married in green, ashamed to be seen. Married in red, you will wish yourself dead. Married in blue, you will always be true. Married in black, you will wish yourself back."

She could not resist an ironic snort to think how Miz Arlene probably wished she had got married in red or black, but what was it about gray? Her brow furrowed as she pressed on to recall the long-ago lines.

From the driver's seat above, Ben, resplendent in a suit of bright yellow satin, leaned to whisper, "Rosa, you better quit gawkin' and get on around and outta my way, 'cause I gotta move on. Other wagons is a'comin."

She obliged, still brooding. Then, just as she started toward the back, she paused to take one more look at Miss Erin. And then she remembered—'Married in gray, you will go far away'.

As the thought struck, an invisible cold mist seemed to descend, showering her with dread. Something, maybe the *obeah* Tulwah said everybody with West African roots had in them, filled her with the chilling awareness that it was so. Miss Erin would, indeed, be going far away. And not just on the trip with her new husband. There was something else. She could feel it in her bones—and suddenly she was scared and did not know why.

The air was perfumed with the scent of all the roses, and despite everything, Erin was impressed by the ambience Ryan had graciously provided. Glancing about, she was assured he was nowhere about. Her mother had sent Ben with a note a few days earlier, reminding Ryan that it was bad luck for the groom to see the bride in her wedding dress before time for the ceremony. Erin was not superstitious but appreciated his respect for her mother's request.

She did not know the man who stepped forward to greet them officially. Vaguely she recalled seeing him at the Rose Ball, where he had been dancing with the young woman who had been with Carolyn Manning at Madame Cherise's. He was wearing wide brown nankeen trousers with a coffee-colored tailcoat, a short waistcoat of yellow brocade, a top hat, and pumps.

Removing the hat, he bowed with a flourish, then took Arlene's hand to bestow an obligatory kiss before straightening to say, "Mrs. Treymayne, on behalf of Ryan Youngblood, master of Jasmine Hill, welcome." He then repeated the ritual for Erin, before introducing himself. "I am Keith Roland, and I'm honored to be Ryan's chief attendant today."

Erin exchanged expected pleasantries as he proceeded to escort them upstairs and into the house. He seemed nice enough, but still she was able to detect an air of subtle condescension in his manner. He, like some of the others, obviously did not approve of the marriage, but if they would only give her a chance, she intended to do her best to make them like her. But, she silently vowed, they would have to give her that chance. She was determined not to be subjected to derision as she had been in Madame Cherise's shop.

She noted that the house was even more splendid than she remembered. It was as though every bit of finery had been brought out to add glitter and splendor to the supposedly auspicious day. Everything was shining, sparkling, from the crystal and china laid out in the dining room they passed, to the objets d'art in the foyer.

The guests they passed were almost obsequious in their rush to greet both Erin and her mother. After all, Erin was to be mistress of Jasmine Hill, a position not to be taken lightly.

Keith took them to the foot of the wide, curving stairs that led up to the second floor. Erin saw that the bannister was draped in pink satin ribbons and adorned with yet more roses. She couldn't help smiling to think of the trouble Ryan had gone to. Taking back the lingerie and exploding as she had to Madam Estelle must have made quite an impression. Perhaps they would have no more problems, now that they understood each other better.

"Miss Erin," Keith was saying, "if you and your mother will go on upstairs, there will be a servant waiting to escort you to freshen up." From somewhere outside the open French doors, the sound of violins tuning could be heard. He turned away with an accommodating nod of dismissal. "Should you need anything, there will be someone to serve you. I'll see you in the gardens in an hour."

An hour! Erin shuddered involuntarily. In just one more hour she would become Ryan Youngblood's wife.

"Isn't this exciting?" Arlene clutched her arm as they made their way. She noticed a tickling in her throat but felt better when she thought of the small flask filled with Tulwah's potion that lay in her pocket. It didn't matter that it made her feel intoxicated. That was certainly better than having a coughing spell and spitting up blood in the middle of the wedding ceremony, she grimly decided.

More roses lined the wide hallway upstairs. Four Negro girls of various ages stood in a line on one side. Dressed in neat gray dresses with long white aprons, they each curtsied in turn and spoke their names. The eldest, Annie, instructed them to follow her.

They were shown to double cherrywood doors that opened into a massive suite that ran the width of one end of the upstairs. Erin could only stare in wonder, for it was far more opulent than anything she had expected. Arlene, easy to express her emotion, scurried all about oohing and ahhing over each piece of furniture, each vase or floral arrangement. They were standing in a sitting room, with doors on each side.

"This must be his room," Arlene announced after a quick inspection. She crossed to the other door, peered in, and instantly cried, "Oh, Erin. You have to see this. It—it's absolutely gorgeous."

Erin went to look and was likewise impressed. The motif was pink and white, with touches of blue. The furniture was all in mahogany, and the huge bed was adorned with a pink lace canopy, edged with tiny embroidered red roses. "It all looks new," she marveled, walking about for closer scrutiny. There was even a writing desk, a sofa and chair situated in front of a cozy fireplace. And, of course, everywhere there were vases of roses and more roses.

"This was Miz Victoria's room," Annie said suddenly, and Erin and Arlene turned to look at her. Nervously, fearing she might have spoken when she wasn't supposed to, she rushed to explain, "Mastah Ryan, he had everything redone jus' this week, said it was only fittin' he and his wife have the same rooms that his grandaddy built fo' the mastah and mistress of Jasmine Hill."

Arlene winked at Erin and could not resist saying, "And you thought he was just doing all of this to impress other people. How many of them will see this?"

Erin made no comment. Obviously, after hearing how angry she'd been over the lingerie, this was a kind of peace offering.

A pleasant-faced woman appeared and introduced herself. Though a distant cousin, she explained that Ryan had always referred to her as his aunt Sophia. Erin liked her at once, for she was fat and jolly and made her think of what Mrs. Santa Claus would be like if there were one.

"I came to tell you it's almost time to begin. Is your lady-in-waiting here?"

Erin blinked, confused. "My what?"

Aunt Sophia rolled her eyes and admonished herself, "Oh, I've been reading too many fairy tales. What I mean is, has your maid of honor arrived?"

Arlene gave a soft gasp. She had not stopped to think Erin would need an attendant. Everything had happened so fast.

But Erin promptly solved the dilemma by cheerily confirming, "Yes. My mother."

"Wonderful." Aunt Sophia clapped her plump hands together, then cried, "Let's start downstairs then, and Erin, my dear"—she gently touched her arm—"I just want you to know I have never seen a more beautiful bride. No wonder, I had my mind on fairy tales. You are truly a princess this day."

"She certainly is," Arlene agreed brightly, as Erin graciously murmured her thank-you.

Aunt Sophia was headed for the door, but remembering all the talk about how her nephew had taken over Victoria's suite and redecorated for his bride, she paused to glance about. "I certainly hope that boy knows what he's doing," she spoke her thoughts aloud, as was her way.

Arlene was quick to ask, "Why, whatever do you mean?"

"Oh, don't mind me." Sophia waved her hands in dismissal of any anxiety she might have caused. "It's certainly proper. I mean, when a man takes a wife, it's understood he takes over the master suite in the house if he is, indeed, the master. It's just that Victoria is going to be in for a shock when she gets home, and . . . ." She fell silent, realizing she had been about to say far too much. Glibly, she continued, "But who cares? Victoria is always being shocked over something, anyway. That's how she is."

Lowering her voice conspiratorially, she continued, "She's not on my side of the family, you see. Ryan's father was my cousin, so she's only related by marriage and never has been a favorite relative. But enough gossip." She looked expectantly from Arlene to Erin. "Are we ready? And, oh, my dear, you are so pretty." She slipped her arm about Erin's waist. "I'm so happy you're going to be in our family."

She was the first person who had seemed genuinely friendly to her, and Erin adored her already.

The path to the formal gardens led from the side terrace of the house, and the way had been generously strewn with rose petals. A trio of violinists stood to one side beneath the shading arms of a huge magnolia tree, and their sweet music wafted with the breeze. Beyond, the sleepy James River flowed lazily toward the sea.

But in between, and beside a fountain filled with floating rosebuds, Ryan Youngblood awaited his bride. When she appeared, his breath caught in his throat, for she was even more lovely than he remembered.

She came toward him, not meeting his gaze, her mother at her side. If she were nervous, it didn't show.

Her mother, he noted with a silent chuckle, was enjoying every minute of her triumph. From the glazed look in her eyes, he suspected she had already been nipping at the champagne fountain. He liked her. She was conniving and shrewd, but she had bravado, and in only a short time, he had grown quite fond of her.

He had even grown fond of the idea of marrying Erin. Things just might work out for everyone's good, after all.

He had also had a few glasses of champagne and the whole world was glowing right then. He didn't give a damn that some of his relatives, and friends like Keith, had told him he was making a mistake. It was his business, his life. As for his mother, he found it hard to remember a time when they weren't sparring over something, anyway. In time, she would get used to the idea of having Erin for a daughter-in-law instead of Ermine.

Neither was he concerned over how Ermine would react. She would have no trouble finding herself another fiancé, and in short time, too. He had never felt any particular longing for her, and she had certainly sent no messages of desire to him.

Erin, however, was another matter entirely, he privately acknowledged as she reached his side. If she would let him, one day, in the not too distant future, he would give her his heart along with everything else he possessed in this world. He just needed time, time for his pride to heal, to get over feeling he had been coerced. But that would come, along with eventually making her return his love. They would learn to cherish each other . . . together. He had so many wondrous hopes as he turned to take her hand and smile down at her with the mirror of his optimism shining in his eyes.

Erin met his enraptured gaze and was stabbed with guilt. Maybe she should have returned the lingerie to him, instead of Madame Estelle. It must have been terribly humiliating for him. But, the point had been made, and now they could get off to a good start with proper respect for each other. It was time to think only of the future and, of course, the tender moment at hand, for the ceremony had begun.

Erin softly spoke her vows, and Ryan reverently answered with his. Then the minister solemnly pronounced them man and wife.

Lifting the short, gossamer veil from her face, Ryan stared at her for an instant, entranced by her compelling beauty, before brushing his lips softly against hers.

Around them, there was light applause, mingled congratulatory murmurs. Tucking her hand in the crook of his arm, he led her to the terrace, where they would meet their guests as they filed inside to the reception.

Erin's heart was pounding as she contemplated how fiercely handsome he truly was. He was wearing a suit of pale blue that complemented his cerulean eyes. The way he smiled at her made ripples of anticipated delight move up and down her spine. Perhaps, she dared to hope, her mother was right, and one day they would know true happiness together. But it would take time, she realized, lots of time. For, despite his good looks, wealth, and respected station in life, Erin still found him arrogant and assuming. It would also take much time to forgive, much less forget, his original intent.

The same people filed by whom she had met at the party the week before. A few seemed a bit friendlier, now that she was officially Mrs. Ryan Youngblood, but there were also those who still smiled with their lips as disapproval shone in their eyes.

When, at last, the line ended, they found themselves surrounded by people. Aunt Sophia appeared to rescue them and see they were served from the sumptuously laden tables. There were roast pigs and chickens, vegetable platters of all kinds, creams and pies and candies and mints. In the center of it all was a tiered cake, frosted in white and decorated with ribbons of spun sugar and topped, of course, with roses.

Aunt Sophia also made sure Erin and Ryan's glasses were kept filled with champagne. She and Arlene were getting on well, sharing continuous glasses of the bubbly drink.

There was little time for private conversation, and Erin was glad, for what could she say? Ryan was behaving as though they'd been engaged for years, and this day was the culmination of all their hopes and dreams. In no way did he act as a man constrained.

By the time everyone had eaten, a full orchestra was setting up in the ballroom as food tables were being cleared away.

Erin realized that for the first time no one was around them. They were waiting for their special table to be positioned beneath an archway covered in roses. Feeling suddenly awkward, she offered shyly, "I appreciate all the lovely roses, Ryan. I'm overwhelmed."

"And so am I," he murmured huskily, sweeping her with his hungry gaze. Then, attempting to overcome the quick rush of desire, he said, "Did you like the traveling suit? Madame Cherise said she was sure she could fit it properly without your having to try it on."

"It was fine." She looked at him then, wondering if he were going to seize the opportunity to bring the other matter out in the open and apologize, but what she saw in his expression was extremely baffling. There was an almost mischievous glow about him, as though he were trying to keep from laughing. Instinctively, she stiffened. Maybe he thought it was all a big joke, but she certainly didn't. Wishing to rob him of his moment, she deliberately made her voice cold as she said, "It would seem that you'd have had the courtesy to inform me you had planned a nuptial trip. Then I could have done my own shopping."

At that, he did give a chuckle. "Oh, come on, Erin. You and I both know that if I had told you, you wouldn't have been excited enough to so much as buy a new handkerchief. You think you're doing me a favor by marrying me, and you're more than willing for me to take care of all the arrangements and pay all the bills.

"As for the trip," he proceeded to tell her as she looked at him, stunned by his bluntness, "I thought it would be pleasant to get away and relax for a while, to give us a chance to get to know each other better away from here. People are going to be nosy and dropping by."

Still tense, she asked, "And might I ask where we are going?"

"I thought Philadelphia would be nice. It's a wonderful city. Good hotels and theaters. Plenty for you to do while I'm taking care of business."

"What kind of business?"

"I'm thinking about investing in a steamship line. Steam is the transportation of the future, but business is the last thing on my mind right now."

He reached to touch her cheek in a gesture of tenderness, but she quickly stepped back, pretending to be glancing around to enjoy the surroundings. Actually, she was afraid that if he did touch her, he would sense her excitement. Philadelphia was where the Free-Soilers were headquartered. It was also where Letty might be, by then.

Ryan frowned at what he thought was a rebuff but then passed it off as bridal jitters. "We'll be spending tonight at a guest cottage on the estate of a friend of mine near Tappahannock. I've sent couriers ahead to make all the arrangements for our journey as to coaches and ferries. I thought you'd enjoy some river travel, so I've leased a small steamship and crew for a cruise up the Chesapeake Bay."

She was impressed but not about to say so.

He led her to their table, and they had no more than sat down when the orchestra began to play a valse. Erin laughed, "I might have known you'd want to shock everyone—again."

"Why not?" he stood, held out his arms to her. "It's my house, my wedding day, my wife."

The guests circled the huge ballroom floor to watch the newlyweds swirl around in the dreamy, rhythmic steps of the dance that would soon be accepted all over the country and known as the waltz.

After a proper few moments, Keith approached to take over with the requisite dance as best man. Ryan promptly went in search of his new mother-in-law for an obligatory turn about the floor.

Soon everyone was trying to do the dance, and Erin was amused that she and Ryan seemed to have started a trend.

She was having a wonderful time till she found herself in the arms of Carl Whitfield. Seeing Carolyn Manning glowering from the sidelines, Erin was annoyed that the woman was even in attendance, then realized that her family and Ryan's probably socialized.

Not wanting any tension, Erin promptly apologized to Carl for cutting the dance short. "I really need to be changing to leave soon," she explained politely.

Arlene saw her leaving to go upstairs and was going to follow, but Aunt Sophia detoured her to help with a fresh bowl of champagne punch.

Rosa had dutifully laid the dove silk suit out on the bed but was nowhere around. Stepping behind the brocade dressing screen, Erin began to take off her wedding gown. Hearing the door open, she thought it might be Rosa coming in and was about to call to her when she heard a nervous-sounding voice. "Please, Carolyn, let's go. We don't have any business being up here, and we just saw her come up here, anyway."

Erin heard Carolyn's retort. "I don't care. I wanted to see what Ryan did to Miss Victoria's suite. She's going to have a fit when she sees this. Just look at it. It's like something out of a bordello." She gave a nasty giggle as she added, "and I'm not a bit surprised."

At that, Erin stepped from behind the screen, wearing only her lace petticoats. She recognized the girl with Carolyn. She had been with her at Madame Cherise's shop. Though Erin wished no confrontation, these were now her quarters, after all, and she was not about to stand by and listen to someone speak so crudely. "Well, I must say I'm surprised, Carolyn," she said. "Do you make it a habit of snooping in other people's houses? I'll have to remember that when I make our guest list in the future."

Mary Susan's eyes widened, and she started to leave, but Carolyn caught her arm to keep her beside her as she fired back, "You've got a few things to learn, Erin Sterling, and as soon as Miss Victoria gets back from Europe, you'll get your first lesson. She'll never put up with you taking over here. You'll find out quickly enough who makes up the invitation lists."

Erin took a deep breath, held it to calm herself, then let it out slowly and said, "I would appreciate it if you would leave now, Carolyn. There's no need for this conversation."

Carolyn lifted her chin defiantly. Sick of hearing Carl prattle on about how beautiful Erin Sterling was, then seeing him dance with her, had been just too much. She was going to put her in her place once and for all. "Oh, yes, there *is* a need for this conversation. You might as well know that using guile to make Ryan marry you does not mean you will ever be accepted socially. You'll be excluded, just as you've always been, just like your mother, and—"

"Carolyn, you stupid little snob." Erin laughed at her incredulously. "Do you really think Ryan will be excluded from any social function because of me? My stepfather was never held in esteem, by anyone, so there was no way anyone would give me or my mother a chance to be accepted. But with Ryan, it's different. He has position already, and he will never tolerate his wife being ostracized.

"So, dear Carolyn, you might find yourself no longer

welcome at Jasmine Hill if you can't conduct yourself in a socially acceptable manner."

For a moment Carolyn could only look at her and blink rapidly in disbelief that anyone could speak to her in such a way. Mary Susan, no longer wanting to be a party to the scene, pulled from her friend's grasp and ran out of the room.

"You'll see," Carolyn warned between clenched teeth, her face a mask of uncontrolled rage. "Miss Victoria will have you thrown out of her room, maybe even out of her house. Ermine will have something to say about all this, too," she called over her shoulder as she headed for the door. Then she paused to glance at Erin's left hand and sneer, "Her ring was prettier, too."

Erin stared after her, bewildered. Who was Ermine? And what ring was she talking about?

Just then, Annie and Rosa came in, chatting happily and only mildly curious over the shouting they'd over-heard as they came up the back stairs. They tried to ignore white folks' business.

"Annie," Erin said in a commanding tone, "who is Ermine?"

Annie exchanged a nervous glance with Rosa as her eyes grew wide with fear.

Rosa shrugged helplessly, indicating she had no choice but to tell her.

Annie swallowed hard, bowed her head as though apologizing for having to be the one to inform her, "Miz Ermine was Mastah Ryan's fiancé befo' you come along."

Erin managed to ask, "What happened to her?"

"Nothin' that I know of. She went over yonder to Europe with Miz Victoria to shop for weddin' clothes and things, and they won't be back till the end o' summer." She dared to offer a saucy smile and say, "She sho' gonna be surprised when she comes back and finds out Mastah Ryan done took himself another bride."

Erin was stunned.

To learn that Ryan had been officially engaged to another woman was astonishing, to say the least. And it certainly explained many things, like why some of the people she had met were so hostile.

But what puzzled her was the awareness of sudden—what? resentment? jealousy?

She wasn't sure; she knew only that she was suddenly curious as to what other secrets were yet to be learned about her husband.

CHAPTER

 14

T**HEY HAD LEFT AMIDST A FLURRY OF WELL-**
wishes, but by the time the carriage reached the main
road, Ryan knew something was wrong. Erin had moved
to the other end of the leather seat, as though attempting
to get as far away from him as possible. He asked if anything were amiss, and she shook her head, turned to look
out the window, and ignored him. Deciding once more
that she was just a nervous bride, he settled back and
closed his eyes. She would learn, sooner or later, that he
was not going to cater to her moods.

Erin was trying to decipher what it all meant. If Ryan
were officially engaged to someone else, how had her
mother been able to cajole him so easily into marrying
her? It was obvious he was a man of independence and
free thinking, a nonconformist. She stole a look at him
as he slept, marveling he could be so relaxed the way the
carriage was jouncing on the road. Her husband. But who
was he, really, this enigma of a man? What was it that motivated him, made him what he was? It was important that
she find out, for he was to be her life from this day forward, an important part of it, anyway.

With each passing day, her own determination grew,
her desire to help the oppressed. Yet, it all had to be done

in secret, and if she were to operate successfully, she would have to learn all there was to know about her husband. It would be necessary to anticipate his every mood, to foresee his reaction to any situation. Yet, as she stared at him, Erin knew, somehow, that Ryan was complex and it would be only with the greatest acumen that she would ever be able even to remotely understand him.

She tried to sleep but was too tense, for there was so much to think about.

Just as darkness descended, Ryan was awakened by the driver calling down, wanting to know where he should turn. Ryan looked out the window, familiarizing himself with the landscape, then replied, "Not much farther. You'll see a road to the right, winding down toward the river." He sat back to smile at Erin. "Were you able to get any sleep?"

"No." She returned to her vigil at the window, grateful he did not pursue conversation. But she heard his sigh, could feel his curious eyes on her.

In the purple glow of twilight, Erin could see that the world about her was quite beautiful. They were fast approaching a tiny vine-covered cottage situated on a grassy knoll with a commanding view of the waterway. It was sheltered by graceful weeping willows and looked cool and inviting.

The carriage stopped at the end of a flower-lined path. Ryan got out and helped her alight.

Erin watched as the servant unloaded her trunk and Ryan's leather valise and took them inside. Ryan told him to return by eight the next morning, because he wanted an early start while it was still cool. He then got back up in his coach seat and took the reins to set the team of horses back in the direction they had just come.

"Where is he going?" she wanted to know.

"There are servants' quarters near the main house."

Puzzled that no one was about, no sign of host, hostess, or servants, she asked why. Ryan explained as he led the way up the walk, "The man who owns this estate is a special friend of mine, as I told you, and he lets me use this cottage sometimes. When I sent word we wished to spend our wedding night here, he was most agreeable and said he'd take care of everything and see that we had complete privacy.

"Do you think you can get by one night without a handmaid, my dear?" he couldn't resist teasing.

She was quick to inform him, "I don't have a handmaid. I take care of my personal needs myself. But what about you? Do you think you can get by without your valet?"

"Of course." He grinned down at her as he reached to open the door. "I have you instead."

"You've got a lot to learn," she muttered, brushing by him.

"And so have you."

Erin chose not to continue the verbal warfare and instead began to remove her gloves slowly as she looked around. They were in a small sitting room, with sofa and chairs positioned before a fireplace, not in use, of course, for the late August day was quite warm. She could see the bedroom through an open door but glanced away quickly, not about to dwell on that.

Before a window with a commanding view of the seascape, a table had been set. Covered with a cream colored linen cloth, place settings were of gold and pink china and elegant crystal and silver. Tapers were burning in an ornate silver candelabra. A bottle of champagne waited in a bucket of cooling water. There were platters of sliced meats—ham and roast beef—as well as cheeses, breads, and fruits.

Erin turned, startled to find Ryan standing right behind her.

"Get used to my being behind you, my darling," he murmured warmly, placing possessive hands on her shoulders as his lips brushed her forehead, "as well as beside you, for always."

She tried to move from his grasp, but he held steadfast. With blue eyes becoming stormy in the soft glow of the candles, he reminded her, "This was what you wanted, Erin. Marriage. It's time for you to get used to being a wife, so you can stop cringing every time I touch you." With that, he released her.

She glared up at him in silence, for there was nothing she could think of to say for the moment.

"Would you like to eat now?" he asked with exaggerated courtesy. "Our host certainly made sure we had everything we could possibly want."

She gave her head a toss, felt her heart pounding in her chest. "No. Nothing for me. I'm not hungry."

Tension descended like an invisible shroud as they faced each other. The only sound was that of a distant whippoorwill calling to his mate, and the kiss of the willow fronds as they brushed the sides of the cottage.

"I'm sure you'll find everything you need in the bedroom, along with your trunk. Why don't you change into one of the gowns I sent you and then we'll have the champagne in here?"

For a moment, Erin could only stare at him in absolute shock and then was barely able to whisper, "The gowns you sent . . ."

"Yes." He was watching her, puzzled. "You did receive the lingerie from Fine Things, didn't you?"

"Fine Things," she helplessly echoed once more. Surely, he was aware she had returned everything. Wasn't that why he had gone out of his way to make things so lovely for the wedding, to apologize for insulting her? Yet, he was behaving as though he knew nothing.

He took her reaction to mean she was registering disapproval of the shop. "Yes, from Fine Things, Erin, and don't look so shocked. You saw the name on the box, I'm sure."

"But—" She began, then fell silent, not sure of what to say.

"If more wives bought their lingerie at places like Estelle's, there might be fewer places like hers operating. Next time, you can pick out your own." He dismissed her as he went to open the champagne.

When she made no move to go, Ryan asked softly, "Are you *sure* you don't need a handmaiden, Erin? I'll be glad to help if you can't manage to undress yourself."

At that, she rushed into the bedroom and closed the door, leaning against it to hear him chuckling to himself. Damn! She cursed under her breath. Why hadn't Madame Estelle told him? And why had he gone to so much trouble? And why had he so easily turned from his fiancé, and—oh! Never had she been so bewildered by so many things.

Ryan was smoldering, and not from desire alone. That, he could deal with. The way Erin was acting was something else, and he was finding it increasingly difficult to contain his anger. Who the hell did she think she was, anyway? He had bent over backward to give her a nice wedding, because he knew she had to be under a lot of pressure. There were, no doubt, feelings of insecurity she had to deal with. He had seen how some of the guests, both at the wedding and the engagement party had looked at her with contempt. He didn't like that, didn't want it, and was stupid enough to try and make it up to her. He'd given her the ring for show, so everyone would come nearer believing his explanations for the hasty marriage. The roses had been his own special gift, a nostalgic reminder of the night they had met. Yet, on their journey here, she had frostily ignored him. And now, when the moment was at hand for the consummation of their marriage, she dared act shocked that he was even expecting it. Damn it, didn't the little vixen know she was driving him crazy?

The champagne cork popped loudly, its contents sloshing over the neck of the bottle to splash on the front of his suit. Irritably, he stripped to the waist, tossing coat and shirt aside. What difference did it make, anyway? Soon he was going to be naked, and so was she, whether she liked it or not.

He was starting to feel like a fool, and he wanted revenge for his pride.

He reached for a glass, cursing to himself. Filling it with champagne, he tossed it down unceremoniously. Staring at the closed door, he made up his mind that if she did not appear in five more minutes, he was going in.

Erin had heard his curses and moved from the door. Her trunk was on the floor beside the dressing screen. There was nothing to do but open it and put on the outfit she had brought as her final retribution for his insult—a dowdy, plain muslin gown that fit her like the feedsack it had been fashioned from.

Ryan was glad his friend had provided several bottles of champagne, because he was well into the second when he decided he'd overextended his self-imposed limit for Erin's appearance. She had been in that room for over half an hour, and he'd not heard a sound. Enough was enough. "Are you going to join me in here, Mrs. Young-blood, or would you prefer that I come right into the bedroom and dispense with courtly preliminaries?"

Erin hesitated, then bit back an angry retort. One day,

my arrogant husband, she silently, furiously vowed, you will know what it means to beg, rather than demand.

She took a deep breath and flung the door open.

Ryan, at first, could only stare in disbelief. She stood there, sable hair brushed to fall loosely about her shoulders, blatant defiance glimmering in her chestnut eyes, the play of a taunting smile on her lips. With hands on her hips, bare feet slightly apart, she gave her head a haughty toss and said, "I pick out my own lingerie, Mr. Youngblood. I thought you knew I returned your selections to Madam Estelle.

"Didn't I make it clear I don't intend to be your whore?" she testily added.

A shadow passed, wiping away surprise to leave fury in its wake. "I never wanted you for my whore, Erin. And, no, she didn't tell me. Maybe," he said slowly, evenly, "she was afraid to, afraid of how I might react to such an insult."

"You—you're insulted?" Erin stammered, aghast that he could even hint at such a thing. "How do you think I felt, receiving lingerie from such a place, picked out by my husband-to-be?"

At that, he blazed, "When are you going to stop playing the role of shy, indignant virgin, Erin? It doesn't become you. I sent you those things, because I was stupid enough to think you might have some passion in your bones, that you might want to try and keep me away from another woman's bed. But I see now I was wrong. You don't care. You married me for material reasons, social position. . . ."

"Why did you agree?" She could not hold back her resentment any longer. She stepped from the doorway. Yes, she acknowledged to herself, he was devastatingly desirable standing there broad-shouldered and bare-chested, the thick mat of chest hairs trailing down provocatively.

"Why did you agree to marry me . . . when you were already engaged to someone else?"

He shrugged. It didn't matter, but he knew he owed her an explanation. "I never wanted to marry her in the first place. That was my mother's idea. She arranged it."

"You even gave her an engagement ring."

Another shrug. "I can afford lots of rings, Erin." Damn, he inwardly cursed himself, he didn't want it to be this way, but she left him little choice but to fight back.

"Bastard! Who the hell do you think you are?"

"I'm your husband, Erin." He started toward her again. "You got what you wanted. Now it's my turn."

Instinctively, she stepped back, even though she really had no fear of his becoming violent. Only carnality, and a glimmer of amusement, was mirrored in his gaze.

He turned the champagne bottle up to his lips once more, then looked at her thoughtfully and said, "I thought we'd be sharing this."

"Drink it yourself."

He smiled crookedly as he shook his head slowly from side to side and whispered, "No, my sweet. I've got something else in mind."

She began to back into the bedroom, feeling uneasy.

He followed her, like a cat stalking prey. He continued to sip from the bottle. "Didn't you learn anything from your previous lesson, my sweet? Didn't you learn who's the master and who's the slave here?

"As for your gown," he sneered, "you don't even need one." His hand snaked out to clasp the neckline and easily ripped the garment from her.

"Damn you," she cried, attempting to cover herself with her arms, whirling about, looking for cover.

For an instant, he could only stare, for the sight of her naked body was intoxicating, paralyzing. He felt himself grow hard, and set the bottle aside to unfasten his trousers.

She watched, angry and terrified all at once.

When he, too, was naked, she could not help but look at him and see the raw proof of his desire . . . and intent.

He gave her a gentle shove that sent her sprawling backward on the bed. He retrieved the champagne bottle and slowly positioned himself beside her.

She looked up at him mockingly and said coldly, "So take what you want and be done with it."

"Be done with it?" he echoed, laughing at the incredulity of such a notion. "You can't be serious, Erin. This is something to enjoy, and savor, like fine wine and champagne . . ." His words trailed away as he took another swallow, before continuing, "I was trying to figure out a way we could both enjoy this, and I think I just found one."

She screamed as the cold liquid dripped slowly onto her breasts, writhing at his touch as he smeared it across her bare skin with his fingertips. "What—what are you doing?" she cried, feeling a warm tingling despite her fury.

"Relax, my lovely. I'm not going to waste good champagne. I'm going to savor every drop." He leaned then to lick one nipple, delighting in the taste of the wine on his tongue along with the feel of her hardening at his touch. He began to suckle gently, rolling his tongue all the while, his hand kneading and cupping the firm flesh. He moved to the other, licking the champagne, then sucking and rolling his lips against her. He was aware of how her heart had begun to pound, and her chest started heaving with her own unbridled longing. Her head had rolled to one side on the pillow, and she was clutching with her hands, arching her back in unchained pleasure.

He knew she was fighting for control, no doubt intending to submit passively and make him the total aggressor.

He knew well how to play that game, for he had invented the rules, prided himself on bringing ultimate satisfaction to any woman he bedded.

He maneuvered to allow the champagne to drip onto her belly, then trickle slowly, sensually, downward and between her legs. He felt as though he were going to burst for want of fulfillment, agonized by the throbbing of yearning to enter the sweet-hot flesh and have the velvet softness wrap around him. But he had also learned self-control in his enjoyment of women and could hold back for hours, if that was what it took to make his partner writhe and moan with ecstatic delight.

Positioning himself, he spread her thighs, pausing to trail a forefinger between. She stifled a moan as he found the pinnacle of sensation. For long, torturous moments, he massaged it with his thumb, watched her half-closed eyes, the soft gasps that escaped her lips, the way her tongue so often licked from side to side.

"Tell me you want me, Erin," he commanded gently, smugness thick in his tone, for he knew she was helpless. "Tell me you want me, and you'll have me, inside you, to take you for my wife, my woman . . ."

Almost violently, she shook her head from side to side.

Clamping her teeth tightly as she fiercely clutched the edge of the pillow, Erin thought how much kinder rape would be at that moment. To render her helpless with ecstatic torture was humiliating and demeaning, and she hated him for it, while at the same time wanting him so fiercely it was like a burning knife in her loins.

Then she felt him withdraw, dared hope he was about to take her then and there, yielding to his own hunger. Abruptly she felt the tormenting trickle of the champagne once more. She cried out loud as his mouth closed over that almost painfully sensitive nuclei of pleasure.

He began to suck and lick the champagne from her delicate flesh, and each touch was fire in her blood. Without realizing what she was doing, she released her hold on the pillow and reached out instead to caress him tenderly as he devoured her. Her legs entwined around his back as she arched yet closer. She could feel a strange sweet-hot needling sensation beginning from deep within her belly at the same time the low gurgling in her throat began to fight its way upward.

Ryan felt it, too, and was not about to give her blessed release, not till she begged for it.

He withdrew, and her eyes flashed open to stare in pained disbelief. Surely he was not stopping, her tormented mind screamed, but then he was looming over her, to lower his body the length of hers, to cover her lips with his. She could taste herself on his tongue, and she returned his kiss with fervor. Their bodies clung together, perspiration slick and undulating, every muscle taut, tingling, every nerve wild and shrieking for release.

She wanted him. Oh, God, she wanted him. Inside her. Forever. Always.

He was further tormenting by allowing his rock-hard member to throb between her legs, not quite touching that burning core that silently begged to be caressed once more. She spread her legs to receive him, boldly reached to cup his buttocks to pull him closer.

As much as he wanted her, Ryan could not help raising his mouth from hers to command hoarsely, "Admit it, Erin. You want it as much as I do."

Erin, far too lost in passion to be incensed by further taunting, could only whisper, "Yes, yes, I want you," and clutch him against her even more. There would be time later to admonish herself for her weakness. For the moment, she could only seek to answer the longing, the calling, of her hungry body.

"Take me," he commanded, maneuvering on top of her

once more and spreading her legs wide. "Take me where you want me to be."

Boldly, brazenly, she reached for him, positioning him. He drove deep and hard, shuddering with his own needs, and she cried out, legs wrapping tightly about his waist. He leaned to cover her mouth with his, then traced hot kisses along her neck before burrowing his face in the hollow between her shoulder and neck. She responded with nibbling kisses to his cheek and ear. He was driving into her relentlessly, his movements urgent, hard. His body was convulsing over hers as though he had lost all control. She pulled him ever harder against her as she felt the needles stab once more, and her buttocks were bouncing up and down in unison with his driving thrusts.

She called his name, gasping, crying, at the wonder that wrapped her from head to toe in a cocoon of smothering bliss. He reached to clamp her bottom and hold her secure, firm, as he drove into her mercilessly, taking himself to his own tower of surrender. Never, he realized through the dizzying shroud that was engulfing him, had it ever been like this, never so dazzling or intense. It was as though something in her was reaching out to pull him inside her and he was drowning.

He cried out but pounded on, and she answered him with her own call for more, and finally, when he thought he was surely dying, he felt the great, gasping shudder and exploded inside her.

They became one.

He gently collapsed on top of her but continued to hold her close. His breath was warm on her neck, and his sweat-damp body melded against hers as if they were truly only one flesh. "Did I hurt you?" he asked her, suddenly remembering it was her first time.

Erin felt a bit embarrassed to admit, "I'm afraid I have

to stop and think about it. I was so . . ." She could not go on.

"I know." Rolling to one side, he looked at her in the mellow glow of the bedside lantern and admitted, "I was lost in the moment, too." They lay quietly for a time, and then, fearing she might think he had somehow surrendered, he pretended to goad, "Tell me. Do you think it will be so bad, being my love slave?"

"Ha! We'll see who's the slave and who's the master," she fired back good-naturedly. It was all so uncanny, this emotion washing over her, tingling, stirring. She never dreamed it would be like this—so good, so right. Wasn't she supposed to feel subservient?

He gazed at her in affectionate wonder, then remembered her anger. "So tell me," he prodded curiously. "How did you find out about Ermine? Not that I was trying to keep it a secret, mind you. It's just that it never came up, and I saw no reason to mention it."

"It's not important how I found out," she replied, reaching to pull the sheet up to her chin, because now she felt a bit embarrassed to be lying next to him naked. It was still all so new, and she was not yet comfortable with the intimacy. "I would like to hear about it, though, seeing as I was warned right before we left that when your mother came home, I'd be facing not only her wrath, but your fiancée's, as well."

"Ermine won't care," he assured her. "She only wanted to marry me for material reasons, same as you. The two of you would probably get on well together. She'll find someone else. She's not an unattractive girl. As for my mother, she'll just have to accept things as they are."

"You really make it all sound so callous, so cold," Erin could not resist saying. "Didn't you ever think about marrying for love?"

"Love?" he scoffed. "There's no such thing. It's fantasy.

Like the pot of gold that's supposed to be found at the end of a rainbow. The rainbow is pretty to look at it, but it doesn't exist . . . just like love," he added with a bitter smile.

"So you really didn't care who you married."

"Of course, I cared. I wanted you, Erin, as I'd never wanted a woman before. Maybe in the beginning, I'll admit my intention was to make you my mistress, but enough about that." He raised up on an elbow to look down at her in amusement as he queried, "Tell me why you were so angry about the lingerie."

She proceeded to do so, mincing no words.

He chuckled. "What a little hypocrite you are. You gave me the impression you didn't give a damn what people thought, yet you panicked that someone would think you wore revealing undies. Well, we'll just take care of that when we get home. You can go to Madame Estelle and tell her it was all a mistake, that you do want the lingerie, after all."

"I'll do nothing of the kind," she cried, pushing him away as he sought to take her in his arms once more.

"We'll argue later," he laughed, crushing her against him. "We've got the rest of our lives to argue, Erin, as well as make love, like this. . . ."

CHAPTER

 15

THEY CROSSED THE RAPPAHANNOCK RIVER BY ferry and proceeded to Westmoreland County alongside the Potomac River. Erin slept most of the way, weary from the long hours of lovemaking. Though Ryan also had cause to be exhausted, she suspected the way he seemed so cool and detached was due to something else. He appeared to be brooding, and she did not know why and was not about to ask. But what could she expect? she pondered. He had only married her to get what he wanted by night. Why should he pay any attention to her by day?

They spent the night at another guest cottage on a bluff overlooking the Potomac River. Again, arrangements had been made in advance, and they were provided with luxurious accommodations, the best wine and food.

"You certainly seem to have some rich and influential friends," Erin remarked as they dined on roast duck and cherry sauce, accompanied by sweet scuppernong wine, which he said was made right there on the plantation.

"My family has always traveled a lot," he said matter-of-factly. "The men, anyway."

"Well, you'll have company from now on."

Curtly, he disagreed. "Oh, I doubt that. You'll be too busy having babies."

Erin felt a needle of resentment. "In case you're interested, I happen to have other interests in life besides a baby every year. I want to get out, see things, do things. I don't intend to have a baby right away. I want to just get used to being married, running a household, and—"

"You won't be running anything, Erin."

She had just taken a bite of cherry sauce. She quickly swallowed and demanded to know what he meant by such a remark.

Carefully, he laid down his knife and fork, wiped his mouth with the napkin before cooly informing her, "My mother is still mistress of Jasmine Hill, and tradition decrees she will remain so as long as she lives. Granted, she's not an easy person to get along with, but it's a large house, thank goodness, and the two of you should have no trouble avoiding each other. But you won't have any responsibilities. She maintains full charge of the household.

"As for your not wanting a baby right away, I think nature will take care of that," he continued, watching her closely to gauge her reaction. "I want as many children as it's possible for us to have. And frankly, I don't know what you mean when you say you want to get out, see things, do things. The only thing there is for you to do is be a wife and mother. What else do you have in mind?" His eyes raked her almost suspiciously.

Erin felt a frantic wave. She was going to have to be able to have some freedom in order to work with Mahalia and the Free-Soilers. "I like to go riding," she said airily. "By myself. I'll be going to visit my mother. And there's church work. She's been wanting me to join her in that. There are all sorts of things I can do with my time, Ryan. Please don't expect me to sit around the house like an old woman, tatting with your mother."

He pushed his plate away. As was his way, he got

straight to the point. "I've changed my mind about taking a mistress, Erin."

She shook her head, not understanding, and demanded, "What does that have to do with anything?"

"I wasn't expecting to have a passionate life with Ermine. I intended to sleep with her for the sole reason of having babies but look to someone else for the real warmth a man needs from a woman. I imagine that Ermine, like a lot of other women, planned to take a lover from time to time for her own diversion.

"But it isn't going to be that way for us," he fervently declared as he got to his feet, walked around to stand behind her and clutch her shoulders possessively. "I've found something in you I never thought existed in just one woman, Erin—warmth, passion, excitement, a keen wit, intelligence. I'm not sure just which quality draws me the most. I only know I have no need of another woman.

"And," he finished with an ominous tone, "I also know I'm not about to share you with another man."

Indignant, she reminded him, "I was a virgin, and you know it. I'm not the type to be promiscuous. You should know that; you certainly tried hard enough to prove otherwise," she added tartly.

He ignored her sarcasm and went on. "Decent women seldom are till after they're married, and find themselves bored. That's not going to be the case with us. I paid a dear price for your body—my pride. I'd kill any man who tried to take you away from me, and if you ever tried to leave me, I'd probably break your beautiful neck." His fingers closed about her throat.

Erin knocked his arms away as she bolted from the chair. Whirling about furiously, she saw the devilish grin on his face, the twinkle in his eyes. "How dare you joke about something like that!"

"Who says I'm joking? Just bear in mind that now that

I've got you, I'm going to keep you, and you won't have anything to worry about." He then lifted her into his arms and headed for the bedroom, ignoring how she held herself stiffly aloof. Nuzzling her cheek, he whispered, "All you do have to worry about is having the stamina to feed my hunger, because I'll never get enough of you."

He laid her on the bed, then delighted in undressing her slowly, savoring every inch of flesh as it was revealed to him. He covered her body with his lips, tenderly, gently, as though paying homage to a rare and fine work of art.

Though Erin reveled in his every kiss and caress, she managed to hold back a part of herself to keep him from knowing just how much she enjoyed and craved his love-making.

That was her secret, and her only weapon against his ultimate goal of total submission.

During the nights that followed, there were many times she would pretend merely to submit, just to enrage and make him exquisitely torture her into begging for bitter-sweet release. Yet, no matter how driven he was to take her, always he was delicate, disciplined, at just the right moments. Never did she feel used or violated. Always, she was completely satiated when it was over.

It was a triumph to her ego to have had him confess he had no interest in ever bedding another woman, but she was not about to tell him she could never imagine herself in the arms of another man.

Despite the closeness and intimacy they shared by night, their days were still a war of wits as they battled each other in their own kind of defensive pride.

Their journey was leisurely. They crossed the Potomac by ferry, then continued on to Washington. They stopped two nights along the way, again at prearranged cottages.

Always, there was utmost privacy, and no host, hostess, or servants, were ever seen.

Washington, however, was another story. There, they stayed at a fine hotel. During the day, they went sightseeing or shopping, but at night, they were entertained in private homes. Erin quickly learned her husband was prominent elsewhere besides Virginia, as she met senators and congressmen, the cream of Washington society. She was delighted to feel so respected and stood proudly, regally, beside him.

When she wanted to know how it was that he knew so many people, he matter-of-factly said he was a graduate of West Point and had fought in the War of 1812. "Military, wars, and politicians seem to go together," he declared with a wry smile.

Erin was enjoying the social whirl and had to admit to being completely happy in her role as a new bride. Still, she was worried about her mother, as well as Letty. Not knowing what was going on back home filled her with anxiety, and one morning she could not resist asking how much longer they would be traveling.

"Aren't you having a good time?" he asked with a frown.

Quickly, she assured him, "Of course. I was just wondering, that's all."

It was early morning, and they were having breakfast in their room. Ryan picked up the envelopes on the table that had been brought in with their tray. Every day, it was the same. Dozens of invitations were delivered to the hotel, as word spread that he was in town. He began to leaf through them, tossing to one side those he had no intention of accepting, deliberating over the others. "Theater. Dinner. A tea party. A weekend of riding and hunting." He shook his head, amused by the variety offered. "Do you like opera? We've been invited to the opening performance of *Faust,* and . . . what's this?" He focused on a cream-colored envelope, opened it with interest, and then nodded to himself. "I think we'll accept this one. Dinner with Representative James Tallmadge of New York and his wife."

"Who's he?" Erin asked but did not really care. All it meant was another night dressed in elegance, clinging to her husband's arm, sipping wine and smiling graciously.

"He's the one who started all the uproar last February over the Missouri territory's preparations for statehood. Congress introduced what they called the 'Missouri Bill', which gave permission for them to draft their state constitution, but Tallmadge wanted two amendments to it—a declaration that no more slaves could be brought in and another stating the children of those already there had to be freed when they reached the age of twenty-five."

"Now I know the name," she said. "The House of Representatives passed both amendments, but they were defeated in the Senate."

Ryan was impressed. He had never known a woman who even concerned herself with political matters, much less one who obviously knew what she was talking about. "How did you know that?" he couldn't resist asking.

She returned his questioning stare with one of her own to counter, "The same way you did, probably. In the newspapers."

"You read the newspapers? The political news?" He was still astonished.

"Of course, I do." She was beginning to feel defensive and realizing that made her angry. "Why do you find that so surprising?"

"Most women don't—" he began.

But she cut him off to remind him tartly, "I'm not most women, Ryan. You'd do well to remember that."

A muscle in his jaw twitched. He resisted the temptation to get into another contest of wits. Standing, he informed her he had some business to take care of and said, "You'll have to entertain yourself today. Here's money if you want to go shopping."

She didn't, but quickly took the money. It was not the first he had given her, and she was hiding as much as possible in the lining of her trunk. By the time they got home, she would have an impressive sum to send to Mahalia.

That night she wore a lemon-colored dress and cape with a flowered band in her hair. Quite dignified, not too formal, she decided, glancing at herself in the mirror. Ryan would be pleased. He had gone over her wardrobe with her, explaining what gowns should be worn for which functions they attended. She was not pleased that he took the position of telling her what to wear, but, since she had not much experience in social matters, decided to yield this once. When they returned to Richmond, however, she would take over her own wardrobe selection.

The evening began with a social hour. Guests enjoyed wine and hors d'oeuvres while chamber music played.

At dinner, she found herself seated to the right of Representative Tallmadge. Table talk was generic, broaching no particular subject. Small talk. Trivia. Erin knew it was because politics or serious matters were never discussed in the presence of ladies. Still, she kept hoping some mention would be made of the situation concerning Missouri, because she was deeply interested now, more than ever, in anything that pertained to slavery.

She knew after dinner it was customary for the men to go into the parlor with their brandy and cigars. The women had tea or sherry in another room and chatted about babies and children and sewing, topics she was not interested in for the time being. Fearing she would never have another opportunity to discuss such a vital subject with so important a man, Erin seized the opportunity during a rare lull in conversation to comment, "I understand, Mr. Tallmadge, that you're the representative who proposed the two amendments concerning the admission of Missouri as a slave state."

All eyes fell on her then, and a tense hush descended in the room. Tallmadge, himself, was taken aback by having a woman broach such a subject. He cleared his throat and murmured, "Yes, that's right."

Erin was undaunted at finding herself the center of attention but couldn't help herself and felt driven to ask, "Well, I'm curious to know whether you've ever stopped to think how, if conditions are set for Missouri that no other state has had to meet, Congress might actually be assuming powers that aren't specifically granted by the Constitution. And . . ." she dared to continue, "I hear there are Southerners who fear it's just the first step, that Congress, with a Northern majority, would one day wipe out millions in slave property with a majority vote."

It was so quiet that the bubbles bursting in the champagne could almost be heard.

A woman seated on the other side of the table, who happened to be the wife of a Southern senator in attendance, was the first to recover. "You sound as though that might please you, Mrs. Youngblood."

Erin glanced to where Ryan was sitting, saw the way he was observing with disturbing concentration. She had been leading up to approach Mr. Tallmadge to consider how it might bode well to require Missouri and all others applying for statehood in the future, to come in as free states. It could be the first step to one day, mercifully, wiping out slavery altogether. Wishful thinking perhaps, she decided then and there, and dangerous for anyone to suspect she thought that way. If she were to be able to assist the underground movement, she could not be known as being in abject opposition to slavery. So, with an apologetic smile to the woman, Erin lied. "Why no, ma'm. I didn't mean it to sound that way at all. My husband owns slaves, and we are both Southerners. In any issue, we would stand with the South. I just wanted to voice our concerns to Mr. Tallmadge."

"That would seem better left to the menfolk to worry about," the woman advised.

Mr. Tallmadge reached to pat Erin's hand patronizingly. "It's refreshing to realize women do concern themselves with our nation's problems, Mrs. Youngblood, but I agree. You leave the worrying to us old codgers and concentrate on what you do best—looking beautiful."

Erin bristled but said no more. She couldn't help it if other women were content to merely adorn life, instead of wanting to be a part of it.

In the ladies' parlor after dinner, Erin found herself somewhat ostracized and left out of the usual conversation. She didn't care. She only wanted to leave Washington before she got in more trouble by her inability to keep her opinions to herself.

Ryan didn't mention what had happened, but the next morning they continued on their way. Erin suspected it was a bit sooner than he'd planned but didn't dare ask.

By carriage they journeyed east into the state of Maryland and on to the seaport town of Annapolis. There, Ryan had made arrangements for his carriage driver to stay at the estate of yet another friend, to work while awaiting their return. The small steamboat he had leased was waiting with full crew.

"I hope you won't get sick," he offered as they set out on their journey up the Chesapeake Bay. "I've seen a lot of ladies spend their time on a voyage with green faces, clinging to the rail."

But Erin was entranced with the sea, reveling in the

smell of the air, the caress of the breeze. They had opulent accommodations in a small cabin below deck, but she enjoyed being outside. Ryan busied himself with going over financial reports that had been sent to him by the shipping company in Philadelphia and was glad Erin seemed content to entertain herself by walking around on deck. Unknown to him, however, she cajoled the vessel's captain into allowing her to watch him as he coursed and charted, steering the boat through channels and canals. By the time they moved on to the Delaware Bay, she had even the crew in awe over how quickly she had learned nearly every aspect of operations and navigation.

In Philadelphia, their first days were spent sightseeing. Built to a checkerboard town plan, the grid of tree-lined avenues ran between two rivers. Erin enjoyed the shops and stores, as well as pouring through historical volumes in America's first library. Ryan was impressed that she was such an avid reader, seeming to commit to memory every single line she read.

She laughed over the etiquette books that seemed to be so popular. Quickly she learned that wealthy and fashionable families in Philadelphia barricaded themselves behind a system of exclusion even more so than those in Richmond.

Social life, she learned, consisted of homes being opened in the evenings for dinner parties, dances, and formal balls. There were even "morning calls," and she learned about calling cards, insisting Ryan have some made before they left town.

But it was not the shopping or social or cultural life in Philadelphia that Erin sought to explore. The very first day Ryan left her to attend a business meeting, she set out on her own. Here, she excitedly realized, she could almost feel the heartbeat of freedom. Every time she saw an obviously free Negro walking on the street, she was struck with the desire to run up to him, or her, and ask where she could contact someone who might know something about a runaway slave girl named Letty. With tears stinging her eyes, she knew that was not possible. All she could do was wander the paved and cobblestone avenues and wonder and wish.

She found herself standing in front of the Arch Street Meeting House where the Society of Friends, the Quakers, met. She had seen them around the city, dressed sedately, but the women, with fine figures and tiny feet, always wore frocks of rich fabrics. They were, she knew, a contact point, but she did not dare make any inquiries. When she saw a man dressed in Quaker attire step out the door and glance at her curiously, as though about to ask if she were looking for someone, she turned and hurried away.

One evening, the owner of one of the shipping firms Ryan had an interest in asked them to his home. Charles Grudinger was a widower, and Erin dared hope since there would be just the three of them for dinner, she might be included in conversation afterward. Instead, Mr. Grudinger's housekeeper, a free black woman he affectionately called Nanny Bess, showed her into the library.

"Your husband told Master Charles that you enjoy reading. You should be comfortable here."

Erin guessed the woman to be in her late fifties. Gray-haired, she was stoutly built, short, with a round, pleasant face. She had turned to leave, but Erin could not resist inquiring, "May I ask how it is that you speak with no dialect?"

Nanny Bess did not hesitate to tell her. "I'm one of the lucky ones, Mrs. Youngblood. When I was only ten years old, my master died, and his widow set all the slaves free. The only problem was, I'd been brought over from Africa on a slave ship, and my parents died en route. I had nowhere to go. My mistress kept me as a companion for her daughter. She taught me how to read and write and speak properly. She grew up to become Mrs. Charles Grudinger, and took me with her. We were together till her death, and then Mr. Grudinger was kind enough to keep me on."

Erin nodded, silently agreeing she was truly lucky. Not many slaves were given such opportunities. Then she saw the way Nanny Bess was staring at her, as though in resentment and asked, "Is something wrong?"

The woman hesitated a moment, then said, "It isn't proper for me to ask this, I know, but I always wonder, whenever I meet someone from the South, just how many slaves they have."

Instinctively, Erin stiffened, and the words were out of her mouth before she realized it. "I have no slaves. I don't know how many my husband has."

Nanny Bess nodded thoughtfully, eyes narrowed.

For a moment, Erin thought she was about to ask her another question she deemed improper, but she abruptly walked out without another word.

Erin wandered around the library but was not really interested in settling down to read a book. Ryan had hinted they might be leaving for home soon, and though she was terribly anxious to return, there was still an empty feeling inside. If she could only have an idea of where Letty might have gone, then she would dare leave a message for her, maybe even some of the money she'd hidden.

She was leafing through a copy of Coleridge's *Kubla Khan* when she realized she could hear Ryan's voice, clear and distinct, coming from the other side of the bookshelf. Quickly moving aside other volumes, she realized not only that the wood was quite thin, but there were hinges on one side. This section was obviously a concealed door into the study.

With a ripple of mischief, Erin pressed as close as she could get, delighted to be able to make out everything the two were saying. Ryan, she noticed, sounded somewhat irate.

"As much as I'd like to get involved in shipping, Mr. Grudinger, I can't afford to get involved in colonization efforts. There's just no way my position as a slave owner, with a large plantation to run, would permit me such a venture. I want to be able to bring valuable horses from Europe to breed with my stock in Virginia, not transport runaway slaves back to Africa.

"And," he seemed regretful to have to say, "there's the question of violating laws concerning runaways. The Constitution contains the genesis, when it states a fine is to be placed on anyone rescuing, harboring, or hindering the arrest of a fugitive."

Mr. Grudinger hastened to point out, "They aren't all runaways, Mr. Youngblood. Some of them are freed blacks with nowhere else to go. The fact is, the census of 1810 counted a total of two hundred thousand of them, and the question now is what to do with them. They're a shadow zone in our society. They're denied citizenship. They aren't considered capable of functioning as part of our white society. They become a candidate for rebellion, and sadly our country regards the freed slave as a public nuisance. The American Colonization Society feels the humane thing to do is transport them back to where they came from, and they're seeking to do just that with government and private funds. I was frankly hoping you'd want to be a part of it. Surely, you can understand the compassionate and humanitarian aspects of such a venture."

"Compassion and humanitarianism don't go hand in hand with owning over three hundred slaves of my own, Mr. Grudinger. I'm sympathetic to the plight of those mistreated by their masters, but I'm afraid I have little choice but to commit to slavery if I'm to continue running my plantation successfully. And to buy into your company, when you tell me your chief cargo across the Atlantic will be slaves, whether freed or fugitives, would make me feel like a hypocrite, especially when we're having a problem with runaways in our area, anyway."

Erin heard Mr. Grudinger give a disgusted snort before he scornfully said, "Yes, I've heard. Several belonging to one Mr. Zachary Tremayne, I understand. Even as far north as Philadelphia, we've heard rumors of his mistreatment of his people, as well as his despicable involvement in the illegal slave trade."

Erin winced; she knew Ryan was probably gritting his teeth right then to think how he was married to the stepdaughter of such a man. Well, she couldn't help it and longed to be able to burst right in on them and say so.

"Miss Erin, would you like some tea?"

She whirled around, felt her cheeks flame with embarrassment to be caught with head awkwardly inside the bookshelf, eavesdroping. She smiled and confessed, "I'm nosy." With a touch of bitterness, she added, "I also resent the way men shut themselves away to talk in private, as though women are too ignorant to be involved in their business."

Nanny Bess cocked her head to one side, eyes narrowed thoughtfully. Quietly, slowly, she began, "I was just in there to ask if they wanted anything. They were talking about sending freed Negroes to Africa. Is that business you might be interested in hearing?

Erin hesitated, then dared admit with a quick nod and nervous whisper, "Yes. Very much, I'm afraid."

"We're all afraid, Mrs. Youngblood. These are dangerous times for my people. May I ask just what your interest is, and rest assured you can speak freely to me. I have no reason to divulge anything and perhaps every reason to keep it secret."

Erin, not sure just how far she dared to go, finally decided there was no risk in telling her about Letty, how they had been close friends, just as she and Mrs. Grudinger had been. "And since I'm here, in Philadelphia, the place I'm told that runaways head for, I can't help wondering if there's anywhere I could go to try and find out something about her, see if she really made it here."

"You say she escaped on the Virginia–North Carolina border?"

Erin nodded. "That's all anybody knows."

"That area is known as the Dismal Swamp, a terrible place, I hear. There're poisonous snakes and yellow flies, ticks, mosquitoes, and redbugs." She shuddered to think of it. "But the slaves head for there, if they can, like it's a second home. Your friend just might have made it, Mrs. Youngblood. There's plenty of her people living in there for that one purpose—to help the runaways."

Erin's heart was pounding excitedly. "Is there any way you can find out for me? Anyone you can contact?"

Nanny Bess said firmly, "No. I give information. I don't ask for any. And I have to be very discreet about who I give it to, because I'm not about to risk bringing trouble to Mr. Grudinger."

"Why would he be in trouble?" Erin could not understand the secrecy.

Nanny Bess had been standing inside the door, but she closed it then and walked over to sit down on the sofa, motioning Erin to take the place beside her. "Now you listen, child, and you listen good," she began in a whispered rush. "Just because a runaway makes it here, it doesn't mean he's safe. Not by any means. Slave hunters and vigilantes follow after them, and, for information, they're willing to give part of what they get for returning them to their masters. That's the reason some of the run-aways try to keep on going, all the way to Africa, but that's not legal just yet. Not if the slave is a fugitive. He's supposed to have papers proving he's free, before he can sign up for the colonization program.

"And there are other dangers, too," she confided, moving closer to ensure she could not be overheard. "Freed slaves live in fear of being kidnapped by whites to be sold back into slavery. Negroes aren't allowed to serve as witnesses against white people, so it's very difficult to stop it. There are even white men, right here in this city, who marry mulatto women and then sell them as slaves when they get tired of them.

"So what I'm telling you, child," she concluded, "is that even if your friend got this far, it doesn't mean she's safe, not unless she's got the money to pay to be smuggled on a ship headed for Africa."

Eagerly, fervently, Erin assured, "If I can find her, she'll have it."

Nanny Bess looked at her in that strange way again, as though trying to decide if she could truly be trusted. But just as she was about to speak, the door suddenly opened and Charles Grudinger looked in, surprised to witness the intimate little scene but not registering any disapproval as he announced, "I believe your husband is ready to leave now, Mrs. Youngblood. Nanny Bess, will you get Mrs. Youngblood's cape for her, please?" He walked out but left the door open.

Nanny Bess moved to oblige but quickly, nervously, whispered, "Find Mother Bethel. That's all I can tell you."

On the way back to the hotel, Erin tried to make her voice casual as she asked once more when they might be going home.

"Soon," Ryan said, sounding impatient himself.

Then to her surprise he recounted his conversation with Mr. Grudinger concerning transporting freed Negroes to Africa and asked if she shared his opinion that it would be hypocritical for him to invest in such a venture. At once, she was wary. Though their nights were tender and wonderful, there was still a feeling of apartness by day. At times, he regarded her with near contempt. So it came as quite a shock that he should ask her opinion on anything. "Since dinner at Mr. Tallmadge's, I've decided that woman was right when she said it's best to leave anything dealing with slavery to the menfolk. I have no opinion."

He looked at her in wonder. "I'm surprised you let that bother you so much. You're normally so outspoken. Besides, you were close to that runaway slave girl, too. Your mother told me your stepfather was taking her away to be sold. He didn't feel it was proper."

"That—that was different," she stammered uneasily, fearing she might say too much. "We grew up together. Letty was bought, along with her mother, Rosa, the day after my mother married Zachary. I was a baby. Letty was about a year old, I think. It seems like I've known her all my life."

"But you didn't like the idea of her being a slave, did you? I mean, you were very upset that morning that he'd taken her away."

"Of course, I was. Wouldn't you be—if someone you'd known your whole life was dragged out to be sold at auction, and you knew you'd never see her again? She . . ." Erin heard the hint of hysteria creeping into her voice and fell silent. Drawing a steadying breath, she said, "It's over now. I just don't want to think about it anymore."

"Do you object to our having slaves?"

"As long as they aren't mistreated. I'd never want you to beat them."

"I never have."

"Zachary does," she said vehemently. "And they hate him. Every single one. I wouldn't be surprised if he wound up one morning with a knife in his throat."

Ryan studied her for a moment, then assured her, "You never have to worry about me mistreating my slaves. I never mistreat anyone, unless they give me cause."

She caught the ominous note in his voice but fell silent. It was times like this, she thought, when his blue eyes grew so stormy, and he looked at her with such glaring suspicion, that she felt uneasy. As tender as he could be when he held her, she feared his wrath if ever she betrayed him. That was all the more reason never to let him know she was involved in any work to help the runaways. He would consider it a personal betrayal.

Still, she knew she had to do whatever she could, and if at all possible, before leaving Philadelphia, she intended to find Mother Bethel.

CHAPTER

 16

ERIN QUICKLY LEARNED THAT IT WAS DIFFICULT, if not impossible, to find out anything about an underground movement in the city of Philadelphia to aid runaway slaves. Even though she made up her mind to try, she could not seem to locate anyone willing to give her information.

First, she returned to the Quaker church, where the man had stared at her as though about to ask if he could be of assistance. She could not be sure it was the same one who answered when she knocked, but the moment she let it be known she was from Virginia, looking for a runaway slave, the door was quietly closed in her face. She never got the chance to ask if he knew who Mother Bethel was.

She went to several other churches, walking much of the time so as not to have to spend the money Ryan had given her for shopping or hiring a carriage. As a result, her feet were aching, but she plodded on.

Starting to feel all was hopeless, Erin received her first encouragement when a minister of a protestant church invited her into his study. It was obvious he was reluctant to do so, for he'd stared at her thoughtfully for a long time before finally waving her in.

He got right to the point. "I hate to see you wasting your time, young lady. While I admire you for your devotion to your Negro friend, I think you've been misled as to how the majority of white Pennsylvanians feel about the plight of the slave, in general." He proceeded to tell her there was apathy, that most people did not care one way or the other. White churches, on the whole, did not give aid to fugitives and were sometimes even hostile on the subject.

"So you see," he finished with a helpless smile, "you just can't make the generalization that Pennsylvania is a haven for these people. The immense burden of antislavery work and fugitive aid is carried out by a very small group of citizens who, understandably, go about their work quietly and cautiously. I'm not one of them, or I'd be happy to direct you to where you might get some better information."

Erin stood wearily, the blisters on her feet making her wince with pain. She hoped she could hide her anguish from Ryan, for he would begin to ask questions as to exactly why she was doing so much walking.

"Thank you," she said, holding out her hand. "You've been most kind, and I appreciate your wanting to help. Perhaps . . ." she ventured, taking one more chance he would reveal the information if he knew it. "Can you tell me where I might find Mother Bethel? I was told to find her, and then . . ." She stopped talking as she realized he was laughing at her. "Is something funny?" she asked, annoyed, for she could find nothing amusing in any of it.

"I would say so. You see, my good woman, Mother Bethel is not a she. Mother Bethel is another name for the African Methodist Episcopal Church, and if someone told you to go there, then you might be headed in the right direction to find news of your friend. It has connection with the Free African Society, which was formed by the Negro community here over thirty years ago to give mutual aid to both freed slaves and fugitives. I'll give you directions how to get there."

Within an hour, Erin was sitting across the desk from pastor Absalom Jones. His dark face grew even darker as she confided her reason for being there. He listened respectfully, and when she finished, gave her a pitying look and said, "Mrs. Youngblood, you are to be commended, and blessed, for caring about this poor girl you speak of, but you must understand I can't tell you anything. Yes, I will admit to you that I have knowledge of people who do help fugitives, but I am not directly involved, so I wouldn't know anything about individual cases."

She had anticipated what he would say and was ready to make her plea. "Will you at least speak to the people you know and tell them I was here asking about a runaway slave girl from Virginia named Letty? If they do know anything at all about her, they could give her a message for me."

Pastor Jones had to think about that. He did not like to agree to anything with a total stranger, particularly when it dealt with the matter of a runaway slave. Still, there was something about the lovely young woman sitting across from him that provoked trust. She seemed so intense, cinnamon eyes mirrored with desperation. With her light bronze skin, she might even have Negro heritage herself. He'd heard that once upon a time, slave traders had brought in a different branch of the Negro race called Mandingos, and they lived in South Carolina in great numbers. A child born of a Mandingo and a white parent had skin light enough to pass for white. There were no other racial characteristics, so these mixed bloods had no trouble passing, unlike the mulattoes, whose light skin was their only hint the color line had been crossed.

He shook away the suspicion. This woman had said she was married to a wealthy and prominent Virginia plantation owner. It was doubtful she had ever been anywhere near South Carolina.

Sensing his reluctance, Erin persisted, "What harm can it do for you to try?"

Still skeptical, he probed, "What is the message you're so desperate to get to her?"

"I want her to leave Pennsylvania," she rushed to explain, desperate to keep his interest now that she had it. "I've heard terrible stories, how even freed blacks are kidnapped and sold back into slavery. And you don't know my stepfather. He's ruthless when it comes to tracking down runaways. Not because he can't afford the financial loss. He has plenty of money. He just doesn't want it said that a slave can ever get away from him, so he'll never stop looking for her.

"I've heard"—she leaned across his desk, encouraged by the concern she saw in his face—"that there is a group that sends freed slaves back home to Africa."

"Freed," he acknowledged. "Not fugitives."

She nodded vigorously. "I know. I know all about that, how the Constitution even sets a fine for anyone helping them, but I don't care about that. If Letty can get on one of those ships sailing for Africa, she'll be free."

A smile touched his lips. "That's one way to look at it and justify breaking the law, but, it takes money to send freed slaves back, and even more to buy illegal passage for a fugitive."

She reached into her purse and drew out the roll of money she had taken from her hiding place that morning. Laying it on the table, seeing how Pastor Jones's eyes widened at the sight of it, she bluntly asked, "Is this enough?"

He picked up the bundle, looked at it, then at her. "This is a lot of money, Mrs. Youngblood."

"My husband is a generous man. He gives me money for shopping and doesn't ask what I buy."

He could not resist saying with a respectful nod, "And, no doubt, money for carriages and doesn't ask why your feet hurt."

"So you saw me limp in." She shrugged. "It doesn't matter. What does, is whether or not you think that's enough to buy Letty's passage to Africa."

For a moment, he could only stare at her in disbelief and shake his head slowly from side to side. Finally, incredulously, he cried, "You don't even know if she made it out of the Dismal Swamp. You don't even know if the Free African Society or the Free Soilers have contact with her.

"And most of all, you don't even know *me*, Mrs. Young-blood."

She met his piercing gaze with one of her own. "Let's just say your position lends character without having to prove it. In short, Preacher, I'm going to trust you to do all you can to find her, and if you can't, then I'd like for you to see the money go to help some other wretched soul." She stood.

"Bless you," he whispered as she made her way out. "And I promise I'll do everything I can. . . ."

But Erin was no longer listening, for she was in a hurry now. The day was drawing to a close, and so was her time in Philadelphia. She was anxious to get back to the hotel before Ryan did. He would want to know why she had not started packing, since they were leaving the next day. Her feet were burning with agony, and she longed for the comfort of a carriage ride back.

But there was no money.

She had given it all away.

And even though every step was torture, Erin had no

regrets, not if it meant freedom, and a new life, for someone.

Maybe it would be Letty.

Zachary was determined not to return to Virginia without Letty. He and his men had backtracked to the area
where she had escaped. There they contacted several informers who, for the right price, would tell which direction a runaway had gone. From one of them they'd
learned Letty had made contact with someone, almost the
very next day, and had headed for the coast. At Norfolk,
Zachary had stood aside while Frank had beaten a Negro
dock worker into admitting a Negro girl had been smuggled on board a boat heading North, toward Delaware.

Zachary had refused to give up, even though his men
urged him to turn back.

"What's one slave, more or less?" Frank had challenged.
"Hell, you can take your pick the next time a ship sneaks
in with a new load from Africa, and you know it."

Zachary had growled that giving up set a bad example.
"Let one get away and another will try. Word is already
out, anyway, that my darkies are runnin' away, even
though I've tried to keep it hushed up.

"No," he vehemently declared, "we got her trail, and
we're followin' it."

And he did so, all the way to Delaware, where he
reached a dead end. Delaware was the only state in the
South where a black person was considered free unless
proved to be a slave. Any inquiries were met with a surly
response, and no physical persuasion did he, or his men,
dare try to use.

Doggedly, after nearly three weeks of searching, there
had been nothing to do but turn back.

Zachary got home late one Saturday afternoon but stopped off at a tavern for a drink. He figured he might as well get it over with, all the taunting the men he caroused with would inflict over his unsuccessful hunt.

He listened to the jeers, tossing down one shot of whiskey after another, pretending not to care, but then something was said that got his attention hard and fast. He whirled on the man who had spoken and demanded hotly, "Say that again. I don't think I heard you right."

The man obliged, having nothing to fear, for he was telling the truth. "I said, at least you got one thing to be thankful for—marryin' off your stepdaughter to a rich man like Ryan Youngblood."

Zachary charged out of the tavern, shoving people out of his way, murder in his eyes. He rode his horse into a lather, all the way home, while his blood was boiling with rage. He knew there could only be one reason why a wedding would take place so fast, especially with him gone. The little slut had gone and got herself pregnant. Oh, was he mad!

Ben, on his way to the slave quarters after closing up the stables at dark, heard a rider coming in. Hurrying up the path to take the horse of whoever was calling so late, he felt his heart slam into his chest as he saw Master Tremayne. Throwing caution to the wind, forgetting his place, he broke into a run, waving his arms.

Zachary reined in so hard his horse reared up on hind legs to paw the air wildly.

"Mastah, mastah, did you find her? Did you find my Letty?"

Zachary brought the horse under control, then dismounted.

Ben was almost in tears as he continued his plea, "Mastah—"

Zachary struck him across the face with his riding crop

and snarled, "Get outta my way, boy. Give my horse a rubdown. Then get the hell to your shack and see that the others do the same. I don't want none of you skulkin' around tonight."

Blood streaming from a gash on the side of his head, Ben could only scramble to his feet and murmur humbly, "Yassah, yassah," and all the while he was choking back tears. It was torture not knowing what had happened to the woman he loved, realizing he probably never would.

Zachary was going in the back door, just as Rosa was coming out. She saw him and instinctively screamed. He looked like someone gone mad, eyes bulging, face a reddening grimace of wild fury. She covered her mouth with both hands in terror and backed away. Grabbing her by her hair and slinging her from the steps and onto the ground, he yelled the same command to her that he'd given Ben. "Get to your place and stay there. I better not see no black faces around here this night. I'm goin' to find out what the hell is goin' on."

He started on inside, but Rosa dared to call out from where she lay sprawled on the ground. "For the sake of Jesus," she shrieked from the depths of her soul, "tell me what you done with my baby girl."

Turning, he stared down at her. "I haven't done anything with her. Ask your Jesus. Maybe He knows where the bitch went."

Arlene had gone to bed early. She had done little but rest in the weeks since Erin had been gone. Tulwah's potion did not stop the coughing spasms from coming but helped bring them under control. Still, she felt terribly weak, and the blood seemed to be getting worse. She supposed there was nothing to do but go back to the doctor and ask for his help; yet, it was so much easier just to drink the foul-smelling, horrid-tasting concoction and let it take her away to a peaceful sleep. At least, she drowsily gave thanks as she snuggled beneath the sheets, Erin was safe. She would be taken care of for the rest of her life.

Suddenly, the door opened, flying back to bang loudly against the wall.

Arlene quickly sat up. Seeing the maniacal look on Zachary's face, she whispered, "Oh, my God!" and then shrank weakly back against the pillows, quaking in terror.

Slowly, he crossed the room. Striking the air with his fist, he raged, "I'm gonna kill that son of a bitch for gettin' her pregnant, and then I'm gonna beat the hell out of her for bringin' shame on this family."

"No! No, you aren't going to do anything." Despite her frailty, and her fear, Arlene quickly crawled out of bed to attempt to explain. "It wasn't like that at all. Erin isn't going to have a baby. It was all very proper. They just wanted to go ahead and get married, and we had no idea when you'd be back, and—"

He grabbed her by her throat and shook her viciously, then flung her onto the bed and roared, "Then damn it, why did you let her get married before I got back? How do you think it looks, my stepdaughter gettin' married and me not here? Makes me look like a fool, that's what it does. Makes it look like I'm not respected around here, that all I'm needed for is payin' the bills."

Arlene could not speak. The coughing had begun, rattling from deep down in her chest. She struggled to reach her handkerchief on the bedside table and the bottle of Tulwah's potion.

"But then that's all you married me for, anyway, wasn't it, you goddamn strumpet!" He knocked her outstretched hand away. "You thought you were so smart, didn't you? A high yeller marryin' a rich man from Virginia! Well, who in the hell do you think you are to make me the laughing stock of Richmond? Don't you think it's bad enough, me havin' to worry folks will find out my wife's part nigger, without havin' to face their snickerin', 'cause my own family don't respect me?"

The coughing was quickly getting worse. "Please . . . Zachary . . . ," she begged, groping for the bottle. "My . . . medicine . . . please."

He backhanded her, knocking her across the bed. Then he threw her on her back and straddled her. With one quick jerk, he ripped off her nightgown. "I knew you was Mandingo, all right, but it didn't make no difference, not with a body like you had back then."

He was panting with excitement as he tore off his shirt. It had been a long time since he'd had a woman. Letty had been the last. He, along with Frank, had had his fill of her the night before she escaped. He'd been leaving Arlene alone, because she always started that damn hacking, but tonight, she was going to remember who was master around here. "You always did drive me crazy. Beautiful. Just beautiful."

She was too weak even to attempt to fight him off, calling on what strength she had to try and breathe. The coughing was becoming a heaving spasm, and his weight on her was only making it worse.

He was about to enter her when, in the bedside lantern's glow, he saw the way she was looking at him. The coughing had finally subsided, and she made only a soft, wheezing sound. But contempt, hatred, and disgust was mirrored in her glaring eyes, and this enraged him. He slapped her and yelled, "Don't you look at me like that, goddamn you! I'm your husband. I've got my rights."

He hit her again and again. Her head lolled to one side, and then he took his pleasure.

Arlene made no move, and, at last, he got off the bed and walked out.

She was good for nothing, he fumed. Always sick. Her and that infernal coughing. Before, he had managed to cope with the misery of his marriage by thinking ahead to the time when he'd have his way with Erin. Sooner or later, he would have been able to convince her she would be wise to keep his bed warm on a permanent basis. If it ever got out she had Negro blood, well, as tense as things were getting, no white man would have her, except as a whore. And for damn sure, he bet Youngblood didn't know about it. Coming from his blue-blood aristocratic background, he'd never marry a woman of mixed color.

Arlene and Erin had pulled it off slicker'n a baby's bottom.

And now Erin was married and gone, and he was bitterly forced to acknowledge he had no one to satisfy his lust. Not even Letty. She had been a prime lay, too. Now he'd have to find somebody else. Start all over. Maybe he would get him a young woman. Have the younguns Arlene hadn't given him. Just as well. He didn't want to sire any high yellers. He wanted an all-white heir to his fortune. He'd worked too hard to see it go to a high yeller, and that's damn sure what would happen if Arlene should happen to outlive him.

But maybe she was dead already.

He'd worry about it in the morning. The whiskey was catching up with him, making his head spin.

He made it to his room and was asleep by the time he fell across the mattress.

Rosa waited nearly a half hour before daring to go upstairs. Even then, she crept along, holding a candle in her hand to light the way. She paused between each step to wait for any sound that would mean Master Zachary was still moving around. She thought she had heard him leave Miz Arlene's room but couldn't be sure, would take no chances.

At last she stood outside the open door and stared into

the shadowed abyss. Not hearing anything, she tiptoed in to stand beside the bed, then froze at what she saw there.

Arlene had been brutally beaten, and a pinkish, blood-tinged froth ringed her partially opened mouth.

For long moments, Rosa could not move. The candle's wax dripped down to burn her fingers, but she didn't feel anything but the anger and pity raging within. A constricting lump of horror held back her screams as she reached out to press her fingers to Miz Arlene's throat to see if she were still breathing.

Then she felt it—a pulse. Weak. But there.

She hurried from the room. No matter that Master Zachary had forbidden Tulwah to come onto his land. No matter that he would probably kill her if he knew she was bringing Tulwah right into the house. Tulwah was the only hope of saving her mistress now.

And when he was through with his white magic, Rosa prayed he would use his black magic on the devil responsible.

CHAPTER 17

Erin awoke with ryan's arms wrapped around her. For a moment, she could not remember where she was. So many different bedrooms in the past weeks. Then it dawned on her. She was home.

Home.

The word seemed as alien as her surroundings.

She lay there for a moment, marveling once more over the opulent surroundings.

And they were in her bedroom, she thought with smug satisfaction, not his.

They had arrived late the day before, exhausted. She would have liked to go directly to see her mother but knew it was too late and too far. Instead, they had enjoyed a leisurely supper, while Annie and Ebner unpacked their things.

Erin had been surprised by how they, along with the other servants, seemed so glad to see them, especially Ryan. Likewise, he greeted them genially. It was certainly different from the atmosphere at Zachary's house, where fear and anxiety hovered almost all the time.

She turned her head to look at him as he slept. For one who could be so remote and distant at times, he was certainly warm and passionate when he made love to her.

How easy it would be, she thought, there in the still and quiet of the early morning, to give him her heart. Yet, she knew that could not happen. Never could she allow herself to be so vulnerable. As he'd said, they each had their own reasons for the marriage. But love had not been one of them.

Careful, so as not to awaken him, Erin disengaged herself from his embrace. She padded softly to the window and pulled back the curtain only a little way so she could look out at the splendorous view. She could see the river in the distance. In between was the intriguing labyrinth, an intricate pathway of hedges that she judged were nearly ten feet tall.

The entire scene was dramatically beautiful, with the rising sun making the waters dance with crystal droplets of gold and emerald. Selfishly, she couldn't help wishing they would always have this privacy, the entire estate to themselves. But when Victoria Youngblood returned from Europe, things would change. Now that they were back, her thoughts turned to that inevitable meeting. According to the impression she had got from Aunt Sophia, and Carolyn Manning's venomous diatribe, it was not destined to be a pleasant encounter.

Ryan's voice intruded upon her reverie. "If you'll pull that cord next to you, Ebner will bring our morning coffee."

"I didn't mean to awaken you." She gave the cord a yank and went to put on her robe. She was wearing a sheer gown Ryan had bought for her at the first place they'd shopped, to replace the muslin garb he'd ripped to pieces.

He got up and headed for the door to the parlor that separated their rooms. She could not help but stare at the magnificence of his nude body. His buttocks were perfectly molded, firm, and his thighs, rock-hard. He had told her he never slept in a nightshirt, preferring the freedom of sleeping bare. He coaxed her to do the same, but she refused. Once their passion cooled, the wall between them always sprang back, and she was uncomfortable then to be unclothed.

"Tell Ebner we'll have breakfast downstairs. The usual for me."

Erin quickly reminded him, "I'd like to visit my mother today."

"Of course. After lunch. This morning I'm going to show you around the grounds. It's time you familiarized yourself."

He stood there, naked, in the middle of the parlor, and she was amazed at his nonchalance.

He went on to say he'd noticed her fascination with the labyrinth. "I'll take you through it. Unless you know the way, you can get lost. So don't ever try to hide from me in there," he added with a wink before continuing toward his quarters.

She was surprised by his good humor. The past few days, he had seemed to be withdrawing from her more and more, and while she didn't like the coldness between them, she had no idea what to do about it and was too proud to try. But, perhaps, she could hope being back home would cause him to behave differently.

As they were having a last cup of coffee after breakfast, a woman servant Erin had not seen before appeared to stand almost imperiously next to her. She was wearing the familiar gray dress with long white apron, but, unlike the others, she wore a white turban on her head. She did not speak, merely stood there holding some kind of paper in her hand.

They were in the breakfast nook, glassed on one side for the glorious view of the gardens, sunshine pouring in on baskets of colorful petunias and geraniums that hung from the ceiling. It was a cozy place, and Erin had been enjoying herself till the strange-acting woman appeared. She looked at Ryan, not knowing how to react. The woman seemed to want something.

"This is Eliza," he said without flourish. "I guess she's second in command after my mother around here, as far as the servants go. She wants to go over the lunch and supper menu with you."

Erin took the paper, glanced over it, and handed it back with a timorous smile and said it was fine. There was just something about the woman that was intimidating. She said as much to Ryan when Eliza had gone.

He explained, "She's very loyal to my mother. She came here with her when she married my father. No doubt, she resents you, thinks you're going to take over. When Mother comes back, she'll realize nothing has changed, and she'll be all right. Don't worry about her."

Erin frowned, but he didn't notice. So! He felt nothing had changed around here. He was married, had redecorated his mother's suite, moved her in, his mother's favorite servant resented her, and he naively felt things were the same. Oh, he had much to learn, and it was going to be a challenge to make him realize it.

On horseback, he gave her a perfunctory tour of the estate that took nearly three hours. The weather was cool, a definite hint of fall in the air, and the day was pleasant. Erin enjoyed it all and was thoroughly impressed, particularly with the way the slaves were provided for. They had their own compound, of course, but it was like a small village. There was even a clinic, which Ryan said was visited one day a week by a white doctor he paid to care for "his people," as he called his slaves. All of them seemed fit and wore adequate clothing. They did not glance away in fear as did the poor slaves on her stepfather's plantation. She was also impressed to see his overseers carried neither whips nor guns.

They left their horses at the stable and walked to the labyrinth. As they did so, he casually explained how it came to be. "My grandmother had it made for my grandfather as a joke. He told me how she would tease him about his sneaking off to the river to launch a boat and slip away to go fishing without telling her. She decided to make it difficult for him to get to the little pier he'd built. So, she had some of the field hands plant hedges. It was done in jest, with no hard feelings, but after it was over with, my grandfather really liked the idea of a labyrinth to make the way a bit mysterious. He made it even more elaborate. Now it's so gigantic that only I, and the sons of the men who originally planted it and who keep it trimmed, know how to get through it. Otherwise, you need a map, and I keep that locked in my desk drawer."

"Why?" she wanted to know at once. "What's the reason for the secret?"

"My grandfather said it could be used as an escape route, if need be, if the British attacked by land. You see, the river bends there, and it's a perfect place to take out a boat. Any other way to the bank means taking a long way around the labyrinth. If there's ever a reason to leave Jasmine Hill in a hurry, the quickest way is through it. I keep it a secret more out of tradition than anything else."

Feeling like an outsider again, she asked stiffly, "Don't you want your wife to know about the escape route?"

His lips were smiling but his eyes were cold as he told her in feigned jest, "No. She might be trying to escape from me."

She felt a chill of apprehension. It was almost as though he were waiting for her to do something to justify his suspicions.

He motioned her to follow and went on to explain, "Actually, it's just a novelty, something to amuse guests now and then. We've had summer garden parties when the more adventuresome would divide up into teams and see which one could make it through the fastest. No one ever succeeds. I always have to go in after them. The gardeners' sons take pride in keeping it up.

"If my mother had her way," he added, sounding annoyed, "it would be plowed up. She thinks it's garish and silly."

"I think it's beautiful," Erin said, and meant it, staring all around in awe at the neatly clipped shrubs. It was like being in a never-ending tunnel of green, but after only a little while she became dizzy, lost in the maze. Ryan knew exactly which turn to take and kept on going, with her close on his heels.

In less than five minutes, they reached a huge grass-covered clearing in the middle. There was a bench and a large birdbath.

"It's a park," Erin cried, delighted.

"I've had very few people even get this far, and if they do, it takes them over half an hour. Sometimes longer."

They rested a moment, then continued on to the river in the same length of time they'd reached the center.

As they stood on the pier, shrouded from view on either side by water oaks, cypress, and bamboo, as well as weeping willows on the bank, Ryan was moved to confide a story from his youth. "I was just fourteen and thought I was a real man of the world. I fell in love with an older woman of sixteen, the poor daughter of a fisherman. Naturally my mother was against it and put her foot down, said I couldn't see her. When I started slipping off in the woods to meet her, she had some of the stableboys follow me. So, I just took her to the center of the labyrinth. They didn't dare try to go in after me. We had all the privacy we needed."

She readily agreed. "Yes, it'd be the perfect place to

meet a lover, all right." Then she saw the strange way he was looking at her and was instantly struck with a flash of resentment. First, Eliza had made her feel anything but welcome in her new home, and then he had brushed over it as though it were nothing. He had let her know he wasn't about to share the labyrinth secret with her, and now he was making her feel defensive. Unable to hold back any longer, she exploded to demand, "Ryan, just what is wrong with you? You make me feel guilty when I haven't done anything."

"See that you don't," he replied calmly, "and you've nothing to worry about. Let's go. Annie can ride with you to visit your mother. I've got business in town, and I don't want you out by yourself."

They walked back without speaking. Ryan ground his teeth together to keep from saying he didn't mean to be so brusque. But damn it, the painful memories were like lockjaw, preventing him from speaking his heart. Simone had not been his to lose. But Erin was his wife, she belonged to him, and he intended to keep it that way, especially since she meant more to him with each passing day.

On the carriage ride, Annie sat across from Erin, mesmerized by the passing scenery. She did not offer to make conversation, which, Erin supposed, probably wasn't considered proper. Curious, she asked, "Doesn't Mrs. Youngblood allow you to talk on trips, Annie?"

"Ain't never been on one with her," she answered soberly, not turning her gaze from the window. "Eliza, she's always the one to travel with Miz Victoria. She's mad 'cause she didn't get to go across the ocean with her, but Miz Ermine, she always takes two slaves with her, everywhere she goes, and Miz Victoria said one of them could do her biddin'."

"Do you like Eliza? She seems a bit unfriendly to me."

At that, Annie did turn to look at her. "You asked me,"

she said, her expression one of bitterness and resentment, "so I reckon I can speak my mind. I don't like her at all. She thinks she's better'n any of the rest of us, 'cause she's been workin' in the big house longer'n anybody else. She sleeps there, you know, in a little room at the back, in case Miz Victoria needs her durin' the night. She don't have no cabin of her own. And all of us, we don't care. We don't want her around, anyway, 'cause she tells everything she knows. That's how Miz Victoria always knows everything that's goin' on."

Since she seemed so willing to gossip, Erin pressed, "Tell me something. How do you think Miss Victoria will react when she comes home and finds out Master Ryan got married while she was away?"

Annie pursed her lips, held back a giggle, then confided, "Well, since you want to know, I'll tell you that everyone is sayin' that's gonna be some blowup. Miz Victoria, she had her mind made up Mastah Ryan was gonna marry Miz Ermine. She ain't gonna like it one little bit."

"What's she like?"

At that, Annie's eyes grew wide and she shook her head firmly and declined, "I don't reckon that would be rightly proper for me to say."

"Not even if I asked you?" Erin gently prodded.

"No'm. I'll just say I like you a lot better." She flashed a toothy grin and settled back to enjoy the ride. "I sho' hope you make me your special slave, Miz Erin."

"Servant," Erin was quick to correct. "Say servant, or handmaiden. Anything but slave. I despise that word."

Annie looked at her, bemused, nodded her head and made no comment.

Erin directed the driver to stop the carriage at the stable, as it was only a short walk to the back door from there. She was happy to see Ben coming out to meet them—until she saw his face. "God, Ben!" She leapt to the ground, not waiting for the groomsman to help her alight. "What happened to your face?" It was swollen, discolored, and a gash on one side had been sewn shut with boiled horsehairs, probably the work of Tulwah.

"I fell down," he mumbled, grasping a harness to hold the horses steady as Annie scrambled out of the carriage behind her mistress.

Erin went to stand beside him and take a closer look. He tried to turn his head, but she caught his chin, held him, and examined it. "That's a nasty cut." She released him. "I don't think you're telling me the truth. That wound looks as if it was made by somebody."

"I fell down," he repeated, almost sullenly.

"Ben, I know something is wrong." She could see other stable workers stealing glances in their direction. "You've got to tell me. Is there news of Letty?"

At that, he seemed to brighten, defiance glimmering, then said so low she had to strain to hear him, "The mastah is back."

"When?"

"A few days ago."

"And Letty? Did they find her?"

He shook his head, then turned to lead the horses to the hitching rail. He did not dare say more and was afraid even to be seen talking to her at all.

Erin lifted her skirts above her ankles and took off for the house. Tension was like a smothering fog. She could feel it.

Rosa was sitting at the table, peeling potatoes, and at the sight of Erin, her eyes grew wide with fear, and she instinctively glanced about the empty room to make sure they were alone.

"I understand Zachary is back, and that he didn't find Letty," Erin said in greeting. "What happened to Ben's face?"

Rosa ducked her head and went back to what she had been doing. "He fell."

"I don't believe that, but we'll talk about it later. How's my mother?"

Rosa mumbled, "She had a bad spell a few days ago. She's been doin' poorly ever since. She don't get out of bed."

Stricken with worry, Erin turned to go to her but felt the need to try and lift Rosa's mood. Never had she seen her so depressed. "I was in Philadelphia," she quickly told her, "and I talked to a preacher at a church that helps runaways, and—"

"No," Rosa cried, looking up at her then, terror etched in every line of her dark face. Wildly, she shook her head from side to side and protested, "I can't listen to that kind of talk. Not no more. I don't dare. I don't know nothin' about nothin'. She's gone. Let her be gone."

For a moment, Erin could only stand there and look at Rosa, completely dumbfounded by her reaction. She was nearly hysterical. Where was the secret spirit that always managed to surface? The woman was petrified. Moving around the table, Erin knelt beside her, saw how her lips were trembling, the way she was fighting to hold back tears. "Listen to me, Rosa. I'm back now, and I'm going to help my mother, and you, and the others, just as soon as I can work things out. But I want you to know that if Letty does reach Philadelphia, she'll no doubt contact a group that stays in touch with that church. Runaways know to do that. I gave the preacher some money to get her to Africa, where there are colonies to help freed slaves and the ones like Letty make a new life. She'll be safe. The bounty hunters will never find her. And you can go to her, too, if you want to. And Ben. But meanwhile, I've got some money for you to give to Mahalia." She reached into the bodice of her dress and withdrew the bills she had slipped out of Ryan's wallet. Later, she would think of a reason to give him, so he wouldn't think she was just stealing from him.

Rosa stared at the money in Erin's hand as though it were an ugly spider about to pounce. Getting to her feet so quickly the chair almost tipped over, she backed away, head whipping from side to side. She drew a steadying breath and nervously rubbed her hands against the sides of her skirt and whispered, "No, Miz Erin. I ain't takin' that money. I can't be involved with Mahalia, or the Free-Soilers, no more. Things has changed. Mastah Zachary, he came back a crazy man. He says ain't no slave ever gonna run away from here again. He says he'll kill anybody who tries, and if he finds out any of us here is workin' with the Free-Soilers, he's gonna kill us, too. I tell you, that man is the devil, himself."

She began to sob, covering her face with her hands. Erin was quick to attempt to comfort her, yet pointed out, "You've got to help me, Rosa. What am I going to do if you don't? How can I get money to Mahalia? I can't go riding over to the farm where she lives and hand it to her."

Furiously, Rosa said, "I can't do it, Miz Erin. I just can't. And you better remember that if anything happens to me, there ain't gonna be nobody around here to look after yo' momma. So till you can get her to move over yonder with you, you better make sure I don't get in no trouble with the mastah."

Erin knew she made sense but also knew there was no other way. At least for now. "I can't leave Jasmine Hill any time I want to, so it's impossible for me to try to meet someone and give the money to them. If I can't bring it here, to you, they'll have to come after it." It did not take much thought to decide on the perfect place. The labyrinth. Ryan had said he kept the diagram locked in his desk. If she could get her hands on that, make a copy, then the person arriving to pick up the money could come up the river by boat and enter the back way. She could slip in the front. Their rendezvous would be in the center.

She explained her plan to Rosa but insisted, "You're going to have to help one more time. I'm going to try to get back here tomorrow with the diagram, and you will have to get it to Mahalia."

Rosa continued to weep softly but knew she had no choice but to agree. "But you hurry, Miz Erin," she pleaded. "You hurry and get your momma outta here and away from that madman. It don't matter about me. I'll get away when the time comes, if need be. You just get her outta here so's she can have some peace before the Lord takes her home."

"I will," Erin vowed. "I'm going to help her and all of you. I promise. Tell me, where is he now?"

"I don't know. He's around somewhere. I ain't seen him since lunch."

Erin went upstairs to her mother's room. When she saw her, propped on the pillows reading, she was alarmed to realize she did appear worse. Her skin was almost translucent against the white linens, and her eyes, as she looked up happily to see her daughter, were lackluster, with deep, dark circles beneath.

They embraced, and when Erin went to sit on the side of the bed to tell her all about her trip she noticed the bruises on her mother's cheeks. "Did he do that?"

"What?" Arlene feigned confusion, then touched the spots with gentle fingertips and said, "Oh, these. I'm afraid I fell out of bed. I was reaching for my medicine in the dark and lost my balance. I'm fine, though, really. Now, tell me about your trip."

Erin knew she was lying but did not want to upset her by making her answer a lot of questions. Instead, she gave a glowing report of her nuptial journey, and Arlene listened, entranced.

Afterward, Arlene held up the pale blue bed jacket Erin had bought for her in Philadelphia and, cried, "It's beautiful. Thank you. And thank Ryan for me, too." With a hopeful smile, she asked, "So tell me. Is he wonderful to you? Are you happy?"

Erin assured her mother that Ryan was good to her. "As for being happy," she said, "I'll just say I'm not unhappy, Mother, and I guess that's all any of us can ask for in this life, isn't it? Not to be unhappy?"

"Oh, I don't know." Arlene sighed wistfully. "I was very happy with your father. There was never any doubt but that we loved each other with all our hearts. My prayer for you is that one day you and Ryan will realize it's happened to you, too, that somewhere along the way, you fell in love.

"It can, you know." She turned to face her daughter, and for the first time, there was a glimmer of spirit revived.

Erin shook her head; she was not as optimistic. "How would I know if it did? How does anybody ever know for sure?"

"It's like a rainbow after a storm, spreading across the sky like a thousand smiles, and you have a good, warm feeling inside that makes you want to smile, too, because you know there just has to be sunshine behind all those clouds.

"And believe me," she continued, "there's no mistaking the magic of a rainbow when you know you're really in love."

She held out her hand. Erin took it and pressed it against her lips, as she wondered if she, too, might one day know the enchantment of the rainbow of love.

CHAPTER

 18

I**T WAS LATE. ERIN DID NOT REALIZE JUST HOW** late till she heard the case clock in the hallway chime midnight.

Tossing and turning beneath the satin comforter, she wondered restlessly why Ryan had not come to her bed. They had enjoyed an intimate dinner, earlier, and a bottle of wine.

They had sat in the parlor sipping cognac afterward, and for the first time, he had talked to her about his mother and Ermine.

He described how they had made the transatlantic passage on the first steamship—the Savannah. "It was supposed to be a very historic occasion," he had said, "the first crossing of a steamship. But I read in a newspaper that only eighty hours after they left Savannah, the coal supply was exhausted, and they had to resort to sails to go the rest of the way. It took them twenty-eight days to reach Liverpool."

Erin inquired as to when they would return, and he'd said he honestly did not know. There had been no word, and since they had been gone nearly four months, he supposed they could be expected any time.

Gingerly, she had asked if he were concerned about

how his mother would react when she heard of their marriage. He had laughed and said since she had never approved of anything he had done in his whole life, he saw no reason to expect her blessings now. Erin wished he would take the matter more seriously. After all, she felt it was important she get along with his mother if she were planning on moving hers into the house as soon as possible. She was just waiting for the right time to do so. After a few more days, when they were settled in, she'd approach him.

They had discussed other things, too, such as how they should plan a dinner party to celebrate returning home from their nuptial journey. Erin bluntly asked if Carolyn Manning could be excluded, but Ryan had shook his head and said he was afraid not. He confided he didn't care for her, himself, but her father and his had been good friends. If a function were held at Jasmine Hill and she were not invited, then her entire family would consider it an insult. He didn't want that. "Just ignore her," he'd said. "Everyone else does."

But Erin wondered about that, fearful of how much trouble Carolyn might cause with her vicious tongue.

They had talked on, and he had shared with her his excitement over the expected foaling of a colt sired by one of his prize horses. He had hired the animal for stud to Quincy Monroe, a plantation owner nearly two hours' ride away. Ryan was supposed to be notified when the birth commenced, because he wanted to be there. He was hoping the mare might be carrying twins, and, if so, Quincy had promised he could have one.

They had shared several nice hours together, and when, at last, he'd got up to extinguish the lanterns and make ready for bed, Erin had gone upstairs with a warm flush of eagerness as she thought of the coming passion in his arms.

But that had been nearly two hours ago.

Erin sighed, then snuggled down to try and sleep. But the truth was, she missed his arms about her, had got used to falling asleep with her head snugly on his shoulder. And, yes, she had to admit with a pleasant tightening in her loins, she missed his lovemaking, as well.

Finally she told herself she really should make sure he was all right. What if he were ill and just didn't want to disturb her? She got up and put on her robe, then crossed the sitting room that separated their quarters.

His door was closed. She hesitated, wondering whether to knock. If he weren't sick and was, indeed, asleep, and simply had not wanted her, then she certainly didn't want him to know she had even been there.

Turning the knob slowly, quietly, she entered without a sound.

The curtains were closed, and she could detect only vague outlines of the furniture in the shadowed darkness. All was quiet. Padding softly, she made her way to the side of the bed without bumping into anything. She could barely make out that he was, indeed, in the bed and apparently sound asleep.

So, she thought with a flash of anger, even though they'd had a wonderful evening together, and she probably felt closer to him than at any other time since they'd been married, he truly had not wanted her.

Well, so be it!

She turned to leave but screamed out, startled as his hand snaked out to grab her wrist. "What took you so long?" he said softly, giving her a rough yank that brought her tumbling down across him.

Erin indignantly struggled to free herself. "Let me go. I thought you were sick, and—"

"You thought no such thing," he laughed mockingly, as he slung her over to the side and rolled to pin her down. "You couldn't understand why I didn't come to your bed."

Her hands pushed against his shoulders as she stammered, "That—that's not true."

He burrowed his lips in the sweet hollows of her throat and murmured, "Admit it, Erin. You want me. Every bit as much as I want you. You're just too damn stubborn to admit it, but this night, my little minx, the truth comes out."

"No, that's not true—" But her ragged gasp of denial was silenced as his mouth claimed hers.

He felt her resistance cease as her lips parted beneath his, allowing his tongue entrance. His fingertips clutched her face, moving to trace tiny circling patterns in the sensitive hollow beneath her ear, igniting hot tingles throughout her body.

Quickly, he manipulated her gown from her, and she was naked, vulnerable to his sensual assault.

Erin felt as though she were being consumed by his ravishing hunger and answered with the yielding of her mouth.

His hand moved down her throat, in burning anticipation of his lips. He wanted to taste all of her, inch by inch. He could feel her quaking beneath his touch, could hear the faint moaning sound that proved her own primal need was awakening and calling to be fed. He drew her along into the quick currents of passion, enticed and driven by the heated throbbing of her body. Taking her fingertips from their clutching of his shoulders, he moved them to his bare chest, and she gasped to realize the burning heat, the way his nipples hardened in eagerness like her own.

He did not have to guide her hands any farther. With a will of their own, they danced downward, exploring. She felt his muscles contract beneath her touch.

Ryan was on fire as his mouth claimed her breasts, lips

opening upon the soft, tender flesh, to assault one taut, hard nipple between his teeth. Erin writhed and twisted in pleasured anguish, lost in the fervored moment. She did not realize her hand had dared go so far till she felt the thatch of hair, the pulsating hardness of his manhood.

In tormenting descent, Ryan's fingers caressed the swell of her hip and the flatness of her belly. He danced on into the warmth between her thighs, finding that special place to roam in soft agony.

Instinctively, Erin's legs parted to allow him freedom to the center of her desire, as her hips began to undulate with the rhythm of his fingertips. He moved up and inside her, and she closed about him hungrily.

Ryan was inflamed with her innate rapacity. "Tell me," he commanded hoarsely, lifting his mouth from her breasts but continuing to lick greedily. "Tell me you want me, Erin. Tell me how much."

Erin felt as though she had been propelled into another world, another realm of being and existence. She did not submit as in the past, when he had provoked unbridled hunger. Instead of surrender, she assaulted. Moving downward, she closed her lips about him and reveled in his own uncontrollable groan of torment. She trailed him with her tongue and teased with nibbling kisses, and when he could stand no more, he forced himself to withdraw from her hungered torture.

Almost roughly, he slammed her onto her back and straddled her. She opened herself to him, arching her hips to bring herself closer to the length of him. He mounted her, and hot eagerness charged through him as he began to probe inside her. He endeavored to be gentle, so she could take all of him, but her body urged him on. With one hand, she clutched his back, nails digging into flesh. Her other cupped one of his buttocks, squeezing, coaxing.

The dizzying awareness of her mutual frenzied fever inflamed his loins, and he penetrated deeper, sculpting her flesh, so tender, to accept his massive hardness.

He felt her climax coming, the shuddering deep within, and this moved him to unleash his own passion, as he burrowed his face into the hollow of her neck to stifle his gasps of ecstasy. She made soft, whimpering sounds as she clung to him, legs squeezed tight around his back, and she gave tender little kisses to his ear.

For long, reverent moments, they lay locked together.

At last, he moved to one side, his breathing becoming easy once more. He held her against him, her head cradled upon his shoulder.

Erin lay awake for a long time, bemused by the maelstrom of emotions within.

Was it nearing the time, she dared ask herself, when the enchanted rainbow would appear?

The next morning Erin awoke in Ryan's bed to find herself alone. She was startled to glance at the bedside clock and realize it was nearly noon. No wonder he was already up and gone, probably out riding.

Still bathed in the afterglow of the awesome passion they had shared, she would have liked just to dreamily lie there in sweet reverie, but knew it was the perfect time to try and find the diagram of the labyrinth.

Returning to her own room, she quickly took care of her morning ablution, remembering, as always, to bathe in the special solution. Her mother had insisted she saturate her skin with it every single day to ensure softness. Erin supposed it worked, for she did have nice skin.

As she headed downstairs, she hesitated to make sure no one was about. Annie would not come till she was summoned and was probably then waiting in one of the rooms at the back of the house. The household servants were very careful not to make any noise until they could be sure their master and mistress were both awake.

Stealthily, she made her way. There was no sound, which meant she probably had this part of the house all to herself for the time being. Any activity would be going on at the rear, in the work areas, or outside in the detached kitchen wing.

She let herself into Ryan's study. It smelled of leather and tobacco and the faint odor of cognac. Dust particles danced in the tiny sunbeams coming in between partially opened curtains.

Quickly she went to his desk. Opening each drawer in turn, she leafed through the contents but found nothing even remotely resembling a diagram or map. The bottom drawer, however, was locked.

Where would he have hidden the key?

And then it dawned on her.

Ryan would presume no one would dare go through his things, so he would not take much effort to hide it. Accordingly, she found it in the center drawer, tucked in a back corner.

Unlocking the last drawer, she found what she was looking for.

She took a blank sheet of paper, laid it over the diagram, and hastily copied it. Returning the diagram, she closed the drawer, locked it, placed the key precisely where she'd found it.

Then, as she rose from his chair, she was startled to find Eliza standing in the doorway. Her expression was cold, her eyes accusing.

With forced joviality to cover her shock and unease, Erin cheerily said, "My goodness, Eliza. You're as quiet as the proverbial creeping mouse. How long have you been standing there?"

Eliza ignored the question. Tightly, she asked, "It's late. Are you going to be having breakfast or lunch?"

Annoyed, Erin chose equally to disregard her query and instead fired another, lifting her chin slightly in a gesture meant to override the servant's imperious attitude. "Did my husband say where he was going?"

"Ebner might know," was the curt response before Eliza abruptly turned on her heel and left.

Erin bit down on her lower lip as she worried about how long Eliza had actually been standing there and whether, from that distance, she could tell what was being copied. Surely not. It was a long way between door and desk.

Putting it out of her mind, Erin returned to her room and rang for Annie. When she appeared, cheerful and eager to serve, as always, Erin asked her to take a seat. She obeyed, suddenly looking a bit nervous.

With a deep breath, Erin began, "Annie, I have to know that I can trust you to keep your mouth shut about anything you see or hear, when you go places with me."

Annie's eyes grew wide, and her spine tingled with curiosity as she was quick to assure her mistress, "Yassum. You don't have to worry about me sayin' nothin' 'bout nothin'. I tol' you before, I want to be yo' slave—" she saw Erin's immediate frown and corrected, "uh, handmaiden. I'll be good and loyal. I promise."

Erin had no choice but to give her the chance to prove it. "I'll trust you till you give me reason not to. Now then, I want you to go to the stable and have a carriage ready in an hour. We're going to visit my mother."

"Yassum," Annie jumped to obey.

Erin called to her again, compelled to ask, "Does Eliza often clean Master Ryan's study in the mornings?"

Annie swung her head from side to side. "Oh, no'm. Mastah Ryan, he don't allow nobody in his study unless he's there, too. That's the only time we're allowed to clean. Can't none of us go in there less'n he's there."

Erin nodded thoughtfully and waved her on her way.

No doubt Eliza had seen the study door open and looked in to see who was daring to disobey the rule. She had probably not been standing there long at all.

But regardless, Erin made a mental note to be more alert to the ubiquitous housekeeper in the future.

During the ride, Erin observed that Annie seemed upset. Her enthusiasm was absent, and instead of gazing happily out the window, she sat with eyes downcast, hands folded in her lap.

Finally, Erin offered, "If something is wrong, Annie, I wish you'd tell me. If I'm going to trust you, you're going to have to trust me back, you know."

Gloomily, Annie agreed with that, then worriedly asked, "But am I gonna get in trouble?"

Erin firmly shook her head. "Not if you just keep silent and do as you're told."

Annie thought about that a minute. "But what is it I'm not supposed to tell?"

With a resigned sigh, Erin knew there was nothing to do but confide in her. She had no trepidation, really, in doing so. The girl was almost fawning in her desire to please, and she'd made it clear she despised Eliza. Candidly, she explained, "I'm going to be helping some of your people who aren't treated as well as you are, Annie." She watched her face closely for any sign that she might react negatively to what she was hearing. When she saw only excited interest, she went on to say, "There may be times when I'll want you to see if someone has left a message for me somewhere close to the house. You will have to be extremely careful in slipping it to me. Master Youngblood is not to know and certainly none of the other servants. Do you think I can count on you to do that?"

With awe and admiration, Annie leaned forward, almost trembling in her excitement. "Oh, yassum. Yassum, fo' sure." Confidence renewed, she rushed on to share the gossip she'd heard from the other slaves. "Miz Erin, I know only too well how me and the rest at our place need to give thanks every day for how good we're treated. It's true, Miz Victoria can be mean sometimes, screamin' and yellin', and one time she slapped me and gave my hair a yank when I accidentally broke somethin' while cleanin', but she didn't have me whipped. I don't know of anybody that's ever been whipped at Jasmine Hill. She threatens, sure as God's in His heaven, that she's gonna beat somebody's worthless hide, but she don't never do it. She might, if'n it won't fo' Mastah Ryan, but he's jest like his daddy, good to the bone, he is.

"No ma'am." She sat back, shaking her head in positive assurance. "You ain't never got to worry about me tellin' nothing."

Suddenly she snapped her fingers and brightly cried, "Are you lookin' fo' a hidin' place for somebody to leave you somethin'? I know just the place—Miz Henrietta's pot."

Erin blinked, sure she hadn't heard right. "Miss Who's What?"

"Miz Henrietta," Annie explained impatiently. "Don't you know about her? She was Mastah Calvin's wife, the one he named Jasmine Hill for. She's buried right there out your bedroom window, almost. You can see her grave when you look out to the left.

"And it's said," Annie continued uneasily, "that when the jasmine is in bloom, and the night air is just sick with that sweet smell, that you can sometimes see her walkin' around down there, sniffin' them flowers, specially if the moon is full, and—"

"Annie," Erin cut in to stop her ghost story, "what about her pot?"

"Her flower pot. It sits right there on top of her grave, in front of the tombstone. My momma tol' me that her momma told her Mastah Calvin had it carved out of marble sent all the way from Italy. He used to have flowers put in it every day when there was any bloomin'. And when there wasn't he'd have paper flowers made up. Momma said her momma said that was one eery sight, seein' them paper flowers stickin' up outta the snow.

"But," she finally concluded, "nobody never put nothin' else in that pot after he died, so it'd make a good place fo' somebody to leave you whatever it is you're lookin' for." She flashed one of her special toothy grins, eyes shining in anticipation of praise.

She received it. "Thank you," Erin said, and meant it. "Now all you'll have to do is tell me when you find a flower, paper or otherwise, in that pot. I'll know what to do then."

Annie was so proud, happily wiggling in her seat to think how she was such big help to her mistress. "What kind of flower you gonna have, Miz Erin?" She wanted to know, anxious to keep the conversation alive, so the good feeling would last. "You gonna have a jasmine? They bloom the longest, but they'd be kinda hard to make out of paper."

Erin did not have to think long on that. She smiled to herself as she whispered, "No. Not a jasmine. A rose."

Always it had been her favorite flower but never more so since Ryan had showered her with so many.

Maybe, by adopting the blood red rose as her special signal, she contemplated, it would help assuage her feeling that she was, in a way, betraying him.

Ryan took the back steps three at a time. Dashing through the service porch, he passed by Eliza as though she were not even there. Through the years of growing up with her watching his every move like a barn owl after a field mouse, so she could tattle to his mother, it was second nature to disregard her at every opportunity. But, after dashing through the house and not finding Erin anywhere, he was forced to address her.

"Did Miss Erin tell you where she was going?"

Eliza was ready with her answer. After all, Miss Erin had not told her, but Annie had, and he didn't ask her about Annie. "No, sir," she replied in the proper enunciation Miss Victoria had taught her, void of dialect. "Miss Erin didn't say anything to me."

He turned away without further conversation. She heard him going down the back hallway toward his study. Tiptoeing behind him, she peered in through the half-opened door, just as she had done that morning, when she'd seen Miss Erin take something out of his drawer and copy it. She didn't know what it was, but maybe Miss Victoria would, and she sure intended to tell her. Miss Victoria was going to be very mad about all of this, anyway. And Miss Ermine wasn't going to like it, either.

Eliza liked Miss Ermine, because after the betrothal was announced, she had made it clear that when she married Master Ryan and moved in, she might be bringing some of her own servants with her, but Eliza would still be in charge, even if something was to happen to Miss Victoria, she had whispered. Eliza knew what she meant. Miss Ermine would be mistress of Jasmine Hill when Miss Victoria passed on, and Eliza was pleased to know she'd still be in charge should that happen and not any slaves Miss Ermine brought into the house.

She could see Master Ryan writing something on a

piece of paper. Moving from the doorway, she eased on into the parlor directly across the hall and waited. In a few minutes, she heard him come out and go up the stairs. Then he hurriedly came back down and left the house.

Eliza went straight to Miss Victoria's room. She wasn't about to think of it as belonging to Miss Erin, because once Miss Victoria got back from her trip, she'd take over again.

She found the note lying on Miss Erin's pillow. She could not read the lines that explained he had received word Quincy Monroe's mare was about to foal, and he was going over there. He might not be back till late, maybe even on into the morning. He would miss her, he wrote, but he would be thinking of how wonderful it was last night, and he hoped when he came home he would find her in his bed again.

No, Eliza could not read. Victoria Youngblood felt there was a certain limit to how learned a slave should be. So Eliza did not know what Master Ryan had written and didn't care. All she knew as she tucked the paper in her apron pocket was that by doing so, she was helping maybe to make Miss Erin unhappy, and maybe she would start thinking how she never should have married Master Ryan. Eliza was also confident Miss Victoria would approve.

Erin was doubly pleased when she arrived at her mother's. First of all, Zachary was nowhere around, and, second, her mother was dressed and sitting on the side veranda. "I'm so glad you're better," she cried with a kiss of greeting.

Arlene, with forced gaiety, replied, "It's such a lovely afternoon I couldn't bear to be indoors." Actually, she had not felt like getting up at all, and only with Rosa's help had she been able to get her clothes on and make it to her favorite rocking chair. But she'd anticipated Erin's visit and did not want to worry her by still being bedridden when she arrived.

Rosa brought mint tea, and Erin noticed she would not look her straight in the eye. She waited till it would not appear so obvious, then followed her inside to corner her in the service kitchen. "I've got the diagram of the labyrinth," she said hurriedly, not giving her a chance to protest or refuse to take it. She stuffed it in the pocket of her apron and continued, "Tell Mahalia there is a grave on the river side of the house. She can't miss seeing it. There's a big tombstone. In front of that is a marble flower vase. When she wants me to meet her in the center of the labyrinth, tell her she's to leave a red rose in that vase. If she can't find one, she's to make one out of paper.

"Tell her," she rushed to finish, "that I'll always have money for her. Maybe not as much as I'd like, but when she's in need, I'll be there with something."

Rosa just looked at her with fear-widened eyes and lips trembling.

"Rosa, just do it!" Erin snapped impatiently. "After this, Mahalia will know how to contact me without involving you."

Rosa managed a quick nod and turned to scurry out the back door and head for the outbuildings.

Erin stared after her with a chilling stab of foreboding. Was there another reason, she wondered, why Rosa was so nervous? She did not know, knew only that something within was urging her to get her mother out of that house of evil as soon as possible.

Erin stayed till there was just enough time to get back to Jasmine Hill before dark. "I'm going to send a carriage for you early Sunday morning so you can come and spend the day with us," she promised, giving her a hug, thinking once more how sickly her mother looked.

Arlene was reluctant to promise. "Maybe. We'll see." Then, suddenly, although she hated to, she felt she had to tell her, "Zachary isn't at all pleased about your getting married while he was away. He thinks it shamed him."

Erin wanted to say he had always done a good job of bringing on his own shame and certainly didn't need to give credit to anyone else. But her mother knew that, and there was no need to cause pain by reminding her. "He'll get over it," she soothed. "Besides, soon it's not going to matter how he feels, because you're going to come and live with me."

Arlene managed a smile but inside felt no optimism, for she could not help wondering how much longer anything would matter.

When Erin arrived home to find Ryan had not returned, she was disappointed.

When the evening wore on, and he still did not come back, she became angry.

When, at last, it was time to go to bed, she went to her own.

It was nearly three in the morning when Ryan returned from the Monroe farm. He was in very high spirits. The mare had, indeed, delivered twins—a colt and a filly. Quincy had obligingly given him his choice, and he'd picked the filly. Erin could choose the name, because he was going to give it proudly to her. She could raise it and help train it and then she'd have a good-blooded mare to ride alongside him around the plantation.

He had ridden almost at full-gallop to get home. Not only was he anxious to tell her about his gift, but he also couldn't wait to find her in his bed. Maybe, he was starting to think with a warmth in his heart, they really were

going to be happy together, and maybe, he smiled to the
night world around him as he rode, she might one day
return his ever-growing love.

The grooms had all gone to bed, and the stables were
dark. He unsaddled his horse himself, gave him a quick
rubdown, because the animal was well lathered from the
hard ride. Then he hurried to the house.

He approached from the rear. Eliza slept in a small
room just off the service hallway, assigned there by his
mother years ago to keep an ear out for his comings and
goings at night. He avoided going in that way whenever
possible and, through force of habit, turned to go in the
front of the house.

He glanced up to the east wing as he started up the
stairs and wondered why Erin had not left a lantern burning for him. Maybe she had decided he would be out all
night. No matter, he grinned to himself, quickening his
step, he was going to wake her up and let her know different, by God!

He entered his room through the door that opened out
into the main hallway and walked in the darkness straight
to the bed. "I've got a surprise for you, Erin," he called
softly, not wanting to startle her from slumber. He
reached out, expecting to touch her soft skin, to feel the
sensual curves of her warm body.

His hand flattened on the spread and mattress.

Blinking in bewilderment, he groped about to realize
she wasn't there. Whirling around, he made his way out
and into the parlor. There was a quarter moon, scant
light, but enough to keep him from bumping into anything. Then, opening her door, he was slammed with disappointment and anger as he made her out, contentedly
sleeping in her own bed.

Was this her way, he wondered bitterly, of reminding
him that she had married him for one reason only—and

that it had nothing to do with wanting him, much less loving him?

He shook his head in discouragement, stepped out of the room and quietly closed the door.

CHAPTER

 19

E*RIN WAS NOT ABOUT TO ASK RYAN WHY HE* never came to her that night, nor did she inquire as to exactly when he returned home. She pretended not even to notice. In turn, he never mentioned the note he had left or asked why she had ignored his request.

In the days following, Ryan told himself it was time he became more involved with the actual workings of the plantation. By so doing, it took his mind off Erin and his brooding over the invisible wall between them. He called together his overseers for reports, then satisfied that all was operating smoothly, he began to devote himself entirely to his favorite pastime, his prize horses.

Erin, meanwhile, looked forward to her mother's visit. She was also ever on the alert for the right time to approach Ryan about the tense situation at Zachary's. But it was starting to look as if the opportunity just wasn't going to come. He stayed away from the house during the day, and if he did come around, he was cool and withdrawn. It was no different at night. His lovemaking was as tender and satisfying as ever, but afterward, they were like strangers. There was never the proper milieu for intimate conversation. As the days passed, she found it difficult to believe that one special evening had actually happened.

She ached inside, but on the outside, she pretended not to care. But there seemed to be so many empty hours with nothing to do. Then she hit on the idea of restoring the garden area around Henrietta Youngblood's grave. It would give her an opportunity to check the spot herself, without anyone wondering why. With fall approaching, there were fallen leaves to remove, anyway. If Ryan even noticed, he said nothing. It was as though he never gave her a thought until bedtime. He began to take his meals in his study, locking himself away for the evening. Erin did not say a word, merely had Annie bring her a tray to the upstairs parlor.

It was on Saturday evening when Erin's patience finally grew thin. All week, she had been cooped up inside the house, save for the time when she puttered around the grave. In the morning, she would be sending for her mother. It was for her sake that Erin wanted to try and make sure there'd be no tension between her and Ryan, for a little while, anyway.

Deciding she was just going to have to talk to Ryan, Erin went to the serving kitchen and told Eliza to let her know when he came into the house.

Eliza did not speak or acknowledge her request.

Suddenly, standing there, the subject of the woman's blatant disrespect, Erin could contain herself no longer. "Eliza, I am talking to you."

Eliza was polishing silverware and did not look around as she dully responded, "I know that. And I heard you."

Erin resisted the urge to stamp her foot childishly for emphasis. "Then act like you hear me." She bit out the words tightly, evenly, fighting to control her rage as the woman insolently continued to keep her back turned.

"What do you want me to say?"

"I want . . ." Erin took a deep breath and let it out slowly. "I want you to say politely, 'Yes, ma'am, Miss Erin, I'll be glad to let you know as soon as Master Ryan comes into the house'. Then, I will be sure that you heard me, and that you will carry out my request."

In a maddening monotone, Eliza sarcastically obliged, "Yes-ma'am-Miss-Erin-I-will-be-glad-to-let-you-know-as-soon-as-Master-Ryan-comes-into-the-house." She still did not turn around.

Erin swiftly walked over to her. Her fury was not motivated by the insolence of a slave to a mistress. Far from it. Her ire was provoked by the fact the woman was deliberately being impudent and arrogant. "Eliza," she began in a heated rush, "servants at my stepfather's house will tell you I am a very easy person to get along with. I make no unreasonable demands. I do not scream. I do not yell. And, most certainly, I have never lifted a hand against any of them. But I want you to know that I won't stand for you treating me this way. I'm going to have to speak to my husband about this."

Eliza did look up then, and the eyes she locked on Erin gleamed with contempt and challenge. "You do that. You just go right on and do that. And the sooner the better, so he can tell you just how it is around here, how I don't have to answer to anybody in this household except Miss Victoria. Not even him. That's the way it's always been. That's the way it will always be. If you want someone to slave for you, then you call Annie. Not me."

Erin was aghast and could not believe what she was hearing. "We'll see about that," was all she could trust herself to say at that moment.

Ryan came in a short while later, and it was Annie who came to tell her so. She went immediately to the study and knocked on the closed door.

"What it is?" he called.

Erin turned the knob, then stepped inside.

Seeing her, he shook his head in apology for his abruptness. "I thought it was one of the servants. They know not to bother me when that door is closed." He was sipping brandy and held up the glass to ask with quiet, almost mocking eyes, "Would my bride like to join me?"

"It seems I'm too far behind to catch up." She could not resist the sarcasm, but seeing the way his face darkened, she wished she had taken a glass. The last thing she wanted to be was a nagging wife, but it seemed they grew farther apart with each passing day. "As a matter of fact," she said hurriedly, "I wanted to talk to you about one of the servants."

At that, he gave a short, brittle laugh. Leaning back in his leather chair, he propped his booted feet on the edge of the desk and pretended to be in deep contemplation before retorting, "Let me try and guess. It wouldn't happen to be Eliza, would it?"

"That's right."

"And you want to complain about how she told you that she answers only to my mother."

Erin sank into the chair opposite. It looked as if she would be there a while. "I see she cornered you the second you walked in—"

"No, no," he was quick to correct, "You don't understand, Erin. Eliza didn't have to tell me anything. I figured sooner or later you would come to me with this, because that's the way it is. And she probably told you it wouldn't do any good to speak to me about it, and she's right. It won't. I can't drag her outside and have her beaten. I can't haul her off to the auction and have her sold. She belongs to my mother, and if there's any disciplining to be done, my mother will do it."

"Did your father have the same lack of authority?" she wanted to know.

"You better know it." He grinned. "Maybe," he softened his tone a bit, "when you meet my mother, you'll understand why. She can be a very difficult woman."

"Well, thank you for warning me."

"Would you have refused to marry me if I'd told you what an ogress she can be? I think not. But don't worry. As you can see, it's a big house. Her quarters are now way in the other wing. If you keep on having trays sent to your room, you'll hardly ever see her."

Erin again yielded to sarcasm to match his. "I might say the same for you."

He raised an eyebrow. "Ah. You noticed."

Their gazes locked in silent challenge, as they came to the brink of yet another battle of wit and will. Erin gave herself a mental shake and was reminded of the other purpose for the meeting. "I'd like to talk about something else," she began, folding her hands in her lap. "My mother."

He lowered his feet then and sat up straight. "Is there a problem?"

Erin admitted she could not be sure. "She's never been one to complain, but she certainly looks weaker to me than when we left. I'm sending a carriage for her tomorrow, because I want her to come and spend the day here."

"That's fine," he agreed, then figuring she didn't want her mother to see how things were between the two of them, he assured her, "I'll tell Eliza we'll have dinner in the dining room."

"Are you sure that will be all right with her? Maybe I'll need to have Annie fix something."

"Eliza will always obediently do what my mother has told her to do, and she knows serving meals is part of her duties. It's when she's asked to do something out of the ordinary by someone other than my mother that she balks."

Erin brushed over that unpleasant subject to get to the heart of the matter. "Ryan, I'm worried about Mother, and frankly, I'd like for her to come and live here with us." She searched his face for some hint of reaction but could not detect anything. "You said yourself it's a big house. You wouldn't even know she's about."

Ryan was struck by his inability to deny her anything. Yet, he felt it was to his advantage not to let her know that and hedged, "Does your stepfather know about this?"

"He ought to," she replied quickly and angrily. "As I said, Mother has never been one to complain, but I know she's miserable. I think he's taking out his anger on her over our getting married while he was gone. She told me he was furious when he found out, because he said it made him look like a fool, and that we went behind his back."

It was Ryan's turn to yield to derision. "But according to your mother, he was the one I was going to have to answer to if I didn't marry you right away." Then, seeing the way her face tightened and her cinnamon eyes grew stormy, he held up his hands in mock surrender. "Okay. I'm sorry. No more. And, yes, if you and she both want it, I really don't see why it can't be worked out."

Erin fought the impulse to jump up and run around the desk to throw her arms about him in a hug of gratitude. Instead, she thanked him and added, "I promise you. She won't be a bother."

He stared at her. Lord, he wanted to get up and walk around to draw her into his arms and hold her and kiss her and then make love to her right then and there on the sofa, the floor, the top of the desk—wherever. It was not just lust that was firing his loins. Oh, no, more and more of late he was being forced to come to terms with the cries of his heart. What he had denied and fought against so long was coming to pass—he was truly falling in love with her.

Refusing to yield to the impulse, he again asked if she'd like a glass of cognac, and this time she accepted.

It was a mellow time, and Erin started feeling as she had on that other occasion when closeness dared surface.

They talked of mundane things—how the weather was really starting to turn cool, and autumn would soon be upon them. She said she'd seen some pumpkins in the fields on her way to visit her mother earlier in the week. He remarked he'd noticed the gardening she had been doing around his grandmother's grave. She told him she was only looking for something to do, because it was boring to be in the house all day by herself.

He astounded her then by saying, lips curving in a secret smile, that perhaps she would like to ride over to Quincy Monroe's farm the first of the week and see her new filly. He didn't mention the night he had originally planned to surprise her with the news. He didn't want to stir the memories of his disappointment over her rejection of his invitation to his bed.

"You're going to give me my very own horse?" she cried, and when he nodded, she did get up and rush around to fling her arms about his neck. "Ryan, I don't know what to say," she cried, laughing at the same time.

"Don't say anything," he commanded huskily, holding her close. "Just show me."

It was so hard at such moments, Erin thought wildly, to hold back, lest he discover how very much she was starting to care. Yet, as long as he wanted her only for his physical needs, she wasn't about to let her feelings be known.

His touch was gentle. He captured her mouth with his, exploring, tasting, caressing, in a tender seduction that sent her senses reeling. She moved closer still, offering herself eagerly, welcoming his hands over her body, yielding to his touch. He lifted her skirt to slide his hand along her bare leg, dancing slowly upward between her thighs, and she began to move, her arms twined about his neck to hold him tight against her.

Sudden pounding on the partially open door caused them to spring apart.

Erin almost tumbled to the floor, and as Ryan quickly grabbed her, they looked at each other and tried to keep from bursting into laughter at the sound of Eliza's irate voice. No doubt but that she'd spied on them before knocking.

"Master Ryan. Will you be taking your supper in there or at the table?"

His gaze lustily locked with Erin's, he called back, "Mrs. Youngblood and I will both be having dinner in the dining room tonight. Have Ebner bring up a bottle of my best wine from the cellar."

They heard only the furious shuffling of her feet as she retreated. As usual, she did not acknowledge her orders.

"I still don't see how you put up with her," Erin couldn't help saying. "She isn't even civil."

"I just don't pay her any mind, Erin. You've got to learn to do that with my mother, too."

His voice had a bit of an edge to it, and she wondered whether the irritation was directed at her, for being annoyed, or if he, himself, were dreading the time when his mother returned. She did not ask, did not want to engage in any kind of serious discussion for the remainder of the evening, fearful of bursting the happiness bubble that had suddenly appeared.

It was later, while she was bathing and preparing to dress for dinner, when Annie suddenly burst into the dressing alcove. Obviously excited over something, she didn't speak but quickly glanced around as though making sure they were alone.

Just as Erin was about to ask impatiently what it was all about, Annie reached into the pocket of her apron and withdrew one of the few remaining roses that were still in bloom.

Erin felt her pulse quicken. The rose could only mean that Mahalia would be in the center of the labyrinth at midnight.

She, too, had memorized the diagram and was positive she could find her way in. The trick would be slipping out of bed if Ryan were beside her, and after their torrid embrace in the study, that seemed a certainty. She told herself there was no need to get nervous now. All along, she'd known that sooner or later the nocturnal rendezvous would begin. She'd just have to take them in stride and not give herself away by being anxious.

Despite her resolve, dinner seemed to take forever. It was nearly ten o'clock by the time they went upstairs, and it was all Erin could do to keep from shaking, because she was so nervous. Sometimes Ryan would torture them both by prolonging their ecstasy, and she hoped this night would not be one of those times.

She need not have worried.

So ravenous was he that he apologized afterward for not being able to hold back, even though she was pleasantly satisfied. "Later . . . ," he murmured, lips pressed in the hollow of her throat as he held her. "Later . . . again, and again . . ."

She had not responded, for she was afraid he would hear the lie in her voice if she attempted to be as eager as he was for more passion later in the night. Instead, she lay very still, pretending to fall asleep right away.

They were lying in his bed. When she finally heard his even breathing, she moved carefully to untangle her arms and legs from about him. By the time she stealthily crept from his room, the hour was quite late. She knew she would have to hurry.

She did not take time to dress but pulled her robe on over her gown. With hair tumbling about her shoulders, she slipped on her shoes. Taking the small amount of money she had been able to get her hands on to give to Mahalia, she was on her way.

She let herself quietly out the French door leading to the terrace. The light of a half moon in a cloudless sky illumned the way as she ran across the lawn. The wet grass licked at her ankles as she lifted her hem. Her heart was pounding, and she prayed Ryan would not awaken to find her gone from his bed. If he happened to glance out the window, he would be able to see her running in the moonlight.

The labyrinth loomed ahead like ghostly sentries joining hands to hinder entrance to the netherworld. Erin supposed she should be frightened. After all, one wrong turn, and she might possibly find herself confused and trapped in the maze. And who would find her? Not Mahalia, for never would she dare call out for help and maybe trap her accomplice as well. What would be her explanation to Ryan when he did, at last, have to go in to lead her back out? So many terrifying contemplations, but all she had to do was think of Letty and Ben and Rosa and all the other tormented souls, and she felt brave enough to continue. If she could help only one runaway find peace, then her efforts would not be in vain.

Within the intricate shrubs, there was scant light. Erin was concentrating so hard to remember the diagram she broke out in a cold sweat. Groping along, arms straight out on either side, she would reach an opening and, by memory, count which one it was and determine whether to turn left, right, or keep on going. She had practiced reaching the center twice in the past days, closing her eyes to simulate the darkness she knew she would have to cope with. She would have liked more rehearsals but was afraid of arousing suspicion. She felt as if Eliza was trying to spy on her all the time, anyway.

She was sure she was going in the right direction, and when, at last, she stepped into the square and saw the benches and the fountain softly gleaming in the moonshine, she gave a soft gasp of relief.

Mahalia was nowhere around, so she sank down on the bench to wait. She felt deeper anxiety to think how Mahalia might become lost on her side of the maze. Erin thought she had memorized that part, too, but hoped it would not be necessary to find out for sure.

Finally, when she heard the sound of cautious footsteps approaching, she breathed a sigh of relief, only to freeze in instant terror as she heard a man's voice softly call her name. "Miss Erin . . . Miss Erin . . . don't be afraid . . ."

Shakily, nervously, she got to her feet and stammered, "Who . . . who are you?" She began to back up toward the other side, preparing to dart back within the shrubs to hide, even if it meant becoming lost.

Quickly hearing, sensing, her rising terror, he called, "Mahalia sent me."

He stepped into the clearing, and Erin strained to see him in the silvery shadows. He was white. She could tell that much. Tall. And he wore a wide-brimmed hat. No facial features could be distinguished from where she stood, but as he also made her out in the shadows and approached, some of the tension began to fade. After all, she reminded herself, the only way he could have known and used the right path to the center was if Mahalia had shown him the diagram. That meant she trusted him.

"My name is Sam Wade, and I'm a Free-Soiler."

"A Free-Soiler," she echoed in relief, then stepped forward to hold out her hand and warmly greet him. "Did you have any trouble coming through the maze?"

"No. The diagram you drew was very clear. I committed it to memory, then took a rowboat from across the river. I spent all day yesterday scouting around to make sure that area, as well as the banks around the dock, was isolated. It's perfect for our needs," he finished, sounding satisfied and impressed.

Erin took the money out of her pocket, suddenly self-conscious to be standing there in her nightclothes with a strange man. "Well, you know the plan. When you're going to be here, have someone leave a rose at the grave. I think every two weeks will be sufficient, and there might even be times when I don't have any money to give you, but this is the best I can do.

So . . ." She allowed her voice to trail off, signifying there was nothing else to say. She did not want to tarry and knew she could not begin to breathe easy till she was back inside the house.

But Sam had other ideas. With a quick shake of his head, he protested. "I'm afraid you're wrong, Miss Erin. It *isn't* the best you can do. There's a lot more you can do for the cause."

As she listened warily, he proceeded to explain that the Free-Soilers had to ask something of her besides money. "This is the perfect spot for fugitives on this side of the river to hide and wait for a boat to pick them up at the dock. They can slip inside the entrance to the labyrinth during the night. Annie can check every morning to see whether a rose has been dropped there. She'll know then there's a runaway in there, and she can get word to you. You can slip out that night, at midnight, and take them through. Leave a rose on the dock. We'll have someone checking every day. They'll drift by, like they're just out fishing, and when they see a rose, they'll know to make a pickup at midnight."

Erin listened dizzily, amazed he had it all planned so carefully, but she was hesitant. "It's too risky for me. And how do you know Annie, anyway?"

"Annie is already involved. She knows all about the Free-Soilers, just like a lot of other slaves, but not one of them is going to tell the wrong person anything."

Grimly, Erin informed him, "The head housekeeper, Eliza. She'll tell in a heartbeat. The other slaves despise her."

He said he was well aware of that. "But everything will take place at night. The only risk is your being able to slip out of the house at midnight, without being seen. I know it's a chance, but it's one you've got to take. There will be a lot of people depending on you for their lives."

"But if I get caught—"

"You won't. Besides, you can teach Annie the way, and nights you don't dare try to go out, she can make the run for you. You can take turns. We need your cooperation," he persisted in near desperation. "We need to know we can count on that rose being placed on that pier to let us know there's a runaway slave who needs to be helped on his way north."

Erin bit her lower lip thoughtfully. She had wanted to help but had not realized just what it would entail, how deeply she would be swept into the underground.

She stepped closer to try and distinguish his features in the faint light. She guessed him to be in his late twenties, early thirties. He was startlingly tall, appeared to have powerful shoulders, as best she could tell. His face was ruggedly handsome, she decided. His eyes were dark and piercing as he tried to gauge what she was thinking of him. His hair was also dark, touching his collar. He was dressed in slouchy clothes, as would be expected of someone prowling around riverbanks in the night. "Just who are you?" she asked slowly, evenly. "How is it you're able to travel about and talk with the slaves and find out so much? And why is it I've never seen you before since you know so much about what goes on here at Jasmine Hill?"

"I used to sell elixir, but now I've broadened my offering of merchandise," he told her in his deep, mellow voice that was so strangely reassuring. Inclining his head in the merest hint of a mocking bow, he grinned, "At your service, of course, madam, but the fact is, I don't ordinarily deal with slave owners, just their overseers and their head housekeepers, butlers, and such."

"Of course," she cried softly then, remembering. "Ben told me about you. He said you told them how a runaway named Micah was safe and living in a colony in Meadville, Pennsylvania."

"Was," he corrected with a lilt of enthusiasm. "I just got back from Pennsylvania day before yesterday, and once Mahalia told me about you, and how you're going to be one of us, I got so busy checking out the river and this place that I haven't had a chance to get the news to Ben that his friend is on the way to Sierra Leone. He got scared when he heard your stepfather had been up that way, spreading the word he was doubling his bounty on his runaways. Micah had been working very hard for a farmer, and he'd managed to save a little bit of money. We were able to get him some false papers saying he was free, so we could get him on board a ship transporting legitimate freed slaves."

"I've heard about that. I was in Philadelphia not long ago, myself." She told him of her meeting with Parson Jones and was surprised when he confided he already knew about it. With a bemused shake of her head, she laughed. "I guess there's nothing I can tell you about me that you don't already know."

He became quite sober. "Yes, there is. I don't know if you're willing to go along with my plan."

Erin knew that, despite the risk involved, she could not refuse. "All right," she said finally, giving him a brave smile she did not truly feel, "but Annie will probably be making most of the runs. If I slip out at midnight too often, sooner or later, I'll get caught."

"It won't be that often. We've a long way to go to help these people, and there just aren't that many willing to take a chance and try and escape. But word will spread. Already we're growing. For a long time, there was just me, and I only came through a few times a year to keep in touch with what was going on. Then we were able to get Mahalia in position. Now we have you." He reached out and clasped her hand in friendship.

Erin squeezed his fingers in return. It was a bond. She was committed. "All right." She sighed in resignation and finality. "Spread the word that fugitives can come to Jasmine Hill to wait for help to move them along on the road to freedom, but, dear Lord, let's hope I don't get found out."

"Let's hope none of us do," he tersely added. "If any of the ruthless slave owners, like your stepfather, find out what I'm up to, they'll hang me, for sure."

Erin soberly, grimly, agreed.

She made ready to leave. "I've got to get back before I'm missed. I'll talk to Annie tomorrow and let her know what we've got ahead of us."

He was about to exit on his side of the labyrinth, but just as she stepped into the hedges opposite, he broached the news he had saved for last. "One more thing. Your friend, Letty, that you were asking Parson Jones to try and locate . . ."

There was something in his tone, a kind of melodic happiness which dared fill her with hope as she whirled to cry, "She made it to Philadelphia!"

"She sure did." He all but sang the triumphant words. "And she's on that ship with Micah, bound for Sierra Leone, and a new life as a free woman. It's what it's all about, Miss Erin. It's what this whole, dangerous business is all about."

She could only nod in agreement, tears of gladness stinging her eyes. She turned to rush back toward the house, but this time, her feet were hardly touching the ground.

She made it safely inside but did not dare return to Ryan's bed. It would not do to awaken him, especially when she was trembling from head to toe with happiness, and he would certainly want to know the reason.

Finally, in her own bed, drowsiness crept over her. As she drifted away, she longed to be lying in her husband's arms, her head cradled lovingly on his strong shoulder.

When Ryan awoke the next morning to find Erin had returned to her own bed, he was furious. Obviously, she couldn't stand to sleep with him. Oh, yeah, she liked the lovemaking, but when it was over, she couldn't get away from him fast enough.

She liked a lot of other things about being married to him, too, he mused as he threw his clothes on, like money and presents and moving her mother in with them to share the luxurious life. But the fact was, she didn't give a damn about him, never had, never would. He was a fool to think it could ever be any different.

In a surly mood, he went downstairs for morning coffee instead of having Ebner bring it up for a leisurely few moments before starting the day. He went all the way to the service kitchen and poured his own.

Eliza ignored him. If he wanted breakfast cooked, he

would say so. She wasn't about to ask, because she didn't care.

He left without a word and went to the stable and saddled his horse himself. One of the stableboys hurried over to help, but Ryan irritably waved him away.

He swung up in the saddle, about to ride off, but one of his overseers called out to him, wanting to know when he'd be back. There was something he needed to discuss about the cornfields, he said, and the harvest, whether Ryan wanted the stalks down for livestock fodder or wanted them to stand in the field for browsing.

"We'll talk tomorrow," Ryan snapped, reining the horse about and kicking him in his flanks to set him into a fast gallop toward the road. He did not say when he would return, because he had no idea. He just knew he had to get away and try to figure out if it was useless to continue to hope his marriage could ever be anything more than what it was—a mockery.

It was nearly noon when the carriage pulled up to the front steps of the Jasmine Hill mansion.

The groomsman leapt down to assist the lady passenger inside to alight, while the driver began untying the large steamer trunks that were laced on top.

Victoria Youngblood stepped down and glanced about. All seemed well. The lawns were manicured, which was a standing edict. Later, she would make sure the gardens were also in order for fall. But, for the moment, she was exhausted. It had been an arduous journey from Savannah. The way stations where they had stopped at night were all small, crowded, and the food had been terrible. All she wanted was to languish in a tub of hot water and then enjoy one of Eliza's scrumptious meals, accompanied by a bottle of the estate's best scuppernong wine. Ryan could take a carriage and go for Ermine later in the day to share the welcome-home celebration with them. She was younger, wouldn't need so much time to recuperate. Victoria had asked the driver to drop Ermine off at her parents' home in Richmond and just kept on going, anxious to reach the final destination.

By the time Victoria paid the fee for the journey, Eliza had spotted her and was running down the steps calling excitedly, "Oh, Miss Victoria, I'm so glad you're home. How was your trip?"

Victoria gave her a nod of greeting, not about to show any emotion, even though she was glad to see her. "It was exhausting," she cried dramatically, going up the stairs. "Have Ebner bring in the trunks, and then draw my bath at once. I'm going straight to my room.

"Oh, and bring me tea," she turned to snap. "And maybe a spice cake, if you have some fresh baked."

Eliza watched her go, smiling triumphantly. Now Master Ryan and his bride would find out who was in charge at Jasmine Hill.

Ebner, who had also heard the carriage rolling in and rushed to see who it was, came running around the side of the house. He saw Miss Victoria going inside and looked to Eliza and anxiously whispered, "Ain't you gonna tell her, 'liza? Ain't you gonna tell her about Mastah Ryan takin' hisself a bride?"

Eliza lifted her chin defensively, dark eyes narrowing in malicious glee. "Why should I? She didn't ask me anything about anything."

Ebner rolled his eyes heavenward and whispered, "Lord, help us."

Eliza snickered and lifted her skirts and hurried to follow after her mistress.

She wasn't about to miss what was sure to happen next.

CHAPTER

 20

VICTORIA OPENED THE DOOR TO THE PARLOR
and was momentarily frozen by the scene that greeted her.
Had she taken a wrong turn, she wondered, and wound
up in the wrong wing? But no, there wasn't any section
of the house decorated in such a way—light colors of pale
rose and light blue, with touches of cream. She preferred
more sedate and darker accents. Even the curtains had
been changed, she noted. Gone were the heavy burgundy
velvet and in their place were white chintz, blowing gently
in the breeze coming in from the river.

She felt a stiffening jolt. What was going on around
here?

She walked about, examining the room, as she tried to
figure it all out. Had Ryan wanted to surprise her by redec-
orating? No. He'd never do that, because he knew better,
just as he knew he wasn't moving into the master suite
when he married Ermine. What, then, had been his motive?

Eliza caught up but hung back so Miss Victoria
wouldn't start asking her questions. She had already
peeked in earlier and knew Miss Erin was sleeping in her
own bed this morning. Master Ryan had been in a bad
mood when he'd left. She had felt the tension between

them lately and was sure it all meant they just weren't getting along. She didn't know what white people did about things like that but was certain it could all be worked out when a man made a mistake and married the wrong woman. Miss Victoria would take care of it all, anyway.

Victoria headed for her bedroom but hesitated in front of the closed door. Some strange instinct was telling her she was not going to like what she found in there. Very slowly she reached out for the knob and turned it, allowing the door to swing quietly open.

Erin was still sleeping soundly, exhausted from all the excitement of the night before. The curtains were closed against the late morning sun. She was lying on her side, face burrowed in the pillow.

All Victoria saw in the dim light was a woman lying in her bed. She was unaware that all of her furniture had been removed from this room, as well.

Indignant rage was a stealthily creeping snake, twining slowly around her body. It began at her toes and worked its way up insidiously to burn and torment every inch of flesh it touched. At last it found its way to her throat, and the rageful scream exploded.

Erin was jolted awake and sat straight up in wide-eyed wonder as she tried to grasp what was happening. The woman who was towering over her and yelling was a stranger, but it did not take her long at all to figure out who she was.

"How dare you sleep in my bed? It's bad enough that my son would bring one of his—his whores into this house," she stammered, choked by anger. "But to use my bed is unforgivable. Now get out of here! At once! Victoria snatched away the satin comforter.

Erin tried to shake away the cobwebs so she could think clearly and attempt explanation. "Mrs. Youngblood," she began nervously. "It's not what you think. I'm sorry you had to find out this way, but—"

Victoria was beyond all reason and shrieked, "Did you hear me? I told you to get out of my bed. Out of my room! I want you out of my house!" Wildly, she whirled to call furiously, "Eliza! Get in here and get this woman out of here, before I lose control and drag her out myself!"

Erin realized it was useless for the moment to try and clear things up. Quickly, she moved to the opposite side of the bed, grabbing up her robe as she did so. Seeing how Eliza gloated as she walked in, she knew then it had all been planned for Ryan's mother to find out in such a shocking way. "Why didn't you tell her, Eliza?" she asked coldly, shuddering with her own fury as she yanked on the robe.

Victoria's brows shot up as she was also struck by that jarring question. "Yes." She turned on Eliza. "Why didn't you tell me there was a whore in my bed?"

Eliza, as usual, was arrogantly silent.

Dimly, Erin thought how Ryan must look like his father, because he certainly did not resemble this ranting woman with eyes like a snake and a nose that was so pointed it seemed to accuse. "Mrs. Youngblood," she attempted again, shock fading and courage returning. "I am not a whore. I am your son's wife. We were married in late August. It's not right that you had to find out this way, and I'm truly sorry."

Victoria swayed, reached to clutch the edge of the armoire for support and dizzily realized it was not hers. Glancing about wildly, she saw that all the furniture was unfamiliar. "That's not true. You're lying." She turned to Eliza in hope of confirmation.

Eliza shrugged and gave an apathetic nod.

Victoria felt the blood rush to her head and a great roaring begin. Stumbling from the room, she whispered hoarsely, "I don't believe it. I just don't believe it. It can't be. Ryan wouldn't do this. I know he wouldn't. It has to be a nightmare, and I'll wake up any second, and it won't be happening." She needed to go where she could think, and asked Eliza, who had followed after her, "Where did he move my things?"

"Into the yellow room on the corner at the far end of the hall."

Silently, Victoria walked out, shoulders stooped, head down.

Eliza stared after her. She wasn't worried that her mistress might be defeated. Oh, no. She knew her so well and was confident that all she needed was time to make up a plan.

Erin came out then and said harshly, "That was a terrible thing you did, Eliza. I knew you were devious, but I never dreamed you would go so far."

Eliza paused to smirk, then followed after her mistress.

Erin wasn't sure what she should do. Damn it, where was Ryan? Hurrying to the bell cord, she gave it a yank, and in seconds, Annie appeared. All the servants had heard by then that Miss Victoria was back, and they were curiously waiting to see what was going to happen.

"Have you seen Master Ryan today?" Eliza wanted to know.

Annie shook her head. "No'm. You want me to go look for him?"

Erin had begun to pace nervously around the room. "I certainly do. Tell one of the overseers to get some men out looking for him and tell him he's needed here immediately." Remembering what day it was, she added, "And you'd better send someone to tell my mother we'll have to postpone her visit today. I can't have her here with all this going on." Dear Lord, she had known the situation would not be pleasant when Victoria Youngblood returned but never had she dreamed it would be this bad.

Annie was out the door to obey, but Erin suddenly remembered her meeting with Sam Wade. She called her back and drew her close to confide the agreement they had made. She wished she could have her take the message to Rosa that Letty was safe and on her way to a new life in Africa but didn't dare. She might not see Rosa, and Erin was afraid to trust just anybody with such information. And she was not about to write a note that could fall into the wrong hands.

Annie listened with interest but frowned when she got to the part about her having to learn the way into the labyrinth so she could aid a runaway to the pier. "I can't do that," she said in horror. "That's when Miz Henrietta's ghost is out walkin'."

Erin had neither time nor patience to listen to such superstitious nonsense. Motioning her to carry on with her orders, she told her they'd discuss all that later. "Meanwhile, you keep an eye out for a rose left at the grave or inside the entrance to the maze. I just can't think clearly right now."

Annie rushed out. She was sorry things had turned out as they had, felt sorry for Miz Erin. She was willing to do most anything to help her, because she liked her, but there was just no way she was going around that creepy place at night.

Victoria sat at the window and stared out at the fields beyond without really seeing anything. At first, she had been in shock, but raw nerves had taken over, and she was starting to get really mad. Her head was still pounding, and if Eliza did not hurry up and get back with that brandy she'd sent her scurrying after, she feared she was going to start screaming and never be able to stop. And where was Ryan? How could he just disappear? She had been home nearly an hour, and Eliza had sent some of the hands to search, but no one could find him.

Finally, Eliza came with the liquor. Filling a glass, Victoria snatched it from her and downed it in one gulp, then wanted another. In a dread voice so cold as to echo from a grave, she asked, "Who is she? I want you to tell me everything you know."

Eliza sat down in the chair opposite and took a deep breath of delighted anticipation. She had been waiting for the moment to inform her that Master Ryan had married the stepdaughter of Zachary Tremayne. Even Eliza knew what a contemptible man he was, the way decent folk shunned him and his family.

Victoria thought she was going to faint. Swaying, gulping the brandy so fast she nearly choked, she recovered to whimper, "It's even worse than I thought. Oh, dear Lord. Dear, dear Lord. I've heard such terrible things about that man. And his wife! Everyone talks about how she's always tried to push herself on people. Brazen. That's what she is. The menfolk think she's beautiful, but I don't think that's what attracts them to Arlene Tremayne." She punctuated her words with a derisive sniff.

Eliza listened, clucking in sympathy now and then. She was feeling more confident than ever that Miss Victoria was going to come up with a plan to correct Master Ryan's mistake.

"What is Ermine going to do? Oh, poor thing. She'll be so humiliated. She probably already knows, doesn't she?" She wildly looked to Eliza for dreaded assurance.

"The wedding was big," she related. "Master Ryan, he even had a party the week before to tell everybody. All your kin was here. Neighbors, too. I want you to know I didn't help with any of it. I pretended to, but I knew you wouldn't want me doing anything. The other servants, they took over and really made things fancy. Master Ryan even gave her a big ring."

Victoria was feeling sicker by the minute. "Then Ermine's parents knew, and they probably told her as soon as she walked in the door this morning." The pain in her head had become a dull throb. "Oh, what could Ryan have been thinking?" she wailed. "Ermine Coley comes from good, blue-blood Virginia stock. It's said her ancestors can be traced all the way back to distant British royalty. Thornton Coley is one of the most prominent attorneys in Richmond, and I can't think of any family more respected. Why, I couldn't have asked for better stock to carry on the Youngblood name. Ryan's father is probably turning over in his grave."

Ermine dutifully refilled her glass and sympathetically offered, "Well, you don't have anything to be ashamed of, Miss Victoria. It's not your fault that Master Ryan is the only one to carry on. I remember how you lost all those babies. Two before Master Ryan was born, and then you nearly died having him and then lost three more later on. You tried. The good Lord knows you tried."

"I certainly did. Ryan should have appreciated that fact, respected it, and accepted that it was his duty, and Ermine's, to have as many sons as possible so the Youngblood name would go on. But how in the name of heaven," she cried, lips trembling, eyes brimming with tears, "could he dare to mix his seed with someone of unknown heritage? I seem to remember that Zachary married Arlene after a trip farther south. She came back with that . . . girl in there, when she was just a baby. She probably didn't even know who the father was. And I'm supposed to accept that trash into my house? I'm supposed to be grandmother to her children?

"No!" She declared vehemently, pounding the chair

with her fists. "I won't do it. There has to be a way to end this madness."

Through the years, Eliza had experienced many similar scenes with Victoria when she was distraught about something. Consequently, she knew much local gossip and was able to remind her of a similar situation. "You told me last year about how Miss Coralee Sutton was sent away by her daddy, because she brought shame on the family after letting a man bed her before he married her."

Impatiently, Victoria snapped, "What does that have to do with any of this?" Suddenly, it dawned on her, and she gasped. "That's how she got him to marry her! She made him crazy for her and held out for marriage. Oh, that cunning little bitch!"

Eliza suppressed a smile to offer instead another cluck of dismay.

"But that also has to mean he can't really be in love with her." Victoria was starting to get excited, as she began to see a light at the end of a long, despairing tunnel. "Tell me, do they seem happy?"

Eliza told the truth, how there did seem to be some tension, and Master Ryan always seemed to be in a bad mood.

"Then it's obvious that now that he's got what he wanted, he regrets what he's done. Oh, my poor boy!" The tears spilled down her cheeks, and she realized it was up to her to get him out of the mess he had got himself into. But she also knew she was going to have to be very careful. Ryan could be quite stubborn. And the two of them had never seen eye-to-eye on many things. If she angrily condemned what he had done, it would only make him defensive, thus making her scheme difficult.

Eliza could tell she had finally come up with a plan and asked excitedly, "What are you going to do, Miss Victoria?"

It was Victoria's time to smile, at last. "First of all, I want that bath and my tea and my spice cake. Then I want you to get busy and prepare a very special dinner."

Eliza was puzzled and said so.

"Don't you see? I've got to help my son make the best of a bad situation. He needs sympathy right now. Understanding. I'll let him know, in subtle ways, that I can understand how a beautiful woman like Miss Sterling could beguile him into marrying her.

"I will also let him know," she added, eyes narrowing with malicious delight, "that I'm ready and willing to help him straighten out his life."

Eliza nodded, feeling a comforting rush. It was just like she'd known it would be. Miss Victoria would take care of everything.

Rosa hated to give the message to Miss Arlene. She had been dressed and ready to go since first light, so looking forward to spending the day with Miss Erin. But, more than that, Rosa knew she wanted to be out of the house when Master Zachary woke up. He had come in late the night before, all liquored up. She had heard him yelling and screaming all the way from the storage room, where she now slept. She knew he would have her beaten if he found out she was disobeying his rule that no slaves were allowed in the house at night, but after that time when he had beaten Miss Arlene so bad, Rosa didn't dare go all the way to the compound. She wasn't about to leave her beloved mistress all alone with that man. If she hadn't found her when she did that night, Miss Arlene wouldn't have lived. It was Tulwah's magic that saved her. Rosa had sent Ben running through the night to fetch him, and he had come and packed Miss Arlene's chest in some kind of poultice to stop the bleeding from her mouth and nose. He had stayed with her till near dawn. He had been back

since, too, but nobody knew that except Rosa, and she
was not going to tell. She suspected he was gathering
wanga for his spell she'd begged him to cast on Master
Zachary. She just wished he'd hurry up and do it, because
things were getting bad. He had beaten poor Ben again,
because he was just so angry over Letty. She feared Ben
was going to run away, and she only hoped he would wait
till Mahalia sent word about the new plan the Free-Soilers
were setting up. If he didn't, and he got caught, Master
Zachary would take particular delight in killing him. He
had already had the whipping post brought out of the
swamp and placed right in the middle of the compound,
and now when he did his whipping, he ordered all the
slaves to gather round and watch.

Rosa shook her head in hopeless despair as she made
her way up to Miss Arlene's room. She figured there just
had to be a special place in hell for a demon like Zachary
Tremayne.

Arlene glanced up as she entered. She was sitting by the
window and had seen the horse come up the road, and
Rosa could tell by the disappointed look on her face that
she already knew there was not going to be any trip that
day to Jasmine Hill. "Did the messenger give the reason?"
she asked dully.

"No'm. He just said Miz Erin said it couldn't be today.
That's all."

Arlene blinked furiously; she didn't want to cry in front
of Rosa. She had been living for this day, because she had
made up her mind that she would move in with Erin and
Ryan if it was all right. She had reached the point of being
absolutely terrified of Zachary and was even starting to
fear for her life. Last night, he had taken her savagely and
brutally.

Afterward, he had shoved her away in loathing and disgust and said, "I'm gettin' sick of you, sick of thinkin' how

you're one-quarter the color of the ones I wouldn't wipe my feet on. You're not good for nothin', anymore, always coughin', always lazin' around. Before, I could look forward to havin' Erin in my bed, but you ruined all that for me."

Sore and bleeding, Arlene had laid there for long hours in anguish, wanting to just die then and there so she would never be hurt or humiliated by him again. When Tulwah had boldly slipped into her room, she had welcomed him. And she had even broken down and cried and told him what had happened. He had a poultice for her to use after he left, and he promised she would not have to suffer much longer. He was taking care of things. She didn't know what he had in mind, didn't care what happened to Zachary. All she knew was that she was ready to get down on her knees to Ryan Youngblood, if that's what it took to escape from the torture and the madness.

She got up and began to undress. There was nothing to do but go to bed and try to sleep. She would take a big dose of Tulwah's medicine. It always made her drowsy.

It was nearly dark when Zachary finally woke up from his drunken stupor. He lay there a few minutes and anguished over the throbbing pain in his head. The cure for that was the hair of the dog that bit him, as the saying went, which meant he needed a drink. Bad. And he was going to have to get up and get it himself from his supply downstairs, because the slaves were supposed to be out of the house at such an hour.

He rolled to his side, about to get up.

And that was when he saw it.

The rooster's half-closed glassy eyes stared at him from where they lay propped on the pillow next to him. The stringy stump of its head oozed blood, and it had run down onto his shoulder.

With a scream and an oath, he grabbed it to fling it against the wall where it exploded in a sickening pulp.

He leapt to his feet, his own blood rushing to his head in a rage of terrified anger.

He knew what it was and what it meant.

Voodoo. Black magic. Evil spirits.

Someone was casting a spell on him, and he could hear the furious pounding of his own heart as he rationalized just who that someone had to be.

His mulatto wife.

Well, he had news for her if she thought she was going to use her African blood to put a curse on him. He'd fix her. He'd put her where she'd be no threat with her *obeah*, ever again.

He was going to do what he should have done a long time ago.

He was going to send her where she belonged, back to her own people . . . and bondage.

CHAPTER

 21

R*YAN KNEW SOMETHING WAS WRONG WHEN HE* saw Ebner waiting at the stable. Quickly dismounting, he turned his horse over to a groomsman and brusquely demanded, "Let's hear it."

"Miz Victoria is back."

Ryan nodded, felt tension creeping. He'd known it could happen at any time, but damn it, he wished he had been there. They started toward the house. "What time did she get here?"

"It was about noon."

Ryan glanced toward the horizon where the sun bathed the landscape in golden hues as it sank behind the western ridge. It was getting late. "Well," he prodded with a sigh of resignation, "how did it go?"

Ebner knew he was talking about the first meeting between his mother and his wife. "Lordy, Mastah Ryan, I don't know." He wrung his hands in a helpless gesture. "Eliza, she didn't tell you' mama nothin' befo' she went in the house. All I know is Miz Erin, she ain't come downstairs all afternoon, but she did send Annie out to the stable to get somebody to ride over to her mama's house and tell her she'd have to postpone her visit today."

Ryan groaned outloud. Damn, that had slipped his

mind, too. In fact, he'd been so lost in thought as he rode aimlessly all day that he didn't even recall where all he had wandered. And he hadn't resolved anything by his brooding. The givens were the same—he loved Erin; she didn't return that love. Still, he had no intentions of ever letting her go, and he'd be damned if he'd wear his heart on his sleeve and wind up feeling like a fool—again.

Ebner continued. "Eliza said Miz Victoria said that I'm to let her know when you got here, and to tell you to go to yo' study and wait fo' her there."

"Fine. Do that." He wanted to get the encounter over with as quickly as possible.

In his study, he filled a glass with whiskey to brace himself for what he felt was going to be an unpleasant scene.

He did not have long to wait. He had just sat down behind his desk when his mother appeared.

He stood in polite greeting. "Welcome home," he began with forced geniality but immediately fell to stunned silence as she burst into tears. He had never known her to cry. Not even when his father died.

He watched uncertainly as she sank to the leather sofa to cover her face with trembling hands. This was a side to her he found himself totally unprepared for. He'd expected screaming, yelling, anything but tears.

Not knowing what else to do, he went and sat down beside her, awkwardly putting his arm about her quaking shoulders. "Listen. I didn't mean for it to be a shock to you. I wish I'd been here to tell you myself, and—"

"No!" she cried sharply, raising misty eyes to look at him in anguish. "It's not your getting married that hurts, Ryan, though, dear God, I pray you won't live to regret it.

"I can accept that," she rushed on, "but what hurts me so is thinking how you must hate me to turn your wife against me, before I even had a chance to meet her and try to accept this marriage." She summoned a fresh attack of grief, shook her head wildly in pretense of being too upset to go on.

Ryan was not only baffled, he was fast becoming agitated by all the mystery. "Will you please stop crying and tell me what this is all about?"

She cried even harder.

He looked up then to see Eliza outside the door, apparently reluctant to intrude. With a sigh, he got to his feet. "Well, Eliza, maybe you can tell me what's going on."

Eliza recited, as she had been coached. "I heard Miss Victoria crying. I'm afraid she's going to become ill if she doesn't get hold of herself. It was a terrible, terrible scene, Master Ryan. I wish you had been here for her."

"Well, if somebody doesn't tell me what the hell is going on, I'm going to get ill, too—in a different way," he added grimly.

Eliza continued her recitation. She explained that Miss Victoria, unaware of his marriage, went to her room, like always. "Miss Erin"—she lifted her chin in a gesture of disdain—"was still asleep, and when she woke up and saw your mother, she had a fit and started cursing and screaming at her to get out."

As planned, Victoria took over at that moment to wail, "Oh, it was awful. Just awful. I've never had anyone talk to me like that in my whole life. Such filthy language! I didn't know what was going on. All I could think of was that you'd brought one of those—those street women home with you, and she was in my bed."

Ryan glared at Eliza, then, and wondered if she'd told about him having Corrisa Buckner sleep in his bed. If she hadn't, she would, but for the moment, she was not meeting his accusing eyes, because she probably knew what he was thinking.

Victoria prattled on. "I asked her to leave, and that's

when she started after me, saying I was the one who had to get out, because she was your wife, and I had no right to be there. She said things were different now, and I'd find out soon enough who's in charge now, and . . . oh, dear, dear Jesus. Your father would turn over in his grave if he knew you'd let anyone treat me this way."

She gave a loud gasp, began to shudder convulsively as Eliza, right on cue, rushed to comfort. Cradling Victoria in her arms, she looked up at Ryan to say worriedly, "I think you'd better send for a doctor. She's real bad. Real bad."

Again, as planned, Victoria threw up a hand in protest and took deep, rasping breaths, as though fighting to get hold of herself. Swallowing hard, gulping, giving her head a brisk shake, she protested, "No. No doctor. I won't air the family's dirty laundry for all of Richmond to gossip about. We'll make the best of all this. Somehow. Eliza, get me some brandy. A big glass." She leaned back against the sofa and closed her eyes, as Eliza rushed to obey.

Ryan sat down behind his desk again and tried to sort it all out. It just didn't sound like Erin, but he didn't know what to believe, especially since he hadn't heard her side, yet.

Victoria sniffed and blew her nose in the lace handkerchief she drew from her pocket before going on with her tale. "I just ran out. I was afraid she was actually going to strike me. She did throw something, a pillow, I think, and she had her hand on the lantern when I ran out the door, getting ready to throw that at me. She just went crazy. If only someone had told me, prepared me for all this, I'd have waited till you got home and talked to you first. But I had no way of knowing you'd moved her into my room, or I'd never have intruded."

"Eliza could have told you."

"She said she didn't think it was her place—"

Ryan couldn't resist a sarcastic sneer. "Well, that's the first time she's ever worried about her place when it came to my business."

Victoria let that pass. "Eliza took me to where you'd moved me." She made her voice tremble as she asked pitifully, "What's to become of me now, son? Where is my place in your life? If I'm in the way, I'll move out."

"That's not necessary," he said tersely.

"I don't understand any of this, anyway. You know I had my heart set on your marrying Ermine. Poor thing! Her heart is probably broken."

"Don't worry about her. She'll be engaged to somebody else by Christmas."

Victoria's eyes narrowed. He might be right. Ermine was a lovely girl, and when word spread she was no longer engaged, the young bachelors of Richmond would beat a path to her door—all the more reason Victoria knew she had to move quickly. "So, tell me about Erin Sterling," she prodded, pretending not to know anything about her. "Who is she, anyway? Where does she come from?"

"Not far from here. Sterling was her real father's name. Her mother remarried."

Victoria wanted to make him say it, "And her mother is . . . ?"

"Arlene Tremayne. She's married to Zachary Tremayne."

"Oh, dear God!" Victoria began to sway to and fro, feigning surprise. "Oh, dear, dear, God! That dreadful man! And his wife! I've seen her. Always pushing herself on people. No one knows anything about her background. Why, there's no way of knowing what kind of heritage your children would have, and—" She looked up sharply. "Oh, no! Don't tell me that's the reason you did this. Tell me she's not carrying your child!"

"Not yet," he replied cooly.

"Well, I find it hard to believe you married her because of love, not when she comes from such questionable background."

He surprised even himself by his quick retort. "Actually, I did."

That was a jolt, and she wouldn't let herself believe it but offered instead, "I can get you out of this trouble."

"There's no trouble, Mother."

A smug smile touched her lips. "I'd say you've got a lot of trouble with a wife who curses your mother."

"I'll talk to her. I'm sure it was just a little misunderstanding."

"I just wish you'd help me to understand what brought all this about," Victoria begged again, taking the brandy Eliza brought.

Gently he asked a question of his own. "When have you ever understood anything I did, Mother?"

Victoria knew she'd get nowhere by arguing. Continuing with her plan, she whispered pitifully, "Then at least tell me what's to become of me now."

"Nothing has changed," he assured her wearily, wanting to end the conversation so he could go find Erin and hear her side. "You're the mistress of Jasmine Hill. Erin knows that. I made that clear to her. As for taking over the master suite, I felt it was the right thing to do. You know I'd planned to when . . ." He let his voice trail, not wanting to bring up the past.

"Yes, yes, of course." She nodded vigorously, hoping she sounded completely submissive, while inside she was burning with vengeful rage.

"Rest till dinner," he urged. "I'll get it all straightened out by then."

For the first time, Victoria allowed a tightness in her voice. "If we're all going to live together under one roof, I can't tolerate her talking to me that way. If she'll apologize, it will be forgotten."

Ryan was quick to say, "I'm sure she'd like to make peace, too."

"Let's hope so." She paused at the door to give him a glance filled with pity.

Ryan found Erin in his bedroom, pacing about in agitation. He couldn't resist the barb, "Well, I guess this is one way of getting you to come to me."

She whirled on him at once. "I don't have the patience for your sarcasm. Ryan, where have you been all day? Why weren't you here when your mother arrived? She went absolutely crazy and charged into the bedroom and accused me of being one of your whores!"

He glanced up to see the way she looked at that moment, hands on her hips, legs apart in some kind of self-defensive stance, he supposed. In her anger, she was even more beautiful. Dark hair tousled wildly about her face. Long, silken lashes fringing coffee-colored eyes that sparkled with fire. Cheeks flushed with anger.

"Well?" she demanded. "Are you going to help me with this? I tried to tell her we're married, but she wouldn't listen, and—"

He reached out to pull her roughly onto his lap. She resisted, but he tossed his empty glass away and used both arms to hold her tightly. "Now you listen." He nuzzled her forehead. "I don't know what happened between you two, but whatever it was, it's best forgotten. We both knew she'd be shocked, and her suddenly showing up, no doubt, took you by surprise. Frankly, I don't think either one of you knew what you were saying. So now I'm going to ring for Ebner and send word to the kitchen that we're going to have a very nice, and very formal dinner tonight to celebrate her return. You apologize, and we start out fresh."

For an instant, Erin could only stare at him incredulously, and finally she was able to find her voice and stammer, "Are—are you out of your mind? I apologize? For being awakened by someone screaming I'm one of my husband's whores? Oh, no!" She shook her head furiously from side to side. "I've nothing to apologize for!"

"Even if it means forgetting the whole damn incident so we can live in peace under one roof?"

"I think we should all sit down together and talk about it, and—"

He released her, nearly spilling her to the floor as he abruptly stood. "Mother isn't the kind who can talk things out, Erin. Even though you might not think it's fair, it's be best for everybody if you'd swallow your pride, apologize, and get it over with.

"You knew," he went on, "when we got married, that she was still going to run the house, and you had no business flying off the handle and telling her she'd learn who's in control now, and—"

"She told you that?" Erin said. "Well, that's another lie, and I'm not listening to any more."

She started to leave, but he grabbed her and spun her around. "All I want to do is smooth things over, Erin. We've got enough problems without this."

"What about when my mother moves in with us?" she reminded. "She's not well, Ryan."

"I know that, but we can't have an outsider here right now, anyway. Mother needs to adjust to our being married."

"My mother may not have that kind of time." Tears stung her eyes and she blinked furiously, determined he would not see her cry.

Wearily, he murmured, "I'll do what I can, if you'll just cooperate."

"I won't apologize for something I didn't do."

He lashed back. "Well, I guess I'm a fool, anyway, to think you'd even give a damn. Hell, you can't stand the sight of me, anyway. Isn't that why you left my bed last night?"

How she ached to tell him the last thing she'd wanted to do was leave his tender, loving arms. The only time she felt safe was when he held her. The only time she knew real joy was when he was near. Yet, she dared not say those things, refused to yield to her heart, silently crying out to him with love. Finally, she drew a ragged breath and lied, "I just like to sleep alone, Ryan."

He raked her with wretched eyes and hotly proclaimed, "It's well I did take you for my wife instead of my mistress. I'd probably have had to find a replacement by now."

Erin gritted her teeth, clenched her fists. "Yes, I suppose it's easier to find another mistress than a wife."

"You aren't very good at either position, my dear." He began to undress.

She retreated, enraged.

Eliza, her ear pressed against the door leading into the hallway, also took her leave. Miss Victoria would be eager to hear how upset Master Ryan was over his wife's refusal to sleep in his bed. It meant they were having trouble, and that was what they were both hoping for between the newlyweds. Miss Victoria would also be very interested to hear how Miss Erin was planning to move her mother into Jasmine Hill.

Erin stewed the rest of the afternoon, trying to decide what she should do. On one hand, she wanted to stay in her room and refuse to come out until Victoria agreed to some kind of meeting between the three of them. But, as the dinner hour approached, her pride would not allow her to hide away as though she were ashamed. Failing to appear would be the same as an admission of guilt. And perhaps more important than anything else was the fact this was her home now, and she had every right to show up at dinner.

Victoria was already seated when Erin went into the dining room. She regarded her new daughter-in-law cooly for a moment as she sipped her wine. Finally, with a smirk touching her lips, she said, "Please wait until Ryan comes in before you apologize for your despicable behavior this morning. I want him to witness."

Erin quietly, calmly, informed her, "There won't be anything for him to witness, Mrs. Youngblood. We both know it was just a misunderstanding. I'd really like to forget it happened, because I want us to get along. I am your son's wife, and—"

"Not for long."

Erin blinked, sure she'd not heard right, but seeing Victoria's smile, the threatening sheen to her eyes, knew there was no mistake. She swayed ever so slightly with shock, for she'd not expected such a threat. "Now wait a minute. You can't—"

"I can. And I will. And get something else straight, Miss Sterling," she added. "I'm not having your trashy mother move in my house. You can get that notion out of your head right now. You won't be living here long enough to make any demands. I promise you that.

"Do you think I want my son married to someone like you? From a family like yours?" Victoria was slowly getting to her feet, her face twisted with rage. "Oh, no, you scheming little trollop. Your days at Jasmine Hill are numbered. You trapped Ryan with lust, but by now he's probably had his fill. He never did stay with one woman very long, so he's no doubt ready to admit he made a mistake. Now that I'm back, I'm ready to do everything I can to help him get out of this mess. You'd be wise, very wise, indeed, just to leave, and—"

"I'm not going anywhere," Erin cut in raggedly, coming out of her stupor to defend herself. "You can't do this to me, to our marriage. I won't let you."

"Oh, can't I?" Victoria challenged. "You'll see. You'll see what power I have over my son."

"Mrs. Youngblood, there's no need for this."

"Perhaps not," Victoria said coldly, thoughtfully. "Perhaps there's an easier way. How much money will it take to get you out of my son's life?"

"You don't have enough money to make me leave Ryan." Before she even realized what she was saying, she blurted, "Regardless of what you think, I happen to be in love with him."

Victoria swayed as though she'd been struck. Another unexpected jolt. And there was no time to think how to react, for she could hear Ryan's footsteps as he came up the hall from his study. Through clenched teeth, she whispered, "You'll wish you'd taken my offer."

Her hand closed about her wineglass, and Victoria suddenly threw the contents into her own face as Erin watched in frozen disbelief. "How dare you?" she began to scream at Erin, wildly swiping at her eyes. "How dare you do such a thing?"

Ryan heard the shrieks and ran the rest of the way to the room. He looked from Erin to his mother, who was soaked in wine. "What the hell is going on here?"

Erin was quick to answer. "She threw it on herself, Ryan, to make you think I did it."

"Are you out of your mind?" Victoria wailed. "Eliza! Eliza, where are you?"

"I'm here, ma'am." Eliza stepped out of the little hallway leading to the service kitchen and promptly cried, aghast, "Lordy, Lordy . . . ," and gave a pitying shake of her head, fighting to keep from smiling, for she'd been listening, had peeked out just in time to see Miss Victoria sling the wine on herself. "Those stains are never going to come out of that gown. Here, let's get you up to your room."

"Yes, please get me out of here," Victoria said dramatically.

The moment they walked out, Erin said furiously, "She's lying again."

"I'm supposed to believe she threw wine in her own face," he murmured incredulously.

"Unless you think I'm the one lying."

"Hell, I don't know what to believe anymore." He ran both hands through his hair, then shook his head in an attempt to clear away the deep pounding that had begun. "I knew there'd be some problems when she got back, but damn it, in one day, there's a goddamn war going on."

"Well, I surely didn't start it."

Suddenly, Victoria burst back into the room, for she had been standing outside eavesdroping. "Oh, yes you did," she exploded. "You started it the instant we met, but don't worry. The war is over, because I surrender. I'm moving out of this house."

Ryan was quick to protest. "Wait a minute. This is all getting out of hand. We need to sit down and talk about it."

"No," Victoria said, tears spilling down her cheeks again. "This isn't my home, anymore. I don't belong here. I can go and live with Cousin Hannah in Richmond. She'll take me in." She left, sobbing wildly.

Erin said tentatively, "Maybe it would be best if she did go and visit her cousin for a while, till we can straighten everything out. She's obviously taking this a lot harder than you thought she would."

He looked at her, stunned. "This is her home, Erin. You think I want to run my mother out of her own home? Jesus! All this is tearing me apart. As I said, you and I had problems of our own without this happening all at once." He slammed out of the room, heading for his study.

Erin started upstairs but changed her mind. She went to him and urged, "We've got to talk about this, Ryan."

He had gone to sit behind his desk, and he looked up at her with wretched eyes. "You know something, Erin?" he asked ruefully, pausing to draw on the cheroot he'd just lit. "I was just sitting here thinking how I don't really know you at all."

"Your mother is lying." She wasn't about to soften the issue. "If you won't believe that, then there's no hope for us, Ryan. No hope that we can ever truly be happy together."

"Was there ever a chance that we could?" he asked with forced sarcasm, not about to let her sense his real misery.

She left him then, because she was afraid that if she didn't, she might unlock her heart—and she did not dare.

Ryan didn't go after her. Instead, he rang for Ebner and told him to go and pack a bag for him, that he would be leaving first thing in the morning for New Orleans. The horse show didn't start for a few more weeks, but he felt that if he didn't get away, far away, and figure out what the hell to do about the maelstrom of his life, he'd explode.

But first, he wrote a letter to Erin, explaining what he had to do—and why. He couldn't just go away without a word. He suggested she go and stay with her mother till he returned. Finally, he confided he did truly care for her. He just needed time to himself to figure out how to deal with it, because he didn't feel she cared for him in return.

The next morning, with hopeful heart that the separation would be good for both of them, he slipped the letter under her door.

Eliza saw the corner of the envelope. It was not quite all the way under Miss Erin's door. Picking it up, she dutifully hurried to take it to Miss Victoria.

CHAPTER

 22

T*HE DAY PASSED WITH AGONIZING SLOWNESS.*
Too angry to leave her room, Erin paced miserably as she
tried to figure out what to do about the maddening situation. She desperately wanted to go check on her mother
but didn't dare leave the house just then.

Annie brought her a breakfast tray, which she didn't
touch. At lunch, because she was starting to feel nause-
ated from not eating, she sipped mint tea and nibbled on
a slice of cornbread, though she really didn't want anything.

She had briefed Annie earlier about the scene the night
before and asked her to be alert for anything going on.
Annie said she knew nothing, but at noon she was able
to report that Miss Victoria was up and about as though
nothing had happened. "Eliza, she had me polish the silver service, 'cause she says Miz Victoria is expectin' Miz
Ermine and her mama for tea this afternoon. And she tol'
the kitchen girls to get some nice cakes and cookies baked
and frosted."

Erin was jolted by that bit of information. Why on
earth would Ryan's former fiancée be making a social call?
Then it dawned on her. Victoria was wasting no time. She

was obviously also not making good her threat to move out of the house. "Have you seen Master Ryan?"

"No ma'am, and I did like you tol' me, I asked Ebner if he knew where he was, and Ebner said he wasn't supposed to say nothin' to nobody about nothin'. But I been lookin' out, like you tol' me, and I ain't seen hide nor hair of him all mornin'."

"Keep watching, Annie. And report back to me if you find him. I've got to talk to him. This madness can't go on."

"Yassum," she mumbled, filled with pity for her mistress. Her fears that there would be bad trouble when Miz Victoria returned were coming true, all right.

It was nearly four o'clock when Annie returned to tell Erin excitedly what she'd been able to find out. "Mastah Ryan is gone, Miz Erin. I talked to one of the stableboys, and he said he left at first light this mornin'. Had a bag with him, strapped on the back of his horse and said he was goin' to New Orleans and didn't know when he'd be back."

Erin couldn't believe he'd go away like that without telling her. She went in search of Ebner. She found him on the back porch, polishing a pair of Ryan's shoes. "Is it true? Did Ryan really leave for New Orleans this morning?"

He saw no harm in admitting what she obviously already knew and confirmed with a nod.

"And he left no message for me? No note? Nothing?"

"Not with me, he didn't. No ma'am." He'd seen Master Ryan writing something when he went to tell him his bag was all packed but wasn't about to say so, because he had no idea what it had been.

Erin was seething. How could he do this to her? Just ride away and abandon her to his angry mother.

Just then, Victoria appeared at the back door. Angrily,

she ordered Erin, "Go upstairs. At once. I'm entertaining guests, and I don't want you around."

Erin yielded to the sudden urge to say, "You know, Mrs. Youngblood, I really feel sorry for you, because we could have been friends. But you don't want it like that. So you go on and have your tea party, and I'll gladly get out of your way."

Victoria laughed. "You'll be out of my way permanently once Ryan comes to his senses. He went to New Orleans to figure out how to get rid of you."

Erin went inside and hurried up to her room, refusing to be goaded into another scene.

She was standing on the veranda when the carriage pulled up in front of the house. She watched as the petite young woman stepped down. She was wearing an olive green dress. Golden curls trailed from her bonnet, and as she happened to glance up, Erin saw she had a lovely heart-shaped face.

Seeing Erin, Ermine turned to murmur something to the older woman who was just alighting. Also elegantly dressed, she regarded Erin coldly, then took Ermine's hand and led her up the steps.

Erin thought about going to the tea party herself and making Victoria miserable, then decided it was a waste of time. She had also realized it was cutting off her nose to spite her face to remain in the house till Ryan returned. She was disappointed and hurt he hadn't taken her as he'd promised, but she knew he was angry, and there was no telling how long he'd stay away. The thing to do was go back and care for her mother, even though she hated the thought of having to be around Zachary.

She told Annie to have a carriage made ready to take her to visit her mother the next day.

It was that very evening, when she'd made her decision

to escape the misery, if only for a little while, that Annie came to her at dusk, excited to report there was a paper rose in the vase on Miss Henrietta's grave.

"That means there's a runaway slave hiding in the labyrinth," Erin told Annie. "And you'll need to go with me to be on the lookout for Eliza or anybody else that might be about."

At once, Annie started swinging her head from side to side. "Oh, no ma'am, Miz Erin, I can't go out there. Not tonight. It's a full moon, and that means Miz Henrietta's ghost is walkin', and I'm scared of ghosts, and—"

"Nonsense." Erin waved away her protests. "It's Eliza you should be scared of. Not ghosts."

"I just can't do it. I just can't. Not when there's a full moon."

Erin knew there was no sense arguing and irritably told her she should be ashamed of herself.

"Can't help it. I ain't goin' around that graveyard when there's a full moon."

Erin went alone. She waited till nearly ten o'clock, to be sure that Victoria would be in her room and asleep. Then she crept out of the house, leaving by the side terrace doors, to run swiftly across the lawn. The night was quiet and eerie, with silver shadows leaping from behind every shrub and tree. The only sound was a barn owl, somewhere far in the distance, and a gentle breeze rustling the magnolia leaves.

Entering the opening of the maze, she stood perfectly still for a moment, waiting for any noise. When there was none, she dared call softly, "Hello, is anyone there? You don't have to be afraid. I'm here to help you."

She heard a soft, anguished moan from deeper within the greenish shadows. Taking a few steps, she gently assured once more, "I'm a friend. I want to help you."

Abruptly, a familiar voice called on a broken sob, "Thank God, Miz Erin. Thank God, you came."

"Ben!" She held her arms open to the dark figure that suddenly loomed. "Ben, what are you doing here?"

"I gotta get away," he gasped, then cried out as she touched him.

"Ben, what is it?" She felt it then, the torn flesh on his back, raked by the lash, the stickiness of blood still oozing. "Damn them to hell, they whipped you!"

"I'm runnin', Miz Erin. I can't take no more. If Letty can make it, so can I. And Mistah Sam, he tol' me to come here if I was afraid to make it along the riverbank, and Lordy, I was. That'd be the first place Mastah Zachary will look fo' me, and I know he knows I'm gone by now, 'cause I been hidin' here since first light this mornin'. I had to wait till dark to put that rose in the pot that Rosa made for me outta paper and chicken blood." He paused for the relief of a nervous laugh before admitting, "I was scairt, too, 'cause I've heard the stories about a ghost a'walkin' there on a full moon, but I'd rather face a ghost anytime than Mastah Zachary, fo' sho'."

"Does Sam Wade know you're here? If not, then I'm going to have to place a rose on the dock, and you're going to have to hide till midnight tomorrow. They won't see the signal till daylight, and—"

"It's all right." He went on to explain that he'd told Sam before hand of the exact time he planned to run away. Sam had promised the boat would be at the pier exactly one hour past midnight, so Erin would have time to get him through to meet it.

"Then let's go." She tugged at his arm. "Stay close behind, and be patient. I've got to count turns and steps and do all kinds of things to remember the right path so we don't wind up hopelessly trapped."

He did as he was told, and just when his heart began

to pound with the fear they were truly lost within the monster hedges, Erin softly cried, "We made it. There it is." She pointed, and in the moonlight, the river danced with thousands of diamond shards. The outline of a boat was barely visible beneath the dying fronds of a weeping willow tree. "You're going to be safe now, Ben. They'll get you north, to Pennsylvania, and you'll be on your way across the ocean to Letty before you know it." She reached for his hand and squeezed happily, confidently.

This time, he did not pull away. He swallowed hard, then dared confide, "Miz Erin, I got to tell you things is bad over there. Rosa said for' me to tell you that if you're gonna get your momma outta there, you best hurry up and do it, 'cause Mastah Zachary, he's gone crazy. Tulwah is using his *wanga* on him, and—"

He was talking so fast, nearly hysterical, and she could not grasp it all. "You've got to speak slower, Ben, and tell me exactly what you mean."

"Tulwah, he's not just a medicine man, Miz Erin. He was a *tonton macoute* in his homeland, and he knows magic, and he's using *wanga* to put spells on Mastah Zachary. And it's workin', too. Rosa, she say he's feelin' poorly, havin' pains and not knowin' why. He beat her the other day and accused her of poisonin' him, and now he won't let nobody fix his food. He fixes it hisself. But she didn't put nothin' in it. Now he don't know it, but Tulwah, he left some hummin' bird meat under his pillow, and that's what made him sick. But he's like a crazy man, she said, and he's bein' real mean to yo' momma. You got to get her out of there."

Enraged, Erin was quick to promise, "Don't worry about anything. I'll take care of her. I'd already planned to go over there tomorrow and stay with her till I can bring her back here."

"No. Not tomorrow. Mastah Zachary, he's gonna be

crazy mad about me runnin' away, and it'll only make things worse if you go. Rosa said to tell you that, too, to wait a few days till he finds out I ain't nowhere around here, and then he'll get a posse together, just like when Letty got away, and then he'll take off. You can go get yo' momma, and Rosa, too, I hope, and get 'em both back here safe and sound before he comes back."

She agreed that made sense, even though she had desperately been looking forward to seeing her mother.

He started from the maze, as the two men in the boat impatiently waved him to get moving. But then he turned back, and in the silver night glow, Erin could see the tears sparkling in his eyes as he fervently whispered, "Jesus bless you, Miz Erin. I'll never forget you."

"And I'll never forget you, Ben. Godspeed." She blew him a kiss and waved him on, holding back her own tears.

Victoria did not sleep well in the room where she'd been moved. Tossing and turning in the unfamiliar surroundings only served to make her even more irate over the situation.

Damn Erin Sterling.

And her mother, too.

After hearing that Erin wanted her to move in, Victoria was sure Arlene Tremayne had been a part of Erin's scheme to get Ryan to marry her.

Hearing the case clock chime twice, Victoria threw back the covers. No need to keep lying there wide awake. What she needed was a little sherry from the bottle she kept hidden under her divan.

Pouring herself a glass, she decided some fresh night air might also relieve her stress and help her fall asleep.

It was a lovely night, but as she stepped onto the veranda that ran around the front and sides of the second floor, she was struck with terror. There, running from the labyrinth, was a figure in white. Her hand went to her throat, and she froze where she stood. She'd heard the slaves' stories about the ghost of Henrietta Youngblood but passed them off as superstitious nonsense. Now, she wasn't so sure, for who would be out there this time of night?

She gripped the railing with trembling hands, then bolted back into the shadows.

Wearing a white robe, Erin was the "ghost" she thought she'd seen on the lawn. Victoria at once admonished herself for allowing her imagination to run away with her, if only for a split second.

But what was she doing out there?

Then it dawned on her.

A man.

The labyrinth would be the ideal place for lovers to meet in secret. Who would think to look there? Perhaps that's what she'd been doing all along, and her infidelity was the reason she avoided sleeping with Ryan.

And now, Victoria realized gleefully, she had a weapon she could use to force Erin to leave. All she had to do was keep an eye on her and actually catch her with her lover. Once confronted, the trollop would have no choice but to pack her bags and get out of Ryan's life once and for all.

Finally, Victoria went to bed, and for the first time since returning home, she slept quite soundly and peacefully.

Nate Donovan looked at Zachary as if he'd lost his mind. In fact, he hoped he had. "I don't think you know what you're sayin'. You're just mad 'cause that slave took off today. But we'll get him. He can't have got far."

Zachary turned up the bottle again, then passed it back

to Nate. They were in his study, and the house was still and quiet. "You're wrong. On both counts."

It was late, but Zachary didn't want to go to bed. Anyway, after the past few nights, he never wanted to crawl in his own bed again as long as he lived. Every night there was something new there. First the cock head. Then a dead bird. And lots of other things. Weird things. And slapping Arlene so hard he split her lip hadn't put a stop to it. Neither had beating the shit out of Rosa.

He turned his attention to Nate once more to voice his fears that he might not be able to find Ben. "Somebody is helping these runaways. Bound to be. Luke Washam had one take off and disappear just last week. Before that, I lost two. There's no way that many could vanish in thin air. And don't forget Letty. She got help once she hit the water. No." He swung his head from side to side in firm resolution. "Something funny is going on, and I got a feeling my high-yeller wife's got somethin' to do with it."

Nate felt a little funny about Zachary confiding that Arlene's grandmother had been a Negro. That was really a shocker, if it was so, but he couldn't imagine a man lying about a thing like that. But wanting to sell her into slavery was another matter entirely, and he couldn't believe Zachary was serious and said so, again.

"Well, I am." Zachary said hotly. "I told you. I been finding stuff under my pillow, under my bed. She's behind the slaves running away, and she's trying to kill me with that voodoo shit. Now I'm tired of jawin' about it. I want it over and done with. So, are you gonna take her and get her to the block, or do I have to find another trader?"

Nate did not have to think long. He figured, what the hell? If he didn't do it, Zachary would find some other trader who would. Besides, it wouldn't be the first time he'd seen a mulatto auctioned off, protesting all the time, because she thought she'd found security at last by marrying a white man and passing for white. But that was different. Those women had known they were taking a chance, and most of them hadn't been married long to start with, and, nine times out of ten the husbands had married them with the intention of having their fill and then selling them off and making some money when they got bored. Arlene Tremayne was a different situation. But no matter. Nate had learned a long time ago not to take a personal interest in any of the human flesh he peddled. "All right," he said finally. "When do you want to do it? I'll need some papers, you know."

"I've got them." Zachary handed over the ownership papers he'd drawn up, as well as the sign-over granting permission to Nate to sell her to the highest bidder. "We do it now. Tonight. I want her out of the house tonight. Then all this voodoo shit will stop, and I can have some peace."

Nate stood, snatched up the papers, and stuffed them in his coat pocket. "Is she asleep?"

"Probably. I haven't heard no sound from up there in awhile. Sometimes she just pretends, though, thinking I won't claim my rights. Hell." He snorted. "Who wants 'em, anyway? All she does is cough and wheeze."

"Did you ever think it might be best to just leave things as they are and maybe she'll go on and die?"

"Meanwhile, I have to sleep with cock heads and dead birds? Hell, no. Get her out of here. Now." He settled back in his chair and this time poured himself a drink from the bottle instead of turning it up to his lips. He wanted to savor the taste of the liquor, while he savored the moment of triumph in removing the bane from his life.

"I'll call Jason in to help. He's waiting outside. We'll gag her, throw a bag over her head, and haul her off. I'd like to make tracks before anybody finds out what's going on."

Arlene awoke as the foul-smelling rag was stuffed in her mouth, and before she could even attempt to struggle, a large bag was slipped over head and shoulders, reaching all the way to her waist. Arms went about her, pinning her own down, so it was futile to resist, even if she'd been able to muster the strength. It was so much easier to let the cloak of terror take her gently away to oblivion.

Zachary grinned as he heard Nate and Jason leave the house. A few seconds later, he heard the sound of them riding away.

It was over.

He was rid of her forever.

And now he could stop worrying about the goddamn *wanga* and *obeah* and all that nonsense. With their priestess out of the way, the slaves would calm down. Maybe he would have a few beaten at the stake tomorrow just to set an example that all the mumbo jumbo was over and done with, and he'd tolerate no more.

He took one last sip of the whiskey in celebration, but nearly choked as he swallowed.

The sound seemed to explode all around him at once, and for a horrified instant, he thought it was all right there in the room. Covering his ears with his hands, he staggered to his feet, whirling around, staring in terror at each and every shadow.

The drums continued. Strong. Rhythmic. A throbbing beat like an avenging, pounding heart.

Voodoo drums.

From deep in the swamps, where he'd never be able to find them.

Zachary ran to his gun cabinet, took out all his weapons, and piled them in front of him as he crouched in a corner. There, he would spend the night in readiness, and if any of the black demons came after him, he'd blast them to the hell they'd come from.

The drums beat even louder.

And soon, Zachary's screams became their relentless echo in the night.

CHAPTER

 23

WITH EACH WORD VICTORIA SPOKE, ELIZA'S knowing grin grew ever wider. At last, she cried, "That's why she was in Master Ryan's study, snooping around in his desk. I saw her there. One day before you came home. She was looking at a paper and seemed to be drawing something at the same time."

"That's it. The diagram of the labyrinth." Victoria felt a sweeping wave of triumph. "Ryan used to love to have parties where guests would try to make their way through, remember? If anyone got lost deep within one of the intricate pathways, he'd have to check his map to find the way. He'd memorized the way to the center and out the other side to the river, just like his father did, but there are so many different corridors and trails in that mammoth growth of hedges that no one could remember each and every turn. Now we know that's what Erin did. She copied his map, memorized the way to the center, then gave it to her lover so he could find his way in from the river.

"Oh, Eliza!" She gave her treasured servant an impulsive hug. "Don't you see? This explains everything. It's all so clear now. Erin schemed with her lover, and her mother, to make Ryan marry her. She wants to move her mother in here, and the two of them will take over. Erin will be stealing money from Ryan to give to her lover, and who knows what else she's plotting and scheming to do?" She gave a shudder of exaggerated horror. "Why, they might even be planning to murder all of us and make it look accidental so they can take over Jasmine Hill before Ryan gets back."

Eliza thought she was getting carried away but didn't dare say so, offering instead, "What do you want me to do?"

"I want you to watch her constantly. Day and night. Every time she leaves her room, I want you to let me know, because I'm going to follow her, and if I can catch her with her lover, whoever he is, I'll confront her then and there and force her to leave. And she'll do it. Because she knows when I tell Ryan, he'll kick her out himself."

"What about when he comes back?"

Victoria's brows drew together. "What about it?"

Eliza was reluctant to point out, "Maybe he won't want her to leave. Maybe he'll just want her to stop doing what she's doing."

They were on the sun porch, and Victoria was finishing her morning coffee. With an airy wave, she dismissed such a ridiculous notion. "He'd want nothing more to do with her, but the important thing is to get her out of here before he comes back and finds out himself and kills both of them. He has a terrible temper, you know."

Again, Eliza knew to keep silent. Despite her loyalty to her mistress, she had the utmost respect for Master Ryan, as did all the servants. They obeyed him because they liked him, and he never had to raise his voice or use the whip. He was forceful and imposing, but gentle and kind. In a way, she even regretted what she was helping to do, for in the past weeks she'd come to feel that despite the tension between the newlyweds, there was also a caring. She hadn't realized that fact till she'd seen him the

morning he left. He had come through the service
kitchen, and though she'd regarded him as distantly as always, she had taken note of the expression on his face.
Sadness. Grief. Confusion. His shoulders were slumped.
He was the image of a man whose spirit had been broken,
his dreams dashed. But Eliza reminded herself she had to
remember how much she also liked Miss Ermine. Miss
Ermine would always let her be in charge of the household. Miss Erin would probably give the duties to that
nit-headed Annie, if she could. No, she silently, solemnly
resolved, with a determined lift of her chin as she poured
her mistress one last cup of coffee, Miss Victoria knew
what she was doing, and Eliza would, as always, do whatever was required of her to assist.

"What I have to do now," Victoria said, taking her cup
and preparing to go back into the house proper, "is find
that diagram myself so I can follow her next time. While
I'm doing that, you go upstairs and position yourself to
watch her door."

It proved to be a very long day for Eliza. There was a
shadowed recess in the wall, halfway down the hall, where
a statue stood on a pedestal. Behind that, Eliza was forced
to hide, for it was the perfect vantage point to see the
stairs, as well as all three doors leading into the master
suite.

She watched as Annie brought a lunch tray. When
she did not come out of the room right away, Eliza dared
leave her hiding place and tiptoe to stand outside the door
and listen. But they were speaking in hushed tones, and
she could not make out what they were saying. Disgruntled, she returned to the little alcove, lest one of the
other household servants happen by and catch her eavesdroping.

Erin told Annie about Ben running away, and Annie listened in wide-eyed fright. She'd heard of many slaves fleeing of late, heard the rumors that many more were planning to do so. Most, it was whispered, belonged to Zachary Tremayne, and she boldly said as much to her mistress.

"I'm not surprised. I know how they've suffered, and that's why I'm risking everything to help them, Annie. I wish you'd feel the same way and get over your fear of ghosts, for heaven's sake."

"I'll try," Annie promised lamely.

"Tomorrow, no matter what, we're going to see my mother. I'm going to stay a few days with her, and I don't care what Mrs. Youngblood thinks."

Annie grunted. "She'll probably lock the door the minute you walk out and not let you back in."

"Then I'd just wait till Ryan returns."

Annie dared to warn, "There just ain't no tellin' what that woman might do. She's evil to the core."

Erin agreed but thought it best to keep it to herself.

When Eliza saw Annie with the tapestry bags, she rushed to inform Miss Victoria that Erin was getting ready to go somewhere.

Victoria was sitting at Ryan's desk, studying the diagram of the labyrinth. "That means she's going to slip away and spend some time with her lover while Ryan is away. No doubt, she'll say she's going to stay with her mother, but I'll be right behind her all the way. She won't know she's walking into a trap, because the instant they rendezvous, I'll have her right where I want her.

"But go back and keep watch," she added, "because she may sneak out during the night. If she leaves her room, you come and find me, no matter what time it is."

Eliza blinked wearily. She ached all over from standing

on her feet for so many hours. "You want me to stay there the rest of the day?"

"And the night, too, Eliza. Who else can I trust? Now get back up there. She could have slipped out while you were in here."

The afternoon passed slowly. Eliza felt as though her legs would no longer support her. She had made sure the rest of the household staff had chores to do that would keep them on the main floor, but still she was afraid to venture out of hiding. Surely, she prayed wearily, her mistress did not expect her to keep watch throughout the night.

When she left her post long enough to serve supper, Victoria was furious. "I told you to stay there."

Eliza could stand no more. "I been there since this morning," she reminded her mistress, on the verge of tears. Lord, she was tired, snatching only a bite of corn-bread when she'd gone up the last time. She'd not even had time to go to the outhouse, and her stomach was grip-ing with the urge. She unleashed her complaints and pro-tests and finished to beg, "Please. Can I just go outside for a while, tend to myself, and have some food?"

"Oh, be gone with you." Victoria shoved back her plate and stood. "I'll go watch. Take ten minutes. No more."

Victoria had not been in place long when she heard footsteps rushing up the stairs. It was nearly dark out, and only a faint light was filtering through the window above the doorway to illumine the stairs. She could see it was Annie coming up, and she ran down the hall, passing right by her without seeing her in the shadows, of course. Victoria was stunned to see she didn't bother to knock on Erin's door but burst right in.

She was even more puzzled to hear her cry excitedly, "A rose, Miz Erin. I found it at the grave."

Victoria then peered out to see Erin reach to snatch the girl inside the room as she anxiously warned, "Hush! Someone might hear . . ." Then the door closed, and Victoria couldn't hear anything else.

Annie did not stay inside long, and as Victoria watched her go back downstairs, she toyed with the idea of having Eliza interrogate her about what was going on. A rose, she had said. At the grave. She had to mean Henrietta Youngblood's grave, because the slaves never ventured near the large family cemetery. But it made no difference where she had found it. The puzzle was that summer was long over. Fall had descended. And winter was right around the corner. There just weren't any more roses in bloom.

Slowly, it began to dawn on her. The rose was probably not real and was a signal of some sort. Of course. The rose meant Erin was to meet someone in the labyrinth. But when? She heard another movement on the stairs just then, saw that it was Eliza, and rushed to meet her and draw her in the opposite direction to her room.

Once inside, Victoria told her what she suspected. "Now you get back there and watch, and don't you dare fall asleep or take your eye off that door for an instant," she said sharply. "The minute she leaves, you come tell me, and I'll be dressed and ready to follow her. Do you understand?"

"Yes ma'am." Eliza wished for the first time she had never gotten involved in any of this. She was now expected to keep vigil all night long, if need be. She found herself suddenly wishing she weren't the head servant, could join the others in the compound for an evening of companionship. They were all gathering to cook a catfish stew in a big cauldron of hot fat. She knew, because she'd heard some of the women talking about how they needed to peel onions and potatoes and roll out some dumplings to add to the pot likker. Someone would play a banjo and there'd be singing and Eliza swallowed against a lump in her throat to think of the fellowship she would miss out on, as she had for so many years. Long ago, she'd crossed that invisible line and chosen loyalty to her white mistress over allegiance to her own people.

And she could not go back.

Erin's heart was pounding louder with each ticking of the clock. She hadn't expected another runaway so soon and hoped it wasn't going to become a nightly occurrence. If so, she'd have to contact Sam Wade and have him make other arrangements. It was too risky for her to slip out of the house every night. She had to send word to him, anyway, that she'd be staying at her mother's for a few days, so he could have someone else watch for the signal.

Just a few minutes before midnight, Erin made her way silently through the house. All was quiet. It was a cloudy night, so the moon gave scant light. Fortunately she knew her way.

Stepping between the opening in the hedges, she repeated her call of the night before. This time, however, there was no answer. Apprehensive, she went farther in, again softly calling out, but only silence, tense and thick amidst the shrubbery, prevailed.

She knew then it had to mean someone was waiting in the center. Hoping it would be Sam, she began to pace and count and find her way in the dark.

When she reached the clearing, there was enough light for her to distinguish shadows, and when one of them moved, her instinct was to retreat within the maze till it identified itself. But before she took even a step, Sam called to her.

The moon had slipped momentarily from behind a

cloud as she rushed to greet him. "Thank God, it's you. I was going to send a message to you by Rosa tomorrow, because I'm going to be over there for a few days, and—" She fell silent as she read in his expression something that filled her with cold dread. "What is it? Something's happened. I can feel it. My mother! Is she—"

"I honestly don't know. I can't get on your stepfather's property to find out what's going on in there. Did you hear the drums last night?"

She nodded fearfully. "What did it mean?"

"Trouble. That's all I can tell you. At first, I thought maybe it had something to do with Ben running away, but Mahalia told me today it was a message that there was big trouble at Zachary's. So I went by there. But I couldn't get past the front gate. One of his overseers stopped me. Said they weren't letting any outsiders in. I asked why, and all he would tell me was that they'd had some trouble with the slaves, and Zachary was getting a posse together."

"Then I've got to get there right away, in case Mother needs me."

"I agree. If there is an emergency, and you need to get in touch with me, I'll be making my regular stops in the north part of the county. The Siddons place. The Bartons. You know where they live."

She nodded.

"I usually camp out at the Bartons. There's a cotton-wood grove overlooking the river, and the slaves know they can find me there around this time. They slip in during the night to fill me in on anything they think I need to know. If you want to find me, or get a message to me, that's where I'll be tomorrow night."

"I'll leave at first light. I'd already planned to go."

"Good. Now you'd better get back inside before your husband misses you."

Ruefully, she said that was no problem. "He's gone. I don't know when he'll be back."

"Is something wrong?"

"His mother has returned from her trip. She wasn't at all happy over finding out about our marriage. I knew it would upset her, but I had no idea how much."

"It will work out. You'll see. Now do you mind if I walk along with you? I didn't come by way of the river. My cart is about a mile down the road from your house."

"Of course," she murmured, not really listening, for she was lost in thought. She was terribly worried about her mother but also grieving with wanting Ryan to be with her. She needed him, and found herself desperately wishing she had let him know that.

Eliza had decided there was no reason to keep standing in the darkness. No one was around, and she just couldn't resist sitting down to rest her weary legs. Leaning her head back against the wall, she closed her eyes and promised herself she wouldn't fall asleep, just rest for a few precious moments.

She sat straight up, realizing with a start that she had fallen asleep. Groggily struggling to her feet, she was further disturbed by the feeling that she'd been dozing for more than just a few moments. What if Miss Erin had slipped out during that time? She couldn't take a chance, had to make sure she was still in her room.

Hurrying to her door, she eased it open. It was difficult to make out anything in the darkness, but she could tell, with a jolt, that no one was in the bed. A check of the adjoining parlor, and even Master Ryan's room, confirmed the growing terror that she had sneaked out.

She was trembling to think how Miss Victoria would never forgive her for falling sleep and letting this happen. And while she might have to report to her Miss Erin had got away, she wasn't about to let her know just when, and how.

She rushed to her bedroom to shake her awake. "She's on her way. She just went down the steps. And she's moving fast. You might not be able to catch her."

Victoria was up in a flash and running out on the veranda. At the corner, she strained to see in the moonlight and whispered, "She's probably headed for the labyrinth. I memorized the map, and I'll go in and try to catch her with him, and—oh, no!" She gasped.

Eliza saw them, too, and her heart sank to her toes.

In the scant light of the moon-tinged clouds, they could make out two figures emerging from the maze. A man and a woman. The man embraced the woman briefly, then broke into a run along the front line of foliage and disappeared around the corner. The woman lifted her hem to hurry across the lawn, coming toward the house.

Victoria's sharp nails dug into Eliza's flesh as she grabbed her arm and pulled her along quickly, quietly, in the shadows of the veranda toward her room. Once inside, with doors closed, she slapped Eliza hard. "You lied. She left long ago. You fell asleep, didn't you? Damn your worthless hide, I ought to have you whipped."

Eliza had begun to cry, backing away as she begged forgiveness. "I didn't mean to. I was just so tired, and I'd been standing there all day and half the night, and—"

"Shut up! I've no time for your sniveling. Now you get back out there and keep watch, and don't you dare fall asleep again, you stupid cow. I want to know at once if she starts out of this house again tonight. If she doesn't, wake me at first light, so I can follow her when she does go. She didn't have Annie pack those bags without reason. She's planning something for sure.

"And another thing," she commanded. "You tell Annie

in the morning she is not to serve Erin again. None of the slaves are to serve her. Do you understand?"

With bowed head, Eliza murmured, "Yes ma'am."

"Now get out of here. I may have you whipped yet."

Anxious to escape her wrath, Eliza ran out.

When she was in her position in the alcove, she was far too angry even to think about being tired. It was the first time Miss Victoria had ever struck her. The first time she'd ever cursed her, called her names. Eliza thought she deserved better, even if she was a slave, after so many years of dogged loyalty.

Bitter, hurt, filled with resentment, Eliza resolved never to forget this night.

Ryan stood at the ship's railing and stared down into the rolling sea. His horse was stabled in the hold, along with those of other owners who wanted their own horses when they reached their destination. In a few days he would arrive in New Orleans. He planned to stay for two weeks, maybe longer. He'd buy the stock he wanted—two mares and a stallion—then bring them back with him. He figured he could manage pulling the trio from Norfolk to Richmond.

Once he'd taken care of business in New Orleans, there would be a few days for pleasure. He liked the food and drink, the gambling, the women. . . .

He laughed ruefully, there in the darkness. The women, indeed. He had left behind the only woman he would ever want, could ever love.

It was a few moments later when the fragrance of perfume came to him just before he saw the girl step out of the shadows and into the scant light. He knew right away what she was—a fancy girl, her kind were called. Slave girls. Mulattoes, most of them. Owned by the shipping lines. They were painted up, dressed in revealing gowns, and placed discreetly on board for the pleasure of male passengers—for a price. Ryan had indulged in the pleasant diversion many times. A warm body to share the narrow bed in his tiny cabinet, to please him in any way he demanded, at his beck and call. When she wasn't servicing him or other men, she would stay out of sight. It angered the ladies to know prostitutes were on the ship.

"It's so sad to be alone on such a lovely night," she cooed, boldly twining her arm about his, brushing her breast against him. "Have you need of a woman to keep you company?"

Ryan felt a stirring in his loins. Hell, he made no apology for being a man. Yet, he knew that just as it was Erin's face he saw dancing there in the silver-splashed waters, he would search for her, too, in the arms of another woman. There could be no real pleasure in pretense. Maybe, in time, his hunger would get the best of him, and he'd yield to temptation. For the time being, he wanted no substitute. It was like craving champagne, only to be served cheap wine. Gently he dismissed her. "No thanks. I'd rather be alone."

When rejected, her orders were to melt away into the night, silently, quietly. She did so.

And he was left alone with his memories of passion unequaled.

CHAPTER

 24

As ERIN APPROACHED THE MAIN GATE OF ZA-
chary's plantation, there was no guard in sight. It was just
as well. She was in no mood for a confrontation. Learning
that Victoria had forbidden Annie, as well as any other
slave at Jasmine Hill, to do her bidding was frustrating
enough, without being denied the use of a carriage. It was
only because the stable hands had not dared stop her, that
she'd even been able to take a horse. Leaving her bags behind, she'd mounted bareback for the ride, silently vowing to borrow one of Zachary's wagons later and come
back for them.

All seemed quiet, and strange, as though an invisible
pall had descended. She could feel the tension in the air,
could see it in the way the few workers in the fields refused
to look at her as she passed. Something was wrong. She
could feel it in her bones. She quickened her pace.

She rode all the way to the front steps and had just dismounted when an overseer hurried up from the field closest to the house. He was carrying a whip, and she noticed
he was wearing double-holstered guns. He was not familiar to her, but then the only one of Zachary's overseers
she knew was Frank, and he was nowhere about.

"Hey, who are you?" he yelled curtly. "What do you want? Tremayne don't want no strangers here."

Instinctively she didn't like him, felt her ire rising over how his ferretlike eyes lingered on her bosom. "I'm hardly a stranger. Unfortunately, he's my stepfather."

"Oh, so you must be—" he paused, gave a nasty-sounding laugh, "yeah, I know who you are, all right."

She started up the stairs. He wasn't worth the effort it would take to rebuke him.

"Ain't nobody in there."

She spun around, felt a sudden chill of foreboding. "Where is everyone?"

"Zach run everybody out and says he ain't goin' back in there himself till we beat all that voodoo-*obeah* shit outta the slaves. He's sick of blood and feathers and dog's teeth and all that stuff they use to try to scare him to death. Me, I don't believe in it. But like last night, when they get to beatin' them goddamn drums all over, it's enough to scare even a nonbeliever."

Erin blinked at him, bemused. "What are you talking about?"

"The slaves decided to try a little voodoo on him. Led by your mother, he believes, and—"

"Where is she?"

"Hell, I don't know. Ask Zach. He's over at the stable gettin' ready to go after another runaway. Says this time he's gonna chop a foot off to set an example to the others, and. . . ." He fell silent, stared after her as she took off running. Well, he didn't have time to mess with her, anyway, even if it was a real pleasure just to look at her. He'd heard she was a beauty, and now he knew it was so.

He turned back to the field.

Victoria watched from the grove of trees just across the road from the gate. She had carefully stayed far enough behind Erin so she wouldn't know she was being followed. Now, however, it seemed the moment of reckoning was at hand, when she could let her know she was aware of her infidelity to her son. She had seen her talking to the white man with the whip. Was that Zachary Tremayne? Heavens, she didn't know, wouldn't recognize the dreadful man, anyway, for she knew him only by his infamous reputation.

She waited until Erin disappeared inside the stable, then kicked her horse into a slow canter. Her lover was probably waiting inside, she figured, and maybe she could catch them in the throes of a torrid embrace. Erin could never lie her way out of that. She felt a shiver of anticipation. Ermine had confided she would be willing to give Ryan a chance to come to his senses but would not wait for long. Ansel Bancroft had proposed, and she could not postpone giving him an answer. Well, she wouldn't have to. After this day, Victoria was confident Erin Sterling would be out of Ryan's life forever and always.

In the field, hoe in hand, Rosa dared steal a glance at Erin as she headed for the stable. Her eyes stung with tears of sympathy and sadness. It was going to just about kill her when she heard what had happened to her momma— if Master Zachary told her the truth. There was no telling what an evil man like that might do. She wouldn't put it past him to be planning to say Miz Arlene had died and maybe he even had an empty grave made up to show her as the resting place. Oh, Lordy, how she wished she could have done something that night to save her, but by the time she'd crept out of her hiding place in that pantry and up the back stairs to find out what that strange noise was, it was just too late.

There were two men, one of them carrying a lantern. By its glow, she'd seen that they'd put a bag over Miz Arlene's head and were carrying her off. She recognized one of them—Nate Donovan, his name was. She knew, because he sometimes came to see Mastah Zachary, and one of the other kitchen workers had told her he was a terrible man. It was said he bought slaves smuggled in from Africa, which was supposed to be against the law.

But she could only watch in stricken horror, helpless. There was no need to go screaming for Mastah Zachary. He was in his study, and she'd seen him talking to that Donovan man earlier, when she went to ask if there was anything else he needed before she left for the night. He couldn't help hearing Miz Arlene trying to cry out through that bag. He knew what was going on all right. He'd been acting stranger and stranger, anyway, since Tulwah had started using his *wanga* to cast a spell on him, and she'd worried it would all go too far. As she watched in terror as Miz Arlene was taken away, she knew her worst fears had come true.

She had then left the house and run down the path to the compound as fast as she could to spread the word. The drums had started, calling Tulwah out of the swamp. When she told him what had happened, his eyes had begun to glow like angry coals. A growling sound came from deep down in his throat, and when it finally exploded from his lips, it had chilled her to the bone. He had started swaying to and fro as if he were in a trance.

Then they had heard Master Zachary yelling all the way from the great house. From fear, he'd melded to anger, and he'd gathered his men to charge down to the compound to stop the drums. They began to whip and beat every slave in sight, and, seeing Tulwah as he melted into the swamp, Zachary screamed to kill him. His men had started to go after him but drew back as the rhythm of the drums ignited the world around them, like wildfire leaping from tree top to tree top.

At dawn, Master Zachary had ordered all the slaves to the fields, to work till dark or feel the lash. He was going to find Ben, and Rosa prayed with every beat of her heart that Tulwah would somehow work his magic and cause him to drop dead before he and his slave-hunting posse could do so.

Her attention turned once more to Miss Erin, as she disappeared from sight. If only she could speak to her, tell her what she'd seen—

"You! Lazy wench!"

Rosa screamed as the lash popped only inches from her face.

"Stop your eyeballin' and get to work or you'll feel it on your back next time."

Rosa started digging with the hoe and ducked her head just as she caught a glimpse of the white woman slowly coming up the main road. She wondered who the woman was but dared not look that way any longer.

Zachary was in the tack room, which he sometimes used as a meeting place for his men. They were gathered about him. He was showing them the coastal area on the map where they were heading, the spot where it was rumored fugitive slaves were smuggled on board boats heading north. Glancing up when Erin stormed in, his men instinctively backed away from him.

"Well, well," Zachary greeted her with a sneer. "Have you finally come home to let your daddy kiss the bride?"

A ripple of laughter went through the others. Erin silenced them with a sweeping glare, then turned her full wrath on Zachary. "You aren't my father. I'm ashamed you're even my stepfather. Now where's my mother?"

A few of the men cautiously began to move by her, heading out, not wanting to be around for the explosion sure to come.

Zachary motioned to the rest to go. He didn't want them hearing Erin's insolence. He called to Frank, "Lead 'em on out of here. You know where to head. I'll catch up with you as soon as I take care of this."

Erin waited till they were alone before repeating her question more forcefully, "I asked you where my mother is, and I want to know. Now!"

Zachary flashed an evil grin as he tapped a finger to his forehead and pretended to ponder, "Well, let's see. They left just before midnight last night. I'd say they're a pretty far piece down the road by now, but I'm not going to tell you which direction. Not that you could catch up with them, anyway."

Erin was cold with fear. "If you don't start making sense—"

"You'll do what?" he challenged. "The best thing for you to do is stop worrying about your moma, because she's gone, and you can't do anything to get her back. The thing you best concern yourself with is making sure that rich husband you and her managed to snag for you don't find out the truth and do the same thing with you that I done to her."

Erin shook her head in disgust. "I'm not going to stand here and listen to this nonsense. I'm just going to ride into Richmond and ask the sheriff to come out here. Maybe you'll talk to him." Her knees were knocking together, and she felt anything but brave as she started for the door. It was obvious he wasn't going to tell her anything, and she was wasting time listening to him. Something awful had happened to her mother. She could feel it in her heart.

"The sheriff won't help no high yeller."

"You just don't stop trying to hurt me, do you?" she asked incredulously. "First you drag Letty off to be sold, because she was in the way of your trying to sneak into my room, but thank God, she escaped. Then you won't tell me where my mother's gone, just to worry me, and now you're making up lies. If I didn't loathe you so much, Zachary, I'd feel sorry for you. But the truth is, you're a contemptible bastard, and I hope the *obeah* succeeds in giving you what you deserve."

His eyebrows shot up. "I mighta known you had something to do with that, too, that you and your momma were in on it together. But it's not going to work. I've got orders out to kill that witch doctor, Tulwah, on sight, and when he's dead, I'm going to hang him by his heels from the whipping post and let the crows eat his eyes out, so the others can watch him rot and see what happens when anybody dares try voodoo on my land.

"As for you, you arrogant little bitch—" He began to move toward her, stepping around the table as she backed away. "If you don't want Ryan Youngblood to find out he's married to a mulatto, you'd best sweeten up to me and give me what I've had a hankerin' for all these years." He began to unfasten his pants. "So you just get them clothes off and lay down on that straw in that stall right behind you and spread them long, pretty legs of yours."

Erin was only slightly terrified by his physical threat. The real horror washing over her came from his words, so easily spoken, as though he actually believed them himself. "You're lying," she protested shakily. "You don't know what you're talking about."

"The hell I don't," he sneered. "Your momma told me about her grandmother being a Negro before we got married, 'cause she said she didn't want no secrets between us. It didn't matter then, not as bad as I wanted her. It was only later, when the fire cooled, that I realized what a fool I'd been and started worryin' about how if we had younguns, they might be colored.

"How come you think she had you wash all the time

in that special water she mixed up?" he went on to taunt. She continued to back away from him, horror mirrored in her eyes as she began to believe he might be telling the truth. "That was supposed to keep your skin light. Worked, too, didn't it? Nobody thought nothing, except you had natural dark coloring. Pretty little bitch, you are, too. Just about the prettiest mulatto I've ever seen. I imagine you fire up Youngblood, too, but I doubt he'll like the idea that you might just one day present him with a son that's black as the ace of spades. That happens sometimes, you know. Blood turns around in generations."

Erin felt the roaring within as she realized that whether or not what he was saying was true, he believed it to be, and that had to have something to do with whatever had happened to her mother. "What have you done with her?" Washed with rage, she looked about wildly for a weapon. He stealthily continued his advance. Blindly, she'd backed into the stall and found herself trapped. And, strangely, in that hysterical moment, she wished for Ryan, knew this would not be happening if he were there. Only he wasn't, and she had to defend herself.

Behind Zachary, she saw the pitchfork leaning against the wall but couldn't get to it.

"I won't say anything," he promised with a hungry grin. "And he'll never know. All you got to do is be nice to me. Just this once. I'll keep your secret just like I kept your momma's. But you might like it. You might find me more of a man than Youngblood, and you'll want more. . . ."

Erin felt sick to her stomach with fear as well as revulsion. With her back pressed against the rough wooden wall, she was trapped.

" 'Course there's the chance he'll hear how I sold her off, because she dared use that voodoo shit, but I'll deny everything if he asks, just for you. I'll say she ran off with another man." He gave a vicious grunt as he suddenly leapt on her, wrestling her to the straw floor, hoarsely crying, "If you don't want to take 'em off, goddamn it, I'll rip 'em off. I don't have all day. I got a runaway to go after, and I've waited long enough—"

Erin fought with all her strength, kicking, biting, scratching, thrashing from side to side as he ripped at her clothes. Her struggles only served to excite him all the more. Around them, horses stamped in their stalls, snorting, rearing up in their own kind of terror over the humans grappling with each other.

Victoria bit down on the fist she had crammed into her mouth to stifle her horrified gasps. The stupor that had held her captive as the shock washed over her slowly released its grip. Her son had married a mulatto. No matter how thin the blood, the thought that her grandchild would not be of pure blood and defined lineage was too repulsive even to contemplate. Dear Lord, she realized with a fresh wave of dismay, if what Zachary Tremayne had said were true, and he had, indeed, sold Arlene into slavery, then Erin was now the daughter of a slave. And by law, Ryan had the right to sell her, too, and, oh, the whole situation was dizzying. She couldn't think straight but knew she had to get out of there as fast as possible.

She ran down the path, to where she'd left her horse. All she wanted to do was get as far away as fast as possible, before the screams of rage lunged from the very pit of her soul.

From the corner of her eye, Rosa saw the woman running away as if the devil himself was right on her heels. She had seen the men mount and ride off, but something cold struck her just then. No doubt, it was her own *obeah* again, the spirit of good rising to defend against evil, to destroy, if need be, and she sensed, knew, Erin was in trouble. The overseer had his back turned just then, and as the others purposely ignored her, she began to creep stealthily from the field. When she reached the path that led to the stable, she broke into a run, and, as she got closer, could hear Erin's cries for help.

In her panic, she stumbled and pitched forward, felt the flesh tear from her hands and knees. Daring to glance back as she staggered to her feet, she was grateful that the overseer had not yet missed her.

Plunging into the barn, she followed the sounds and reached the stall in time to see Zachary slam his fist into Erin's face. She lay very still then, and he was jerking her legs apart for his full assault upon her body.

Without thinking what she was doing, Rosa saw the pitchfork hanging on the wall and snatched it down. Holding it high, ready to plunge into Zachary's back, she screamed. He turned just in time to thrust himself upward, catching her knees with his shoulder and sending her sprawling backward.

"Try to kill me, will you? You goddamn wench!" He tore the pitchfork from her and, as fast as the wink of an eye, drove it into her stomach and jerked it out again.

Erin had stirred as Rosa's terrified scream split the air, and she flashed to consciousness in time to see Zachary make ready once more to plunge the silver prongs downward. She was on him in a flash, flinging herself against his back and reaching around to gouge her fingers into his eyes. He dropped the tool. In painful desperation he sought to yank her hands away. He swung, striking the side of her head. She fell backward, but he had lost his balance, dropped the pitchfork, and when he fell to the side, a sharp steely prong pierced his cheek.

With a yowl of pain and a gush of blood, he freed himself, staggered to his feet, and ran from the barn.

Stricken, Erin gathered Rosa in her arms, not knowing what to do. The blood was pouring from her stomach. Sobbing, she vowed, "You'll be all right. I'll get Tulwah, and he'll take care of you. Just be calm, and still."

"No, Miz Erin," Rosa whispered faintly, a crimson trickle at one corner of her mouth. Her eyes were glazing over, and she couldn't focus, couldn't see the face of the young girl she'd loved ever since Erin was little. "It's almost over, child. I'm goin' home. But you find your momma. They took her away. . . ."

Erin pleaded, "Don't try to talk now, Rosa, please."

"Got to talk, 'cause you got to find her. That trader, Donovan. He's the one you gotta find. But you got to get out of here now. The mastah, he'll hurt you bad. You got to run."

Erin shook her head. She wasn't about to leave Rosa, no matter her own danger. She also knew Zachary was hurt bad, and he'd be no threat. Not for a while, anyway. "I'm going to get help for you—"

"No!" Feebly, but with determination, Rosa reached out to touch her cheek in farewell. "I'm goin' now, and so are you. Far away. 'Cause you wore gray on your weddin' day, Miz Erin, and that means you'll go a long, long way . . . and you'll find your momma. I know you will. . . ."

Her head rolled to one side, eyes frozen in death.

Erin felt herself slipping away, the throbbing pain in her head from Zachary's blows becoming more intense. Her vision was becoming blurred, and there was anguish in her side from where he'd kicked her as she fought him. There was nothing more she could do for Rosa, so she concentrated on getting away before he came back.

But where could she go?

Would Ryan even want her if he knew the truth about her heritage? Oh, dear God, she prayed so, for in the moment of reckoning, as Rosa had slipped away, and her own life seemed to ebb before her, she knew with stark, cold, awareness just how much she did love him.

But now it might be too late for him ever to know that.

She reached out and caught the railing, pulled herself to her feet. Sam Wade would help. All she had to do was make it back to her horse and ride to where he was camped. But the effort was too much. Finally her knees buckled, and her legs gave way.

She slumped back down into the bloodied straw, falling beside Rosa's lifeless body.

Drifting to merciful, peaceful oblivion, Erin was not aware of the footsteps creeping from the shadows.

CHAPTER

 25

E<small>*RIN STRUGGLED TO AWAKEN, TO PULL FREE OF*</small> the cobwebs that seemed to hold her captive. Her head was pounding and there was a terrible ache in her jaw, and she didn't know why.

She also had no idea where she was.

Despite the pain, she managed to sit up and glance around. She seemed to be in a crude hut of some sort. The air was a bit fetid, and damp, and she could smell the richness of the earth beneath her pallet of straw and corn stalks.

Through a small opening a few feet away, a flickering campfire could be seen. She could tell it was nighttime, but not by the sky, for a sentineled ring of trees and scrub brush shut out any glimpse of horizon. It was the monotonous drone of the crickets and tree frogs that told her the day had long since ended.

As she tried to figure out what it all meant, something else needled amidst the throbbing in her brain. It was a darkness looming, slowly changing to a hazy cloud, transcending to a whispering mist, and, finally, a swirling haze that parted into stark reality. A cry escaped her as the macabre scene reappeared in her anguished mind—Zachary's brutal attack, Rosa's tragic death.

Covering her face with her hands, she sank back to the ground and allowed her grief to take her away in painful lament. But she cried only for Rosa, not Zachary's taunting of her mixed blood. That made no difference, not to her, anyway, for she was the same person she'd always been. So was her mother, God help her, whatever her cruel fate might be.

"Oh, God, does the injustice never end?" she wailed out loud, lost in her misery.

"No, my child. Not till freedom begins." Tulwah moved from the shadows, where he'd been sitting, waiting for her to awaken.

Startled but unafraid, she realized then where she must be—the swamp and Tulwah's hideaway. She glanced up at him through laced fingers and asked, "You brought me here? But why?"

"To save you from the devil." He touched gentle fingertips to her swelling beneath her left eye. He had made a poultice for her bruises out of boiled dogwood bark and toadskin shavings and applied it off and on throughout the day. There was some discoloration, he noted, which would probably get worse before it got better. He went on to tell her of the danger that now existed for her. "Tremayne was injured by one of the pitchfork prongs that killed Rosa. He's sworn revenge on you."

"On me?" she scoffed, incredulous. "What about revenge on him for murdering Rosa?"

"There's no punishment for a man killing his own slave. You know that. I've heard he has a terrible wound. He almost lost his eye."

"I wish it'd been his black heart instead."

"So do many others, my child."

"What about Rosa?" she hesitated to ask. "You didn't leave her there, did you?"

"She's at peace. They buried her this morning."

"This morning? Then—"

"This is your second night here, and I want to go now and get you something to eat. You are weak and need to get your strength back."

She moved to get up but winced with pain. Dimly, she remembered Zachary had kicked her side as he knocked her to the ground. A rib could be cracked, or broken, but she'd just have to move easy.

Tulwah warned, "You shouldn't try to move around."

"I have to. Don't you see?" She looked up at him beseechingly. "The longer I stay here, the farther away Nate Donovan gets with my mother. I've got to go after them."

"That's already taken care of. I sent word to Mahalia, and she knew where to find Sam Wade. I'm told he's already sending messages to trusted contacts in places where she'd likely be taken for auction. Donovan, it is said, likes to turn his mulatto women over to traders along the coast. They're very much in demand as fancy girls on passenger boats, as well as waterfront places of pleasure."

Erin clenched her fists and cried, "It will kill her. I know it will."

"If the consumption in her lungs doesn't take her first. I'm going to get your food now."

Erin didn't want to offend him when he brought the soup but was leery of anything he concocted.

He saw her reluctance and couldn't resist an amused smile. "It's only chicken and water. No bat wings or eye of newt."

She took a sip and realized it was, indeed, nothing but chicken soup, as he'd said. "I'm sorry," she offered, "but I'd heard—"

"That I'm a witch doctor?" he finished for her with a chuckle. "A *tonton macoute*?"

She nodded. "One of his overseers told me how Zachary claimed my mother was leading the slaves to use voodoo against him."

"It was voodoo, but she wasn't responsible. Neither were any of the others. I was the one, and I won't give up trying to rid the earth of that devil."

Erin sipped the soup slowly, thinking as she did how educated Tulwah seemed, how well he spoke English. Finally she yielded to her curiosity and asked how that came to be.

He told her how he'd been born in what the English and French colonies in the Antilles referred to as the Sugar Islands. He never knew his mother. She, no doubt like his father, had been kidnapped from their homeland in Africa and taken to the island of Santo Domingo to work in the sugarcane fields. At birth he had been taken to a central nursery, where babies were tended by slave women too old to toil in the cane fields from daylight to dark. He didn't know the date of his own birthday but supposed he was only five when declared fit to begin his own life as a laborer.

It had been while he was in the fields that he'd learned of voodoo. It happened that when Negroes were kidnapped down in the Congo or Angola, witch doctors of both sexes were often transported as well. And they brought with them a dark knowledge of obscure and insidious things. They were experts in vegetable poisons, and they found in the florid vegetation of the Sugar Islands appropriate substitutes for the leaves and roots of Africa. They were able to take revenge on those who mistreated them, and others of their own race lived in awe and fear of their power. "They cast spells and created superstition, and when one of them took me under his wing and taught me all he knew, I was an avid pupil."

Santo Domingo, he went on to explain, was, in 1791, the richest colony of France. But there had been much cruelty to the slaves. "For certain serious crimes, they were nailed to the ground, with crooked sticks strapped to each limb, then slowly burned alive. For lesser crimes, they were castrated, or maybe had half of one foot chopped off with an ax. Sometimes they were whipped till their bodies were raw and then had pepper and salt rubbed into the wounds."

Erin shuddered at such barbarity.

"The slave uprising," he said, "was planned by the *hungans* or, the priests and priestesses of voodoo. Within two years, the white planters were swept from the island, and the free people of color realized voodoo could also be used to unite and inspire slaves all over the islands.

"The drumbeats—" he paused to smile in the infiltrating glow of the campfire outside, "that people regarded as being used just for dance rhythms, resumed roles they'd played in Africa, sending messages across hundreds of miles of territory and summoning slaves to revolt and fight.

"By that time, however, I'd been taken in to work as a houseboy by the family of a high-ranking officer of one of the French government's agencies. They took me with them when they fled to Europe. Being somewhat in the other classes of society themselves, they wanted more than an ignorant cane worker to present as a domestic servant, so they sent me to school to be educated."

"But how did you get here?"

"My master died and left many debts. I was sold along with the rest of his valuables at auction, by his widow, to settle his estate. Eventually I was brought over on a slave ship, auctioned again. The man who bought me was superstitious, and it was quite easy"—he gave a proud, toothy grin—"to use my knowledge of voodoo to convince him he'd live a much longer and healthier life if he freed me.

"But even with papers stating I'm no longer a slave," he finished on a bitter note, "I'm still forced to run from the devils, as you must now learn to do yourself."

Erin shook her head. "I'm not running, Tulwah. I'm going home, to Jasmine Hill, so I can continue to do whatever I can to help the runaways on their way north. Like Ben. Zachary won't dare come on Ryan's property to try and hurt me. I'll be safe there."

"Unless you get caught," he grimly reminded her. "A mulatto, married to a white man, helping fugitive slaves, would likely be tarred and feathered."

Even though a cold chill began to creep along her spine, Erin lifted her chin in a brave gesture and avowed, "That's the chance I have to take, Tulwah. You said it yourself—injustice won't end, till freedom begins."

Sadly, she could not help thinking of another injustice, one she'd committed unto herself, by attempting to deny her ever-growing love for Ryan.

Now she could only pray it was not too late to let him know that.

Victoria was uncomfortable. She didn't like being in the dirty, dusty warehouse. During the late summer, it was used to store tobacco, and the air was still thick and heavy with the pungent odor of the golden leaves. On Saturdays, however, as well as many weekdays during the winter months, it was used for slave auctions.

She particularly did not like trying to push her way through the crowd of rough-talking men who'd gathered to bid on the slaves of their choice. Neither did she like the whimpering sounds of those being dragged up onto the platform.

Finally reaching a far corner, away from everyone, she curiously stood on tiptoe to catch a glimpse of what was actually going on. Her pointed nose wrinkled in distaste as she watched the burly auctioneer prying open the mouth of a big buck to prove he had good teeth, which meant he was probably healthy. She winced as she heard how much he sold for—five hundred dollars! Good heavens, she was glad that generations of slaves were bred at Jasmine Hill, for it meant they were amassing a fortune in human flesh. There had been times, and still were, when she felt stricter rule should be enforced over them all, but Ryan, like his father and grandfather, insisted there would be no whipping of slaves.

A Negro girl, hardly more than twelve or thirteen, she guessed, was being dragged up onto the platform. When she saw the auctioneer flash a nasty grin and rip the front of her blouse open to expose her large breasts, Victoria turned away. She could hear the jeers and snickers from the men and knew it was no place for her, a lady of class and breeding. At least that's how Richmond society would regard the Youngblood family until they found out there was a mulatto now in the fold.

Oh, damn you, Ryan, she fumed, as she gave a man blocking her path a poke with the tip of her umbrella to get him out of the way, why did you have to marry the wench? After all, she knew he'd bedded other women before without feeling honor bound to marry them. She knew that by tales Eliza told her. She even knew he'd sneaked some whore into the house while she was away. Better, she was reluctant to admit, if he'd married her instead. She was probably all white. And it made no difference that she'd figured out Erin was only one-eighth colored. Erin's children, Victoria's grandchildren, would be considered one-sixteenth . . . oh, to hell with brooding about it. She was going to make sure there were no children, by God, not sired by her son, anyway. Why, the main reason she'd chosen Ermine Coley for his wife was due to her royal ancestry, no matter how far removed.

The two would produce fine children to carry on the Youngblood name.

She approached a man in faded overalls who was busy picking his teeth with a pocketknife. Trying to hide her disgust, she inquired, "Would you please direct me to Mr. Nate Donovan?"

Hooded, bloodshot eyes flicked over her with contempt. Tightwad blueblood. No doubt, she was looking to buy slaves that were smuggled in fresh from Africa, to try and save paying top dollar on the block for legal trade. But no matter. Donovan knew how to deal with her kind and still make a buck. "In there," he all but snarled, nodding toward the door beyond.

Worthless peasant, Victoria silently condemned as she swished by and pushed the door open, not bothering to knock. This was not a place, she felt, where courtesy was called for.

Nate glanced up and had the same reaction as the man outside. Impatiently he snapped, "If you want to buy a slave, you'll have to bid out there like everybody else." He went back to what he was doing, which was reading the roster for the day's sale. He'd brought the Negroes in himself, but this time they were all legal, having been consigned to him for sale to pay somebody's debts. He was hoping for a good price, because his commission on consignment wasn't much, but reminded himself he wouldn't even have them if it hadn't been for being in the right place at the right time. He'd handed Arlene Tremayne, along with two other mulattoes, over to someone specializing in the desirable light-skinned women. It just so happened that this contact was looking for someone to take the others.

Victoria crossed the room and brought her umbrella down across his papers with a loud smack. She met his instant, violent glare with one of her own and cried,

"Damn you for your insolence! I'm not here to bid on slaves. I'm here because I know you for the unscrupulous trader you are, and I have a job for you."

If she were a man, he'd have knocked her on her pompous butt. Since he figured her to be well-to-do, he'd get back in the best way to hurt her kind. "Whatever it is, lady, if I agree to·it, it's gonna cost you plenty."

Unmoved, she cooly assured him, "I will pay you anything you ask and give you a bonus for a job well done."

He raised a skeptical eyebrow. "If that's the case, then there might be a bit of a risk involved. What have you got in mind? I'm no hired killer, and—"

"Oh, I don't want anyone killed, for heaven's sakes!"

"Then get on with it. I've got an auction going on outside, in case you didn't notice."

She glanced around the room to make sure there were no other doors and no windows through which they could be over heard. She whispered, "No one must ever know we made this bargain."

"We haven't made a bargain."

"We will. All I want you to do is get rid of someone for me."

"And I told you I'm not a hired killer." He was losing his patience.

She drew a sharp breath and decided it was best to just come right out and say it. "I want you to do with my daughter-in-law what you did with her mother."

He shook his head, bewildered, and more than a little annoyed. "I don't know what you're talking about."

"I'm talking about Arlene Tremayne."

He licked his lips nervously, not about to admit to anything and wondering how she knew so much. Zachary had promised he'd keep his mouth shut, especially about Donovan's part in it. But now he knew who the arrogant bitch had to be—Erin Sterling's mother-in-law. He continued to hedge, "I still don't know what you're talking about."

"I was there, Mr. Donovan," she said icily, leaning so close he could feel her breath on his face. "I was outside the stable just as Zachary Tremayne started to attack Erin. I heard him tell her about her mother, how he sold her into slavery to be rid of her."

"That don't mean I had anything to do with it," he cried.

"I have a lot of money, Mr. Donovan. When I want something, I pay for it. Without explaining the circumstances, I made some inquiries as to who should be contacted for such an unpleasant task. And your name kept coming up.

"Now then." She smiled confidently. "What I want you to do is take Erin and reunite her with her mother. Make sure they both go far, far away."

He watched, wide-eyed, as she opened her bag and took out several large bundles of money. He'd made some big deals in his lifetime but never so much at one time. "I'm not saying you're right, but now it's my turn to ask questions. What about your son? From what I hear, he's not a man to mess around with. Does he know about this?"

Solemnly, she shook her head and confided he was out of town. "It has to be done before he returns. Ryan can be quite stubborn. He fancies himself in love with her, and I can't be sure it will make any difference when he hears about all this. We have to move fast."

He looked from the money to her. "I don't mind admitting I'm tempted, but the truth is, Mrs. Youngblood, I don't like the idea of selling off a man's wife without his consent."

"Scruples, Mr. Donovan?"

"Yeah, if you want to call it that."

"Perhaps it's time to discuss the rest of our little deal.

Perhaps it will set your mind at ease." She reached into her bag to draw out another bundle and laid it on the table as his eyes grew ever wider. "This is payment for being a good actor, because you're going to convince Erin that it was her husband who wanted her sold after learning she'd deceived him. You are to tell the same story to anyone who works with you. If she believes that, she'll hate him to her dying breath and will never try to contact him, much less return to Richmond.

"When he comes back," she finished, "I'll just tell him she ran away with another man."

"Will he believe you?"

"Why wouldn't he? She won't be here. What else is he to think? I'm not worried about him hearing about her mother. She's not exactly in our social circle, you know."

No, he didn't know, Nate answered silently, and he didn't give a damn. All he knew was that for the kind of money lying on the table, he'd do just about anything. He put his hand across it, eyes locking with hers as he gave a nod of assent. "You say when it happens."

"As soon as I find out where she is."

"Tremayne is looking for her, too."

"Let's hope he doesn't find her before we do, but if he does, you'd better be prepared to move fast to get her away from him and proceed with our plan."

"For sure!" He laughed. "Because he wants to finish what he'd started when she stabbed him with that pitchfork, and if he messes her up, I won't get as good a price. She'll go for plenty as a fancy girl."

Cooly, she advised, "I'm not sure I know what you're talking about, Mr. Donovan, but I'm confident I don't want to.

"That's your bonus, by the way," she added, preparing to leave.

He shook his head; he wasn't sure what she meant.

"The bonus I promised. You get to keep whatever she brings at auction. She's all yours."

Nate's heart began to pound with excitement. Lordy, she'd bring top dollar, for sure. "Look, I want to get this over with quick as we can. You got any idea when your son will be back?"

"Don't worry about him," she called as she walked out of the office. "He hasn't been gone very long, so it will be awhile."

Ryan woke up feeling as if he hadn't been to sleep. Tossing, turning, he had spent a miserable night. After a few drinks, he'd realized he was on his way to getting drunk, and to hell with that. It didn't solve anything, and when he sobered, usually with a headache, he always felt terrible.

He sat up to look out the porthole and see what kind of day it was going to be, not that it made any difference. The sun was glistening on the rolling azure waters, with not a cloud in the sky. A glorious late fall day. He slammed his head back on the pillow and stared up at the ceiling. The pitch and roll of the ship made his stomach lurch slightly, reminding him that he hadn't eaten very much since boarding several days ago. He wasn't seasick. He wasn't hungry. He wasn't anything except miserable.

"Damn it!" he swore, leaping from the narrow bed and starting to pace around in the restrictive cabin. He didn't like feeling as if he had run away. He'd fought a goddamn war and come out alive, only to become a coward in affairs of the heart. And why? Because once upon a time he'd had the misfortune to become involved with a scheming, conniving bitch. Instead of coming out of it stronger, he'd let himself become mired in self-pity and self-doubt. He should have stayed and fought for Erin's love, by God, instead of using the trouble with his mother as an excuse to retreat from reality.

He heard the voice of the deck steward as he passed by his door.

"Port call. Port call. Wilmington, North Carolina. Port call in two hours."

Suddenly Ryan knew what he had to do. Or, maybe more importantly what he could not do, and that was keep on going all the way to New Orleans, to waste a lot of time trying to make up his mind about what he already knew.

He loved Erin.

He was going home to let her know it.

CHAPTER

 26

E*LIZA WATCHED FROM A WINDOW AS ERIN CAME* slowly up the walkway. She looked worn, weary, and as she drew closer, Eliza could detect a large blue and purple bruise on the right side of her face. She noted, too, how she'd take a few steps and then pause as if she was in pain and clutch her side.

Eliza suspected she'd been beaten, but who could have done it? And why? A lot of strange things had been going on, ever since Miss Victoria had ridden out to follow her. That had been three days ago. When Miss Victoria had come back, she was pale as a ghost, shaken, and even crying. Real tears this time. Not like when she put on for Master Ryan to make him think her heart was broken over his marriage, hoping to make him feel bad. Eliza figured she was crying with anger, because she'd stood outside her door and listened to her cursing and stomping around. She'd even smashed some things against the wall. A vase. A crystal powder box. Eliza knew because she'd had to clean up the mess, of course.

Eliza didn't dare ask what was going on, and she was even more puzzled because Miss Victoria had always shared her miseries. This time, however, she wasn't saying anything, and if she did, it was to yell and scream.

She had got rid of Annie, too. Eliza had eavesdropped as she asked her about the man Miss Erin had met in the maze, but Annie swore she didn't know anything. She pretended not remember telling Miss Erin she'd found a rose at the grave. She heard the sound of several slaps, and Annie crying, and then Miss Victoria told her to report to the overseer in charge of the field workers, and if she ever set foot near the big house again, she'd be taken to auction and sold.

As Erin crossed the porch, heading for the front door, Eliza hurried up the stairs to announce she was back.

Victoria suppressed a smile as she closed the book she was trying unsuccessfully to read. She couldn't concentrate. All she could think of was getting rid of Erin, and, finally, the moment was at hand. "Listen to me carefully," she said, her voice ringing with excitement. "Go to the stable and find that boy, Thaddeus. Tell him I said, 'It's time.' He'll know what to do."

"She looks like somebody beat her," Eliza felt the need to inform.

Victoria's eyes glittered as she exulted, "Well, then, she must be very tired and in need of rest. After you've taken my orders to Thaddeus, you can take her some tea. Since we want to make sure she relaxes, you can lace her tea with some of the laudanum the doctor gave me for my nerves."

"The way she looked, she won't need anything to make her relax."

At that, Victoria flared, "I didn't ask for your opinion, Eliza. I told you what to do, and I expect you to do it."

"Yes ma'am," Eliza bit out the words, turned on her heel to go, but was furiously ordered to turn around.

"Now you listen to me. I'm starting to sense reluctance in you to obey my orders, maybe even rebellion. I don't like that, Eliza. I don't like it one little bit. And I'm warning you, if you continue this arrogance of yours, I'll have you taken to the block."

Eliza's eyes widened, and she cried, "You'd do that to me? After all these years, you could sell me off?"

Victoria lifted her chin and snapped her fingers. "Just like that, if you give me cause. Now get out of here and do what I told you to do. And make sure you put plenty of laudanum in her tea. I want her to get a good night's sleep. And send Ebner to me."

Eliza was hurt and angry again. It wasn't right for her to be treated like that. Not right at all. She had always regarded her relationship with Miss Victoria proudly, as a rare and special kind of friendship. But, sadly, bitterly, she realized she'd been wrong.

She hung back in the shadows of the upper hallway and waited for Miss Erin to get inside her room before moving to obey Miss Victoria's orders. She didn't want to see Miss Erin, because for some reason she couldn't understand, Eliza felt sorry for her.

After sending Ebner to answer Miss Victoria's summon, she found Thaddeus to gave him the message. As he nodded in compliance, she couldn't resist wanting to know, "What does she mean? It's time for what?"

He thought a minute. Miss Victoria had told him he better not tell anybody what he was supposed to do, but like the rest of his people, he knew not to cross Eliza and get her down on him. "Well, I ain't supposed to tell," he pointed out, so she'd appreciate him obliging with the information, "but she means it's time for me to ride into Richmond to the big 'bacca warehouse and find Mastah Nate Donovan and tell him the same thing—that it's time. For what? I just don't know." He finished with a toothy grin.

Eliza knew a lot of things about what went on in the world out there, and one of them was that Nate Donovan was believed to be the meanest slave trader around. It was said he'd tear a suckling babe from his mama's teat if he had a buyer for it. And while she might not know what was going on, she was sure if it had anything to do with Nate Donovan, it could only mean trouble.

Thaddeus watched as she headed back to the big house and thought how he couldn't ever remember seeing her with her shoulders stooped as if she were carrying the weight of the world. Well, he just wasn't surprised at anything, anymore. The drums were beating every night, and he'd heard Tulwah was working his *obeah* at the Tremayne place, and things were real bad over that way. So, it was only natural, he guessed, that the pall had spread to Jasmine Hill. He only hoped Master Ryan came back soon, because he was sure he'd find a way to keep the evil spirits away. He was a good man. And Thaddeus liked Miss Erin, too. He was worried about her, because when she'd come walking up a little while ago, she looked like something one of the barn cats had dragged in. But Master Ryan would fix everything. Thaddeus was sure of that.

He jumped on his mule and took off to obey his mistress.

Eliza looked from Ebner to Miss Victoria and fearfully asked, "But why? Why do you want Ebner to tell Miss Erin that Master Ryan is back, when he's not?"

Victoria gritted her teeth. More and more lately she was starting to question Eliza's loyalty. It wasn't anything particular she could put her finger on. There was just an air about the old woman that made her wary. Testily, she cried, "I don't have to explain myself to you. Now I want you to make sure all the doors to her room are locked and remain locked."

Eliza bit her lip. Evil. It was all evil. And she wasn't

even sure what it was but knew she had to obey without question.

Erin realized it was probably useless to pull the bell cord but did so anyway. She supposed she would have to fend for herself till Ryan returned, as Victoria obviously intended to make her life miserable. Well, no matter. Personal discomfort was of no consequence. All she was concerned with was her mother's whereabouts. Oh, dear God, she only hoped Tulwah was right when he said Sam Wade had secret contacts, and he would be able to trace where she'd been taken. Legal wheels would then be put in motion to free her from whatever fate had befallen.

She went to the window to look down at Henrietta Youngblood's grave. From such a distance, it was difficult to see whether a rose had been left in the vase. Of course, she'd have to go to the labyrinth opening to check on that site. She couldn't depend on Annie to do it for her, either. It was all up to her now, and she was so tired.

How she longed for a bath, but the tub was empty, and she lacked the strength to bring up water pail by pail, herself, especially with her injured side. Tulwah had run experienced fingers over her rib cage to probe, and sensed, he said, a cracked bone. She would have to take it easy for a while. Well, she grimly reflected, turning away from the window, what other choice did she have? All she could do was wait, and pray.

She removed her soiled clothing and put on a robe. Her stomach gave a hungry lurch. Surely, she could make it back downstairs to the service kitchen and find some cold biscuits, anything to quell the gnawing emptiness.

Just as she was about to leave the room, there was a soft, almost hesitant knock at the door. She hoped it wasn't Victoria, spoiling for another confrontation. She just wasn't up to it.

She was surprised to find Eliza standing there holding

a tray. "I saw you were back." She kept her eyes down, not looking at her. "I thought you might like some tea and spice cake."

"I would. Oh, thank you, Eliza." It was easy in that grateful moment to forget every unkind thought she'd ever had about the woman. She waved her in. "This is so nice of you. I didn't know what to do with Annie forbidden to serve me. I was going to take a bath, and—"

"I can get you some water," Eliza was quick to offer. She figured she could do that much, and maybe Miss Victoria wouldn't find out about it. The poor girl, she noted, looked awful. The bruise up close was worse than she'd thought. And her eyes were dull, with dark circles, and the little puffiness revealed she'd been doing a lot of crying.

Erin smiled, shook her head in wonder. "You're an angel."

Eliza hurried out, not wanting Miss Erin's gratitude or praise. It made her feel guilty, and she wasn't sure why. All she knew was that she felt like whatever bad things had happened, or might happen, she somehow had a hand in causing them, and she didn't like the feeling. Not at all.

Erin set the tray on the table next to the bed, then propped herself against the pillows. She gulped the tea eagerly. It was wonderful to have something besides Tulwah's heavily herbed potions, even though she noted a rather slick taste to Eliza's brew. But no matter. It was still delicious. She poured another cup and nibbled at the cake with equal relish, knew that by the time she'd had her bath, she'd feel like going to look for the symbolic rose. Maybe, she dared hope, Sam would be back with good news.

She realized that getting something tasty in her stomach made her feel optimistic. All she needed was a few moments of rest, and she'd be fit and ready for anything. The only thing that could make her happier in that relaxing moment was to be able to lay her head on Ryan's shoulder and feel his arms, so tender, so protective, about her. . . .

She closed her eyes, took a deep breath—and that was when she heard the sound of a door slamming loudly, and she sat straight up, alert and alarmed. It seemed to have come from the direction of Ryan's room.

She got up and went into the parlor, glanced about to see a few of his personal belongings scattered about—the cheroots he enjoyed with brandy, a glass, a book he'd been reading. Her heart leapt with joy to think he was back. But why hadn't Eliza told her?

Running to the connecting door to his room, she was stunned to find it locked. Ryan never locked his door! She knocked loudly, happily calling, "Ryan! It's me! Let me in. I have to talk to you. Oh, I've missed you so. . . ." Tears of joy were filling her eyes, and she bounced on her toes impatiently at the sound of footsteps responding to her call.

A key turned, and the door jerked open, but instead of Ryan's dear face, she found herself looking into Ebner's bodeful eyes.

"Ebner, where's Master Ryan?" She tried to look around him, beyond him, into the room, but he stepped this way and that to block her view, as well as entry, should she attempt. "I thought I heard him in here."

"You did." He made his voice sharp, brusque, impatient, wanting to get the lying over with. "He said his trip was delayed due to some sudden, urgent business, but he's not here now."

"When did he return?"

"Yesterday."

She shook her head in an attempt to dispel the creeping

shadows, for she was feeling terribly sleepy and unsteady. "Does he know I'm home?"

"Yassum. He knows."

"And he didn't come to me?" None of it was making sense, unless—

No!

She would not allow herself to think, even for a moment, that he'd turned back because he'd somehow heard about her mother and was angry. It just couldn't be so. "I want to come inside." She made her voice strong, even though she was feeling weaker by the moment. "I'll wait for him in there."

Ebner swallowed hard and made himself stand very straight in an effort to look imposing. "He said you wasn't to come in."

"But that can't be." She swayed and caught the door frame to steady herself. "You have to let me in. . . ."

Quickly, swiftly, Ebner reached to grab her under her shoulders and gently turn her about to guide her back to her room. She was slipping away fast, he knew. No doubt from the laudanum Miss Victoria had Eliza put in her tea. He helped her all the way to her bed, and she was only able to protest feebly as he sat her down and lifted her legs up.

"Ebner, why?"

She looked up at him, pitiful and beseeching. He handed her another cup of tea, just as Miss Victoria had ordered. He was to get her to drink as much as possible. "I don't know." He gave the answer he'd been told to give to any of her questions. "He seemed real upset. And mad. He said not to let you in, that you were the last person he wanted to see right now, that he needed time to think about what he was gonna do, what he had to do," he emphasized, as instructed.

Erin could almost hear her heart breaking. Dear God,

it could mean only one thing—that he had somehow heard about her mother passing for white and now faced the reality she was also of mixed blood. She was hurt and disappointed for many reasons. Mostly because she'd dared to think she knew Ryan to be a liberal and beneficent man, one to whom it would not have mattered. Now she sadly feared she'd made a terrible mistake in judgment.

Ebner was heading for the door. Erin struggled to get up and follow him. She had to see Ryan, talk to him. If she told him the secret in her own heart, how she'd come to realize she loved him, and how deeply, perhaps it might make a difference. There had been times when she felt he really cared for her, and if they could only talk. . . .

Ebner walked out, and she heard the sound of a key turning.

"No." She stumbled to fling herself against the door and twist the knob, but it was locked. Slapping her palms against it in protest she said, "Please, Ebner. Don't do this to me. I have to see him, talk to him. I have to tell him I love him."

She went to the hall door and cried to find it, too, was locked from the outside. Moving to the French doors leading to the veranda, found the same. There was no way out. But why? Why was Ryan doing this to her? Did he think she'd known all along and kept it from him? Did he now despise her? Hate her?

A heavy, invisible shroud was descending, making it difficult to think. A great roaring had begun in her head, and she felt as if she were going to collapse if she didn't get off her feet. Wearily, slowly, she made her way back to the bed, lifted the cup and saucer in hopes the tea would help clear her head so she could think of some way to fight this nightmare.

She was not aware when the cup fell from her lap, the remaining drug-laced tea soaking into the mattress. Neither did she hear the saucer when it clattered to the floor beside the bed as her hand dropped to one side.

Eliza unlocked the door to bring in the first pail of water. Two of the downstairs servants were coming up behind her. Peering into the room and seeing Miss Erin was sound asleep, she waved them to go back. There would be no need for a bath. As much laudanum as Eliza had poured into the tea, Miss Erin would not need anything before morning.

Victoria kept a vigil at her parlor window. And yes, she silently avowed, it was still her parlor. Tomorrow, every reminder of Erin would be removed. She would tell Ryan her motive was to ease his pain. It would have been awful, she planned to point out sympathetically, for him to have to come home to face his wife running away with another man and then have the added torment of being surrounded by memories of his broken dreams.

There was much to do, she thought excitedly, besides temporarily moving herself back in where she belonged. The divorce shouldn't take long, not when Judge Tillingham heard Ryan's tale of woe. But Victoria didn't intend to wait till then to start making plans for the wedding. She intended to consult Ermine as to her thoughts on how to redecorate the master suite. Maybe the connecting parlor should be turned into a nursery. Ryan and Ermine wouldn't need a private parlor all their own. They were going to be a close family, and they would all gather in one of the rooms downstairs.

Victoria just felt so much better about everything, now that the nightmare was nearly over. At first, she had to admit, she'd gone to pieces, not knowing what to do, but then she realized perhaps it was best she hadn't caught Erin with another man. She might have lied her way out of that, and Ryan might have been so foolish as to believe her. After all, he'd admitted he loved her. But hearing the deep dark secret, Victoria had known she could take no chances. Nate Donovan was providing the final solution.

She wasn't worried any longer about gossip, either. If her circle of friends and associates were even to hear about what had happened to Arlene Tremayne, they would have the decency not to mention it around her. Also, they'd have much compassion for her when the story spread about Erin's alleged adultery. In time, it would all be forgotten anyway, and she and Ryan and Ermine, and all their wonderful and beautiful children, would live happily ever after.

Victoria was satisfied she had taken care of everything. Checking on Erin herself, several times, she had found her sleeping so soundly that calling her name did not even penetrate her drug-induced stupor. Ebner had reported he'd followed Victoria's orders, so when Erin did awaken in her new surroundings, she'd remember—and blame Ryan.

At last Victoria saw Nate coming up the road. Gleefully she rushed to meet him at the steps and lead him inside. "She's drugged," she assured him. "Laudanum. She won't know anything. All you have to do is pick her up and get her out of here."

"I'll tie and gag her, anyway, just to be safe," he said, following her as she took up a lantern and headed for the curving stairs leading upward.

Victoria unlocked the door and held up the light so he could see his way to the bed.

"Yeah, she's out." He nodded, satisfied, then proceeded to take a rag from his pocket and stuff it in her mouth. Quickly, he bound her hands and ankles, finally hoisting her over his shoulder.

Erin was not aware of anything that was happening.

"Say good-bye to your daughter-in-law, Mrs. Young-blood." Nate laughed as he headed out.

"Not good-bye," Victoria said gleefully, "good riddance!"

CHAPTER

 27

JASON HARNABY LOOKED AT ERIN AND KNEW, BE-
yond a doubt, she was the most beautiful woman he had
ever seen. And if she were a mulatto, which was the reason
Nate said her husband was getting rid of her, then mixed
blood had served her well. She was truly a sight to behold,
and her husband was a goddamn fool.

Nate had placed her in a corner of the grist house during the night. Jason was there, because they were awaiting
the arrival of yet another mulatto who was being sold by
her husband.

Nate wanted her left tied and gagged, because he wasn't
about to take any chances on her getting away, especially
since they were hiding out on her stepfather's property.
That was when Jason was jolted to find out who she was.

Nate had left, saying he was going to ride out and see
what was holding up the other one. He wanted to get
moving at first light.

Jason thought Erin favored her mother. A lot. Her
mother was bound to have been a head-turner in her day.
She wasn't so bad when he'd seen her maybe a week ago,
either. Sick and pale and beat down in spirit, she was just
a shadow, but with proper rest and food, she might come
out of her miserable state.

Erin stirred, moaned, as the first rays of morning light streamed in through the grist house windows. Jason knelt beside her and began untying her wrists. Damn it, it wasn't right leaving her trussed up. He didn't see any harm in letting her arms free.

He felt her stiffen, cringe, and turned his head to see she was awake, pop-eyed with fear. She started making whimpering noises against the gag stuffed in her mouth. "You don't need to be afraid," he soothed, removing it. "I'm not—"

Erin screamed. Again and again. Jason had no choice but to stuff the rag quickly back in her mouth as he tried to tell her she had nothing to fear from him. "I'm not going to let anything happen to you, and—"

"What the hell is going on in here?" Nate lunged through the door and crossed the tiny room to cuff Jason on the shoulder and send him sprawling backward. "I told you, goddamn it, she stays tied and gagged till we get her to the coast. I'm not taking any chances with her."

Jason bit back his anger. So many times he'd wanted to ram his fist in Nate Donovan's face but didn't dare. It was to his advantage to play the role of big, clumsy, dumb ox, because it prevented a lot of tension he didn't need. "I'm sorry. So sorry." He shook his head wildly, as though overcome with contrition. "I forgot, boss man. I thought since we'd be leaving soon, she might need to tend to herself."

"You don't get paid to think," Nate growled. "I decide when these wenches hit the bushes, remember?"

"Yes, boss." Jason shuffled away, shoulders hunched, in pretense of spirit broken.

Erin's wide-eyed glare changed from terror to anger, as Nate taunted, "Well, now, you don't look like you feel so good this morning, Mrs. Youngblood. But, I reckon that's what happens when you let your husband make your tea.

"My goodness, you look surprised;" he continued with a chuckle. "Surely you didn't think your mammy made that drink that knocked you on your pretty ass, now did you? Why, no, ma'am, she didn't. It was Mister Ryan Youngblood himself who made that tea, and a very special brew it was, too. I gave him the recipe myself.

"You see—" he dropped to a squatting position beside her, trailed a fingertip down her cheek as she struggled in revulsion—"when a wife finds out her husband wants to sell her, 'cause he's decided he doesn't want to be married to a high yeller after all, she can sometimes get pretty upset and make a lot of noise. And it's best to keep things as quiet as possible, 'cause it's embarrassing for everybody. You understand? Like with your mother. Zach fixed her a cup of my special tea, and I just carried her out in the middle of the night without a fuss."

Erin had stopped struggling. She lay very still, absorbing his words with every nerve, every fiber of her being, to hold and preserve and remember and fuel the fire of hatred and revenge with every breath she would live to draw in this life.

Nate saw, knew her reaction was what he was after, and enthusiastically continued. "Yeah, when Zach got word to your husband before he got out of town about your great-grandma being a full-blooded Negro, he just about went crazy, he was so mad. And he understood and appreciated Zach's reasoning for telling him, too. He said he wouldn't have been at all happy to have a little high-yeller baby, maybe even a full-colored. So Zach, he put him in touch with me, and, well—" He smiled, pinched her cheek, and stood up. "You're on your way to a whole new life, sugar."

He walked away, silently congratulating himself for a tale well told.

Erin was rigid. It was as though her veins had been embalmed with liquid malice.

So this was to be Ryan's revenge for his wounded pride.

How foolish she had been to think it would make no difference to him.

And, as she had come face-to-face with the monster responsible for abducting her mother, there had been further revelation.

Erin knew she was capable of killing another human being.

She watched, unflinching, as the other man returned a short while later. Obeying orders, he hoisted her over his large shoulders and carried her out into the early sunlight. It was cold, and she shivered despite her self-induced paralysis of wrath. He felt it and assured her, "I'll see that you get covered with something once we're on our raft and sailin' downstream. Even if I have to take off my shirt and cover you with that."

She didn't want his kindness any more than she wanted his shirt. It didn't matter he'd tried to befriend her by untying her hands just before that devil had come in. He was still the enemy.

Coming out of her rage long enough to take in her surroundings, she was further assaulted by the indignity of it all to realize where they were—the old grist house. How fitting and ironic that it was also the place where Ryan had first approached her with seduction his intent. Oh, how she wished now he had succeeded. Far better it would have been, for never would it have come to this final tragedy.

"My name is Jason," the big man told her as he laid her on the raft and whispered, "I'm going to look after you."

I'll bet! She let her hatred show in her eyes. He winced and moved away at shouted orders from his partner to cast off.

Turning her head, she saw the girl lying next to her, eyes closed. But Erin knew she wasn't asleep, because tears were running down her cheeks, and she was trembling. She wished she could comfort her, but what would she say even if she could speak? Any hope attempted would be futile.

Erin noticed that, unlike herself, the girl's mulatto status was obvious. Though her skin was light, it was still the telltale mocha shade. And her black hair was wiry. Was her husband selling her, too, she wondered in shared pain.

She watched as the big man called Jason used a long pole to shove the raft away from shore, and soon they were caught up in the rushing current—to where? Erin did not know, was actually too lost in the poison of her loathing even to care. Only yesterday, she had felt remorse at never having confided to Ryan her love for him. Today, she yearned for the chance to convey her hatred.

As the morning passed, Erin struggled to come to terms with the fierceness of the turmoil within. She commanded herself to channel her energy from anger to the will to survive. Ryan Youngblood and everything he had ever represented was no longer a part of her world.

She comforted herself with the knowledge that this was the way her mother had been taken, and therefore, her destiny would be the same. They would be reunited, Erin would lend her strength, and together they would find an escape from the madness that had befallen.

The raft was stopped and tied at the jutting knee of a cypress at water's edge. Erin's chief tormentor roughly untied her and led her ashore to tend to her personal needs behind a clump of bushes. "Don't try to run away," he warned. "If the moccasins don't get you, I will, and it'll be the last time you get to relieve yourself till we get where we're going."

Erin was not about to attempt escape, not when she was hopeful of finding her mother. The other girl, however, did make a break for it, and Nate promptly caught her and beat her mercilessly. Then he threw her roughly back on the raft and cursed her as he tied her so tightly Erin could see the blood oozing from around the ropes.

She noticed, also, that the other man, Jason he'd said his name was, watched the cruelty with narrow, condemning eyes. He even dared glance her way in shared sorrow for the girl, and she began to wonder just what his part was in all of this. Still, she was leery and not about to trust anyone.

At dark, they pulled up to shore, and she heard Nate tell Jason they would camp there for the night and said he anticipated reaching their destination by noon the next day. Jason wanted to know if he'd be left there to handle the sale.

"Afraid so," Donovan responded. "I've got to meet Burgess and the others below Norfolk tomorrow night. There's a smuggle shipment coming in from Florida. Prime beef, I'm told." He gave a nasty laugh. "Good, raw-boned women straight from Ghana. We're gonna have us a little party before we brand 'em and take 'em to auction."

"Selling at Tarter's place?"

Erin wondered if it were her imagination as she heard Jason's question, or if there were really an edge to his voice.

"Yeah. It's the safest. Only the most trusted traders know about it, and we always have a good turnout. I'm getting my pick of the litter, as usual, to take back to Richmond for my regular buyers."

Erin felt sick to her stomach. Slaves smuggled in to be sold cheap. That was Donovan's stock in trade.

Tossed to the side of the camp like extra firewood, Erin could only wait to see what would happen next. She could smell smoke, knew a fire had been started. Then there came the sound of bacon sizzling. She could smell the delicious aroma, and her mouth began to water. Her only nourishment the day before had been the few bites of Eliza's spice cake—and the tea.

After a while, Nate appeared to yank the gag from her mouth. "Well, aren't you going to start screaming and yelling now that you can?" He started untying her wrists.

Her steady, venomous glare was her silent message of warning.

He gave a mock shudder. "My, my, those dark eyes do flash fire, don't they? I'll bet you burn in a lot of places, don't you?" He pinched her breasts, and she slapped his hand away. He snickered. "Maybe you need to have that fire put out, sugar baby, and I'm just the man to do it."

Despite his threat, Erin would not give him the pleasure of showing fear.

He went to his other prisoner. "Well, well, Lucy Jane. I reckon you've learned your lesson, and I can untie you long enough for you to eat."

The minute her gag was out of her mouth, she began to sob wildly, clutching the front of his shirt as she begged, "Please. Let me go. This isn't fair. If I'd known he was going to sell me, I'd never have married him. I was safe in New York. No one cared that I passed for white. But he said he loved me, and he promised me—"

Nate suddenly squeezed her throat to silence. "I don't want to listen to any of this shit, you hear me? 'Cause I don't care. My job is to see you sold to the highest bidder, take my cut, and give the rest to your husband. You'll bring a nice price for a fancy girl, unless I have to keep beating on you, and if that happens, you'll be sold to a whorehouse, where you'll be used up within six months and then have your throat cut before you're tossed out in the ocean to feed the sharks. If that isn't what you want, you'd best just cooperate and keep your goddamn mouth shut."

She rolled to her side and covered her face with her hands and wept.

"Bastard!" Erin hissed, unable to keep silent any longer. "I hope you rot in hell—"

He backhanded her, sending her sprawling to the ground. Straddling her, he cried, "I don't listen to that kind of talk from slaves, understand? Now didn't you just hear what I told Lucy Jane over there? The same goes for you, too. And your husband won't give a damn what I decide to do with you, because I don't have to give him any money for what I get outta you. *He* paid *me* to get rid of you. That makes you mine to do with whatever I choose, and you'd best remember that and hold that sharp tongue of yours."

He laughed, a nasty, guttural sound and began to squeeze her breasts roughly. "You like that, sugar baby? You want some more?"

Suddenly, Jason appeared to announce tersely, "Supper. They haven't eat all day, Nate."

"Sure, sure." He got up. "We might just finish this later."

Erin cringed, but at the same time did not miss the sympathetic way Jason was looking at her.

She ate the bacon and eggs, but not as ravenously as Lucy Jane. She had no appetite, despite the gnawing in her stomach. Nate had a jug of whiskey and guzzled that between bites of his food. She knew he was well on his way to being drunk and could only pray he'd soon pass out, because there was no mistaking his intent as he stared lustily at her every so often.

When they finished eating, Nate retied Lucy Jane, gagged her, and dragged her to one side and told her she might as well go to sleep. He walked over to Erin and grinned. He started to unfasten his trousers.

Jason glanced up sharply from where he was sitting near the fire. "Ain't you forgetting something, boss?"

Nate thought a minute, then made a face. "I was hoping you'd forget about that."

Jason's giggle was forced, but only he knew that as he got up and shuffled over. "Now how could I forget a thing like that? Besides, you were the one that said we should take turns with who gets first choice, and since it's my turn this trip, I choose her."

Erin closed her eyes and dared to think it might be a blessing if she just dropped dead then and there.

Irritably, Nate went to his liquor jug and took a long swig before heading over to where Lucy Jane was lying in terror.

Jason lifted Erin in his arms and said, loud enough for Nate to hear, "I'm takin' her in the bushes. I ain't like you. I don't like an audience."

But Nate was paying no attention. He was busy untying Lucy Jane's legs and positioning them the way he wanted, as she sobbed against the gag in her mouth.

Erin was gathering her strength to resist with everything she had, the very second she was untied. But strangely, in the deepening twilight, as Jason walked farther and farther from the campsite, she sensed an anxiety in him, and frantically wondered what it could mean.

At last he laid her gently on the ground. Dropping to his knees beside her, he leaned over so close she could feel the warmth of his breath against her skin. "Listen to me, girl, listen good, because I can't take a chance on him sneaking up behind me and hearing this," he whispered.

Erin bit back an oath. She wanted him to believe her submissive, so he'd untie her, yet wondered why he was acting so weird and not attacking right away.

"Midnight rose," he said, eyes anxiously searching hers for response.

Erin was stunned. It had to be a trick.

"You know what that means, don't you? Midnight rose," he repeated, taking on a desperate note. "Come on, Erin, I know about you, because we're fighting for the same cause. The slaves have started referring to you as Midnight Rose, because a rose left at a special place at Jasmine Hill is a signal to you for help."

She did not realize she had even been holding her breath till it escaped her in one, long, ragged sigh. "How . . . how did you know?" she stammered.

He started untying her, as he spoke rapidly, rushing to confide everything while he had a chance. "I'm a Free-Soiler, too, Erin. I only pretend to be a big dummy so Donovan won't suspect anything."

With hands free, she clutched his to beg, "Tell me what happened to my mother. If you were with him, when he took her, then you'd know."

He nodded vigorously, happily. "Oh, yes, I was with him, all right, all the way to the coast, and as soon as he took off, so did I, heading straight north for my first contact point, and that's where I left your mother."

Erin swayed in stunned disbelief, prayed she wasn't dreaming, that he spoke the truth, and her mother was, indeed, safe.

He saw her reluctance to believe after the nightmare she'd been through. "Erin, it's true. Arlene is safe."

"Bless you," she was finally able to whisper through her

tears. "Bless you, Jason. Dear God, it's just unbelievable. All of it."

"I managed to get word to Sam Wade which route I sent her on, and I imagine he'll be right behind her to see she gets on the first ship out—"

"Out to where?" she wanted to know at once, alarmed all over again.

"I felt it would be taking a chance merely to put her in a colony somewhere. Your stepfather is a vicious man, and I wanted to make sure if he found out she hadn't wound up where Nate was supposed to deliver her, that he'd never be able to find her. That's why I recommended she be sent to Africa."

"Africa?" she echoed incredulously, stunned, unable to envision such a destination for her mother. Worriedly, she pointed out, "But she's sick, and she'll never be able to make that long a voyage."

"There was no other choice, and she agreed it was the only thing to do. She's got a lot of spunk. A lot of courage. She was plenty mad over what Tremayne did to her, and I think maybe she figured it best she get out of the country as fast as possible, or else she might be tempted to go back and take revenge on the son of a bitch. She also knew for your sake, she couldn't go back and make trouble. She even told me she was praying Zachary wouldn't tell you about your mixed blood. She was afraid you'd hold it against her."

Erin was quick to let him know, "I'd never do that. I love my mother, no matter what, and none of it was her fault, anyway, though I wish she'd told me long ago. I'm afraid her prayers went unanswered, because he told me, just like he told. . . ."

Jason sensed her distress and put his arm about her shoulders in an awkward gesture of comfort. "I know all this is hard to swallow at one time, but you've got to get hold of yourself so we can concentrate on getting you out of the country, too. For several reasons.

"You see," he rushed to explain, "I just can't help every single slave I come in contact with, though God knows I wish I could, and only me and Him knows how it tears my heart out not to be able to. About the only time I can is when it's an unusual situation, like Nate having other business to tend to and sending me off to the auction. I'll divide up the price I get for one sale, tell him it was for two, and one slave goes free."

"Dear Lord, how awful it must be for you to have to make the choice."

"You just don't know. I usually make my decision based on which one I figure to be the heartiest and able to stand up to the brutal life of a slave, and I send the weakest to the underground. But in special cases, like your mother's, it's a lot easier."

"Because she's in poor health."

"No. Payment was up front. Like with you. Zachary paid Nate to get rid of your mother as quick as he could, because of the voodoo he blamed her for."

"That's nonsense."

"Well, it doesn't matter to me. All I know is Nate got his money, so he didn't care what happened to her, and he turned her over to me and said I could keep whatever I got at the sale for my pay. The same is true with you. Your husband paid him just like Zach, so when he takes off in the morning, all I've got to do later is lie about how much you sold for, to some buyer from farther south, and he'll never know the difference."

"And neither will—" she hesitated, not about to speak his name, "someone else. But what about Lucy Jane?"

Jason hated to have to say, "Her husband is hoping to get a good price for her. That's why he married her, so he could sell her. It's not the first time he's done this, I'm told."

Erin's heart went out to the poor girl. "Then what's going to happen to her?"

He gave a reluctant shrug. "I'll have to sell her."

"No," Erin cried then. She reached in the pocket of her robe, which she'd been wearing at the time of her abduction. Evidently, it had happened during the night, or Nate would have noticed her diamond ring had he been paying attention. Thank God, she'd had her wits about her enough when she awakened to twist it about so it blended in with her wedding band. When she'd been allowed some privacy to tend to her personal needs later, she'd slipped it off her finger and into her pocket. She handed it to Jason. "Take this and whatever you can get for it, tell Nate that's what you got for Lucy Jane."

He looked at the ring in wide-eyed awe and knew, without a doubt, it would command quite a price, more than enough to represent payment for a mulatto sold at auction. "Are you sure you want to do this?"

"Do you think it means anything to me now? Take it. Whatever is left over, use it for the cause."

"You can be sure of that."

Erin was overwhelmed at his dedication and courage, and said so.

"Well, I'm impressed with you, too. I hear you've done a lot of good things yourself."

"I only wish I could have done more. I had the perfect setup with the labyrinth, the way it opened out to the river for easy getaway. I guess I should have known it was too good to last."

"Don't look back. Just be grateful I was the one helping Nate this run. Sometimes he gets one of his other men to go with him, and if this had been one of those times, you'd have had a miserable fate, believe me."

"Like what Lucy Jane is enduring right now?"

"Don't worry," he said with a proud grin. "Your husband isn't the only one who knows how to drug somebody. I imagine Nate is passed out cold by now, and Lucy Jane is giving thanks and crediting all the liquor he drank."

Erin was washed with relief, but also stung by the reminder of betrayal.

She was thankful that freedom from a fate probably worse than death was only hours away.

And she was grateful beyond words to think that soon she might be able to find her own way to Africa and be reunited with her mother.

Yet Erin could not deny the vindictive emotions smoldering within. Maybe, once upon a time, she had dared to believe she might be falling in love but was bitterly reminded that even as the best wine could make the sharpest vinegar, so could the deepest love turn to the deadliest hate.

The next morning, it was just as Jason had predicted. Nate took off, looking like death warmed over. Lucy Jane quickly confided to Erin that he'd passed out before he could ravish her and been too miserable when he awoke later to finish what he'd started. So he'd retied her ankles and secured her to a tree, while he slept off his whiskey.

Erin told her what had actually happened, all about Jason's secret, and by the time she'd finished sharing everything, Lucy Jane was sobbing with relief and gratitude.

When Nate left them, Jason took them on the raft the rest of the way to Jamestown. There, he rented a wagon and horses to get them quickly to Yorktown at the mouth of the York River and the Chesapeake Bay. He left them only long enough to make his contact, then returned with a kind-faced old man who would escort them to the next point along the secret way north.

"This is the part I hate," he told them gruffly, fighting against the tears sparkling in his china-blue eyes. "Seems in just a little while, I really get attached to my younguns. That's the way I look at all of you, don't you see? Like you were my very own, just like we're all God's children, no matter what color we are."

Erin and Lucy Jane both threw their arms about him at once. Clinging together in emotional farewell, they knew they would never forget him.

Erin didn't want to leave her new friend, just as she knew it would be with deep regret when it was time to part ways from Lucy Jane.

It would be harder, still, to set sail eventually from America, for she longed to stay and do her part for the cause. Yet she would never know real peace till she found her mother.

Only then would she be able to concentrate on the future and bury the past completely.

Everything looked peaceful, Ryan thought as he rode slowly up the main drive. The air was crisp, cool, and all around the leaves were splashes of brilliant color as autumn made ready to bow out, yielding to winter right around the corner.

He was tired, because he'd stopped along the way only a few times to sleep. He felt driven with the need to get home as fast as possible.

He didn't see any of the workers around the stable, but then he remembered it was Sunday, and traditionally Youngblood slaves were allowed to rest that day, except for a few of the household and kitchen staff.

Anxious to get to the house, he rode straight to the

front hitching post. Later, he'd see his horse got a rub-down.

He took the steps two at a time and flung the door open to call, "Hey, where is everybody? Erin? Mother?"

Eliza appeared in the doorway to the back hall. Her knees were knocking together, and she could feel her hands becoming sweaty. Lordy, she wasn't going to be the one to tell him.

"Well, where is everybody?" Ryan was so happy to be home, he was even glad to see her.

"Church," was all she could trust herself to say, not about to reveal it was only Miss Victoria she was talking about.

Ryan was glad to hear that. If Erin and his mother were attending church together, then that meant they were getting along a little bit better, anyway. "Well, I'll just ride over and meet them."

Eliza walked out on the porch to watch him ride away.

He was going to be awful hurt, she knew.

Once again, she was washed with guilt to know she was partly to blame.

CHAPTER

 28

V ICTORIA WAS AWARE ALL EYES WERE UPON HER
as she sat with head bowed during most of the morning
worship. She pretended to be praying, and, of course, everyone regarded her with pity. After all, word had spread
like butter on hoecakes how her daughter-in-law had run
away with another man. Disgraceful, folks said, especially
coming right on top of the mystery concerning Erin's
mother's sudden disappearance. It was even being whispered Arlene might have been guilty of an indiscretion
herself. Zachary Tremayne wasn't saying, but then no one
was asking him, because the fact was, few people cared
what happened to that wretched man and his family. Victoria, however, was the object of profound sympathy.

After benediction, Victoria maintained her doleful expression as she turned in response to the tap on her shoulder from the pew directly behind. "Miss Pearl," she said
serenely, in acknowledgment of the old lady, "you're looking well, praise the Lord." She held out a gloved hand.

Miss Pearl Whittington took it to clasp between both
of hers, faded blue eyes brimming with tears as she tremulously whispered, "You're a strong woman, Victoria
Youngblood. Most women would take to their bed with
the vapors."

For the first time, Victoria was grateful for the outspokeness of the elderly. Everyone around paused to listen as she seized the opportunity to detail her misery. "Don't think I'm not tempted." She dabbed at her nose with her lace hanky. "I'm so embarrassed. So ashamed. To think my son would marry someone who could do something like that."

Miss Pearl snapped, "You've nothing to be ashamed of. Nothing at all. The girl came from a trashy family. We all knew that. Like Adam, Ryan was tempted by forbidden fruit."

Murmurs from those gathered agreed.

Sophia, Ryan's cousin whom he referred to as his aunt, frowned with disgust as she stood in the aisle. She had been charmed by Erin and could keep still no longer. "I disagree."

Everyone turned to stare, and Victoria clamped her teeth together, stiff with indignity at the intrusion. "What do you know about it, Sophia?"

"I was at the wedding. "I met her, and her mother. Both lovely people. Ryan married her because he loved her, and that's where the pity should be directed. It doesn't help to tear Erin and her mother to pieces."

"But she ran away with another man," someone standing close to Sophia said shrilly.

At that, Sophia lifted her chin to respond, "I don't know that for a fact. Do you?"

The woman who'd spoken hurried on her way without further comment, and those standing around Victoria began to move away, also, including Miss Pearl. Sophia hesitated only long enough to accept Victoria's scathing glare with a curt nod, then she, too, walked up the aisle.

Victoria was seething. After all, it was her intent to save face for Ryan by making everyone think he'd been manipulated into marrying Erin and love had nothing to do with it. While she didn't dare come right out and say so, the inference would be Erin had made him crazy with lust. Ermine, being of good morals and class, could understand and forgive such temptations of the flesh, and the devil, but if she thought for one minute love had been involved, Victoria knew she could forget her dream of seeing the two married.

Absorbed with her musing, Victoria was not at first aware of the excited buzzing among the congregation filing out ahead of her. Neither did she notice how they were stepping to one side in the narthex of the church, clearing the way for her.

Finally glancing up, she was at once alarmed, quickening her step and pushing aside those who hadn't already got out of her way.

When, at last, she saw the object of everyone's attention, she gasped and swayed, clutching her Bible to her bosom with trembling hands. "Ryan!" She was barely able to choke out his name, as she saw him rushing up the stairs, two at a time, grinning broadly.

He spoke in perfunctory greeting as he glanced all about, finally forced to ask, "Where is she? Where's Erin?"

Victoria was well aware of once more being the center of attention, only this time she was anything but pleased. "She—she's not here," she managed to stammer amidst the meddlesome faces of the onlookers.

"What do you mean—she's not here? Eliza said you'd gone to church, and I naturally assumed she was with you." He felt apprehension creeping as he noticed how everyone seemed to be waiting for something to happen. Taking his mother's arm, he could even feel her tension as he led her swiftly down the church steps and away from vigilant ears.

Victoria had never dreamed it would happen like this and hadn't expected him home for several, several weeks.

By then, she'd have got rid of Erin's things to make it appear she'd taken them with her. There were just so many loose ends to take care of.

"What is it you don't want to tell me?"

The story she'd not had time to perfect came tumbling out with hysterical edge. "She's gone. Ran away with another man. They were meeting in the labyrinth. I tried to catch him, but I couldn't. It was all a scheme. She and her mother planned the whole thing. To try and get your money. Maybe take over Jasmine Hill. I'm not sure. All I know is once she found out I knew, she ran away. So did her mother. Nobody's seen them since." She shook her head wildly from side to side, and the tears sparkling in her eyes were genuine, but not evoked by sympathy for his anguished reaction. Victoria was merely frustrated by being caught unawares.

He steered her to her carriage where a groomsman waited. Tying his horse behind, Ryan got in beside her for the ride home.

"Ryan, I'm so sorry," she began, once they were on their way. She was feeling a bit more sure of herself, since he seemed to wither in despair rather than go into a rage. "It all happened so fast. I think it must've been going on all along, but you just didn't see it. I wouldn't have noticed myself, except I happened to be sick one night, and I walked out on the veranda for some fresh air, thinking it would make me feel better. I saw her coming out of the maze."

It was getting easier, she realized, except for having to make sure to keep the happy lilt from her voice as she went on with her lies. "When I mentioned it to Eliza the next morning, about how strange it was Erin could even find her way in and out of that place, she remembered having seen her at your desk, copying what looked like a diagram."

Ryan's teeth were clamped together so tightly his jaw was aching. He felt as if every nerve in his body were raw, being pulled, stretched, torn apart, as he listened to the nightmare revealed.

Victoria shook her head as though deeply dismayed. "I just didn't know what to do. From the day you rode off, and Eliza heard her laughing over a letter she told Annie you'd left her, she turned into a shrew. I just locked myself in my room and wouldn't come out. Poor Annie, she even begged to be sent to the fields to get away from her, and, of course, I let her go. Eliza was the only one strong enough to withstand her abuse, bless her.

"But then—" she paused for effect, as though it were painful to have to continue, "when I saw her coming out of the maze the next night with a man, actually saw them embracing, I knew I couldn't allow it to go on. No matter the consequences. I ran out there, but by that time he had left, and when I told her what I'd seen, she tried to deny it. But the next morning she was gone. She knew I'd tell you, so she ran away with him."

His brain was roaring, as the cruel words attacked— laughing over a letter . . . saw them embracing . . .

"Of course, I had to make sure she'd actually run away," she proceeded to fabricate. "After all, anything could have happened, I suppose, but after seeing the two of them together, there was no doubt in my mind she'd taken off with her lover. Anyway, I went to see her mother, and that's when I found out she'd apparently gone with her, and that's when I started thinking maybe her mother had known about it all along."

If his mother knew of Arlene's earlier threat when she manipulated him into the marriage, she'd realize just how justified her suspicions were. Ryan felt as if a fist had been slammed right into his heart. God, how he wished he knew who the bastard was. In that moment, he knew he was capable of killing him with his bare hands.

Victoria fell silent for a few moments to allow him to absorb it all. She thought she'd done a good job, though it made her a bit nervous, the way he was acting. She'd expected him to blow sky high and rant and rave and threaten to wring Erin's adulterous neck, if he ever got his hands on her. But never had she expected him just to sit there in cold and stony silence. His hands, she noticed, were clenched so tight his knuckles showed white.

Deciding to embellish a bit, she made a tsk-tsk sound of sympathy and commented, "Her lover became rather bold, too, daring to leave a rose as a signal he was waiting in the labyrinth."

Ryan felt as though he'd been slapped by his own hand.

Only that morning, as he rode along in the crisp, cold air, he'd been struck by an exhilarating idea sure to delight Erin. He'd wanted to present her with a perpetual symbol of his love, and he wouldn't even wait till spring to get started. He would ask the gardeners to start working right away. They would remove all but a few of the jasmine bushes that grew so abundantly and replace them with roses. All colors. All varieties. Bushes. Trellises. Vines. Anywhere and everywhere. The predominant shade, of course, would be blood red. For it had been in a rose garden where first he'd met his beloved, and thus, would he rename the plantation—Rose Hill.

Victoria jumped, startled at his sudden, growling cry. "What did you say?"

Her hand flew to her throat in fear as she looked at him, saw his eyes bulging, the cords standing out on his neck, the way he was starting to shake all over. He'd pressed his fists together, as if he were squeezing with all his might to destroy something deep inside him. "I—I said," she stuttered, "th—there was a rose. I heard Annie tell her she'd found a rose at the grave. I think it was a signal, because she met him later, and—"

"Stop!" He leaned out the carriage window to yell up at the driver.

With a sudden lurch, the horses were reined in, and Ryan bolted out the door. Victoria watched, stunned, as he ran to untie his horse. Mounting, he swiftly dug in his heels to send him into a thundering gallop.

Victoria poked her head out the window to command the driver shrilly, "Don't just sit here, you ninny! Get after him. Fast!" She braced herself as the horses took off and the carriage began to rock from side to side. A knot of terror rose in her throat, but not over the precarious ride. She was afraid of what Ryan might do.

He rode at breakneck speed.

Eliza heard him coming up the road. So did Ebner. And both of them exchanged looks of wide-eyed wonder as they stood together just inside the front door.

Ryan rode right up to the porch, dismounting only when he reached the door. Without so much as a glance in their direction, he charged upstairs.

Then they heard it—the sounds of glass breaking and furniture smashing as Ryan commenced to destroy what was left of his dream.

Eliza began to weep. Lord, it wasn't right, none of it.

Ebner winced with each sound from above. "Sweet Jesus," he muttered over and over. "Oh, sweet Jesus, help that poor boy."

By the time the carriage pulled up and Victoria leapt out to charge into the house, all was silent. She looked from Eliza to Ebner, who wouldn't meet her terrified, questioning gaze. Rushing by, she made her way upstairs.

Ryan was standing at the window of what had been Erin's bedroom, hands bruised and bloody. The room was in shambles.

Aghast, Victoria lashed out, "Have you gone crazy? How dare you—"

"Yes, goddamn it, how dare I?" he cut her off to rage. "How dare I think she loved me! Never," he roared, "never mention her name again. And tomorrow, I want every rose on this property destroyed."

Victoria stared after him as he left to cross to his room, slamming and locking the door.

What was it about the roses that upset him so?

With a sigh, she supposed it didn't matter. And she really didn't care about the mess. Eliza would clean it up. Maybe she'd invite Ermine over for tea in the next few days, so they could start planning how to redecorate. Ryan would get over it all eventually.

But still, she couldn't help being curious about the rose and why it triggered such a violent reaction.

Erin was still amazed to think how Philadelphia was such an important harbor, when it lay nearly 110 miles from the sea. At the junction of the Schuylkill and Delaware rivers, one of the crewmen on the flatboat that took her on the last leg of her journey explained it was due to the shipbuilding there. He said the masts, spars, timber, and plank came from the state itself. The wood of the mulberry came from the nearby Chesapeake, and the evergreen and red cedars were imported from the Carolinas and Georgia.

"The distance from the sea doesn't really matter," he'd boasted, "though there is some objection due to the river freezing in the winter. But that's just for a few weeks. Besides, the greatest port in Europe, Amsterdam, is inaccessible almost all winter long. When the water warms just a wee bit here, fleets of merchants are waiting to go out and come in. There's fine corn and flour and pork and beef, lumber and iron. Little time is lost, and trade actually increases those months."

Erin had a flash of memory about Ryan's interest in Philadelphia shipping but pushed it back. She didn't want to think about those days when she foolishly thought she might be falling in love with him.

On arrival in the city, Erin and Lucy Jane said tearful good-byes. Lucy Jane would continue north to join her family, vowing if ever she saw her husband again, she would kill him.

Erin could so easily empathize, for she had the same sentiments for Zachary. "Just try not to look back," she echoed advice she constantly gave herself. "Thinking about it keeps it alive. It's best to let it be dead."

"I wish you luck finding your mother. How long do you think it will be before you can get passage?"

Erin said she honestly didn't know. "I don't have any money, and the American Colonization Society, I understand, doesn't have enough funds even for the freed slaves, who've got the legal right to go. I can't expect help there, but I'll probably try."

"What do the runaways do that want to get out of the country if the society can't help them?"

"They have to find a way to get smuggled on board."

"So what will do you?" Lucy Jane hated to leave her new friend, whom she'd learned to love as a sister in the past weeks.

"When I was here a few months ago, I left some money to be used for people in situations like mine. Maybe others have donated to the cause, too, and I can find assistance there."

"But what if you can't?" Lucy Jane persisted.

"Don't worry. I guess I could always get work as a fancy girl." She winked, and they both laughed, but deep down Erin was frightened as she wondered what would happen if, indeed, there were no aid available from Mother Bethel.

With Lucy Jane on her way, Erin set out from the harbor, walking all the way into the city. Her feet were soon blistered and aching. Though she looked and felt dowdy in the gray muslin dress and black wool cape Jason had managed to find for her back in Jamestown, she was grateful to have even that much. She'd been cast out of her home with only her gown and robe. Ryan could have had the decency at least to send along the clothes she'd brought with her. But he had no decency, she thought with bitter rage, promptly admonishing herself for allowing his memory to invade once more.

Her stomach rumbled with hunger. Food had been scarce on the flatboat. The four-man crew got the bulk of the rations for the two-day journey from the bay. Erin knew it was only fair. After all, the men were working, and she and Lucy Jane were riding free, thanks to the owner being a secret Free-Soiler and willing to provide passage for the last leg of the journey to freedom. Still, she felt weak from not eating, and the way to Mother Bethel Church was long.

It was nearly sunset when she got there, and her heart sank. The building was dark and no one appeared to be around.

Fearing she couldn't stand up much longer, and not wanting to pass out in the street, Erin dragged herself across the lawn and into the shadows. Much better, she felt, to rest on church grounds but could not deny being afraid. Never in her whole life could she remember feeling so alone.

There was a small porch at the rear, and she managed to make it there before she collapsed wearily to the stone floor.

And that was where Pastor Jones found her early the

next morning, shivering from the cold in her exhausted sleep. It was not unusual to find the destitute and homeless on the church's doorstep, but he was startled to recognize Erin. Despite her dirty, shabby clothing, and her mussed, stringy hair, there was no denying she was the same lovely young girl he'd met some time back.

He shook her awake, and she couldn't tell him why she was there, not right away, for her teeth were chattering too fiercely. He helped her inside and wrapped her in a blanket from the sofa in his office while he got a fire going in the grate. At last, with a mug of steaming coffee, huddled before the warmth of the blaze, she was able to explain.

He listened sympathetically to her tragic tale of woe, wondering how any man would want to rid himself of one so lovely, as well as intelligent, no matter what her heritage.

His heart went out to her, and it was with deep regret he had to deny her plea for help. "I know it doesn't seem fair after you gave so generously when you were here before, but that money was used to help others like yourself, and we just don't have the funds right now. I'm sorry, Mrs. Youngblood."

"Sterling," she corrected, more sharply than she intended. "I don't consider myself to be Mrs. Youngblood any longer."

"I can certainly understand that."

"And I can understand a shortage of funds. I'm just grateful you and I together were able to help Letty. I heard she got away safely. And my mother, too. Now I've just got to find a way to follow after them. I'd best get started."

"Not till you've had something to eat. At least, I can offer you a hot meal."

"Which I will gratefully accept."

It was later, as she prepared to go, that Pastor Jones clasped her hands to offer up a prayer for her safe deliverance. He then worriedly asked, "What will you do, my child? Where will you go? Why not stay here, and we'll take up a special offering, and—"

"No." She shook her head, politely cutting him off. "There's no time. I've got to leave Pennsylvania as quickly as possible and follow my mother. She's sick, and she'll need me to take care of her. All I know is she was sent to a place called Sierra Leone, in Africa."

"It's a British colony in West Africa that's been openly receiving freed blacks for the past thirty years or so."

"Do you know much about it?"

"Only that it was initially a private venture of antislavery humanitarians. They were hoping to accomplish two things—a home for unwanted ex-slaves and a base for legitimate trade into Africa. The trade venture didn't work out, though. The colony wound up being taken over by the British government. It's still a haven for free slaves, however, and your mother will be safe there."

"That's a comfort. I'm sure my stepfather will never stop looking for her if he finds out she wasn't sold into slavery as he intended."

"Do you have to go there, too? We could use you here, Erin."

"I know, and believe me, I'd like to help, but I feel driven to try and find her, Pastor Jones."

Soberly, somberly, he whispered, "I pray that you do, my child. I pray that you do."

Pastor Jones insisted she take money for carriage fare. Temperatures had dropped even lower, and the skies were cloudy and overcast with the threat of rain. A chilling wind was blowing in from the channel, and it was no kind of weather to be out walking, especially in her weakened condition.

When the carriage pulled up in front of Charles Grudinger's house, it was nearly dark. She hadn't meant to fall asleep at Mother Bethel, but after eating so much of the delicious meal Pastor Jones had prepared for her, she had curled up on his sofa and slept all afternoon. He had not wanted to awaken her, feeling she needed the rest.

Dressed as she was, Erin did not dare go to the front entrance. Instead, she went to the door that opened to the alley in the rear, where deliveries and service calls were made.

Nanny Bess peered out a window in response to her knock, calling sharply, "Who is it? We aren't expecting anyone."

Erin gave only her first name.

Promptly opening the door to motion her inside, Nanny Bess exclaimed, "Glory be, I'd never have known it was you. What on earth has happened? Your clothes, your hair. . . ." Her voice trailed off; she was embarrassed because she'd gone on so. It was obvious the once glamorous and richly dressed young woman had fallen on hard times.

Erin proceeded to tell all, and Nanny Bess listened with eyes growing ever wider with each word she spoke. "I need to talk to Mr. Grudinger," Erin finished in pleading. "I don't have any money. Mother Bethel can't help, either. And I've got to get to Sierra Leone and find my mother. I was hoping, praying, he'd grant me passage on one of his ships."

They were sitting in the kitchen. Nanny Bess had guided her to a chair at the table. She didn't say anything as she took Erin's wet cape and offered her one of her robes. Finally, when Erin was warm, comfortable, and holding a mug of steaming coffee in her trembling hands,

Nanny Bess told her Mr. Grudinger was not well. "The doctors think it's his heart. He seldom gets out of bed anymore. He's gone to sleep for the night, and I don't want to wake him up.

"In fact," she admitted, "I'm not sure it's a good idea even to let him know you're here."

"But why?" Erin was desperate to know, a sinking sensation in her stomach. "Surely, he'll help me, and I know he was involved in transporting freed slaves back to Africa, and—"

"That didn't work out." Nanny Bess cut her off brusquely. "The Colonization Society was having money problems, so he got involved with packet services, instead."

"I don't know what you're talking about. All I do know is that I don't have anywhere else to go, and if he can't, or won't, help me, then I've got to try and slip on board to stowaway and hope I don't get caught." Her voice cracked with emotion.

"That won't be necessary. Mr. Grudinger has been generous to me through the years, and my needs have been few. I have money saved, and I can book your passage on one of the packets myself. He owns two of them. But they also carry cargo, and they don't sail from port till they have a full load. There's only room for about twelve passengers, but I'll see what I can do about getting you on the next one out."

"Thank God," Erin breathed a sigh of relief, but sensing there was something she wasn't being told, she asked suspiciously, "Why don't you want him to know I'm here?"

"Because I'd have to tell him everything, how your husband sold you into slavery, which technically makes you a fugitive. He wouldn't dare let you go on one of his ships, then. He'd be afraid he'd lose his contract with the government to carry mail if it became known he was illegally transporting runaways.

"Whether you like it or not," she hastened to add, "Mr. Youngblood is a rich and powerful man. Quite well known and highly regarded. If he finds out you escaped and were brought North, you can be sure he'll have people looking for you. Mr. Grudinger would not want to be involved."

"But you will help me?" Erin felt the need to be assured, reaching to clasp Nanny Bess's hand.

"Of course I will, but I wish you were going to stay here. I could use your help."

Erin shook her head. "That's not possible."

Nanny Bess understood, then dismally shared her own fears. "Mr. Grudinger isn't going to live much longer, and I won't have a home myself when he's gone. But that part doesn't worry me. What does, is wondering what I can do to help Mother Bethel."

"You'll find a way," Erin assured, reverently adding, "Your kind always do."

Nanny Bess flashed a wide grin and impulsively reached to hug her. "And so does yours! I won't be at all surprised to see you back here one day. I'll sure be praying it happens."

"Maybe. Right now I've got a long journey ahead of me." Pain assaulted her as she remembered Rosa's dying prediction that she'd go far, far away, because she'd worn gray on her wedding day. Sharing the superstition, she offered the comment, "I don't believe in things like that, but it makes me wonder."

"Maybe it works both ways," Nanny Bess voiced her hope. "Maybe it'll bring you back again."

CHAPTER

 29

SEVERAL MORE WEEKS PASSED BEFORE GRUD inger's packet in the harbor was fully loaded with cargo. Erin passed the time by helping at Mother Bethel in exchange for a cot in the basement, since Nanny Bess stuck to her resolve that it was best Mr. Grudinger not know she was about. There was much to be done at the church, anyway, where the homeless and hungry were fed daily.

Erin liked working from dawn till dark, so that when she finally went to bed, she was too exhausted to dream. For despite her resolve to forget the past, she miserably had no control over her heart during sleep. So many nights she would awaken from having envisioned Ryan's strong arms about her, only to weep in sorrow for what was, what might have been.

She was glad when word came of a definite departure, for winter had descended, and no one could be sure when the river would become ice-locked and impassable.

Nanny Bess went to the dock that morning to see her off. She'd provided new clothing and money to help Erin become established once she reached her destination. "This packet, the *Freedom,* goes directly to Liverpool. From there, you'll be sailing off the coast of Portugal.

then Africa, and finally reach Sierra Leone in about another ten days after you leave England."

Erin tried to express her gratitude, but Nanny Bess said it wasn't necessary.

"We're all in this together, child. Helping each other. That's what it takes to get through this life."

Erin hadn't thought much about Nanny Bess providing her with false papers of identification, listing her under the assumed name of Miss Edith Starling. But she realized why that was necessary when the captain obligingly showed her the information he had to keep on all his passengers: their age, sex, occupation, and nationality. So, there would be no document of Erin Sterling ever having crossed the Atlantic.

As on her previous voyage, Erin fell in love with the sea. While the other passengers gathered in the saloon for card games and such, she delighted in following the crew about, fascinated to observe the inner workings of the ship.

The captain, Dolan O'Grady, invited Erin to his quarters each night after dinner. While he enjoyed his daily allowance of one glass of brandy, along with a cigar, Erin listened, entranced, as he told her all about his life at sea, what it was like to be on a packet line.

The term *packet,* he told her, came from the way cargo was bundled—in packets. It came to signify a ship that sailed on schedule, which meant such a vessel could be counted on to deliver the most urgent of cargoes, such as important mail and time-pressed passengers.

Dizzily, Erin challenged herself to memorize every detail.

"What ye' be wantin' to learn all the technical points for, lassie?" Captain O'Grady wanted to know one evening as she proudly recited all she'd learned.

With a shake of her head and a twinkle in her brown

eyes, Erin laughed. "Who knows? Maybe one day I'll run a ship of my own."

The packets were all tubby in appearance. Sturdy construction was required, Captain O'Grady emphasized, for no matter what its size or role, there was no more demanding a job for a ship than year-round service on the Atlantic. Erin was amazed at the cost, which ranged from forty to fifty thousand dollars per ship.

Captain O'Grady agreed. "Aye, that sounds like a lot, but a packet carrying a full cargo can earn as much as twenty thousand in freight alone in a year. Then there's maybe an additional ten thousand to be had from passengers and mail. Why, even allowing for maintenance costs, a packet can still pay for herself in just a couple of years.

"As for me," he divulged, "I might make only forty dollars a month in salary, but I get five percent of the income from cargo, and another twenty-five percent of the passengers' fares, and Mr. Grudinger even gives me a cut of the fee for carrying mail. Thirty times the earnings of a seaman, a captain's responsibility is worthwhile, me lassie."

He was pushing the *Freedom* at top knots, in hopes to cross the Atlantic before a bad winter storm attacked with banshee winds, blinding snow and mountainous seas that could roughly wash the decks for hours at a time.

"Packet sailors," Captain O'Grady proudly boasted, "are the toughest of the tough. They can stand the worst weather, the worst food, on the least amount of sleep.

"All they require," he added with a wink, "is a bit more rum than most."

Ryan put on the fancy new suit his mother had had tailored for him: black waistcoat, gray striped trousers, white shirt, ruffled collar, red satin cravat. He wasn't impressed over the outfit any more than he was the dinner party she was having. In fact, he just plain didn't give a damn about anything anymore.

Ebner appeared to tell him the first guests were starting to arrive.

He poured himself another drink from the crystal decanter on his desk. Even though it had been nearly two months since Erin had gone away, he still tortured himself by imagining her sitting there, copying the diagram of the labyrinth so she and her lover could meet in the center.

Goddamn it, he cursed, how could she have done it? All those nights they'd made wonderful, passionate love, and she'd seemed so willing, so responsive, only to leave his arms later to go to another. How blind, how stupid, he'd been.

Ebner cleared his throat and uneasily repeated, "Mastah, yo' momma said I was to tell you to come on out and greet your guests."

"They aren't my guests, Ebner. It's her party. Let her worry about it."

"Mastah Ryan, suh . . ." He approached reluctantly, fearfully. "Mastah, I know it's none of my business, but I just felt I had to say somethin' to you, 'cause me and you, we've known each other a long time, and—"

"Just get on with it," Ryan snapped impatiently. He was getting fed up with the way the servants crept around, as if they were scared to death of him. Maybe he was irritable, but he'd never been cruel to them. They had nothing to fear, and they should know that.

"Mastah, I'm worried about you."

Ryan laughed. "What on earth for?"

"Well, suh . . ." Ebner wasn't sure how far to go in voicing his concern. "You're not takin' care of yourself, and I'm worried 'cause you just aren't happy no more."

"Of course, I'm happy," Ryan fired back sarcastically. "Why wouldn't I be happy? I've got extremely competent overseers who keep Jasmine Hill running quite efficiently. My mother runs the house with the help of Eliza and a whole staff of good servants. And all the slaves are well taken care of, and they seem satisfied with their life. There's not a thing I have to do. I can just sit here night and day and drink, and nobody cares."

"I cares, suh."

Ryan looked at Ebner over the rim of his glass and knew by the valet's concerned expression it was so. "Well, I appreciate it, Ebner, but there's no need to worry. I'm fine." His smile was forced.

And Ebner knew it.

Ryan tossed down the rest of his drink and stood. "Well, I suppose there's nothing to do but get this evening over with. How many did my mother invite, do you know?"

"I heard her tell Eliza she'd invited all of Miz Ermine Coley's family. I counted Eliza settin' places fo' nine."

Ryan groaned. That meant Ermine's parents and both sets of grandparents, and he smelled a rat. His mother hadn't told him it was strictly a family gathering, and if the grandparents were included, it meant the pressure would be on him to announce a new wedding date tonight. He wasn't ready. He hadn't even gone down and signed the papers the family attorney had prepared that would free him legally from Erin. Damn it, he just wasn't ready for any of it, and most of all, despite the pain and anger, he wasn't even ready to stop thinking about her, wanting her, and, most anguished of all, to stop loving her.

Ryan reached to pour himself another drink. He knew he was going to need it.

"Suh, I wish—"

"Yes?" Ryan glared at him then to communicate that enough was enough. He might have to tolerate his mother's nagging, but he didn't have to listen to his valet, for God's sake.

Ebner withered. "Nothin', suh. I'll go tell Miz Victoria you'll be along."

Ryan continued to sit there scowling in his misery. He had called on Ermine three times in the past three weeks, but only to pacify his mother. He supposed he did have to get on with his life but first had to find a way to cast aside the haunting memories. Yes, God, Erin had been a beauty, but more than that he could not forget how they'd enjoyed each other, shared talk, humor. He'd liked being with her more than any woman he'd ever known. While passion was exciting between them, there were other moments, as well, moments when he delighted in just being with her. But it was over, he reminded himself, and it was only torment to keep thinking about her.

The door opened, and he looked up, frowning, prepared to face his mother's anger that he hadn't answered her summons. But it was Ermine who breezed into the room. Stunning in a gown of red velvet, she came straight to him to twine her arms about his neck as he rose in polite greeting.

"So, here's where you've been hiding," she cooed, nuzzling his chin with her lips.

Tiny, petite, she was standing on tiptoe. The top of her head barely reached his shoulder. Keith, who like Ryan was tall, had once confided that diminutive women made him feel even more masculine, but Ryan experienced the opposite reaction. They made him feel clumsy, awkward. With Erin he'd felt comfortable, for she was tall, and when they embraced she had only to lift her lovely face to his, and. . . .

He gave himself a mental shake, attempting to fling away the cobwebs that sought to hold him forever captive.

Ermine sensed his tension. "Is something wrong? Aren't you glad to see me?" She sniffed, shuddered, and drew back. "Oh, Ryan, you've been drinking."

"Of course, I've been drinking." He laughed, settling back in his chair and lifting his glass. "That's what a man usually does in his study at the end of the day . . . he drinks."

"But"—she gave her golden curls a shake of protest— "you drink too much. Your mother says so. You didn't even come out to greet me and my family, because you were in here drinking, and that upsets me."

He frowned. Now he remembered what he'd tried to overlook in her before: she nagged, which reminded him of his mother. "I'll be out in a minute."

Petulantly, she dropped to his lap and declared, "No. I won't go back out there without you." She began to nuzzle his neck.

Ryan wondered which annoyed him the most: her little-girl whine or her nagging. He also wondered how anyone so pretty could be so unappealing at times. Yet, the way she was wrapping herself about him brought a stirring in his loins. It had been a long time since he'd had a woman. Right after Erin had left, he'd gone to see Corrisa but wound up paying only for a sympathetic ear. The harsh reality was that he didn't want anyone else but knew he damn well had to get over that.

Ermine surprised him suddenly by dropping her hand downwards to caress. "You want me, don't you, Ryan? You always have. Your mother wants us to set the wedding date tonight. That's why she invited my grandparents, so we could make it all official with a family toast. And the sooner we do it, the better, because I want you, too, as I've never wanted any man. . . ."

She kissed him then, with passion that surprised. With her hand between his legs, her breasts rubbing against him, her tongue parting his lips, he felt himself grow hard. He gathered her tighter against him, yet, despite the surging desire, he was still assailed by the torturous reminder this was another woman he held, not the one who could turn his blood to liquid fire.

Ermine pulled back to say seductively, "If you'll come out with me now and get all the formalities over, we can slip away later by ourselves. It'll be so good, my darling. And you'll forget all about that little trollop that cast such a spell. I'll kiss you all over, and make you crazy for me."

She pressed her hot, moist lips against his, but he abruptly pushed her away. "Erin was no trollop, Ermine."

Her laugh was mocking. "Oh? Then what do you call her? Whore? Harlot? It's all the same, and I'll make you forget her—"

He abruptly set her on her feet. "That's enough, Ermine."

"Oh, really?" She bristled with indignant anger. "I'll have you know I've been embarrassed and humiliated by all of this, but I've tried not to say anything to you about it, because I agreed with your mother you had to have been under some kind of spell, and that whore," she paused to emphasize, "just drove you crazy with her depraved lust. I can understand, and I can even forgive you, but there is a certain limit, Ryan, and I won't have you defending her. Do you understand me?

"Now then," she continued, satisfied that his silence was a sign of capitulation, "let's forget this unfortunate scene and join our families to celebrate. I already have my wedding gown, you know, and Mother can get everything together in a short time. You need to go sign those papers your mother had drawn up, and I'd say we can get married in about three weeks."

Ryan started laughing. Once he started, he couldn't stop. He threw his head back and roared with amusement

to think he could ever have been even remotely tempted
to bind himself for life to such a shrew. More than that,
he knew he was crazy to think he could ever marry any
woman until the day he could truly forget the only one
he'd ever loved.

Frightened by his bizarre behavior, Ermine ran out to
fetch Victoria and tell her that her son had gone crazy.

Ebner, however, was standing outside, and he'd heard
much of the conversation. Not because he was trying to,
but because he had nowhere else to be for the moment.
It just broke his heart to know his master was suffering
so. Oh, Lord, how he wished he'd never had to obey Miss
Victoria and tell Miss Erin that awful lie. He didn't know
what it all meant, but maybe she wouldn't have gone away
if he hadn't done it. There was just so much he didn't understand.

Eliza appeared then, and they exchanged wretched
glances of shared misery before melting into the shadows
as they heard Miss Victoria approach, footsteps clattering.

Ryan made no move, nor sound, as his mother unleashed her frustration. Ermine, she said, was convinced
he was having a nervous breakdown. She and her family
were leaving, and her father would have a doctor sent out
as soon as they got back to Richmond. Ryan needed help,
she said, for his humiliation over the actions of that whore
had taken its toll.

Victoria raged on. "Ermine is a very understanding and
sensible young woman. She wants for you the same as I
do, for you to get hold of yourself and get on with your
life." She went to the bell cord and gave it an angry yank
to summon Ebner. "I want you to go to bed now. I'll have
Eliza make you some tea, and you try to rest till the doctor
gets here."

Ryan still did not speak. He was standing at the window, staring out at the misty night. A fog had rolled in from the river, and a chilling wind was blowing, rattling the windowpanes.

Victoria interpreted his silence as evidence he was allowing her to take over. Maybe Ermine was right, and he was actually having a mental collapse, though she feared he just wasn't getting over Erin as quickly as she'd hoped.

Annoyed that Ebner had not responded to her call, she hurried out to find him.

Ebner made sure Miss Victoria was gone before entering the study. "Mastah Ryan . . ."

Ryan did not respond.

"Mastah Ryan, I got to tell you somethin', and I don't want your momma to hear it."

At that, Ryan turned to look at him with lackluster eyes. "Go on."

Ebner took a deep breath, mustering his courage before whispering, "There's a rose at the grave."

Ryan blinked. At first, not understanding.

"A rose," Ebner repeated. "At Miz Henrietta's grave."

Ryan came to life then. His mother had said she thought Erin's signal to meet her lover in the labyrinth had been the placing of a rose at his grandmother's grave. He wasn't sure what it meant now, in the dead of winter, but, by God, he intended to find out.

Opening the French doors, he bolted across the terrace and leapt to the ground. He could barely find his way across the lawn as the fog swirled about him, absorbing him into the night.

At last, he groped and found the entrance to the maze. He only hoped he could remember the way himself, for it had been so long since he'd gone inside.

Then, just around the first corner, he saw the glow of torchlight and knew with a jolt it wouldn't be necessary to go all the way in. Whoever was there, whoever had left the signal, was already waiting.

He turned, only to be slammed with bewilderment to see Eliza standing there, holding the torch aloft. Beside her was Annie. And, as he wondered what it meant, Ebner appeared, out of breath from trying to keep up, to take his place beside them.

"Mastah Ryan," Eliza began bravely, for it seemed she'd been preparing herself for this moment a long, long time—no matter the consequences.

"Mastah Ryan, there's somethin' you gotta know."

CHAPTER

 30

ERIN HAD HAPPILY SPENT SO MUCH TIME WITH
Captain O'Grady and his crew, that she hadn't cultivated
any lasting friendships with the other passengers. Accordingly, when the *Freedom* reached Liverpool, there were
only perfunctory farewells exchanged as the others disembarked.

Captain O'Grady had not wanted to pry into Erin's personal life, nor her reasons for going to Sierra Leone. Yet
curiosity got the better of him after so many weeks spent
together, and when they left England, he began to ask
subtle questions. He was frankly puzzled as to why a beautiful young woman was traveling to such a distant port,
alone.

Though at first she'd been repulsed by his admission
of previous involvement in slave smuggling, Erin was
gradually able to forgive, as his deep regret was so painfully obvious. Her feelings of aversion yielded to a close
friendship. And, as a result, she was finally able to confide
her own haunting past.

He shared her pain, and tears glimmered in his sea-gray
eyes. "But Sierra Leone is no place for you," he declared,
anger taking over. "No matter what your dastardly hus-

band did, you're no slave. You could have stayed in Philadelphia and been safe."

"Probably, but my mother couldn't."

"She doesn't belong there, either. It's primarily for blacks captured from slave ships. Not that it's all that primitive. Aye, there's a good settlement growing there, to be sure. Some of the liberated Africans have become traders, and then there are priests and doctors and lawyers. It's not uncivilized, by any means, but I must say it would take a lot of adjusting for a genteel lady to call it her home."

With a bitter smile, Erin pointed out, "I don't think it'd be hard, at all, Captain, if she had nowhere else to call home."

At last they were sailing off the coast of Africa. Captain O'Grady took time to point out to Erin the different regions they passed—Morocco, the western Sahara, and Mauritania. Dense jungles blanketed the coastal plains, with miles of virgin forest, humid and thick with magnificent trees and precious woods. Beyond was a secondary forest with mangrove swamps and bird-swarming marshes. Then the plains seemed to rapidly rise to form the huge plateau which stretched on into the interior.

They passed Cape Verde, with its smooth green hills, its long strip of shimmering sand, and its dangerously concealed Almadia Reef. Captain O'Grady said they were passing the area known as Senegal. Next would be Guinea, and, soon, their destination of Sierra Leone.

Erin stood at the ship's railing to experience the thick shroud of muffling heat, the density of seething vegetation. Also drifting to greet her was the stench of dead crabs lying in the mud at mouths of rivers and decaying coconuts half buried in the sand by natives trying to rot the fiber of the hard shell free.

Her heart began to pound with excitement as they

sailed on up the mouth of the Sierra Leone River, framed by the vision of mountains darkly rising in an arc beyond the bay. Now and then fork lightning slashed high above the shadowed waters as thunder rumbled among the towering peaks.

Captain O'Grady told her, "When this part of the world was discovered by the Portuguese, they thought the thunder sounded like a lion roaring, so they named it 'Sierra Leone', which means 'Lion Mountain'."

"Beautiful," Erin murmured reverently. "Everything about it is beautiful."

He gave a soft chuckle. "Not everything, lassie. Some of the stories are real ugly. Like the famous outbreak of 'human leopards' just before the turn of the century that took place in the high country. Natives got dressed up in real leopard skins and went around dismembering victims—or eating them."

"Cannibalism?" She shuddered.

"Not really. The purpose was for their group to gain strength, so it was said. Even today, one tribe will blame such a ritual on another tribe, the reason being it's the worst thing you can say about anybody around here. It's also said half the shipboard slave revolts were caused by the natives thinking they were being taken over the sea to be eaten."

Erin, who had heard of many legends also, offered one in return. "Africans who've never seen a white man think they're a kind of sea monster, since they come from over the horizon in big ships, where they don't believe there is any land."

"Sea monsters." He gave a snort of disdain. "Well, they're not far wrong in thinking that, are they?"

Erin's gaze raked the shoreline, cluttered with the thatched huts of the natives, the squat mud-brick government buildings. Now that the actual moment of arrival was at hand, she was starting to feel apprehensive. What if her mother wasn't there? She voiced her fears outloud, "I don't even know where to start looking for her."

"I think"—Captain O'Grady grinned and pointed to the crowd gathering—"she will find you." He went on to explain how the arrival of a ship was a big occasion in the village. Everyone showed up at the waterfront to watch the unloading of supplies and possible new inhabitants—missionaries, workers, and, of course, freed slaves coming home.

Erin was ready the moment the plank was in position. It was nearly dark, little time left to be recognized, especially when her mother wouldn't even be looking for her.

She was about to disembark when Captain O'Grady caught up to place a restraining hand on her shoulder and warn, "Don't stray too far, lassie. Give me time to finish my duties, and I'll go with you to look for her. We can check at the port office and ask to see the list of arrivals a month or so ago. If she's here, we'll find her. Just be patient."

But Erin had waited too long, and she stepped eagerly onto the plank.

That was when she heard the frantic scream.

"Erin! Dear God! I don't believe it! It's her! It has to be!"

Captain O'Grady again grasped her arm but not to hold her back. Instead, he was steering her as fast as possible down the slanted board to make sure she didn't stumble and fall in her desperate, near-hysterical descent to shore.

Ahead, pushing through the crowd of onlookers, he saw the crying, shouting woman. A white man in a dark suit was guiding her, helping clear a path through the sea of bodies.

At last, Erin and Arlene melted in an embrace that seemed to last forever to those looking on. Sobbing, weeping, that they couldn't bear to end the moment for fear it would disappear and not be real, after all, but merely another dream of torment.

Captain O'Grady recognized the man who was accompanying Arlene Tremayne. Elliott Noland was the adjutant governor, in complete authority of the settlement when His Lordship the governor was away in the mother country.

The two exchanged uncertain glances, not knowing what to do. Finally Elliott sought to draw them away from the harbor by offering his carriage to take them to his home. "Captain O'Grady, you're welcome to come along. We can all have dinner."

"Yes, please," Erin begged, turning to him, then remembering to introduce her mother.

"No, no." He shook his head, smiling, warmed by the love radiating between mother and daughter. "I've much to do back on my ship. . . ." He was already backing away, unnoticed as Erin and her mother were lost once more in each other.

Elliott took them to his quarters, a small, but adequate house built of stone imported from England. The cottage was perched on a hillock overlooking the bay. He guided them inside as Erin marveled over how Arlene seemed to be glowing with good health.

"You have color in your cheeks, and your eyes are shining, and you've even put on weight. I can't believe it. And you haven't coughed once!"

Arlene looked to Elliott then. "Tell her. As you told me."

He was only too glad to oblige. "Doctors in England report consumption can be relieved by a change of climate. Your mother told me how she'd suffered back in America, in Virginia, and since she's had few, if any, symptoms since arriving here, we can only assume our hot, humid weather has her on the way to being cured."

Arlene sat down on the little settee in front of the window. By day, the view was glorious, but darkness had finally descended, and only a purplish abyss was offered.

"Enough about me." She beckoned Erin to join her. "How on earth did you find out where I was? Did they get word back to you? the Free-Soilers who helped me? And why are you here? What about Ryan. . . ."

She fell silent, for she knew her daughter so well, knew the anguished shadow that appeared in her eyes at the mention of his name, was projected all the way from her heart. "Something's wrong. Tell me."

Erin did so. From beginning to end. When she finished, they wept in each other's arms once more.

Elliott figured if ever two women needed a drink, they did. He picked up the little silver bell on the table by the settee to ring for a decanter of sherry.

A few moments later, the servant responded—and promptly screamed.

Erin shrieked, "Letty! Oh, God, Letty, I don't believe it!"

Elliott chuckled, shook his head, gave up, and went to get refreshments himself.

Erin was forced to repeat her tragic tale to Letty, who then shared her own experience of traveling north and then across the Atlantic. Arlene joined in, and they were lost in recounting their adventures.

Elliott provided the sherry, as well as a hastily concocted stew. But no one was really hungry, for they were too lost in one another, in sharing sorrow, as well as triumphs.

Then Letty asked the question Erin had known would come, and dreaded having to answer.

"How is my momma?"

Erin knew there was no easy way. "Oh, Letty . . . ," she began. "I'm so very sorry, but—"

She didn't have to finish. Letty knew by the look on her face, the tone of her voice. She began to sob wildly and threw herself into Arlene's waiting arms.

"I wish I could have saved her as she saved me." Erin went on to reveal how Rosa had rescued her from Zachary's brutal assault but declined to admit it hadn't been his first attempt. No need, she felt, to add to her mother's grief over having been married to such a monster.

She told, also, how Ben had escaped, how she'd helped him on the first part of his journey, and prayed he would make it the rest of the way. There'd been no word, no way of knowing his ultimate destination.

"At least she's at peace," Letty lamented. "Can't nobody ever hurt her again."

"Or us, either," Arlene said with forced optimism and joy as she gathered both in her arms. "We're all free here, and we've got a new life—together. Let's just be grateful for that and promise ourselves never to look back."

Erin wished that were possible, dared to think in time perhaps it might mercifully come to pass. Yet, she was still haunted by the pain, the searing ache for revenge. But what stung the most was the undeniable fact she had loved him so.

It was nearly dawn when they finally, wearily, ended their emotional reunion.

Letty retired to her room to deal with her grief in her own way.

Elliott showed Erin to a spare bedroom, adjoining her mother's.

Weary, worn, anxious for sleep, Erin could only wonder vaguely about why her mother was staying here, in the house with the adjutant governor of Sierra Leone. She hadn't missed the way Arlene just seemed to glow when he was around.

Something was happening between the two, and Erin was pretty sure she knew what it was. She was gladdened to think her mother had been able to open her heart once more to love.

As for herself, Erin knew the door to her own heart was bolted shut.

Ryan had gone straight to his mother when Annie, along with Ebner and Eliza, yielded to her conscience and told him everything she knew concerning Erin.

Victoria, however, maintained they were lying.

"I'll have them beaten! How dare they say I drugged that little trollop, that I had Ebner lie about your being here when you weren't! That's absurd!"

He towered over her as she sat on the parlor divan, awaiting arrival of the doctor Mr. Coley had promised to send.

Ryan did not like the way he was feeling at that moment, as if he wanted to reach out and wrap his fingers around her throat and choke the truth out of her. "Yes, it is strange they'd dare lie about something so serious."

"I—I'll have them beaten," she said, repeating her threat. "They just want to make trouble."

"You won't lay a hand on them. I gave them my word. I also promised to free them, pay their passage north to escape you, and the likes of Zachary Tremayne, the goddamn son of a bitch!" His voice rose as he struck the air with his fist. "Now you tell me, damn it, what you know about Erin's disappearance. And stop lying! I know you had Eliza lace Erin's tea that night with laudanum. Then you had Ebner lock her in her room after telling her I was back and didn't want to see her.

"I also know," he raged on, "that Eliza took the letter

I'd left under her door and gave it to you, which means Erin never got it and, no doubt, thought I'd gone away without a word. Now what happened after that?"

Victoria wished she could cry, but she couldn't muster a single tear. She was too infuriated with Eliza and Ebner's betrayal. It probably wouldn't make any difference, anyway, because Ryan looked as if he were capable of absolute mayhem as he waited for an explanation. Desperately, she groped for a way to absolve herself. "Did Eliza lie and say she didn't see Erin coming out of the maze with a man?"

"She told me about that night, but it doesn't mean Erin was guilty of adultery, Mother."

Stunned that he could defend her, Victoria indignantly challenged him. "Well, what other reason would she have for stealing the diagram of the maze and meeting him out there in the middle of the night? And what about the rose at the grave? That was a signal. It had to be."

"It was." He gave a curt nod. Annie had told him everything, and he knew the significance but wasn't about to tell his mother. She had no business knowing Erin had been helping runaways, and now he found himself wishing they'd been close enough for her to share her secret with him, and also that he'd had the conviction to stand beside her and help.

Victoria frantically wanted to know. "Then why—"

"That's not the issue, Mother. Now, I'm going to ask you one more time—what did happen to Erin? Where is she now? I know she didn't run away with another man."

"The slaves know so much," she said flippantly. "Ask them."

"They don't know. You'd already banished Annie to the field and the compound and threatened to send her to auction if she dared come around the house again. I also know you sent Eliza and Ebner to the compound the night Erin disappeared. You obviously didn't want any witnesses. Now tell me, damn it," he roared, and she shrank back against the pillows in fear of what he might do. "What have you done with my wife?"

"You have gone crazy!" she said with forced authority for despite her squirming apprehension, she knew he'd never strike her, his own mother. "Ermine was right. I hope that doctor hurries up and gets here before you go berserk as you did that other time and start smashing things. I swear, Ryan, I'll sign papers to have you sent away and locked up with the insane. I won't tolerate—"

"Do you even know where she is?" He grabbed her chair and shook it, afraid if he touched her he might actually lose control. "Or did you just pay somebody to take her away and do whatever they wanted with her? Was it Zachary Tremayne? Did you pay him to do it?"

She leapt to her feet, pushed by him, and ran to the door before yelling, "I don't know where she is, and I'm glad. You'll never be able to find her. She's gone from your life for good, and one day you'll thank me."

He walked out into the foyer to stand and look after her as she rushed up the stairs. Quietly, ominously, he promised, "I'll never forgive you for this, Mother, and if I don't find Erin, you can forget you have a son."

He rushed to saddle his horse and ride out, oblivious to the chilling darkness. Despite his boiling urgency, he had to yield to the pace set by the stallion, least he stumble and fall.

As he rode, he tried to push down the rising ire over not being told sooner. But, as Ebner attempted to justify, they'd all been too afraid. Eliza had even admitted her own selfish reasons for wanting the marriage to fail, but too late she realized the tragic consequences of her meddling.

All right, he fumed amidst the stygian cold, he knew that Erin had not left him for another man, but now he was faced with finding out exactly what had happened so he could go after her. He figured to get Tremayne to tell what he knew, and hopefully he'd have a clue as to where to start searching.

At last, Tremayne's house loomed against the horizon, framed by the light of a waning moon.

Something, some invisibly creeping spider of foreboding, began to inch its torturous way up Ryan's spine.

What was it about that shadowed structure that birthed such sudden alarm?

And then he knew.

The silence.

Like a giant fist choking and stifling the sound of every living creature in every direction, the silence was a suffocating blanket of terror.

Ryan moved the horse forward at a steady pace, but he was glad he'd strapped on a holster and was armed.

He rode to the front steps and dismounted. Making his way up, there was not even the noise of a distant cricket to break through the deadly still. It was as though not even the wind dared blow across this unholy land.

The door opened with a creak. Stepping inside, he could smell the dust, the muskiness, of a house unkempt. "Tremayne," he yelled from the dark foyer. "We have to talk. Now!"

From upstairs, he heard the creaking of the heart-of-pine flooring as someone stirred. A moment later, there came the sound of footsteps in the hall.

Ryan waited at the foot of the stairs. Gradually, he was able to make out the glow of a lantern, becoming brighter as the man bearing it came closer.

"What the hell do you want?"

Zachary Tremayne stared down at him from the second-floor landing, lamp in one hand, rifle in the other.

Ryan did not mince words. "My wife."

Zachary realized that Youngblood's being there could only mean trouble.

Nate hadn't told Zachary the details, but he knew Erin had been disposed of as Arlene had, and he was glad, because if he'd been able to get his hands on her, he would probably have beaten Erin to death for the scar she left on his face. But Youngblood, according to Nate, didn't know of Erin's fate; his mother had taken care of that.

Zachary pointed the gun. "She's not here. Now get out. I don't want no trouble."

Ryan started walking slowly toward the stairs but kept his eyes on Tremayne. "Where's *your* wife?"

"She's not here, either. Now I told you, I don't want trouble," he repeated, an edge to his voice.

"Tremayne, till I find Erin, everybody's got troubles." He started upward.

Zachary backed away from the railing. "I swear, I'll shoot. Now you get on out of here. I didn't have anything to do with what happened to Erin. All I wanted was to get rid of Arlene, so the voodoo would stop, and it did, 'cause I let the slaves know if it didn't, I was gonna start peelin' hide and hanging a few of 'em. And it worked, 'cause things have got quiet. Real quiet. And that's the way I want it. Now git!"

Ryan continued his ascent.

Zachary watched in wary silence and kept the gun pointed.

Even in the scant light, Ryan could see the hideous scar. "How'd that happen, Tremayne? Did one of your slaves finally give you what you deserved?"

Zachary bristled, eyes narrowing with rage as he sought revenge for the disfigurement Erin had caused. "No, it wasn't a slave, Youngblood. At least, she wasn't one then. But I reckon about now she's getting what she deserves, working as a fancy girl somewhere."

Ryan didn't know what he was talking about but felt the hairs standing up on the back of his neck. "Maybe you'd better explain."

Zachary had slowly leaned to set the lantern on the floor so he could hold the gun with both hands. He could get away with killing Youngblood by saying the man had broken into his house. Or maybe he'd just drag him deep into the swamp and let him rot there. But first, he wanted to enjoy taunting. "Sure, I'll explain, and then you'll be glad you can't find the high-yeller bitch.

"You see." He licked his lips in delighted anticipation of being able to tell him at last. "Arlene's grandmother was a full-blooded Negro, so that makes her mulatto. You hear what I'm saying', Youngblood? You married a woman with Negro blood! Why, she's nothin' but a slave passin' for white, and you were fool enough to fall for it. But not me! I knew all along. Arlene told me before we got married, and it didn't matter till she got so sickly, but I sent her where she belongs, into slavery. I figure that's where your high-yeller wife wound up, too, and—"

With a savage cry, Ryan lunged, and when he did, Zachary pulled the trigger. Ryan had anticipated and dove to the side. As the gun fired, he felt the whizzing heat mere inches from his head. His arms snaked around the man's feet and toppled him backward. They grappled for the gun, rolling over and over, and they kicked the lantern over but didn't notice as oil spilled and flames shot across the floor.

Ryan landed a sound smash to Zachary's jaw but caught a blow to his chin and was dazed long enough for Zachary to grab the gun by the barrel. There was no time to position and fire, but he brought the stock down in a deadly arc.

Ryan saw it coming in the glow of the hungry licking blaze and rolled just in time. Zachary lunged again, but

Ryan was ready, butting him in the midsection with his head and knocking him breathless.

With a smashing fist, he put him all the way out.

Slowly, Ryan got to his feet. Smoke was blinding, for the fire was rapidly spreading. He stumbled through the gray, choking fog, groping for the stairs.

He was about to descend when he hesitated over whether to let the bastard burn to death.

He turned back into the smoke.

With great effort, he dragged Zachary all the way downstairs and out into the yard.

Gratefully gulping in the sweet, fresh air to cleanse his parched lungs, Ryan stared down at his unconscious foe. "Sometimes life is worse than death, damn you," he muttered before turning away. "If there's a God in heaven, I've a feeling he'll show you hell on earth."

Victoria reclined against the pillows, feeling absolutely wretched. With Eliza and Ebner gone, the other household servants were not as competent, and she was having a terrible time with the vapors.

The doctor had come and gone late last night, assuring her he'd return some time in the afternoon to examine Ryan and try to diagnose the extent of his mental disturbance. Meanwhile, Victoria could only pray Ryan would not learn the truth. It might take a bit longer, but if he couldn't find that wretched girl, which she was sure he'd be unable to do, he'd eventually have to get over her and get on with his life.

She guessed he'd gone tearing off to the Tremayne farm. She only hoped Tremayne would tell him about Arlene. Maybe then, he'd realize it had all happened for the best and just give up. For certain, she'd pretend not to have known and, as would be expected, have some kind of attack. Never would she reveal she'd known all along, for then he might suspect she did have something to do with Erin's disappearance. For the time being, it was the word of slaves against hers, and they weren't allowed to testify against white people, anyway, in a court of law, so she was not about to lower herself to contradict any accusation they made.

She yawned, stretched, and decided not to spend the rest of the day in bed worrying about it all.

Flinging back the covers, she sat up—and that was when she realized Ryan was standing in the doorway.

"How—how long have you been there?" she asked, unnerved, grabbing her robe from the foot of the bed. "Heavens, as crazy as you've been acting lately, I don't like the idea of your sneaking up on me this way." She also didn't like the way he was staring at her, as if something in him had died, and just the shell of him was left.

In a dull monotone, he stated rather than asked, "You knew, didn't you."

"Knew what?" she asked sharply, irritably, as she ran trembling fingers through her hair.

He walked over to the bed, and as he came toward her, Victoria instinctively shrank back.

Pulling the covers up to her chin, she was starting to experience fear of her own son. His blue eyes were the color of frost on a January morning, narrowed to ominous slits beneath the frown that creased his forehead. He looked worn, haggard from a sleepless night, yet, there was no slump of weariness to his posture. He stood straight, tall, a fierce resolve emanating as he demanded confirmation of the suspicions that had riddled him during the seemingly endless night.

"Somehow—I don't know how—you found out about Erin having Negro blood. You made arrangements to have her sold into slavery to get her out of my life, as Zachary Tremayne had sold her mother."

Victoria could not conjure the shocked reaction she'd planned, for she was far too terrified. She could only shake her head wildly from side to side, eyes bulging, lips working nervously but silently.

"You knew it wouldn't matter to me," he coldly continued, "because you read the letter I'd left for her and knew I loved her, that I'd still love her even if I found out the truth about her being a mulatto."

Victoria finally found her voice, thin, squeaky, feigning horror. "Oh, no! She can't be . . ."

When he did not respond, she became braver, more sure of herself, daring to think maybe he was coming to his senses.

"Oh, my son, I know how this must hurt you, but be glad she did run away with another man. What if you'd had children? It could have been a disaster. Why, the baby might have been dark-skinned, and—"

"Don't you understand?" He looked at her incredulously, as though he'd never really seen her before. "It wouldn't have mattered. Nothing matters to me except my love for Erin. And you—" he sat down beside her— "are going to tell me exactly what you did with her, and you're going to tell me the name of the person who helped you do it."

Victoria broke down.

The tears and the screams and the sobs and the pleas to forgive were genuine.

Ryan sat unmoved, waiting for her to realize he had no intention of relenting.

Finally, when she saw there was no way out except for the truth, she told him everything.

And when she was done, he got up and walked to the door.

Victoria ran after him, stumbling in her desperate haste, falling. She reached out to clutch him about his ankles as she begged, "Ryan, don't go, please. You'll thank me one day for ridding you of her. She's where her kind belongs, and you're only making a fool of yourself, and me, and the Youngblood name. Please, son—"

He kicked free of her hold, moved quickly out of her reach, then stared down at her, not with hatred or loathing, but abject pity.

Still, he knew he had to speak the words that were needling his soul.

"You have no son . . . and I have no mother."

CHAPTER

 31

E*RIN WAS FASCINATED WITH THE VERDANT* beauty that was Sierra Leone. The low-lying, flat coastal area was said to extend for over two hundred miles, and, though it was extremely swampy in places, inland regions quickly became dramatic with wooded hills rising to the Loma Mountains near the Guinea border.

The language, she quickly found, could be a problem among many tribal groups. Yet, there were enough British people in residence that communication was adequate for her needs.

Elliott Noland was an amiable guide, helping her to become acclimated. She learned that the main crops of the region were rice, coffee, cocoa, palm kernels, and kola nuts. The local pastime of the natives was sharing horror stories of slave catchers in the remote hills, and the ever-present danger of man-eating leopards.

Letty was given the job of cooking for the governor and his staff, in exchange for room and board. Erin, given shelter there along with her mother, was grateful not to have to eat the local diet of crushed corn, parboiled fish and, most unpalatable of all, crispy, dried caterpillars.

She knew the climate had to be the primary reason he

mother's health was so improved, but there was no denying Elliott had something to do with it also.

While Arlene filled her days with helping to teach native children in the settlement school how to read and write, and Letty had her hands full in service to the governor and his staff, Erin found herself growing restless. With too much time on her hands, days blended into weeks of feeling there was no real purpose to her life. Finally, she tried her hand at teaching but was dismayed to realize it just wasn't her calling.

She volunteered to work with the churches, yet did not feel truly needed. The village was bursting with British missionaries, and she was only in the way.

Loneliness set in, along with thoughts of how useless she felt in Sierra Leone and how much she could be doing at home.

One night after dinner, as she and her mother and Elliott sat on the porch overlooking the wine-dark ocean, a strange and eerie sound began from somewhere behind them in the hills. Slowly, it spread, rising in crescendo, voices moaning and wailing in a kind of chant.

"*Morna,*" Elliott affirmed reverently. "It always gives me goosebumps, no matter how many times I hear it."

Arlene murmured, "And such a sad and lonely sound. I'll never forget the first time I heard it."

"Would someone please tell me what it is?" Erin was spellbound.

Elliott obliged. "It's a chant that legend says began on the Cape Verde islands and spread throughout Africa. It's supposed to convey the sadness and loneliness of wanting to go to a mysterious, faraway place, where waves, which represent eternal peace, never cease. Those who chant believe they can actually hear the waves crashing on some distant shore, that the sound is calling them to it. True happiness can only be found by going there, and the chanting echoes the will of the soul to obey."

A beautiful but sad tale, Erin thought. She could not refrain from asking, "What happens when no one ever goes there?"

He smiled cryptically. "Who can say they don't? Where a person goes in his heart is a very private thing."

Erin thought about that. It was only native music, a leitmotiv. Yet, in that instant, it was so easy to imagine she could also hear the eternal waves, only the sound was Mother Bethel, calling her back.

Arlene saw the misery etched on her face and exchanged a concerned glance with Elliott as she probed, "Is something wrong? Does the chanting upset you?"

"What upsets me is feeling absolutely useless." Erin saw no reason to hold back any longer. She'd accomplished what she set out to do; she'd found her mother. Now she was assured of her happiness and health and confident Elliott Noland would ensure it continued.

"Then you aren't happy here?"

Erin framed her answer carefully, for she did not want to upset her mother. Neither did she wish Elliott to think her ungrateful for the way he'd taken her in and given her shelter. "That doesn't have anything to do with it. It just bothers me there's no purpose for me here, while there's much I could be doing back in Philadelphia."

"Like what?" Arlene wanted to know. She was terrified to think of her returning to America and said so. "If Ryan was cruel enough to sell you into slavery, he'd be ruthless enough to try and track you down if he found out you'd escaped. The Free-Soilers told you that. Have you forgotten so quickly how awful it was to have to run from your own home?" Her voice broke, and Elliott reached to put his arm about her in comfort. They'd had some long, inti mate talks the past weeks, and he shared her concern about Erin's growing restlessness.

"He won't find me. I'll take another name, the one I used to come here—Edith Starling. Erin Sterling will no longer exist. And even if he did look for me, he'd never be able to find me. I know only too well how the underground works, how secretive it can be. I'll have a new identity, a new life."

Arlene heard the enthusiasm, the spirit, returning to her daughter's voice. She didn't approve but had learned her lesson about interfering in Erin's life. "Is your mind made up?"

Erin nodded. "I'd like to go back on the next packet."

Arlene bit her lip, determined not to cry. Elliott squeezed her hand. "Well, then," she hesitated, waited for his approving nod. "I guess it's time to tell you we're going to be married. We realize I'm not legally divorced from Zachary, but in God's eyes, I feel I am, and that's all that matters. I'm never going back there, anyway."

Erin was delighted and said so, confident her mother's future was secure. "Now I can go back and know you're in good hands."

Letty was extremely upset to hear of Erin's plans. "I'm going to miss you something fierce. Even after I got here and knew I was safe, I was still lonesome. Then your momma came, and we'd talk about how wonderful it would be if you and my momma and Ben were all here. Now that's not going to happen."

Erin understood but reminded her, "We've got to be grateful for what we've got in this life, Letty. What if none of us had escaped? Think of the misery then."

Still, Letty grieved over her leaving.

News of a packet arriving came the day after Arlene and Elliott's wedding. Excited, Erin rushed to the pier with everyone else to greet those arriving. When she saw the name on the bow—*Freedom*—she couldn't believe it, then realized how the time had passed. She had arrived in Sierra Leone in early spring, and it was almost July.

Captain O'Grady was the first one down the gangplank. He gave her a big bear hug. "Aye, ye look fit, lassie. Almost like a real native."

Erin laughed at that. She no longer used the bleaching water, but her skin had darkened only from the sun. She'd learned, as her mother had, that their heritage was not evident in the coloring of their skin, and she wouldn't have cared anyway.

She was about to tell him she'd be making the return voyage with him, when all of a sudden Letty, standing right beside her, gave a loud shriek and took off, frantically pushing her way through the crowd. Erin stood on tiptoe to see over the heads of those in front of her. As she recognized the tall, dark-skinned man hurrying down the gangplank, waving his arms wildly, she knew the reason for Letty's reaction. "Praise God," she whispered, herself shuddering with emotion.

It was Ben.

Erin waited till the excitement of Ben's arrival died down, and he and Letty had slipped away together, before telling Captain O'Grady her news.

He was as enthusiastic as she'd hoped he would be. "The Free-Soilers need workers like you, lassie. It's just a shame there's not more money to book passage for those that need to make a new life once freed, and an even bigger sin that we can't help the fugitives.

"I guess," he went on thoughtfully, soberly, "since my time with you, all the memories of those days I'm not proud of came rushing back, and I've found myself wishing there was something I could do to make up for it all. Hearing you're going back to help perks me up a bit, all the same."

"Well, we might find a way for you to help, too," Erin commented mysteriously, not about to say more just then. The wheels were turning, and she had ideas but needed to formulate them with Mother Bethel and Charles Grudinger.

Sadly, Erin and Arlene said their farewells.

Arlene broke down and cried, Elliott's arms about her to comfort. "I don't mean to carry on so, to send you away like this, but I'm so afraid I'll never see you again."

Erin, likewise, was emotionally choked but mustered strength to say fiercely, "That can't happen, Mother, because we live in each other's hearts, and that means we're always together, and always will be."

They clung together one last time.

Each had responded to the call of the *morna*.

Nate slept in a room adjoining his office. He knew it meant trouble when Zachary showed up at dawn, and not just because of the unusual hour. Zachary reeked with the stench of smoke, his face was streaked with soot, and he looked as if he'd been in a fight.

Nate thought he was prepared to hear any explanation, but his blood ran cold when Zachary uttered only one word as he slumped into a chair.

"Youngblood."

"Goddamn!" Nate sat down opposite, instinctively reaching for his whiskey jug to take a big swallow before asking, "What happened?"

Zachary helped himself to the jug before revealing, "He was looking for Erin—"

"After all these months?"

"He's onto something. Don't ask me what. All I know is he showed up at my place late last night, asking questions. I was there by myself. Even my overseers were gone, 'cause another slave took off yesterday. We were out all day looking for him, and I was tired and went home to get some sleep but made them stay out there.

"I had a gun, and I told him to get out, but he was able to jump me, and the next thing I knew, I woke up in the front yard, and the house was burned to the ground. The bastard must've left me there to die. I dragged myself out but can't remember it."

Comprehension dawned, and Nate cried sharply, "If he went to you for answers, that has to mean his mother didn't tell him I was the one she hired to take care of his wife. I'd like to know exactly what she did tell him, but I don't dare contact her, and I doubt she'll come to me.

"The thing I got to worry about," he went on, more to himself than Zachary, "is whether Youngblood might just be able to track his wife down. I was hesitant to get involved in this shit, anyway, even with all the money involved, but his mother swore she'd make sure he didn't suspect a thing. Now that he does, if he finds her—finds out what happened and how I had a hand in it—I'll go to prison . . . if he doesn't kill me."

"Well, like you said, he don't know about you. If he had, he would have come after you instead of me."

"True." Nate nodded, his mouth a thin, grim line. "But now I've got to make sure the trail stops with you, that he's hit a dead end and can't go no further."

"It's been months," Zachary said. "There's no way he could trace her now. What you better concern yourself with is him being able to badger his mother into telling him about your part in it."

"That doesn't worry me, because I'd just deny it. It'd be my word against hers. She hasn't got any proof."

"What about me?" Zachary flared. "It's my house got burned down, and I didn't have anything to do with what happened to Erin. Hell, I've had a tough time lately, anyway, what with Arlene stirring the slaves up with voodoo. And now I've got to start all over. I just wish to hell I'd gone on and killed the bitch!" He banged his fists on the table in frustration.

"Maybe you'll get your chance. I think it's time we tracked them both down and made sure neither one of them ever talks. Then we can rest easy. You can go to the law about Youngblood burning down your house, and he'll have to pay for it."

Zachary liked both ideas. He'd get a new house, and he'd also stop worrying that Arlene could reach him from wherever she was with her evil spirits. The drums still echoed sometimes at night, and it made him nervous to worry she might be having messages sent to the slaves to keep them stirred up.

Nate strapped on his holster. "Let's go find Harnaby. He'll set us in the right direction."

"You mean you don't know?" Zachary cried, getting to his feet to follow. "But you took them both off, didn't you? Hell, you ought to know who bought 'em."

"Harnaby took care of that. I had some other business to tend to." He saw the way Zachary was looking at him, and snapped, "Anybody can take a slave to market, damn it!"

"Well, I'll just breathe a lot easier when we find out exactly where they went to market."

Ryan stood in the shadows of an alley just across the street from the warehouse. He was already there when Zachary rode in, for he'd been trying to get himself under control before confronting Nate Donovan. He'd wanted just to charge in and try to beat the truth out of him but knew it was best to move slowly. Then he saw Zachary, and even deeper rage washed over him as he realized the two must be in cahoots with each other. Why else had

Zachary gone straight to Donovan after what had happened?

Ryan tried to figure out what they would do. After all, Zachary had come to tell Donovan about Ryan's visit the night before, that he had found out Erin had not left him by choice. They would, no doubt, try to prevent him from finding her, knowing there would be hell to pay when he did. So he waited, giving them time to decide what to do.

And when they made their move, he was right behind them.

He followed stealthily as they walked the few short blocks to a rundown hotel on a side street not far from the warehouse. When they went in, he waited a few moments, then hurried to the desk to slip the clerk money and ask which way the two had gone. Second floor, he was told, to see a man named Harnaby. Corner room on the alley. Ryan knew he was in luck. He had spotted a rickety stairway to an outside entrance there.

He wasted no time in going around to creep up the steps. The window to the corner room was open a few inches.

Crouching to listen, he heard an angry voice, figured it to be Donovan's, as it didn't sound like Zachary's.

"What do you mean you think Kaid Whitlock bought Arlene, and you can't be sure who bought Erin? Who paid you the money, goddamn it?"

Jason Harnaby knew he had to think fast, but they'd woken him up, and he was groggy, unprepared. "I can't remember. It's been awhile."

"Been awhile, my ass!" Zachary screeched. "You better think and think good, mister, 'cause Ryan Youngblood has gone crazy, and he's out for blood. He tried to kill me last night. Burned my house to the ground. Somehow, he's found out his wife didn't just disappear on her own, that she had a little help, and sooner or later, he's going to find out who gave her that help, unless we find her first and shut her mouth for good."

Ryan gritted his teeth and slowly began to maneuver his gun from the holster.

"I told you," Jason whined nervously. "I just don't remember."

"Like hell you don't!" Nate slammed him with his fist to send him sprawling back across the bed. "You better remember, goddamn it, 'cause we ain't got no time to waste. Now there's only two traders on the coast who deal with mulattos—Whitlock and Silah Bannister. Which one was it? They're miles apart, and you better not send me to the wrong one, you dummy son of a bitch." He hit him again.

Jason knew he was trapped, couldn't lie his way out, because even if he stuck to his story that he couldn't remember, when they went to Whitlock and Bannister, they were going to find out he hadn't showed with either Erin or Lucy Jane, and if they checked further, would find out he'd been missing a few slaves every time he was supposed to be turning them over for sale.

The two men stood between him and the window, but if he could make it, dive through, it wasn't a dangerously long fall to the ground. He could get away, escape to the North, lose himself in the underground as the fugitives had. Even if he didn't make it, there was no way he'd give them even a hint of the direction he'd sent anybody, ever.

Zachary had not been wearing boots when Youngblood had taken him by surprise during the night. He'd had to get a pair from Frank's cabin. He'd also taken a knife, which he'd slipped inside one boot and now was slowly withdrawing. Advancing toward Jason, he snarled, "Maybe he'll start remembering if I start cutting. . . ."

Jason lunged then. Throwing out his arms to send

them stumbling to either side, he dove between them, heading for the window.

Zachary threw the knife and missed, but Nate was quicker, drew his gun and shot him in the back.

Jason fell, just as Ryan reacted to crash through the window, gun in hand. He didn't want to kill, not yet. He still needed information and feared the one who had it was dying at his feet. But Nate had a gun, and Ryan had to defend himself. He fired.

He had meant to hit his wrist but Nate moved as he pulled the trigger and took the bullet right in his heart. He was dead before he hit the floor.

Zachary, unarmed, froze where he stood.

"Don't move," Ryan commanded tightly. Dropping beside Jason, he felt his throat for a pulse. Weak, but it was there.

Just then Jason stirred, moaned. Zachary saw Ryan's attention diverted and seized the opportunity to bolt out the door.

Ryan let him go. He was of no use anyway. He bent over Jason, knew he was dying. "Listen, Harnaby, you've got to help me. Erin is my wife, and you've got to tell me where you took her. You're my only hope."

Blood trickled from his mouth, as Jason managed a feeble sneer, struggling to vent his loathing for the man who had sold her. "You won't . . . find her." He strained to whisper past the smothering mist that was moving over him. "Can't get your money back . . . you bastard . . ."

"My money back?" Ryan echoed in wonder. "You think I had something to do with any of this? That's why Donovan and Tremayne were here, remember? Because I'm after them. Now talk to me."

It was getting dark. Jason tried to remember what they'd said, but there was a terrible roaring, and he couldn't think. The man looming over him was becoming only a gray shadow. Yet, just before the creeping mist completely obliterated his vision, he saw the man's eyes, the mirrored anguish of the desperate quest before him, and somehow sensed he was telling the truth.

But there was not time to explain it all to him, for invisible hands were reaching inside his chest to tear out his soul and carry him along the narrow tunnel he found himself looking into, with that strange and eerie light waiting at the end. His lips moved, but no sound came, as he prayed to last long enough to send him after her.

"Come on, Harnaby." Ryan gave him a gentle shake as he saw how his eyes were starting to glaze over, becoming transfixed as death made ready for triumph. "You've got to tell me where to look. I swear to you I knew nothing about this. Only God and I know how much I do love her. . . ."

Ryan choked to silence, knew he had lost.

But then, with his last, labored breath, Jason spoke his final words. "Philadelphia. Find . . . Mother . . . Bethel."

Outside in the hall, where he'd stood listening just in case Jason did reveal anything before he died, Zachary felt good for the first time in a long time. So often, he had wished he'd just gone on and killed Arlene and been done with it. She was responsible for the voodoo, just as Erin was to blame for his scarred face. Now the house was burned to the ground. His partner in the illegal slave trade that had helped make him rich was dead. He was left with nothing. And he wanted revenge. While Jason's dying words meant nothing to him, he knew Ryan Youngblood wouldn't stop till he figured them out and trailed Erin to wherever she was.

And where she was, there Arlene would be also.

He could then kill them all, and would have his vengeance.

CHAPTER

 32

C*APTAIN O'GRADY WAS OVERJOYED THAT ERIN*
planned to make Philadelphia her home. On the return
voyage they grew even closer. She was the daughter, the
family, he'd never had. He knew, too, that once she got
a foothold and entrenched herself in the secret activities
of those dedicated to helping the oppressed, she'd be in-
valuable.

He assured her there would be many reasons for her
happiness in the city, for it was a progressive one, teeming
with growth. There were literary clubs, theaters, dancing
schools. The Pennsylvania Academy of Fine Arts had been
founded.

Erin was most impressed, however, at hearing the first
public school for Negroes had just opened. She had secretly taught Letty to read and write, and now freed slaves
migrating to Philadelphia would have the opportunity to
be taught in a real classroom, by dedicated teachers.

Erin was hungry to hear news of happenings in America
during her nearly four-month stay in Sierra Leone. The
Missouri Compromise had become official. Maine had
been admitted to the union as the twenty-third state, with
a ban on slavery. But, what impressed and excited her was
hearing how Congress had passed legislation making

trade in foreign slaves an act of piracy. No longer would the penalty merely be seizing the ships of those involved. Henceforth, American citizens found guilty would be sentenced to death.

She had told Captain O'Grady on the first voyage how there had always been suspicion her stepfather was involved in the trading of slaves brought into the country illegally. Hearing of the new law, she vehemently voiced the hope, "If he gets caught now, they'll hang him, thank God."

"The thing to do now," he said, "is to get as many illegal slaves as possible back to Africa."

Erin surprised him with an adamant shake of her head. "I disagree. I've had a lot of time to think about it, and even though there are groups who feel free Negroes are better off being sent back due to slaveholders saying they make other slaves restless, I say it's more important to get the fugitives out. At least the ones freed have a chance for a new life. Those running away risk getting caught and beaten, or maybe having a foot chopped off. Dear God!" She shuddered. "We've just got to find a way to smuggle more of them out to Sierra Leone."

Worriedly, he reminded her, "Erin, helping runaway slaves is a crime. Even in Delaware, the only state in the South where a black is considered free till proved to be a slave, they're running advertisements in newspapers for runaways, offering rewards for their apprehension. I agree with what you want to do, Lord knows, and I'm willing to help in any way I can, but we've both got to be careful."

At that she laughed. "If I were careful, I'd still be in Sierra Leone."

Captain O'Grady was deeply impressed by her dedication, for he knew, sadly, it was fired by the scars of the tragedies in her own life.

It was late August when, at last, they reached Philadelphia. Erin planned to head straight to Mother Bethel to offer her services once more in exchange for shelter.

As the plank was being positioned for disembarking, she noticed something strange. They were directly in front of the Grudinger dock facilities and warehouses, but she was puzzled by the lack of activity, the way workers lazed about indifferently.

Captain O'Grady came out on deck himself to shake his fist and curse the lack of efficiency. "Get this ship secured, you hear me?" He called down furiously, "My men are anxious to be done and take their leave."

The dockmen snickered among themselves, and Erin was even more bewildered. It certainly wasn't that way when she'd left, and Captain O'Grady said he hadn't experienced such difficulty when he embarked several months earlier.

Once ashore, they quickly learned the reason.

"Grudinger died," the captain of a ship docked beside the *Freedom* brusquely informed them. "A couple of months ago. He left everything to a free black who worked as his housekeeper. That raised a few eyebrows, to be sure. Right away, she got lots of offers to buy her out, but she refused, insists on running the line herself.

"Well, you can see how it's going." He gestured to the slothful workers. "They're not taking orders from a woman, particularly one who's black."

Erin was openly distressed to hear of Mr. Grudinger's passing and secretly delighted to learn of Nanny Bess's inheritance. Maybe, Erin mused, excitement building, she could do something to help since Nanny Bess was reportedly having problems. After all, she'd been passing for white all her life, without even knowing it. It shouldn't be hard to do so again, she thought with a sly grin.

She hurried on her way to find Nanny Bess, after assuring Captain O'Grady she'd see him before he sailed again.

"To be sure," he called after her, "because I won't be leaving till I've got a full cargo, and from the way these blokes are moving, I'd say it'd take several weeks to get loaded even if I had one."

Nanny Bess burst into tears at the sight of Erin standing on her doorstep. "Bless you and praise God," she exclaimed, hugging her and pulling her inside. "You don't know how I've thought about you all these months. The captain, he came by to pay Mr. Grudinger a visit when he was last in port, and he told me how you found your mother and that she's well. Has something happened?" She was struck by sudden alarm as to Erin's reason for returning.

"Oh, no. Everything is fine. My mother is happily in love with a wonderful man, and I imagine by now Letty is married, thanks to Ben making it there safely. You had something to do with that, too, didn't you?" She gave her a quick hug of gratitude.

Nanny Bess sighed. "Yes, I did, but it might be the last one for a while. I'm afraid I'm a failure, Erin."

"You aren't thinking about giving up, are you?"

"What else can I do? I can't get any work out of the dockmen, no cooperation from the supervisors, and I've got a sneaking suspicion some of the other ship owners are responsible. They'd like to see Grudinger Shipping go out of business, so they can divide the cargo and packet contracts between them.

"And, frankly, yes," she admitted wearily, "I am seriously considering selling out. I can turn the money over to Mother Bethel. I still have the house and my savings, so I don't really need it, and maybe it will do some good there."

"But not nearly as much as you and I can do with Grudinger Shipping Lines."

Nanny Bess did not share her enthusiasm. "Those men won't like working for a white woman any more than a black, and it would be worse, still, if it got out you're a mulatto. The latest word from Missouri is that mulattoes and free blacks are being barred from that state, according to their constitution, and—"

Erin impatiently waved her to silence. "Hear me out. Please. All I'm saying is that there's nothing to lose by trying. Just give me free rein, and I'll find a way to stay in business."

"But why? What's the point?"

"The point is, we've got to succeed, because we need all those ships, all those packet contracts, to keep the line running. Somebody has got to help the fugitive slaves out of the country, Nanny Bess. You've been able to get a few out, sure, as paying passengers, with false papers, but we need to move larger numbers, faster."

Nanny Bess sat down, folded her hands in her lap, and gave a dubious nod of assent. "Well, the least I can do is listen to what you have in mind."

"I haven't worked out all the details, but what I need from you now is your full cooperation. You have nothing to lose, Nanny Bess, because you've already admitted to yourself you're defeated. Give me a chance. That's why I came back here, to help these people, and I can do it. I know I can."

Erin's determination was infectious. Nanny Bess grinned broadly. "Okay. I'll do it."

Erin wasted no time. Early the next morning, she went to the waterfront. She had pulled her raven hair back into an austere bun at the nape of her neck. Nanny Bess had provided a pair of Mr. Grudinger's reading spectacles that made her appear older, as well as stern and imposing. A drab old dress found in a trunk in the attic, once belonging to the late Mrs. Grudinger, completed her drab, unattractive appearance.

Curt and to the point, she introduced herself to the bewildered supervisors as Miss Edith Starling, new owner of Grudinger Shipping Lines. "But from now on this company will be known as the Morna Lines." She had no intention of sharing the reason for the name. The true meaning was her precious secret.

The men quickly learned she knew what she was doing. By the end of the day, she had fired two for insubordination, replacing them with older, retired seamen, recommended by Captain O'Grady. He was delighted with what she was doing, and enjoying her charade. It was all he could do to keep from bursting out laughing when he overheard the grumbling dockworkers describe her as Vinegar Face.

At a clandestine meeting in the basement at Mother Bethel, arranged by Nanny Bess, Erin met with leaders of the Free-Soilers, Captain O'Grady and other seamen proven trustworthy, to outline her full plan for aiding fugitive slaves.

There would be a special hold in two of Morna's packet ships for their transport to Sierra Leone, she explained. To ensure complete security, the designated ships would not run on regular schedules. The crew of each vessel would be hand-picked by the captain and sworn to secrecy. On those specific voyages, there would be no paid passengers, for once at sea the Negroes could be released and move about freely, returning to their hiding place only if the ship were stopped by the authorities for any reason.

Someone voiced concern over how so many could be loaded on board, even at night, without arousing suspicion.

Erin had thought of that, also. With a confident smile,

she suggested Mother Bethel's people were going to have to learn carpentry. "The fugitives will go on board as cargo, in crates. Three to a box should be sufficient. With a dozen crates loaded, three dozen runaways will sail to freedom."

There was a murmur of admiring consent, as everyone realized her plan could work.

"What about a signal?" Nanny Bess wanted to know. "It's risky to be carrying messages back and forth between Morna and Mother Bethel. People might notice and start wondering why, but we have to know when a ship is ready to sail, so we'll know exactly when to load the crates."

Erin had also foreseen that important aspect of the operation. It was with an inner tremor that she told them, "A rose will be the signal. Every night, close to midnight, you're to have someone walk along the waterfront where our ships are docked. Make sure you send a different person each time, to avoid suspicion. I will leave the rose at the pier in front of the ship that will sail at midnight the next night. When you see it, you'll know to load the crates the next day."

Another ripple of approval went through the room, and it was Captain O'Grady who echoed the opinion of all by reverently declaring, "It's beautiful. Perfect. A midnight rose to signal a voyage to freedom."

And also, Erin thought, it was a perfect means to vindicate a bittersweet memory.

CHAPTER

 33

NANNY BESS HUMMED CONTENTEDLY AS SHE dusted bric-a-brac in the parlor. Everything was going well. Erin was seldom at home, working day and night at the waterfront. The business had grown since she had taken over, and in addition to the sailings to freedom, the regular runs of cargo to Europe were becoming more and more frequent. She was capable, knew what she was doing, and people liked to deal with her.

The only thing that worried Nanny Bess was the way Erin was totally dedicated to her work. It was her whole life. She took no time off for relaxation, much less socializing. Not that men got any romantic notions, anyway, the way she presented herself. And it just wasn't healthy, how she locked herself off from life, all because of that swine, Ryan Youngblood.

Hearing the loud clang of the knocker, Nanny Bess laid down her dusting cloth. Smoothing her apron, she went to the front door, opened it, took one look, and quickly started to close it.

"Nanny Bess, what's wrong?" Ryan immediately stuck out his foot to block the door. "Surely, you haven't forgotten me, after all these years."

Nanny Bess commanded herself to be calm, lest she

arouse instant suspicion. "Yes, of course, Mr. Young-blood," she said in an attempt to recover. Swallowing against the dizziness, she continued, "We've just had some robberies in the neighborhood lately, and I'm leery about who I open the door to." Dear God, she could hardly think past the giant roaring that had begun in her head and felt herself breaking out in a cold sweat.

He wondered why she had even opened the door if she were all that afraid, but let it go.

He stepped into the foyer without being invited, for he had no reason to think he wasn't welcome. "I need to see Charles. Since it's so late in the day, I thought he'd be here instead of his office. I came all the way inland this trip, and . . ." He paused, struck by her strange behavior. "What is this all about?"

Not about to reveal the real horror, she drearily informed him, "Mr. Grudinger passed away."

It was Ryan's turn to be taken aback. "I'm sorry," he said. "I didn't know. I've been out of touch with everything lately. I've had some personal problems, and. . . ." He fell silent, not knowing what else to say, afraid of saying too much.

Despite his sorrow at hearing of his friend's death, Ryan was more concerned with his relentless quest. He had learned much on his trek north, paying plenty for the information, of course. He now knew Mother Bethel was actually a church rumored to help fugitive slaves. He'd dared hope Jason Harnaby's dying clue meant Erin had escaped and gone to Mother Bethel for aid. Filled with renewed hope, he became even more determined to find her, no matter what obstacles he'd have to surmount. He was wondering if he dared ask Nanny Bess for help in the wake of her bizarre behavior.

Nanny Bess was regaining her self-control, and fear was quickly melding to anger with the reality that standing before her was the monster who had coldly, cruelly banished her dear friend to slavery. "Is there anything else you want?"

He blinked, snapped from his musing by her sharpness and ventured to request, "Do you suppose you could put me up for the night since you're keeping the house open? I'm sure Charles would approve," he finished with a lame smile. Actually, he was hoping she would warm up a little, so he could try to find out how much she knew about what went on at Mother Bethel.

She was quick to refuse. "I'm afraid that's not possible. Someone else owns the house now. I work for them."

"I see." Curious, he probed, "By the way, when did Charles pass away?"

"A few months ago."

His brow furrowed. "His estate must have been settled fairly quickly if the house has already changed hands. What about his business? When I was here last time, we discussed my investing in it. Could you by any chance give me the name of his attorney? If it's still for sale—"

"No. It sold, too. Now if there's nothing else . . ." She held the door open wider, indicating he should leave.

Ryan reluctantly stepped out on the porch. Knowing it was now or never, he said bluntly, "Just one more question. Do you know where I can find a church known as Mother Bethel?"

She slammed the door in his face.

Leaning back against it, she could hear the pounding of her own heart, there in the stillness of the house. Oh, how she chided herself for not being more composed, but it was all such a shock. Somehow, he had found out Erin had escaped and traced her to Philadelphia. Worse, still, he knew Mother Bethel had something to do with it.

She had to warn Erin, lest he be suspicious and wait outside in the shadows and see her when she came home.

It would be late, too, because Erin had said that morning before going to the waterfront that she wouldn't be back till after midnight. A ship was ready to sail the next night and the signal had to be left.

Nanny Bess peered through the sheer curtain that hung on the glass windows beside the door. She was relieved to see Ryan walking down the street. That meant his next step would be to try and locate Mother Bethel, which he'd be able to do as soon as he found out it was really the African Methodist Episcopal Church he was looking for.

She knew, with rising panic, she needed to warn Parson Jones, but Erin had to come first.

Ryan had wanted to kick the goddamn door down and do whatever it took to make her tell him what the hell had her so spooked. And why had she looked at him as if he were scum? He'd never been rude or unkind to her in all the times he'd visited Charles. And she might have had a bit of compassion. After all, hearing of his friend's death had been a shock.

Later, he vowed, struck with resentment, he would go back and get some answers. For the time being, he was exhausted and needed a good night's sleep.

Tomorrow, by God, he would start out on his own to find Mother Bethel.

Hailing a carriage-for-hire, he clamored on board.

"Where to, sir?" the driver wanted to know.

Ryan leaned back against the smooth leather seat and jocularly said, "Unless you know where to find Mother Bethel, take me to a good hotel."

"Which do you prefer, sir?"

He sat up straight, not sure he'd heard right. Slowly, he repeated himself.

"I heard you, sir," the driver said patiently. "So, where

do you want me to take you? A hotel, or to the African Methodist Episcopal Church?"

A short way behind, someone else hailed a carriage.

"Just follow that one up there," Zachary ordered tersely, "and it will be worth your while not to let them know they're being followed."

He was tempted to advise the cabby it would probably cost him his life if he did.

Zachary was a driven man. In the past weeks, as Ryan had doggedly trailed Erin to Philadelphia, he had been close behind. No matter that his plantation was probably falling apart back in Richmond. With his partner dead and his house burned down, he was thinking only of revenge.

If Youngblood succeeded in finding Erin and Arlene, he would have it at last.

Erin walked slowly along the pier. She found the sound of the gentle lapping of the water against the pilings soothing, melodic. She drank of the pungent air, shivering with the ecstasy of the world—her world.

What a long path she'd trod to reach it, she mused, and how long ago, a lifetime ago it was, even to contemplate that other time, when she had reveled in the glory of a man's arms, a man she so foolishly believed shared her dreams, her love.

The sad reality was that never, ever, would she have thought it mattered to Ryan that she could be considered mulatto. True, he was a slaveholder, but by necessity and heritage, not choice. A kind man. A gentle man. With compassion for those in bondage. Or so she thought.

Erin had tried to cast him from both mind and heart but had failed. She continued to be haunted by thoughts of what might have been, the happiness that could have been theirs.

So it had come to this, she sadly accepted, pressing the silken petals of the fragrant rose to her lips.

Loneliness.

Emptiness.

The only joy in life to be found was in helping others escape misery, while she seemed doomed to encapsulation within herself.

Midnight Rose.

That's what they were calling her—the Free-Soilers, the Quakers, Mother Bethel's followers.

Midnight Rose—the enigmatic zealot. Dedicated and devoted. Admired and respected.

But Erin cared nothing for the praise. To her, working day and night for the cause was a panacea for a heart that would not heal.

And despite all resolve the memories came whispering back, memories of a warm spring night, when her heart had first been invaded.

She kissed the rose, quickly knelt to place it on the pier.

That was when she heard Nanny Bess frantically calling to her from the shadows. She hurried over, apprehensive. "I'm here. What's wrong?"

Nanny Bess was standing by the office door, the glow of a lantern above revealing her stricken face. Erin tensed. Whatever it was, it was bad. Giving her a gentle shake, for she appeared to be in a stupor, Erin said, "Come on. Tell me. Quick."

Nanny Bess, out of breath from running after leaving the carriage, could only sob, "Oh, God! Oh, God!"

Placing an arm about her shoulders, Erin tried to draw her into the office.

Nanny Bess pulled back, shook her head in protest as the words came out in a frenzied torrent. "He's here! Ryan is here! In Philadelphia. He came to the house. He wanted to see Charles. I told him he was dead. Then he wanted to stay the night, but I said no, and then he asked if I knew where to find Mother Bethel. Oh, God, Erin, don't you see? You've got to run!"

Erin could only stare at her in horror, blood turning to ice, every muscle, every nerve in her body rigid.

"He's here! Ryan is here!" Nanny Bess repeated, voice rising hysterically. "You've got to leave. He can claim you're a runaway slave and take you back, do whatever he wants to with you. Nobody can stop him. Don't you see?"

Woodenly, Erin began to nod, for she knew Nanny Bess was right. Finally, she summoned her voice past the constricting lump of terror. "I'll leave with Captain O'Grady tomorrow night. It's my only chance. But what do I do till then, if he knows about Mother Bethel? I can't go there for refuge. And I don't dare go back to the house." She was frantic.

Nanny Bess lifted a trembling finger and pointed to the outline of the *Freedom*, majestic in its silhouette against the fog rolling in. "There. Go on the ship and stay there. Alert Captain O'Grady, and he'll post guards to make sure Ryan can't get on board. It's your only chance. Hurry. Go now. I'll pack your things and bring them tomorrow."

Erin was wild with fear but also stricken with worry over what would happen to Morna Lines. "I might not come back. It won't be safe for a long, long time. You've got to keep the ships sailing, Nanny Bess. You've got to keep getting the fugitives out to freedom. You're going to have to become Midnight Rose." Erin's voice broke.

Nanny Bess was sobbing, clinging to her. "I will. I swear it. You've worked too hard, and, oh, child, please, just go and get on that ship. It's the only safe place. When you tell Captain O'Grady what's happened, maybe he'll pull anchor and sail at dawn, and—"

"No!" Erin wouldn't hear of it. "I've left the signal. The crates with the fugitives will be loaded late tomorrow. We sail at midnight then. Not before. Now get back to the house, in case he comes around again. Be calm. And I'll see you when you bring my things on board."

"Godspeed." Nanny Bess tore from her embrace, blew her a kiss, and disappeared into the night.

Erin turned and ran as fast as her trembling legs would carry her, and she did not stop running until she was on the *Freedom* and pounding frantically on Captain O'Grady's cabin door.

Ryan walked aimlessly along the pier. Haunted, restless, he was more puzzled than ever after his visit to the church.

He had spoken with a preacher by the name of Absalom Jones, and when he introduced himself, Jones had got that same gleam of hatred in his eyes that Ryan had seen in Nanny Bess. Why? What provoked such instant animosity?

He got nowhere with his questions. Jones denied any involvement, of any kind, with runaway slaves. Further, he claimed he'd never heard of an Erin Sterling, or anyone by the name of Arlene Tremayne. And he had expressed indignant concern that any such rumors about his church should exist, for the congregation, he assured, was God-fearing and law-abiding.

Ryan had finally exploded and said all he wanted was to find his wife, and that was when Jones leapt to his feet and demanded that he leave, saying if he didn't he'd have no choice but to send for the law, because he'd have no trouble at his church.

So Ryan had been walking the streets of Philadelphia ever since, finally wandering down to the waterfront. He was filled with despair; he didn't know which way to turn.

It was a dark night, with no moon, but a few lanterns burned for safety and security.

Head down, shoulders hunched, misery personified in every nerve in his body, Ryan fought the impulse to just jump into the cold, black waters and give it all up. What was life, anyway, without the woman he loved? It was hard enough to live without her, but to have to live with the knowledge she believed him responsible for her fate was more than he could bear.

Suddenly, he froze, blinked, shook his head to clear it, told himself it was only his mind playing cruel tricks. Then he was running, stooping to snatch up the single red rose lying on the pier.

Somewhere, a church bell tolled the hour.

Twelve times.

Midnight.

It all came rushing back, like tides eternal. A rose had been Erin's signal in Richmond.

Could it be?

He looked up to see the ship—the name, visible by the lantern, on her bow—*Freedom*.

It was all starting to come together. Erin had to be responsible for the midnight rose. It explained everything, why Nanny Bess had reacted as she had, even the preacher. Erin had escaped, and she was here, in Philadelphia, and they hated him, loathed him, held him responsible for her having been abducted in the first place and believed he was trying to hunt her down, take her back.

It also meant Erin was somewhere close by, and by God, he was going to find her!

In the shadows, watching it all, stood Zachary. He wasn't sure what was going on, what Ryan had found there on the pier. It looked like a flower of some kind. And he seemed excited, so he had to be onto something.

Maybe it would be time soon.

Time for vengeance.

Time to bring out the black powder he'd been waiting to use for such a long, long time.

CHAPTER

 34

T HERE WAS NO ANSWER.

Erin knocked harder, louder, but no sound came from within the cabin.

A movement just down the narrow hallway caused her to jump, startled. Whirling about, she recognized one of the crew. "Norman, where is Captain O'Grady? I've got to see him right away."

He cocked his head to one side in puzzlement over why Miss Starling was on the ship at such a late hour. She looked terribly upset. Surely some bloke wasn't trying to assault her. What man would want to, less'n he was drunk? She was so dowdy and plain, and always cold and standoffish. "He's not on board," he finally told her. "Him and the others went ashore to make a little merry, being I'm told we sail tomorrow night. So's I don't look for them back much 'for day."

Erin pressed her forehead, her palms, against the door.

"Is there something I can do?" he asked, hoping there wasn't. Whatever was going on, he wanted no part of it. Even though he was on duty, he figured he could sneak a bit of ale as a treat, since he hadn't been able to join the others for revelry, and he had some waiting.

Erin tried the knob. It wasn't locked. "I'll wait inside." She stepped in and closed the door behind her.

Norman scratched his head. Something funny was going on, but he wasn't going to worry about it. If she wanted to stay in the captain's quarters for the night, so be it. He could hear that mug of ale calling.

Back on deck, he settled down. The night was passing slowly, but he didn't care. The ale was relaxing, and he saw no harm in dozing. It would be hours before the others returned.

It was sometime later that he heard a noise like someone slipping up behind him, but he wasn't quick enough, and a hand clamped across his mouth before he could get to his feet.

"Just be quiet and don't move. All I want is information." With his other hand, Ryan held the knife so the blade would gleam ominously in the starboard lantern just before the man felt it against his neck.

Norman whispered frantically as the cold steel touched his flesh. He wasn't about to die defending a bloody ship. "Take what you want. I don't care . . ."

Ryan said, "I'm not here to steal. I told you, all I want is information. Lie to me, and I'll slit your throat."

"Anything. I'll tell you anything."

"I'm looking for a woman. Her name is Erin Sterling. I have reason to believe she's around here somewhere. You know her?"

"Never heard the name, I swear."

Ryan pressed the knife a bit harder. "I told you, goddamn it, don't lie to me."

"I'm not, oh, God, I'm not." Norman's teeth were chattering, and he felt his bladder relax, the warm trickle of urine down his legs. "Don't kill me, please. I swear, don't know anybody by that name. The only woman on board is named Starling, and she's that way—" He strained to point to the ladder that went down to the crew's quarters.

Starling, Ryan thought. Sterling. Of course she'd changed her name. She considered herself a fugitive slave. Tensely he commanded, "Where is she? How do I find her?"

"Down there. First door on the right. Sign outside says Captain."

"Is he in there, too? Your captain?"

Norman managed to assure him no one else was on board.

Ryan didn't want to hurt him but couldn't take any chances on him sounding an alarm, alerting Erin. He would not risk losing her, now that he was sure he'd found her.

One swift blow to the back of his neck and the crewman slumped forward, unconscious.

Ryan hadn't hit him hard, and the man wouldn't be out long, but figured there was time to get to Erin before he came to.

He crossed the shadowed deck to hurry down the ladder.

Zachary waited in an alley next to the building that housed Morna Shipping Lines. He chuckled softly to think how Ryan's obsession had made it so easy to stay close on his trail without being noticed. The fool hadn't suspected all these months that he was being followed. Cocky, arrogant, his kind so smugly thought no one would ever challenge them.

But Ryan Youngblood, Zachary gloated, was soon going to learn different.

Anyone who had ever known Zachary Tremayne would not have recognized him as he waited for the ultimate glory of revenge, at last. The voodoo had taken its toll on his gullible mind, and he was a man possessed. Wide bloodshot eyes, a constant drool from his slightly parted lips, a lurch to his step, he was manipulated by the dementia within.

He had seen Ryan go on the ship, so he knew that was where Erin and Arlene were hiding. There had been no time to go back to where he'd left his pack mule on the outskirts of town and retrieve his black powder. But he prided himself in being smart, knew a bit about the ways of the world. All he had to do was break into a warehouse and find a cache there. He knew there would be ice in the river in the winter, and passage would have to be blasted clear for ships. The method would be the same as on the Rappahannock back home—saltpeter, sulphur, and charcoal, all blended to make black powder.

Now, with a pail in each hand and a long fuse wrapped around one arm, he stepped out of the alley, cackling to himself, and crossed toward the ship.

Ryan quietly turned the doorknob but was not surprised to find it locked. He wasn't about to call out, because if she was in there, she wouldn't let him in, and she might even have a gun and, in a panic, start shooting. He had to keep reminding himself that, to her, he was the villain in all of this.

He braced himself against the wall opposite, gave a mighty lunge, and crashed through the door.

Erin screamed. She backed against the wall and screamed and screamed again. She picked up a half-empty bottle of rum and threw it at him. He ducked in time, and it smashed against the door.

"You've got to listen to me." He started toward her, hands outstretched in a pleading gesture. "I had nothing to do with it. I didn't know—"

That was all he had time to say before he felt a sudden, sharp blow to the back of his head, then slumped to the floor.

Norman stepped across his body, held out his hand to her, and urged, "Come on. Let's go. I don't know what's going on, but I saw another man out there, and we've got to get out of here now."

Erin forced herself to obey, staring down at Ryan as she hurried out of the cabin. It had all happened so fast, but now she had a chance to escape. Gratefully, she took Norman's hand and allowed him to lead her out.

"Up the ladder." He pushed her in front of him. "Quick. The bastard hit me, thought he knocked me out, but I was just dazed. I followed him, got him just in time. Now we got to hurry 'cause there's no telling what his partner will do if he catches us."

Partner, Erin's brain screamed. That had to be Nate Donovan. "You're right. We have got to get out of here. We'll hide till Captain O'Grady gets back. . . ."

She pulled herself up and out on the deck. With Norman right behind her, they raced for the loading plank and ran down.

Reaching the pier, Norman cried, "Come on. Run!" He took off, not waiting for her. His job was done. He'd saved her from that madman. The rest was up to her, because he feared any second a bullet was going to hit him in the back.

Erin dared hesitate, to turn around and take one last look, as though saying good-bye forever to the past and any shreds of love she so foolishly harbored for Ryan. It had not been enough to banish her from his life, his home. Oh, no, he had to twist the knife of contempt a little deeper, denying her freedom forever. He had doggedly followed her, probably intent on shackling her himself, dragging her to an auction block, humiliating her, effecting the final degradation of the soul.

"Damn you, Ryan Youngblood!" The oath ripped its way out of her heart. "Goddamn you to hell—"

She froze.

Satan was not yet through with torment, for her eyes were playing tricks. Not enough to have the demon, Ryan, on her trail. Now the loathsome image of her step-father loomed from up there, at the ship's railing. He was waving a torch, and he began to run down the plank toward her.

"Don't worry, it's almost over," he called as he came.

Erin could not force her legs to move, to carry her out of the nightmare, she could only watch in disbelief, trying to tell herself it was all a mirage. It could not be happening. Why would Zachary be here?

"I've got them both now," he screamed in glee, leaning to set his torch to the wooden planking. "You're mine now, and nobody will ever take you away from me again."

Erin felt herself choking on the constricting knot of terror in her throat. He was setting fire to something. A trail of some kind. It was sputtering, slowly but surely upwards.

"Oh, God, no!" She came alive then, realized it was a fuse, and the ship was about to blow up, and Ryan was still on board.

She charged for the plank. Zachary leapt in her way. Possessed by strength and spirit she never knew she had, Erin gouged his eyes with her nails at the same instant she brought her knee up into his crotch, hard. "Get out of my way."

He doubled over in anguish but still struggled after her as she continued toward the ship.

The acrid smell of the burning fuse struck her nostrils, urging her onward. She had no idea where he'd set the black powder, and there was no time to look in the darkness. The only trail was burning and might set off the explosion before she could find it.

She started down the ladder but tripped and fell. A sharp pain stabbed her ankle, but she dragged herself up, limping, forced herself to keep going.

Reaching the cabin, she dared feel a rush of hope to see that Ryan was up on his knees, struggling to stand. Grabbing him about the waist, she pulled him up, frantically shrieking, "Get out. Now. Zachary lit a fuse, and the ship is going to blow any second."

It was like ice water in his face. He asked no questions, took no time to wonder what the hell Zachary Tremayne was doing there. "Let's go." He started toward the door, only to realize Erin had fallen, was clutching at her ankle, obviously in pain, unable to walk. With one, swift movement, he grabbed her and threw her over his shoulder and bolted out, down the hall, and up the ladder.

Zachary had dragged himself on board and was staggering forward to try and block them from making it to the starboard railing but was not fast enough.

"I'm right behind you," Ryan yelled, dropping her overboard. Without hesitation, he made good his promise and dove after her.

Erin hit the cold blackness, felt it reaching out to wrap about her, pulling her downward into a clutching abyss. It would be so easy, her heart pleaded, to surrender to the peace.

She had saved Ryan's life; he had, in turn, saved hers. But why?

What was the struggle for?

She felt a hand twisting in her hair, pulling her upward, ever upward, as the ascent to reality began.

Then they were surfacing, and Ryan was dragging her

along, swimming as hard as he could against the current, trying to get as far as possible from the ship.

And in the eerie light, just before it blew, they both saw him—Zachary—at the railing, waving and shrieking maniacally.

Then came the tremendous explosion.

Erin closed her eyes against the sight of flying bits of burning sail and wood all around her, grimaced against the sizzling sound as debris struck water.

She let the clutching, clawing fingers of oblivion take her away.

Eager hands were waiting to help them from the river, as a crowd gathered in response to the noise and fire.

Once ashore, however, Ryan would not let anyone keep him from Erin, and he knelt to gather her in his arms and cover her face with kisses as he fervently, feverishly whispered, "Hear me, my darling. It wasn't my doing. Any of it. I swear to you."

Erin's eyes fluttered open, and she could see the truth on his face in the glow of the burning ship beyond.

He saw the tenderness in her gaze and dared hope she did believe. "You saved my life." He offered a grateful smile. "That's got to mean you care a little."

Her ankle hurt, and she was sore and bruised from hitting the water but still managed a soft laugh, could reach up to twine her arms about his neck. "I forgot to hate you, when I remembered I love you."

"And only God knows how much I love you, Erin, and always will."

"The rainbow—it's there, smiling in the sky," she whispered, just before his lips claimed hers.

He did not know her meaning. There would be time later to understand.

As he held her and kissed her, a gentle breeze wafted, mysteriously delivering upon them a victorious red rose.

New York Times best-selling author, Patricia Hagan, has published sixteen books with over ten million copies in print. She is a former television journalist and presently resides in North Carolina with her husband, Eric.